HELMET of FLESH

Also by Scott Symons

CIVIC SQUARE
PLACE D'ARMES
HERITAGE

HELMET of FLESH

A NOVEL BY

SCOTT SYMONS

NAL BOOKS

NEW AMERICAN LIBRARY

Publisher's Note

This book is a work of fiction. Names, characters, places, and incidents either are the product of the author's imagination or are used fictitiously, and any resemblance to actual persons, living or dead, events, or locales is entirely coincidental.

For information address McClelland and Stewart Limited, 25 Hollinger Road, Toronto M4B, 3G2, Canada.

Financial assistance of the Canada Council and the Ontario Arts Council toward the publication of this book is gratefully acknowledged.

Published by arrangement with McClelland and Stewart Limited

NAL BOOKS TRADEMARK REG. U.S. PAT. OFF. AND FOREIGN COUNTRIES REGISTERED TRADEMARK—MARCA REGISTRADA HECHO EN HARRISONBURG, VA., U.S.A.

SIGNET, SIGNET CLASSIC, MENTOR, ONYX, PLUME, MERIDIAN and NAL BOOKS
are published by NAL PENGUIN, INC.,
1633 Broadway, New York, New York 10019

Library of Congress Cataloging-in-Publication Data

Symons, Scott, 1933—
Helmet of flesh.
I. Title.
PR9199.3.S97H4 1988 813′.54 88-1753
ISBN 0-453-00600-0

Designed by Leonard Telesca

First Printing NAL Books, August, 1988

1 2 3 4 5 6 7 8 9

PRINTED IN THE UNITED STATES OF AMERICA

For Kebir—Marrakshi
And for Tony—Colonel emeritus

DESIDERANTES
MELIOREM
PATRIAM

ACKNOWLEDGMENTS

Some novels may well be written as a personal tour de force. This one wasn't. Brewed over a period of fifteen years, it received help far beyond anything the author could muster on his own. The fishing folk of Newfoundland gave it their song. Morocco gave it joyful locale, and a force of sentience beyond anything North America readily knows. And Moroccans themselves endowed it with what dance it has.

During the years of writing, the author was resoundingly broke. A wide range of people and institutions have been generous with outright gifts: businessmen and women, writers, media people, restaurateurs, a Toronto bank and even civil servants. That in itself is a story I would like to tell someday.

As well, the Toronto Arts Council has been helpful. The Ontario Arts Council generous—and patient. And the Canada Council.

The book would not have whatever comeliness it may possess without the steadfast editorial eye of Charles Taylor, Jim Jamieson, Peter Buitenhuis, and Aaron Klokeid. Bill Glassco's sense of drama, as of dialogue, certainly marks it. And one man has hovered like holy harpy over every scene and page. Canada knows no other editor of his stature—Dennis Lee.

Responsibility for the contents rests fully with the author. A companion volume will follow, n'shalla.

CONTENTS

HELMET of FLESH

1
MARRAKECH

The street dissolved and he was standing in an immense open square. A sound like tambourines exploded about thirty yards away.

As he approached, the loose throng became a small crowd perhaps forty feet in diameter. He circled it, finally making his way to the center. Saw a group of men, black men dancing to the sound of the instruments. A kind of pantomime, of animals and birds as much as of people. Their feet strumming the earth. His eyes caught the rhythm, the line of tumultuous black legs, some with yellow slippers. And felt a tingling in his own feet.

Seven or eight dancers wrapped in white cloth, waists bare, small beaded caps on their heads. They were interweaving like dancing birds with yellow flashing feet. Two were pummeling small drums, the tambourine sound. And a deeper drumming, two others hammering large skin drums with sticks, great bent sticks, almost clawing at the drums. Hands, sticks, the skin of the drums, like one flesh thudding to the dance. And among the drummers, a man with an instrument made of bone or tortoiseshell, feathers and ribbons flailing from its shaft. Like a wild banjo, with the drums, tambourines . . . clatterdiclack-and-booommm. Like horses across cobblestones, two more men banging on spoons. Yes, big spoons they banged together. Clatterdiclack-and-booomm, the earth lurching in their gallop. And jumping . . . the youngest of the dancers jumping now into the center of the circle, swaying in the gallop of this motley orchestra. His hands raised to the sky, neck arched back, waiting . . . his thighs pivoting to the drums.

The drums stopped; music stopped. The crowd, silent as the

boy—was he seventeen?—dropped to the ground. The banjo man stepped forward in a yelp, dancing around the flailing banjo ribbons, feathers. The boy quivering on the ground beneath. The drums started up quietly, slowly increasing tempo, the other dancers palming the earth with their feet. Drums rising, banjo man wailing, and the hammering spoons—clatterdiclack-and-BOOOM—as the boy shot straight into the sky, knees clutched to his chest. And back to earth. And as he huddled there, the dancers slammed the ground with their feet . . . BOOOM, the boy hurtled up to the sky again. And back to the shuddering earth.

York's head was spinning, his body expanding with the dance . . . BOOM, the boy into the sky again, bullet of flesh. York shook his head, glanced around. Yes, the crowd swaying too. Mostly Moroccans—swarthy faces, turbans, burnooses swaying in the clatterdiclack. A few white faces, in Moroccan garb, young: hippies gone native, complete with beads. They too were trying to follow the dance. And a handful of people stark still: people in suits, white shirts or dresses. With a start York realized they were his own kind, tourists. . . . BOOOM! The boy shot to shoulder height in the air, and at the summit of his leap the music ceased and boy snapped his head back, arms back, his body suddenly unfurling across the sky . . . soaring elegant and slow in an arching backward dive, black-and-white flesh and loincloth coasting, erection clear through the shimmering cloth. His body completed a full back flip and he descended with a moan, clutching the earth like a shot animal.

"*Jeeezzus*, I shoulda had one of that!" The tourist closest to York was ramming furiously at his camera, waiting for the boy to repeat his trick. But the trick was over, and the boy was working his way around the crowd, holding out a hat to collect money.

"Do you want a guide, m'sieur?" A young Moroccan, looking odd in blue blazer and a lapel button saying GUIDE.

"No thanks, I just want to stroll. . . ."

"I show you all the sights, the Souhk, the Koutoubia, the palace—for the pleasure of the eyes, m'sieur! Mebbe mareejuana, hashish?"

"No, no." York strode off, ducking the fresh offer of a guide every few feet. Until he was once again mingling in the throng of the marketplace. . . .

Marrakech! It was like a waking dream. He wasn't going anywhere, wasn't looking at anything now. Just sauntering, immersed in a rhythm which had begun with that wild dance.

A body brushed close, almost jostling, yet never. A current of bodies like fish swimming, all part of the same tide. And the sway of the robes: blue, brown, long flowing robes—burnooses, were they? York, sensing his own walk, gathering the rhythm of these robes and bodies. Feet in the same yellow slippers as the drummers, patting the ground, slip-slap. Bodies flowing, as if the dancers had heightened the walking rhythm of this marketplace. York, not thinking at all, scarcely realized he was content.

Gradually he noticed the small shopping stalls that ran along beside him. Dozens of stalls, he seemed to *hear* first. As if the trinkets, leather, clothes were chattering at him, plucking some chord in his eye through his ear. He paused at a stall, one with leather bags and belts. Wondering why he had stopped. Till he saw the vendor pummeling on a drum, catching York's ear, drawing him in. He grinned and sidestepped, drifting on.

Soon he was at the end of the stalls, swerving left, down into another market area. Always the throng, clusters of people here and there. As he passed one group his body went tense; strange. He half turned, saw a man holding a writhing, black-hooded snake against the sky. Someone on a flute accompanying this dance of man and undulating cobra. He grimaced and lunged on.

In moments he was at the end of the market, entering a covered alley, protection against the glare of sun. Already past six, yet the sun still brilliant, angling its way through a latticed ceiling, splashing walls, rugs, pots. "You want a rug, best rugs . . . we make special price for you"—vendors shouting, darting out to clutch York's arm, or waving a plate, a jar. He ducked, pushing farther into the melee of wares, cries and people. Pausing at an antique shop—spree of silver knives, scimitars, massive jewelry—items abruptly embossed in his eyes, less objects than acts. Knife seeking the flesh. Necklace the throat. Animate, these antiques, messengers from another place and time. He stood listening, his body swaying in their chant.

As he turned to move on, his eyes were struck by blue. One of those robes; dark youth in a blue burnoose. The young man carrying the color like a prince. York gazed at the face laughing at his wonder. The chocolate face so friendly, sharing its portable blue, sharing the handsome young man who walked with him arm in arm. A few seconds of unspoken mirth, and then gone in the flow of the teeming alley. York stood amazed, the colors, music, vivacity of eyes all around him. Other young men strolling by, arm in arm or hand in hand, unknowingly sporting their colors like impromptu birds of paradise.

For another half hour and more he followed his senses through the maze of colors, the hovering incense. Past luggage and leather, marquetry shops whose tables spun like roulette wheels. And the winding alleys themselves, spinning like the displays. More jewelry, floating balls of amber, and always the ritual knives. A vendor rushing out with a glass, offering, "Come in, come in!"

York found himself inside the boutique, sitting on a low stool, sipping tea. Mint tea, strongly sugared. It was all fragrance and talk, the vendor chattering, his objets d'art seeming to talk as well. York fending off vendor and jewelry with his glass of tea. "For the pleasure of the eye!" While York mulled through the tea and the seething sounds and sights he'd just experienced. Aroused in a way that left him wary.

Now the vendor was pressing a large curved knife with an ivory handle into his lap. Knife so agile speaking. Saying . . . Suddenly York was up, out the door, pressing on through the alleys. Past strident rugs, a blast of pots, a stand filled with stuffed lizards, animal skulls and tails, and what looked like a shrunken hand. York paused. Where did this market end? Where had he started? A spot of sky a few yards on, and soon found himself back in the open square again. He had come full circle without realizing it.

The sun was ebbing now, the final light rippling across the square, throwing everything into relief. Much of the crowd was gone, the snake charmer too. It all felt calmer, and York relieved, strolling again, humming with the sinuous rhythm that had followed him all through the market like an invisible partner. A small crowd coming up on his right. As he approached, he saw balls coasting up against the pink sky, soaring one after another above the heads of the crowd. A juggler, rotating the balls in flight, clapping his hands, laughing and dancing. A companion keeping the rhythm on a small drum as the juggler added colored batons to the spinning balls. Five, and six, batons and balls whirling red, green, black in the sunset, the juggler always laughing. York laughing too now, his feet tapping time, his head rolling with the batons and balls. Up and around and down, his eyes flying with them, then falling to a halt. Captured in another pair of eyes across the circle of the crowd. Caught in a pair of eyes. . . . Ridiculous. York tried to pry his gaze free. He wanted to see the batons and balls still whirling against the sunset. But now he was swimming in someone else's eyes. Swimming as he had on his walk. Didn't even see the person, just the eyes; deep eyes, like a jungle pool. Didn't know if it was a woman or a man, old or young.

He jerked his head to one side, freeing himself. Then glanced back again through the sailing batons. Saw a young Moroccan in faded blue jeans, khaki army shirt, a dark red handkerchief knotted at his throat. He was swaying in time with juggler and drum, eyes delighted. Maybe twenty: tall, with a slim torso. His face as open as his eyes, and carnal in a way York could barely grasp.

York felt awkward, as if he had invaded this stranger somehow. But no; he hadn't been seen. The young Moroccan was still swaying with juggler and drum, his face transparent, gentle. For a few seconds York stood stock-still, basking in such openness. Then backed away from the crowd.

But as he moved off, something hit his eye. A harsh-angled body on the far side of the circle. Smart pressed jeans, leather jacket, white boots. Chunky body, square jaw. A tourist—aged thirty? Studded belt, aggressive stance. His entire body pointing in one direction, toward the young Moroccan. Cowboy tourist shunting ahead along the line of stare as if not moving at all, straight toward the Moroccan . . . halfway there, sliding toward his prey.

Without thinking, York spurted forward, cutting directly into the path of the macho tourist. Breaking his stare, bringing him to a halt. Tourist glared at York. But York continued on around the circle to stop beside the young Moroccan, protecting him from the tourist.

The Moroccan was still watching the juggler, face still open, like a dark warm muzzle in the sunset. Body swaying, oblivious to the small incident. The juggler was now whirling a set of plumed batons, like flying orchids. The young Moroccan following the movements of the juggler's hands with his own, as if apprentice to the act. And doing so, brushed against York, turning to see who he had bumped and grinning to share the juggler's dance.

"It's like sleight-of-hand," York blurted. The young man laughed and, stepping back a pace from the crowd, began to imitate the juggler, his huge hands tossing make-believe batons into the air. Such mirth in the lad's body as he danced around the imaginary batons. York felt clumsy just watching him. Suddenly the boy turned and tossed the batons to him. For a second York didn't understand. The boy nodded his head at York's hands. Till York reached out and caught them, began to juggle the invisible batons—the boy dancing, clapping as he did. Soon they were tossing the batons back and forth, the boy's eyes laughing when York tried to imitate his dance as well. Seconds later they were walking away from the circle together, as if they had just shared an intimate conversation. Though the Moroccan hadn't said a word. Walking toward the caravan of stalls York had passed earlier, with their spangle of buckles and belts and pendant wares chattering in the eye.

Another young Moroccan had planted himself in front of York, a large OFFICIAL GUIDE button on his shirt. Brandishing a sheaf of pamphlets—*The Magic of the Marrakech Medina.*

York stopped, and his young friend fell back. The guide jumped at York's hesitation, seizing his arm. "You must visit the K'toubia, the Mamounia Gardens, the Mirador, the Agdal."

Suddenly the young Moroccan bounded between him and the startled guide. And when the guide tried to step around him, simply butted with his entire body until the guide ebbed away, cowed. York was delighted by this method of disposing of unwanted people. More delighted still when the young Moroccan turned to him, and drawing himself erect said, "I'm Kebir; I'm a Marrakshi!" So proudly, so gently, that York wanted to whoop. But all he could do was babble out, "I'm York, York Mackenzie of . . . Osprey Cove."

They strolled on together. The stalls popped back into view, strident as parrots. All part of the flow of the market, the prance of the juggler, the rolling walk of the tall young Marrakshi. York felt happy, as if he had reached a pact with this young man. He wanted to think. But the flow of the market carried them on to the center of the square, toward the place where York had seen the dancers, that demented banjo with its tail flailing, the canary feet stomping the earth, the boy sailing into the sky. The dancers long gone now, but the site made him nervous. In fact, the entire marketplace made him nervous, even as it fed him rare peace. He wanted to reach out and touch the young Moroccan beside him, see if he was real. After all, the young man had said virtually nothing except his name. . . . And what *was* his name? York about to ask, but looking up, he saw golden balls bursting in the sunset, floating atop the tower he had seen while driving in from the airport, presiding over the market square.

"It's the Koutoubia, our mosque, a thousand years old," the Moroccan lad said quietly, as if he were unwilling to disturb the tower. "And this square is the Djema-el-Fna. It means 'the place of the dead.' "

The soft voice spoke again. "I am Kebir . . . Ka-*beer.*" York smiled and took Kebir's arm. "You are a Marrakshi. *You* are my guide!" At which Kebir started juggling the invisible batons again, dancing, till York was laughing aloud and stamping his feet in time. And only when they stopped did he realize he was exhausted, as if he had been jumping invisible hurdles in the hours since his arrival in Marrakech.

They agreed to meet two hours later. Kebir knew York's hotel. "I will come to your window at nine."

"Ask for me at the desk, or buzz my room."

Kebir shook his head. He couldn't enter the hotel.

"All right, I'll listen for your call. How will I know?"

Kebir didn't answer but began to juggle with his huge hands again, face alight. Then he was gone, dissolving into the dusk like a tawny antelope.

York stood stunned, ignited. He turned toward his hotel, walking pensively. His body thinking more than his mind. And turning, beheld that immense tower rising like a chant above the palm trees, surging in a single thrust up to the golden balls atop. For an instant he stood, almost expecting the tower to say something. Floodlit now, monolithic sentinel over the marketplace.

York felt a sudden urge to bow. Instead, he turned and, ducking a calèche that whinnied by, made his way to the hotel.

The massive glass doors swung shut behind him. For a moment he stood in the lobby, silence flooding over him. Even the Moroccan objets d'art in their glass cases were quiet here; all he could hear was the tick-tock of the grandfather clock. He slumped into a lobby armchair to rescue his mind. . . .

Crazy coming here, to Marrakech! It had all been so abrupt. Only hours before he had been in London, visiting a friend. On a break from his hideaway lair in Newfoundland. Suddenly he was on a plane to Morocco. Had it just been a whim, the longing for sun?

He'd thought the trip would restore him. But had sat numb on the plane, knowing he couldn't cope. Couldn't cope with London—much less with Canada, or John. How would he manage Marrakech?

I'm an exile, he was intoning silently as the plane landed, galloped along the runway. An exile in my own country. Then, stumbling to his feet, trying to assemble wits, baggage, he pushed himself toward the exit. Flames spurting in. . . . No, just a blast of Moroccan sun as he bumbled down the gangway. It's all a mistake, shouldn't have come. A baton bounced at his eyes. . . . No: barrel of a Sten gun. And silhouetted behind the gun, a soldier pointing sternly toward the air terminal. York had nodded as casually as he could, walking with plausible briskness to the terminal.

But if the trip had been crazy; the taxi ride into Marrakech was insane. Climbing into the midget taxi, announcing grandly, "To the Hotel Fauzi." Taxi careering through the countryside.

York had gaped as carts, turbans, waving children flared by. Taxi driver shouting "Allah" as a donkey ambled straight across the road, enormous erection flashing in the sun. When York opened his eyes again there were flamingo walls forty feet high—Marrakech! They hurtled through a massive portal, into a parading avenue, lush trees, mansions, and sudden melee of cars, bicycles, carts. Taxi driver invoking Allah, apparently guiding the car by prayer as it hurtled around a large fountain. And on down the mall toward a tower, flesh-colored tower rising above palm trees. And gone, as the taxi wheeled left into a final riot of bodies, donkeys . . . and stopped dead. No brakes—just dead halt.

Only when he saw his bags passing through a pair of massive glass doors did York realize there had been no accident—he'd arrived at the Grand Hotel Fauzi. He followed his bags through the door, the taxi driver shouting after him something that sounded like "Drams!" or "Deerams!" Shouted the same thing at the hotel desk, received payment and departed in a final flourish of Allah. And York had slumped in a large leather armchair in the lobby, grateful for stillness and shade.

After a moment he had seen man-sized palm trees in brass pots, which soared up from the center of the lobby. Stairwell draped with red velvet curtains cascading from the floor above. And strange objects on the walls, bright as birds, all feathers and bones and shells. Dominating all, a huge grandfather clock that looked like a fugitive from Versailles.

The pudgy manager had eyed York with doubt, announcing the daily rate as "Twenty-five deerams, with breakfast." York had no idea of the value of a deeram. But he knew he couldn't afford a hotel as opulent as this. He had registered slowly, trying to sort himself out.

NAME:

York Mackenzie (right, though he disliked his family name—too darned Scottish).

CITIZENSHIP:

Canadian.

HOME ADDRESS:

Skinner's Lane, Osprey Cove, Newfoundland. (If he could call it "home": Home was a house trailer, with a John and a Farley.)

BUSINESS ADDRESS:

Skinner's Lane, etc. (He had no business. And what business did they have asking all these damned questions?)

LENGTH OF STAY:

Two weeks. (??? As long as his money held out. At least his return ticket was open.)

PURPOSE OF STAY:

Tourism. (Had come to look orgasm in the eye, that's what his diary said. But his diary always exaggerated!)

DATE:

September 11, 1971. (So far as he could tell.)

The more he filled out the damned form, the more agitated York felt. What else did they want to know? He was thirty-six, dark brown hair, ten pounds flabby and fifteen thousand dollars in debt. What else? Exhausted from writing another bad book. Divorced, thank God. And still blighted by three university degrees, none useful. . . . But the form was done, and minutes later York was in his room, lying on the bed in his underwear. He tried lighting his pipe, calm down.

He felt like a fugitive, but from what? From journalism, maybe—been a journalist too long, before trying books. But his books felt like journalism too. What the hell did he want? He desperately wanted not to think about any of it.

He was about to get all this down in his diary when a rising din from the street below interrupted. He rammed the window shut, fell back onto bed, grabbed for his diary.

Shee-itt! Sten-guns at the airport
  Taxi-driver a kamikaze
  Hotel manager eyeing me like a spy

Why didn't I stay in London?
  Why didn't I . . .

I've got to get things straight! 3 continents in 10 days.
  —John sitting in Osprey C. jealous of my vacation
  —London battering the remains of my nostalgia, & Marrakech the remains of my sanity
  —my book clawing at my vanity
  —& me clawing at the whole fucking Canadian Protestant plausible Gliblib gynarchical joy-hating. . . .

Another blast hammered the window. York glared. What the hell was out there, a circus? a revolution?

> I can't goddamn cope. I need some different kind of nervous system—immunity from psychic rabies, the 20th century, myself. I must be goofy or religious or something.

But that last line only upset him more. He crossed it out. He took his spiritual life seriously, though didn't admit it. At least not to his friends. Besides, they were successful, and York was a failure. He didn't admit that, either, though he was proud of it. After all, success was easy: a matter of efficiency. But failure took imagination. He liked that, aphoristic. Wanted to gather a book of aphorisms, his own. But was never entirely sure what an aphorism was. Best make a note. . . . But his pen had fallen from his hand, lost in the percussion of Marrakech.

When he woke, it was London he saw—Nelson's iron lions in Trafalgar Square, Eros in Picadilly, and the palace where a queen still reigned in defiance of reason. He had awakened to London, but what he heard was Marrakech!

Yes, that was how he came to Morocco, memories and madness in his flesh. And Marrakech had forced him up from bed, out into the street. Nearly spun off his feet by carts, bicycles, donkeys. Gradually working his way into the flow, the worst heat of the sun done; it was well after five. He could see market carts tottering with vegetables, a general store with wares piled in tipsy pyramids, a man crouched on the pavement selling teapots. He hurried along the tumbling street, ears perked to a rising harangue of music, drums, strange tambourines. Then that wild dance in the marketplace. And the juggler. And Kebir.

Now here he was, full circle, back in the Hotel Fauzi. Trying to make sense of it all. The lobby itself like an art nouveau theater set. The only sound the tick-tock of the orante grandfather clock. And the clucking of the pudgy French manager, eyeing York. Must be quite a sight. He glanced down at his corduroys, T-shirt, scruffy shoes—Osprey Cove attire. Not up to the Grand Hotel Fauzi.

York brushed the hair out of his eyes, scowled at the grandfather clock. Decided to retreat to his room. He was climbing the majestic stairwell when a figure lurched toward him, swarthy, stocky, beard jutting defiantly. The figure paused, squinting, challenging him. York stepped back. The figure too stepped back, head cocked to one side, interrogating: figure in brown corduroys, black T-shirt, scruffy shoes. It was in the large mirror buried at the head of the stairwell. Lunged on down the hallway to his room.

For a moment he flopped on the bed. Then rose to dispute the mirror's report by taking a shower, washing armpits with extra care, and trimming that Machiavellian beard. Got out fresh clothes for later use. Then lay down, to forget everything.

Goddamned drums again. Din of drums, flutes, dancing feet, though the window was closed. He reached for his diary.

> My body *pummeled* by sounds! Crazy. I've been raped by a marketplace (the sounds are *inside* me!). That weird dance they did. Carnal shamen.
>
> *Must* get notes on all of it. Marrakech—complete antidote to Canada.
>
> Kibeer—or is Kabere?—Marrakshi! Presented himself like an entire city. Can't remember his face. Resonance, his face had a *resonance!* Like the marketplace. Like . . .

But he couldn't find the words. It worried him. Must calm down. Should have brought something sane to read. Then remembered the essay, a piece he was writing for a Toronto magazine—summary of his new book, really. He'd brought the first draft, to revise during his vacation. He rummaged in his valise . . . found the envelope with John's photos of Osprey Cove in it—exactly what he didn't want right now: more of John! Finally located the file with the new dust jacket, and his essay. And turned to the opening page.

> Canada is a case of psychic perjury. More precisely, the much vaunted "Canadian identity" is a case of self-perfidy.
>
> Let me be perfectly clear. Canada is held up in the modern world as an example of material success and wealth, of social adjustment, of multiculturalism, of benignly tolerant liberalism. In short, of social justice, as our intelligentsia like to say. As well, our nation considers itself a happy balance between the New World and the Old. We are the New America, the last best chance.

> Yet the blatant truth is that modern Canada is a failure—worse, it is a self-willed failure. And this failure occurs at the worst possible level: a failure in *being*, an ontological failure. Because the so-called "Canadian Identity" is an exercise in willed self-identification. But will kills being, and . . .

He read on, determined. But the more he read, the more upset he grew. The piece made fine sense; his native land was certainly a "wealthy state that satisfies greed, but not the hunger of the heart." Yes, but . . . He flung the pages across the room.

Truth was, whenever he thought about Canada, he became angry. Then he'd make up one of his lists of enemies.

> —the civil service ("uncivil disservice")
> —the media ("propagate them*selves* as 'celebrities' ")
> —the new national literature ("shallow tracts for the times")
> —The Liberal Party ("Gliblibs")

He loathed them all. And every time he thought about it, he'd start ranting. "The great fulminator," as one of his friends had said, "The Archbishop of York, always sermonizing." Well, he'd come to Morocco to get away from all that, fleeing his own ideas as much as Canada. "Canada is in exile from me!" he'd say with bravado. But it hurt.

And now he lurched up from bed, almost contrite. Gathered up the scattered pages. Yes, what he was opposed to was clear. But what the hell was he *for?* He was for roots, that was it. Respect for the rooted traditions of his culture. And for millennial parliamentary traditions, as opposed to—as opposed to the narcissism of a media presidency. . . . So far so good; he was for respect, as opposed to mere respectability. But respect for what? Well, for public decency. And private gentleness. He was a Tory . . . a radical Tory. Could vote Conservative or New Democrat. Just couldn't vote for those goddamn Gliberals! They shat on life. But beyond that, what was he *for?* He squirmed, scratched his balls, always a sign he was thinking seriously. And realized—he was for joy, that's what! Joy, not mere happiness; happiness was joy for pigs. . . . But what was joy? The celebration of life—

with the angels as cheering squad, and a daily joust with the gods as setting-up exercise. . . . Good definition. But he wasn't very good at what he proclaimed. Nor very brave.

He lay sweating on the bed. No longer heard the din from the street. Just the dismal din in his brain. His mind focused now. But no longer saw the dance in the marketplace, nor the juggler's legerdemain . . . no longer saw Kebir. He was angry and exhausted again. He yanked the pillow over his head for a few moments of peace. The last thing he remembered thinking was that Canadians were closet Republicans.

He was awakened by a faint rumble. The sound enveloped him, and he rolled over on his stomach to stifle it. But the rumble increased, like the purr of a panther, rising to a soft roar. York rose with it, up off the bed as if lifted . . . up and over to the window. What time was it? He opened the window, peered out. Dark, a velvet dark. And the rumble again, flowing in through the window, into his gut, like the call of a giant cat, but nothing the overt ear would catch. York's sleepy gaze followed the sound—over to the right, a feline shadow by the second streetlight. The shadow moved forward, became a pair of eyes under the flickering street lamp, a pair of big hands juggling. Kebir.

"I'll be right down," York heard himself shout. He retreated from the window, realizing he was all but naked. He dressed quickly, was almost out the door, but turned back. Wondering why till he put on the pendant, a two-headed falcon on a silver chain. Gift from John. "Add it to your talismans, Yo-yo; it's full protection!" York chuckled, and made his way out into the warm night. Over to the street and lamp where he'd seen Kebir. . . . No one! Then about ten feet ahead of him, popping out of an archway, arms and legs awhirl, stopping with a laugh right in front of him: Kebir.

They made their way toward the market. Past a cluster of boys playing marbles under a street lamp. A large movie ad of a karate muscleman, complete with whip and black leather boots reminded him of that macho tourist who had been stalking Kebir. Well, Kebir would never know. And on past the sound of Bob Dylan's voice snarling through a jukebox. MILKBAR, the sign read. "Mostly for tourists," Kebir said, "but a good place to meet."

At the end of the street the market flared up—the chattering lights of stalls still open, the calèches trundling by, a pervasive music. To the left, ignited against the sky, the sentinel tower gazing down. And on their right, a large café riding out onto the street. A few tourists, lots of young Moroccans. But Kebir shook his head and soon they were in the center of the plaza, flowing along with the crowd. A spicy fragrance hovering in the night.

They passed a stall piled high with furs and eyes, tongues and hooves . . . and a wide-eyed head, severed head of a ram atop all. Only when he saw the steaming rice and seething soups did York understand it was an open-air restaurant. Kebir was moving on past more stalls, mini-restaurants bivouacked under the stars and their own propane lights. Did Kebir propose to *eat* here? York was sure it was a center for bubonic plague. But Kebir had stopped, his body pointing to the right: a final stall a little larger, much cleaner. There were two lamps, four large benches and a brazier over which a man was roasting a flank of meat. Best of all, there were no eyes, heads, entrails floating around on bloody platters.

As they approached, several young Moroccans jumped up to embrace Kebir. Kebir flashed his disarming smile but kept his eyes on York. On him?—more like over him, a protective beam, as the whirl of friends radiated out to welcome them. York suddenly enmeshed in a babble of eyes, spontaneous grins. While Kebir stood watchful, York felt like a dog being sniffed, licked, finally approved. And just as suddenly they were all seated around one corner of the stall in a hush. Then the smallest one nodded at a huge ebony man with an omnivorous ivory smile, saying, "That's Jareeda!" And Jareeda nodded proudly and looked at the one in a purple shirt. "This is my friend Hassan!" Each naming the next rather than himself, as if more courteous. While Kebir nodded gravely, intoning, "This is my friend York of Ospree Cove." The others echoing, "York of Ospree Cove, York of Ospree. . . ." Their voices almost chanting while their eyes danced around York, never directly at him.

"Please, you are from Ospree Cuv and what is Ospree Cuv?"

York laughed. The hideout of a pair of public enemies. . . . "It's a fishing village in Newfoundland."

"Do you fish much?"

"Not if I can possibly avoid it!"

"Where is Newfoundland?"

"In Canada."

"Please, where is that?"

"In North America."

"You are American!"

"No, thank God, no!"

Voices babbling, as York blessed the fluent French that allowed him to join their play. Because their questions were less questions than laughter shared through words.

Kebir touched York's arm, motioning to pyramids of food rising in the center of the stall. Platters of rice, vegetables, segments of meat. And as Kebir presented the array of food his friends fell silent, releasing York. But he couldn't make head nor tail of it. "Kebir, I'll eat what you do." His friends nodded and started in again. "Do you live alone in Ospree? Is this your first time in Marrakech? What is that necklace, please?" Scarcely awaiting replies, but smiling as York's eyes followed their questions from face to face. And by the time York had explained that his necklace was "for good luck," the food had arrived. Meat kebabs on sizzling skewers.

Someone said, "Bismillah," and Kebir initiated the eating by passing York the largest piece of meat from his own plate. The others nodded. When they weren't talking they were touching each other. Once York had tasted the food the conversation rippled back. "How do you like Marrakech?" "I love it, but it scares the hell out of me!" "Why does it scare your hell out?" "Because there's so much noise, I can't see what's happening." "But *we*'re what's happening." They all bounced in glee, as if pumping mirth into York. And for the first time he could see beyond their little circle. Jareeda taking fresh bread and passing it into the dark, a small pair of hands reaching out and grabbing for it. "Allah karim." While Kebir quickly finished his meat, his long fingers wiping his lips with impossible elegance.

Dinner done, they sat over mint tea in a silence that was its own conversation. In sheer contentment York lit up his pipe. The flame caught Kebir's face in silhouette. Kebir sitting as if in a permanent trance, swaying gently with the sounds of the night.

"You are happy when you smoke your pipe." It was the smallest boy, Abdou, grinning. York nodded. The boy held out his hand, and soon York's pipe was going around their circle, puffing and coughing and smiling.

"It's not hashish," one said.

"No, it's *not* hashish!" But it increased their affection.

Finally Kebir stood up. And the big black, Jareeda, joined him, and little Abdou. York paid, and as they left he saw children scurrying in from the shadows to eat the rice he'd left on his plate. The four of them strolled on into the market. They paused at one of the stalls, and York felt someone watching. It was a picture: a large open hand with an eye in the palm. And a snake coiling through the fingers of the hand, with a scorpion underneath. York backed a pace. Kebir whispered, "It's the Hand of Fatima, to protect the shop."

"To protect the shop?"

As they walked on, Kebir explained, "From the Evil Eye."

"The what?"

"The Evil Eye sends out waves, like poison." York looked dubious, but Jareeda nodded insistently, whispering that his aunt had been paralyzed by the Eye. Kebir nodded too and seemed unwilling to discuss it further. But York was still curious about the picture. "Are there scorpions in Morocco?" Yes; the brown ones were painful. But the big black ones could kill. In Marrakech? No, in the south, like the cobras. York resolved to remain in Marrakech. They walked on in silence.

They were perhaps a hundred yards from the great tower and began strolling towards it as though it had called. They crossed the market road into a small park of palm trees. A young couple brushed by under the trees, arm in arm, Moroccans. York noted quite a few younger men walking hand in hand or arm in arm. It seemed natural, though it made York self-conscious. As if his presence were preventing Kebir and his friends from doing the same. The silence under the trees was palpable, only a rustling overhead like the rubbing of crepe, the shifting of palm leaves in a slight breeze drawing them closer together. Kebir a looming presence at York's side. A bird whooped once, and again, sharp night call. Suddenly they were all linked arm in arm. Kebir at York's right, little Abdou and Jareeda on his left. Swaying through the small palm park toward a light at the end of the tunnel of trees. York caught in the warmth of their linked arms.

As they reached the final trees, he felt a surge inside him. Abdou blurting, "There it is!" The tower burst into view again as they stood there, arms linked, palms rustling over their heads. The tower scrutinizing them.

The main boulevard lay directly between them and the tower. They crossed it, an empty calèche wallowing past, a stray bicycle. The pressure in York's spine mounting, and behind his ears a low drumming as the tower came closer. They passed to one side of it, strolling alongside a low wall into an unkempt garden grown over a body of ruins. Walking till they came to a portion of the wall with no vines on it, just beyond the aureole of the floodlit tower. Jareeda hopped up to sit. Little abdou followed. Silent in the sultry privacy that enveloped them, the tower watching high above.

A car honked sharply nearby, and York's mind shunted fearfully into abrupt focus. What in God's name was he doing here? Then felt the eyes in the dark: gentle, almost mocking—Kebir's eyes gazing down on him, reassuring, holding him. And as quickly as it had come, York's fear dissolved in the ripple of laughter that rose from all four of them. And borne by the laughter, they linked arms and strolled on, the bushes seething beside them.

As they ambled farther into this lunar garden a copse of junipers closed over them, nave of an impromptu cathedral. A large bird screeched and lumbered through the protesting palm leaves. Again a wall provided a bench, Jareeda and Abdou hopping up to sit. This time York followed. Kebir stood silently in front. And again York felt trapped, but now without fear. The trap was a wall of flesh, their own. . . . Now he simply felt timid, acquiescent in the adventure of the night. He glanced up, Kebir's amber eyes wide on him, eyes one could swim in.

York did not know how long he and Kebir remained fast in each another's gaze. But when he turned, he saw that the others were gone. Kebir took his arm, and they strolled slowly into the burgeoning juniper and bushes and red flowers, geraniums, which seemed to spurt up behind his eyes. Kebir swung to the right, under an alley of low palm trees, ending in a closed arbor. They had to stoop to enter, but inside it was airy, like the lair of a large animal. And as York stood up inside this green cave, he saw it through a gap in the foliage—the tower, rising over

Kebir's shoulder. And seeing it, heard the sound again. Heard it rising inside his body, up his spine, the rumble, the same purring roar he had heard when Kebir had called to him, calling through his sleep, raising him from his bed and into the night. Sound of the tower. And to see the tower was also to see Kebir standing erect, eyes still and waiting.

Again York sensed a frontier to be passed. Suddenly he was limp—just from getting this far, from following the inner language of Marrakech, of Kebir and his friends. For an instant he beheld the calm yet virulent tower, and the red flower that was the handkerchief at Kebir's throat, and the impassive eyes. He held his hands out toward Kebir. "I am York of Osprey Cove." Saying it this time with quiet pride. Kebir smiled, raising his hands forward. "I am Kebir . . . Marrakshi!" And with that they were holding each another.

A moment later they lay in the coarse grass, their bodies entwined. Overhead, the geraniums, and the opening to the sky with the tower jutting up. Their own towers of flesh out and touching. Till Kebir rolled York onto his side, their pants down. And York felt one of the red flowers expanding in his eyes, as he felt Kebir's cock caressing the inside of his buttocks. Reaching out, he felt the jab of a cactus on his hand, and pulled back. Back onto the probing head of Kebir's cock. And the rumble up his spine as before. For an instant a sharp stab of pain, then he saw only the tower, spotlit and bright. Shifting slightly, his head arched back, his eyes yoked to flower and swaying tower as Kebir started to move in a way York did not know. Kebir moving in time with the beat of his heart, the motion growing from within, till he had created a circle of light inside York.

Kebir clasped closer, taking York's erection in his large hand, stroking gently in rhythm with his inner motion. And York found himself arching farther toward Kebir, and inhaling the scent of the geraniums. Till Kebir furrowed deeper and York felt an unraveling that started in the small of his back, up his spine, striking a knot in his neck he hadn't known was there. And with this saw the marketplace, the dancing yellow feet, the boy cusping the sky in a swan dive over the world, that prince in the blue of blue and the juggler whirling his batons into the eyes of Kebir—all contained within the watching body of the tower that stood over them, and inside him.

Suddenly the tower flared, growled. Kebir tightened his grasp, teeth sinking into York's neck and moaning as his warmth sped into York, and York flowed into their joined hands.

They lay in silence, then slowly ebbed apart. Kebir brushed the leaves, earth, grass from their bodies. And sat in the sanctuary of the copse, gazing into each another.

Later, walking back through the marketplace, York wanted to arrange a meeting the next day. Yet didn't want to breach their silence. Kebir stopped, pointing to the tourist Milkbar. He held up his right hand, four fingers outstretched. For a second his eyes held York again. And then as York was about to touch him on the arm, good night, he was gone.

York walked the remaining yards to the hotel alone, knowing without knowing: tomorrow, in the Milkbar, at four o'clock. The massive glass doors of the Grand Hotel Fauzi closed behind him. Tick-tock, the ormolu grandfather clock nodded. The velvet ramp of the stairwell bore him up to his room. Up past the large mirror showing his face suffused, in a trance. But he didn't see.

For a while he lay silent on the bed, in his clothes, still hearing the purr, still seeing the tower. When he finally undressed, he felt the stab in his thumb and first finger. Needles from the cactus plant. He hadn't even noticed. Slowly he worked them out of the flesh, watching the blood startle the sheets. He turned out the light, numb. Then heard a scream, an almost inaudible yet piercing scream. It was winding out of him, out of his body. And as suddenly as it had started, it was gone.

2
THIS IS MY BODY

He woke slowly, the bleat of sheep outside his window. Yes: clearly sheep, and a rooster crowing. He propped himself up. Saw blood on the sheet. Sat upright, his hand stinging. "I am Kebir, Marrakshi," the words tumbling through his head. Oh, Christ.

For a moment he sat there, trying to think. Glanced at his watch—nearly ten. Just time for breakfast. He jolted himself out of bed, grabbing for his clothes, diary, and at the last moment his essay. Then he was stumbling along the hall, down the cascading stairwell and pell-mell into the dining room. Apparently in time, because someone was still eating. For a few seconds he stood, rattling his papers as if to defend himself.

"You just take a seat wherever; there's no maître d' on duty." The voice of the other guest, amiable English accent.

York nodded, approached the row of low tables ranged in front of a long red divan. Like large coffee tables. He sat at the next table but one from the guest, wanting privacy even as he wanted company. And ordered breakfast: croissant, marmalade, café au lait.

He sipped the coffee, browsing through his article. "A willed failure of being constitutes perjury, self-perjury. . . ." But the words passed inanely before his eyes. His finger tracing the serpentine inlay of the tabletop as he tried to concentrate.

"Best hurry if you want more coffee." The Englishman again. York glanced over. "Dining room closes in a minute, and you seem to be lost in thought."

York managed a grin. "I was noticing the design of this tabletop. It feels like the music in the marketplace."

"Now that's a remarkable notion for 10:09 A.M.!" The other guest smiled. A youngish man, white shirt, paisley ascot. "But forgive me—"

"Don't apologize. I don't know anyone in Marrakech except Kebir." How his thoughts blurted out.

"Allow me to present myself. James Goodison. Down from London for a sniff of the sun." The Englishman bowed slightly in his seat.

"I'm York Mackenzie, from . . . Osprey Cove."

"Osprey Cove? Now that's a town I'm not familiar with."

"In Newfoundland."

"My, we *are* a ways from home base. Come to visit your friend here?"

"Friend? Oh . . . he's showing me the sights."

"Quite right. Always helps to know one of 'em. Guide in an exotic land." James's eyes beamed approval. But York wished he hadn't mentioned Kebir. Changing the subject, "What do you do in London?"

"I'm in, communications." And stopped, as if unwilling to discuss business matters. "But what do *you* do in this Cove of yours?"

"I've just finished writing a book. My second. Being published next month. . . . About culture in Canada."

"Didn't know there was any. What's it called?"

"Identikit Canada."

"How clever of you." Was James joking?

York reached into his file. "Here's the dust jacket, for what it's worth. I got one just before leaving."

James nodded amiably, held out his hand. "It certainly won't be overlooked, in scarlet and black." And turned to the blurb on the back.

> IDENTIKIT CANADA is a bombshell in the complacent garden-party of Canadian culture. In a series of provocative, wide-ranging essays, York Mackenzie tears the facade from subjects as diverse as fiction, the Canadian identity, and our national museums policy. You may agree or disagree . . . but IDENTIKIT CANADA is certain to be *the* topic of excited debate this season.

York watched James anxiously. He was proud of the new book, though something about it made him uneasy. Like the abominable prose in that blurb; would James realize it wasn't his own? But James's face remained impassive as he read on.

> YORK MACKENZIE is one of Canada's most fearless and controversial new spokesmen. His 1968 first novel, *Media Madhouse*, proved to be a true roman à clef, and roused both the ire of media pundits and the praise of the new generation of "tuned-in" readers. His celebrated column "Culture Commentary" ran in a Toronto newspaper for two years. It has given substance to this new book of iconoclastic essays, which is bound to increase his host of admirers—and enemies.

James pursed his lips. "I can see you're what they term a celebrity. But do they ever say who you *are?*" York pointed to the biography on the inside flap, feeling more and more uncomfortable.

> York Mackenzie was born in Toronto in 1935. He has a degree from the University of Toronto, with further studies at Oxford and the Sorbonne (Paris). He taught history at Lakefield College in Ontario, prior to a brilliant career as a journalist in newspapers, radio and television. Presently he lives in Newfoundland.

For a moment James sat musing. Then he remarked, "Very North American, don't you think?" York squirmed. "But I fear I'm no further ahead with Canadian culture, which is *your* expertise, apparently." Silence. York wished he'd never shown that dust jacket. Yes, it *was* garish, and the photo was pretentious, making York look like a pundit, or a spokesman or whatever they'd said. James rattled the dust jacket like a trophy. Finally saying, "I presume your own prose is better than this presentation." York nodded gratefully. "I do have a small piece here, some of the themes of the book, if you like. . . ." He passed a portion of his essay over, and retrieved the culpable dust jacket, hiding it quickly in his file.

James began to read the text. Now and then he tapped with

long elegant fingers on the table as if to mark a point. York watched his face. Handsome English features, almost a Van Dyck portrait, though pockmarked on the right jaw. Shimmering blue-gray eyes, the paisley ascot matching them. And manicured hands, with a gold ring and crest cut in sapphire blue. Refined club-type, York decided. Usually impossible to approach, except on vacation like this.

"By Jove, you don't mince your words!" James had already skimmed the few pages. "But what precisely do you mean by this: 'Canada is an ontological failure'?"

York hesitated. "Well, you see, Canada is a nation of apprentice cynics—"

"Now that's jolly good. An epigram. Put *that* in!" James turned, gazing at York as at a newfound object. "I'm here doing research myself, on the Glaoui. Know anything about the Glaoui?"

"What is it? Archaeology?"

"It's a *him*, my dear York. The Glaoui was feudal overlord of Marrakech and the mountains beyond." James paused, drawing himself erect. "Marrakech, Ouarzazate, the entire Draa Valley was his personal fiefdom . . . La Berberie!" York nodded. *Marrakech* was the only word he had recognized. "The Glaoui was the last great warlord of North Africa, nailed the heads of his enemies to the walls of this city. In our own time."

"Hallooo, young whippersnapper! Been hunting all over for you." A voice boomed across their tables as a large, blond Englishman of about fifty strode through the dining room, taking the seat opposite James.

"You *are* hearty this morning, my dear Colonel." James glared at the newcomer.

"It's the air, the air. Beats soggy old London, what?" The Colonel sat with aplomb in blue blazer, khaki trousers. "But where's m' coffee?"

"You're too late for coffee." James smiled.

"Too late? It's *never* too late for coffee!" The Colonel pounded the table till a boy appeared. "I'll have some coffee right away . . . no, make it tea," he blared in wobbly French. Boy bowed and disappeared. "Now see here, James, about our little trip. We've got to be off early mornin', ahead o' the sun." And for a moment the Colonel and James spoke of the Atlas Mountains, the rugs of Ouarzazate, some special restaurant there. And of Gnaoua dances, and a voodoo cult that used hashish down in the Draa Valley. York couldn't help overhearing; the Colonel talked as if barking orders to the world.

Now the waiter was back, bearing the tea on a brass tray. The Colonel nodded approval, sipped, and bellowed, "B'god, *subversion!*" Silence. "It's that minty stuff!" And roared at the waiter, no longer endeavoring his French, "*English* tea . . . *English breakfast tea,* don't you know?" James translated. The waiter bowed and disappeared with the offending cup.

"What's this? More of your Glaoui investigations?" The Colonel pointed at the papers on the table.

"Belongs to the Canadian gentleman there, a book he's writing. If you'll pacify yourself, I'd rather like to introduce him." James gestured at York, who rose as if summoned to court. "Colonel, this is York—of New-found-land . . . and this is Colonel Anthony Napier, a Napier of the Peninsular Wars, no less!" The Colonel, looking as surprised as York felt, nodded curtly.

"York writes books about Canadian culture," James purred.

"A bona fide man of letters in our midst." The Colonel glanced askance at York. "James has an odd weakness for culture. If you're not careful he'll have you doing research for him."

"Research?"

"On that old Berber reprobate, the Glaoui. James is obsessed by the man."

"Colonel, please. T'hami el Glaoui was the *glory* of Morocco." James was about to hit stride, but the waiter had arrived with the new tea, and everything stopped while it was tested. The Colonel sipped, winking at York. "It'll do."

The Colonel was growling, but his eyes chuckled. York noticed a long scar on his left cheek. A war wound?

"Did you come to Marrakech alone, or in array?" The Colonel turned toward York again.

"Alone, mostly." York beginning to enjoy the company. "But he has a Moroccan friend as guide."

"My dear James, I'm sure the gentleman can answer for himself. He does look of age!"

"Younger than some of us, Colonel." Ah, the English banter, at once trivial and with a touch of ferocity. But the Colonel was discussing their trip again. " . . . be into the mountains by noon.

Do our fieldwork as we go. Our friend from the Hôtel des Amis can't come, unfortunately. . . ."

"But we must have someone who speaks the language out there, deal with the natives." James was vehement.

"My dear fellow, you'll have to act as map reader *and* native-placator." The two lapsed into more talk of the Moroccan mountains—the old trade route from the Sahara, Timbuktu . . . still a few of the old order in power up there . . . shaman country! Obviously the Colonel was an old Morocco hand. York pretending to eat his croissant. He found himself longing to go on the adventure with them. *This* was what he had come for.

The Colonel had finished his tea, however, and the two men rose to leave. The Colonel gave a curt nod, James a slight courtly bow, and they were gone.

York sat dazed. He picked up his papers, and drifted back to his room. His mind floating somewhere between Newfoundland, London, and the eruption of Marrakech.

> THE COLONEL: Pusser military type (army crest on blazer). The kind who *lead* their troops into battle. Probably a Guardsman. Yet a touch of Friar Tuck.
>
> JAMES: Very upper-class. Eton and Oxford? Intellectual. In communications—BBC? Doing research on a Moroccan warlord. . . . A figure out of Evelyn Waugh.

York contemplated his notes. They seemed clear; meant his mind was focusing again. Keep on and he'd be fine. Yes, might even get a short story out of Morocco. Always hoped to write real short stories—powerful. Not like his first book, which was less a novel than a social hand grenade. Trouble was, you met people like the Colonel and James for a few moments, then never saw them again. He tried to imagine what their trip into the mountains would be like.

> Royal procession, complete with their English clubman banter. Staying at posh tourist spas (I couldn't afford that). Yet steeped in Moroccan lore & arcanae (sp?).

Heartened by such lucidity, he tried to encapsulate Kebir:

KIBEER: All body language. Superstitious, believes in the Evil Eye. His face was . . .

Why do I shy away from thinking about Kiber?

Marrakech blocks thinking, that's it (Canada blocks emotions!). It's the music, everything here is music. Even that tabletop at breakfast. *Voilà*—K's face is . . . *music!*

He put his pen down, couldn't think about Kebir because Kebir then vanished. Try Marrakech. At least get that straight.

MARRAKECH: All I've seen is one teeming marketplace. A vast open square filled with everything from snake charmers & peanut vendors to native dancers. At the far end, an enclosed market area filled with dozens of small shops & fleas.

The market proper is apparently known as "the Place of the Dead." (Why?)

The old quarter surrounding the market looks like a pre-Elizabethan town, all higgledy-piddledly.

And dominating everything, the mosque tower (Kootoobya?) a 1000 years old, is like a carnal cathedral spire!

Yes, that described what he knew of Marrakech. But it didn't present what he felt.

Marrakech is like Hieronymus Bosch in the flesh. People aren't going from one place to another. They're like Roman candles, sparklers, detonating where they stand.

A bit better.

Marrakech is all curves and chaos.

London is all cozy enveloping gray & right angles, & whispered silences. In London you form tidy lines. In Marrakech you dance!

In *Canada* . . . (I refuse to think about Canada!).

His mind had drifted to London now. Something he wanted to remember. He'd made a mental note to make a note of it, then forgotten. Hell. . . .

> In London I went back to the Victoria & Albert Museum. Several times. As if hunting for something, didn't know what. On my final day found myself in those early period rooms. An Elizabethan room, all oak paneling & an enormous bed—"The Great Bed of Ware." Its posts like giant thighs, an uprising. I sprang half hard just seeing it.
>
> Knew I was on to something. And went through all the "period rooms" in chronological order, checking—Jacobean, Queen Anne, various Georges, Victorian.
>
> They kept getting thinner . . . all the tables, beds, decor. Net loss of flesh (& also of my hard-on!).
>
> *Thus:* Jacobean was still tumescent, but Queen Anne getting prissy, and by the late 18th century (Hepplewhite, etc.) it was all a theorem of the mind, *disembodied.*
>
> Worse: by the Victorian period all furniture was muffled, smothered under drapes—a ruling matriarchate (Hide All Hard-ons!).
>
> Knew I'd found it! I double-checked, traced back thru all the rooms. By the time I got to the Elizabethan my body was roaring again. "Great Bed of Ware" like a trumpet behind my balls!

He stopped; after writing in a burst, no longer knew what he was saying. It often happened like that when he was excited. But he was always excited when it came to a national issue, such as his own erection—his "oracle," as he fondly termed it.

> Eureka! Those period rooms revealed the tragedy of the Occident: the collapse of the English-speaking orgasm . . . from 1500 to 1900!
>
> *Thus:* In Tudor England, an orgasm big enough to blast the Pope out of all England!
>
> —but under Charles II, a very "cavalier" orgasm, frolic & frippery (as in Restoration comedy!).

—under Queen Anne . . . Eros reduced to the tea table, and to rhyming couplets (e.g. *The Rape of the Lock!*)
—by the end of the 18th century everything reduced to a cerebral twitch.
—under Vicky . . . the high point of masturbation, all that was left!

Got it—essay on *The Devolution of the Occidental Orgasm!* Using antique furniture as evidence, irrefutable.

Yes, his fingertips now tingling like the end of his oracle. Sure sign that he was on to something major. He lay back, closed his eyes, musing. Suddenly saw it—the Great Bed of Ware. And looming above the giant bed: mosque tower of Marrakech. Could see it clearly, superimposed over the bed.

He sat smack upright. Such "sightings" happened when he was dozing or musing; he always felt it was a message. And what was the message of the Great Bed and the Marrakech tower? What had he been taking notes about? Orgasm!

The Great Bed of Ware, last English-speaking orgasm as large as that tower . . .

He shuddered, remembering last night, the stab of cactus, stab of Kebir and the roaring tower. The "sighting" confirmed his notes!

Those period rooms give concrete evidence of a decline in our capacity for *celebration*. Correlative to our increase in *cerebration!*

Splendid. He always claimed the English language was trapped inside mere syllogisms of the mind—a kind of secondhand Cartesianism. Which made for efficient bathrooms and computers, but bad life. Then he'd discovered what he termed sensibility syllogisms: evidence not through the mind, but the fingertips. Through the eyes, the senses, and his beloved oracle. Though didn't mention this last much. Even to his friends, who by and large viewed a penis as a portable urinal and pleasure machine, of incidental use for procreation if and as necessary. But now—

> *The phallus as oracle.* At the V. & A. it caught the English culture, dormant since Tudor times! *Q.E.D.*

He paused, lost again just as he'd stumbled on to something major. Back to work, his oracle still tingling.

He closed his eyes again. Saw the flaring red hair—John. Didn't want to see John right now. But John waving, shouting something. And a pair of eyes hovering above John, eyes gazing, *knowing*. Then gone. And York confounded by all these messages.

He drew up a list of what he'd "seen," and studied it. Knew it was important, or he wouldn't have had two in a row. Rare occurrence, that. But what did it mean? He was ready to doze when he remembered his talismans. He roused himself, found his valise. There they were—the small red rubber ball. And the Anglican *Book of Common Prayer*, from his father's funeral. And finally John's two-headed falcon. "Because we're the Lords of the Two Ways," John had said.

John scoffed at York's silly talismans. But York took them seriously. Listened to what they said. He looked at them for a moment now. The one he should consult would declare itself. Cedric's ball? No, it was silent. But the *Book of Common Prayer* was muttering. He picked it up and retreated to bed, opening the book at random.

> *God is gone up with a merry noise, the Lord with the sound of the trumpet.*

The first lines he saw. He certainly wasn't feeling merry at the moment. And how did they shed light on his sightings? He shut the book in frustration.

Enough! He thrust the diary aside and slumped back to rest. Wasn't ready to confront Marrakech again. Something about it frightened him. Something voodoo in the very way Moroccans walked, talked, an accompaniment to something he hadn't fathomed yet. Not to mention that sights in Morocco were like sounds, and sounds were sights and music, like a drug pervading everything.

He closed his eyes, shut it all out. But the music kept right on.

Not Moroccan music now, but a plainsong. A soaring plainsong. And someone running toward an enormous building with domes, towers.

It was himself he saw . . . hurtling up the long steps not three days ago, through a straggle of tourists, past a bemedaled guard who hissed, "It's already started! No visitors now!" But York churning on through the giant pillars just in time: there was the swaying line of scarlet, filling the arches with plainsong. Choristers following the silver cross that flashed overhead. Cross that was York's, Cross where his God had died to rise again. It was for this he'd come running despite the flu that had hounded him from Osprey Cove, and the pain of his departure from John. Running like God's own fool to reach St. Paul's Cathedral in time. . . .

The chanting line of red dissolved into the choir stalls. The Cross gone with them, up to the hidden altar. And York on his knees, grateful. As if he'd kept a life-or-death rendezvous, as if this might be the last communion service ever held.

> *Cleanse the thoughts of our hearts. . . .*

The words of the service resounding from beyond the altar screen and up into the arches. As York marveled—"Cleanse the *thoughts of our hearts*"—who would dare make such a declaration in the modern world?

> *Lord have mercy on us, and incline our hearts. . . .*

The *thinking* heart! He followed the words up into the vaulted ceiling. Then fell back into the chair, clutching his *Book of Common Prayer*.

> *We remember before Thee, O Lord, all Thy servants departed this life in Thy faith and fear. . . .*

Words spiraling around him. The voice from the altar:

> *The benefit is great if with living faith we receive that Holy Sacrament . . . so is the danger great if we receive*

> *them unworthily, for then we are guilty of the Body and Blood of Christ. . . .*

The words, ominous words. What did they mean? If you took Communion in bad faith, were you really guilty of murdering Jesus Christ? And was that true of love, even of sex, in bad faith—you murdered your mate? His thoughts blasphemous as the service surged on.

> *You who intend to lead the new life. . . .*

The very title John had given his diaries, in Osprey Cove.

" 'The New Life'; that's what we're leading, Yo-yo." Suddenly York was eager to write John, tell him this Communion was central to their love.

> *Draw near with faith. . . .*

But now he saw John, himself and John going to their cathedral in Osprey Cove, the Citadel of the Salvation Army. They'd gone each Sunday to give thanks, till that day John had said, "You go for both of us, Yo-yo. You go pray; I'll work out on my barbells." They had lost their communion-beyond-the-flesh then and there, because John never went again.

> *Come unto me all ye that labor and are heavy laden.*

The singing prayer surrounded York as he realized, no use telling John that his, York's, central faith had been renewed. John couldn't share . . . at least not this. "You're an Anglican, I'm an androgyne," he had said, laughing, as York trudged off alone to the Sally Ann cathedral in Osprey Cove.

> *. . . A full, perfect and sufficient sacrifice . . . for the sins of the whole world. . . .*

He was on his knees again, the prayer of consecration thrusting him there, his breath deepening despite misgivings. Yes, he would take Communion as hope for John-and-York.

Grant that we receiving these Thy creatures of bread and wine. . . .

The wine, the bread converging as flesh, blood, somewhere up behind the rood screen now . . . *snap-snap.* Could hear the cracking of the bread for the first communicants . . . *snap!*

This . . . is my Body, given for you. . . .

Blue and gold of the dome glinting closer. Yes, for John.

This is my Blood. . . .

Cathedral shadows rising in front of York, gliding forward, guiding York to the towering rood screen, up the steps into the choir loft with its deep stalls where the choristers knelt in chant. Directly ahead, the baroque pillars around the altar. Three green-robed priests:

The Body of Christ, the Body. . . .

Words as gentle as petals, ferocious as knives. And if he received these unworthily, was he guilty? The line shifted forward. He fell into a free place at the altar rail, gazing at the Cross above as if it must sprout blood.

Thisss is the Body of Chrissst. The Body. . . .

Priest sibilant above him, York reaching forward as the bread dropped like flame into his hands, but got the bread to his mouth. His tongue dry, the flesh of bread jamming sharp into his palate.

. . . Feed on Him in thy heart. . . .

The gleam of silver at his nose.

Blood of Chrissst . . . the Blood, shed for you. . . .

Priest holding the silver cup forward. York, about to take the chalice, hands trembling. Abruptly wrenched himself away from the rail, turned tail and fled down the long nave, out.

When he opened his eyes all St. Paul's and all London were gone. Only the *Book of Common Prayer* still beside him, lying somewhere on a bed. And through the window, a mad street cackle—Marrakech.

He lurched up, glanced at his watch, nearly three o'clock. He was meeting that young Moroccan at four, in the Milkbar. Just time to take a cold shower, douse the churning film in his head.

The shower definitely woke him. And when he returned to his room, it hit him sharply. He'd spent several hours abed, half awake, half dozing. One of his crazy seances: ideas, notes, messages, sightings, the whole damned bit. It felt foolish after the cold shower. . . . He fled to his diary.

> For over three years everything I've seen, touched, remembered, became John.
>
> Even a visit to St. Paul's becomes St. Paul's vs. John—like a black Mass!
>
> Maybe I've lost the prerogatives of the Occidental mind: which are, not to *feel* anything. But I want to feel *everything*, and then know it, and know from it.
>
> Why not admit I'm a nut?
>
> At least I got as far as Marrakech. If I'm crazy, might as well be crazy here in this aphrodisiac. Knew that before. I came here on an orgasm odyssey, just wouldn't admit it.
>
> Don't know which is worse—N. American heterosex, or gay sex! Heterosex strung out between that cowboy in the Marlboro cigarette ad and the New Woman, a real iron cunt, itching to rule. They deserve each other.
>
> Gay sex worse, if anything. I view my cock as an oracle; the gay boys view cock as object, something to be consumed. No wonder I shy away from them.
>
> Men like Socrates, Michelangelo, Julius Caesar, et al were not *gay*. There's something more.

Yes, a cold shower did wonders for the brain. Though his notes felt angry, and he didn't approve of anger.

> Fact is—it was *sumptuous* within Kibir last night! Left me joyous.
>
> Kabeer's eyes don't look *at*, they *behold!*

Commotion from the street. He staggered to the window: two young Marrakshi fighting over a rooster. Rooster making a racket, as were several hens in a nearby cart. He flopped back on the bed.

> Got to find a place where I can make *calm* notes. A hotel Kabir can visit, and his friends. . . .

Focused at last, York decided to shave. He tried not to see the somber purple rings under his eyes. Eyes like a mandrill's arsehole, he thought, and promptly cut himself with the razor. He was hiding behind his notes so as not to confront Marrakech. Write that down!

He jammed on his clothes, started down the hall, down the flying stairwell and across the empty lobby. What kind of a hotel *was* this? He tripped over the rug in front of the manager's desk, pivoted, and crashed straight into the bright glass doors.

"Crikey Moses—a flamin' dervish!"

A large man picked York up, barking, "Kill yourself that way, crackin' into a glass door!"

York stood stunned. A second voice announced, "Just the man we're looking for!"

They carried York over to the leather armchairs in the corner of the lobby, setting him down with care. "No use to man or beast if he can't walk through a door straight!" The bluff Colonel sitting opposite him, straightening his tie. James dusting off his suede shoes with a handkerchief.

"Did you get our note, y' goat? James left it at the desk."

"No, I didn't think—"

"Well you'd best start thinking, because . . ." The Colonel hesitated. James leaned forward. "We want you to join our little safari."

"Your little—"

"Into the Atlas Mountains. Couple of days scouting."

"Scouting?" York's head was still throbbing from his collision with the door, the hefty Colonel.

"Scouting the land, local customs, varia." James nodded sternly. York remembered how much he'd wanted to accompany these two Englishmen when he heard them at breakfast. But now he felt happy to stay in Kebir's city.

The Colonel was looking dubious. But James intervened. "We could use an extra hand aboard, a sight safer, don't you think?"

The Colonel nodded. "Well, yes; if we go much beyond Ouarzazate, it could be dicey."

"You'll never stop at Ouarzazate, my dear Colonel; you *like* it when the land turns black!" James smiled.

The Colonel grinned. "I suspect, my dear James, you just want a writer aboard to help in your study of the Glaoui!" The Colonel winked at York. York couldn't resist. These two men knew Morocco in a way he never would, chance of a lifetime. And he'd do Marrakech when he got back. He nodded; yes, he'd go!

James looked pleased. "By the by, if you want to bring your friend as interpreter, guide—please do. Does he speak Chleuh as well as Arabic?"

York nodded. Whatever it was, he hoped Kebir could speak it. And it meant Kebir could come on the trip.

"Splendid!" the Colonel said. "We now have an adjutant *and* a batman." With that he rose and barked, "Muster here tomorrow, nine hundred hours sharp!" And paraded out the great glass doors, followed by the elegant James.

York sat probing his head where the door had struck. These two Englishmen were right out of Kipling. The grandfather clock intoned four o'clock. Four! He wobbled out the doors into the jagged sun. Past goats, donkeys, bicycle carts, propelling himself toward the Milkbar. What a fool he was, smashing into the Colonel like that—yet how fortunate! Someone tugged at his knee. A peddler with no legs . . . trying to sell him a secondhand frying pan. No, he didn't *need* a frying pan.

He started running down the street, trying to remember where the Milkbar was. Till he saw the muscleman again, the movie ad. And a jukebox piping loud, "*How many roads must a man walk down . . . ?*"

The Milkbar. York peered in the door, through dark faces, black halos of hair, hippy jeans, blue burnooses, all enveloped in a haze of sweet acrid smoke. But no Kebir! He slumped at a table by the door, fending off the hurt. No reason why he should have been here. Nothing between them except a quick trip into the bushes. York's perpetual false innocence, that's what John would say. Then his shoulder flinched under long fingers. He whirled around to the quiet eyes embracing him, eyes with a touch of mirth.

Kebir broke into a smile and drew York farther into the café, shooing some younger Moroccans from one of the benches so they could be in peace. They sat silent, Kebir smiling, York pacified yet wary.

Glancing up, he caught Kebir's dusky face, like an animal in shimmering jungle. Kebir swaying invisible in his seat.

He looked again. Was Kebir really there? He most certainly was, his eyes declaring, "When I say I will come, I come." Kebir floated a hand through the smoky air, capturing a waiter. York settled for Moroccan tea, Kebir for a milk shake.

He gazed around the Milkbar through the haze of marijuana smoke. At the far end that hand with an eye in it, framed on the wall. Yet the milk shake counter and the large jukebox were straight out of some American in spot.

Out of the smoke, a pair of hands placed a steaming glass before York, large white one in front of Kebir. As York drank the sweet tea he felt a pact between East and West in this strange little Milkbar. The dark-face, pungence of flesh. Such fullness to their lips, mobile, succulent. And hands everywhere, never still, always dancing. A white face, young American girl beside her Moroccan lad. Her blond hair a luscious foam beside the dark skin. The desire in her eyes that of the entire Milkbar.

They finished their drinks, the jukebox sounding, "Hey Jude, don't be afraid. . . ." York sank back on the divan, felt Kebir's eyes on him. Suddenly they were laughing. And York remembered he wanted to change hotels. "Kebir, the Fauzi is so damned noisy, pretentious."

Kebir merely nodded, finally got up, went to the door. York followed, wondering what was going on. Kebir didn't glance back, but wove his way along the noisy street, into a narrow lane. The noise and light subsiding further with each twist into the side alleys. Women bundled in white huddled along, side-stepping endless garbage. York followed Kebir as quickly as he could. But another turn—and no Kebir! Nothing but silence and the pervasive smell of urine.

"Ami . . . ami d'Ospree Cuv!" Voice from high in a vine some yards ahead. He walked on, looked up: eyes of a big cat, high up in the vine. Kebir beckoning. An archway hidden under the big dangling vine led into a steep stairwell up into brightness. A courtyard of small palm trees, red geraniums. And Kebir jingling a pair of keys. York followed to the end of the balcony; Kebir unlocked a plank door into a whitewashed cubicle. Inside, a straw mat, table, chair, low bed and sink.

The cool silence enclosed them. York sat on the bed, the straw mattress crackling under him. Kebir closed the door, leaving the room ignited here and there by rays of sun through the shutters by the sink. York kicked off his shoes, fell back on the bed. Didn't want to go anywhere. Just lie in this monastic cell with the sound of their breathing.

Kebir settled on the small chair at the foot of the bed, his arm draped endlessly over the back. A harmony of blue and black in shirt and jeans, a spurt of red handkerchief at his throat. His entire body, toes to head, male Mona Lisa, a smile in the undulance of his long body. York sighed, his breathing growing longer as if in waking sleep.

Kebir rose like smoke, over to the window, opening the shutter slightly. The sun sprayed through the grill and Kebir dissolved in the light, reappearing as enflamed silhouette. York caught the image out the corner of his eye, image of Kebir burning. Felt it as flames down his neck. . . . Yes, Kebir standing in the angle of sun—listening to the distant hum of the marketplace. He was sideways to the window, oblivious to the flames around him.

York's entire body facing Kebir now, yoked to the auto-da-fé. Kebir's body swaying almost invisibly, a hidden sway that sent silent drumming down York's back, shuddering his cock. Kebir's long body shimmered from within in waves, though his legs were still, and his head leaning against the arabesque grill of the window.

York leaned forward, his whole body an eye following the subtle motion. Kebir's entire body flowed. All save one part. And

York's gaze fell there, the point where the backbone disappeared into the cleft of the buttocks.

Slowly Kebir closed the shutter, blocking all but a few shafts of light. And with his back still to York, took off his shirt. His torso striped by the rays of sun like a zebra in the jungle. And the drumming rising inside York. Kebir, back still to him, kicked off his sandals, then in a single sweep of arm stripped off his pants. As if he hadn't moved at all. Still standing serene at the window, with that blurt of red at his throat. York's vision fell upon shoulders, spine, the dimple of back, the taut buttocks. Kebir pivoted, facing the bed. His eyes dilated, limpid, as he slowly walked toward York. Slowly the hands, Kebir's hands, raised forward, palms open, as he approached the bed. Till he was standing over York, gazing down calmly: eyes given, hands given, cock raised.

York barely registered it before he felt his testicle growl, and looking down saw Kebir full-length beside him. Seconds later they were naked in each other's arms.

He closed his eyes in joy and fear. Joy at falling farther into Marrakech; fear, because he still half expected to be murdered. Ever since descending from the plane, into the sun and Sten guns, he had expected—coveted, even—the quick bite of death. Didn't have time; his toes were happy. Kebir's toes playing against his own, like a cat. He opened his eyes but Kebir was now with his back arched into York's belly. Strong sinuous line of Kebir's back, starting at his shoulders, funneling down into the cleft of buttocks. Blue-black buttocks splurging York's eye as he contemplated the summons of Kebir's back. His hard-on, spectral white, nuzzled there. And the low chant as his cock furrowed deep.

> *The benefit is great if with living faith we receive the flesh. . . .*

Words burgeoning as he lay, a visitor in Kebir's flesh.

For a moment York lay still, flowing with Kebir's breath, their bodies in unison. And with each breath Kebir closed deeper around him. York surveying that black, arched, crepuscular landscape, mountains and valleys of Marrakshi named Kebir. And rising in that landscape, a giant red tulip on a black stalk.

Tulip quivering, swelling at the touch of York's eyes. And Kebir levering his body in an arch across York's waist.

This is my Body and Blood. . . .

Kebir's glance was a summons now. York saw his own hand move across the dark belly, fingers clasping the full body of Kebir's cock, till Kebir flicked his head back in a moan. And turned his eyes full to York, increasing the rhythm of his rise and fall. York clasping the black god-cock more and more firmly, rising and falling his hand. And Kebir breathing more deeply as he thrust more sharply down. Kebir moaning as York detonated and the black tulip blossomed, spewing white petals into the air, splashing down on their shoulders in musk.

Kebir sang with a jugular warble; York lay trepanned. For a moment they were completely still, only their linked eyes alive. Mirth rising, breaking into mutual laughter. York took his forefinger and traced the line of Kebir's nose and lips, his finger wet with sperm. Then traced a small cross on Kebir's forehead, as he had so often with John.

Kebir rose, gliding over to the sink. He splashed himself with water.

"You are a smile!" Kebir's soft voice as he returned from the sink. Yes: York was sprawled across the bed, smiling from head to toe. "The sign you made on my face—"

"It's the mark of my God."

Kebir quiet, tracing the line of York's thigh with a finger. Their cocks modest now. "Mark of your God?"

"The sign of the Cross."

"It protects?"

"Yes."

Kebir seemed pleased. For a while they lay in each other's arms as the light dwindled with the falling sun. The hotel so peaceful, simple. "Your friends can come here, Kebir . . . we'll bring snacks, talk."

Then suddenly he was up, dressing, sitting at the end of the bed looking serious. "The mark of your God will protect me?"

York nodded.

Moments later they were out in the courtyard, meeting Kebir's friend, the manager of the hotel. York felt awkward meeting anyone now. But the manager acted as if they had been there to rest or pray. York booked the room for a week. Then they were outside. The lanes empty now, except for one stray dog covered with sores and flies.

Kebir loped ahead, that odd stride of his effortless yet swift. York trundled after, his body feeling lucid and grateful. Soon there was a sparkle of lights and they emerged into the marketplace, a large café looming on their left.

They had started across the street when a voice piped up. "Ahoy, Osprey Bay! *Ahoy!*" An English voice shouting at them, an elegant figure rising, paisley ascot. James, summoning them to his table on the terrace. York hesitated, waved. Then turned back to join him.

"Good to see you out on the town, my dear York! You Canajuns need to let your hair down." James gestured to a pair of chairs. He had the best table, riding above the brouhaha of the night and commanding every face that passed.

"This, I presume, is your . . . friend?"

"Oh, yes . . . Kebir, James."

"James Goodison. And what splendid sights has Kebir been showing you?" James regarded York's clothes as he spoke: finest Newfie attire. York twitched in his seat.

"We've been looking for another hotel."

"Quite right. One can't receive Moroccan friends in the Fauzi. Boring rule." James tapped his fingers appreciatively and summoned a waiter. In seconds a bottle of rosé and three glasses appeared. James poured the wine himself, sniffed it. "Le gris de Boulaouane, best Moroccan rosé . . . French cépage." He raised his glass. "Here's to our jaunt into the mountains. I presume Kebir can join us?" York flinched; he'd forgotten to ask. But James was already chatting in fluent French to Kebir. And Kebir smiling calmly, as if he'd known about it all along.

"Jolly good: Kebir does speak Chleuh, as you said. It's Chleuh country down there, you know. But why didn't you tell me his father had served with the Glaoui?" James raised his glass, emptied it. York wondered how James could have learned more about Kebir in two minutes than he had after a whole day.

"You *are* silent tonight, my dear York! Marrakech has drawn you into its web."

York nodded. "Marrakech *does* something; I can't think in the ordinary way here!"

"Who wants to think in the ordinary way? Besides, you just need a holiday!" For a moment they sat surveying the night throng. York sipped his wine; Kebir left his untouched. James nodded to several of the passersby.

"I see Kebir is a good Muslim." York was baffled. "He won't touch the wine I gave him. That'll be useful on our trip. Just thought I'd test him; no offense." James was clearly an old Moroccan hand.

"My dear York, you missed that *wonderful* beggar who just went by."

"Beggar?"

"The one on a trolley cart—his clothes."

"Clothes?"

"A single plastic bag! Keep your eyes on the beggars in Marrakech; one of the sights. Tourists come here for the sights, and they never *see* anything. Just the Koutoubia or the marketplace. They don't probe the people! Remarkable people, Moroccans: one hand on the Koran, the other in your pocket."

Kebir was up from his chair now, bowing imperceptibly to James. York followed instinctively. James looked slightly miffed. "You have a rendezvous?" Yes. "Well, don't forget: tomorrow at niners in the lobby!" Then, just as York was leaving, James clutched his arm to whisper, "Congratulations! He's got such eloquent hands!" And with that York was weaving through the flurry of street and market, chasing Kebir's endless lope.

They crossed the market, evading peanut vendors, peddlers, a final snake charmer. And when he saw the gaslights, the steaming piles of rice, York realized that Kebir was returning to the little restaurant of last night. But first he halted, gazing at York almost sternly. "Never go into the mountains alone. Always with a Moroccan!" Drawing himself up to his full height.

York stammered, "But how did you know I *wanted* you to come—when James asked?"

Kebir smiled. "Your eyes, ami."

And now they were at the restaurant, Kebir's friends bouncing up to greet them. Big black Jareeda, and little Abdou, and another face York half recognized. This time Kebir sat down across from them, so he and York had some privacy. After ordering, he rubbed his hands, laughing. "Your friend James makes words dance."

"You mean—?"

"His hands and body, they move when he talks. Most Europeans don't know how to dance with words." York laughed too, then fell silent. Then Kebir telling Jareeda about the trip into the mountains, and little Abdou asking if he could come too. The kebabs arrived. Kebir took one of the sputtering skewers of meat, passed it into the shadows beyond the stall. A small boy darted in, grasping it with a blink of delight.

"What's it like in the mountains?"

"It will be *Morocco.*" Kebir, eyes unblinking but a smile crossing his face.

They ate in silence.

"I must be home early, ami." Kebir's soft words jolted York. He wanted to explore the city tonight with his friend. For an instant he felt jealous; did Kebir have a rendezvous elsewhere?

Kebir rose, his eyes dropping briefly on York. Chuckling as he said, "I must tell my family we're going to the mountains. Jareeda will walk you through the Medina." Then he departed, leaving York faintly guilty and bereft. Suddenly he was up and running. "Kebir . . . look, here's twenty dirhams. Buy something to wear for the trip." Kebir stood silent a moment.

"You make your gift the Moroccan way. Otherwise it is . . . James's way."

York stood stupidly.

"Good night, friend from Ospree Cuv."

York lumbered back toward the little restaurant. For a moment he was lost; all the stalls looked alike. Then saw their stall, Jareeda protecting York's remaining kebabs from a band of waifs. He stood watching a few seconds, fighting back tears. Idiotic. And went to take his seat, Jareeda greeting him in a huge smile. "You like Kebir, m'sieur York."

"I respect Kebir!" The words jumped out of him.

"You are lucky. Kebir sees even when he's not looking."

York continued eating in silence. When he reached his last skewer of meat, he held it out into the dark without thinking. And like chipmunks, a pair of urchins whisked it away as a prize.

"Kebir is already teaching you." Jareeda approved. York blinked. "Tourists don't even see our children."

York couldn't defend tourists, nor himself.

"What will you teach Kebir, m'sieur York?"

York silent. Finally—"I don't really know anything about Kebir." Idiotic.

Jareeda pursed his giant lips, pondering. "His mother makes a good bstilla."

"A what?"

"Pigeon pie. She's famous for her pigeon bstillas." Jareeda sat back, proud of his information. Little Abdou added eagerly, "His father has a shoe store." Jareeda leaned forward again like a conspirator. "His father was in the army before." Then whispering, "The French Army."

"Ah."

"Yes, for the Glaoui." Still whispering.

"The great warlord of Marrakech?"

"You know about T'hami el Glaoui?" Jareeda delighted.

"No; that is, I . . . but Kebir, what does he *do?*" York's question sounded foolish. Did it matter what Kebir did?

Jareeda leaned forward again. "Kebir is twenty—like me. He was very good at school. He was at school until two years ago." Was that it? Jareeda patted York's arm as if to comfort him, trying to see what York was asking. Little Abdou spoke up. "I'm seventeen. . . . Something bad happened to Kebir at school." Jareeda nodded, then frowned at Abdou. York sat silent, trying to light his pipe.

"What do *you* do, m'sieur York?" Jareeda asked.

"Me? I guess I write books."

Jareeda nodded solemnly.

Abdou's face lit up. "Will you write a book about Kebir?"

York shook his head. "I couldn't write about Kebir."

"Why not? He's my friend!"

Such irrefutable reasoning. York pondered. "I couldn't write about Kebir because he talks so little!" Felt pleased with this, yet inane. What *did* he want to know about Kebir? He wrestled with his pipe, which refused to light. "I don't even know how to spell Kebir's *name!*"

"His name?" Jareeda nodded mysteriously. "It depends. . . ."

"On what?"

"On how you want to spell it." Jareeda bouncing in his smile.

"Please, how do spell Kebir?"

"Ahh . . . *K'-b-i-r*. Or you could spell it *K-e-b-i-r*, m'sieur York. Or . . . *K-e-b-e-e-r*. It depends."

York had dropped his pipe in dismay.

"It's an Arabic name, m'sieur York, maybe Chleuh too. It isn't French at all. So you can't spell it right in French, or English, or Spanish."

York was staring at Jareeda. "How do *you* spell it?"

"I never spell it, m'sieur York."

"Why not?"

"Because Kebir is my friend." Jareeda immensely satisfied.

York sat baffled. They must be pulling his leg, but neither Jareeda nor Abdou looked amused; in fact, serious. Abdou whispered, "If you write Kebir's name on a piece of paper, you might harm him."

"*Harm* him? I don't want to harm him. I shall spell his name K-e-b-i-r!"

"Then you *are* going to write about Kebir, m'sieur York!" Jareeda bounced up and down triumphantly.

York was stymied. "No, I wouldn't dare."

"You scowl such a lot, m'sieur York!" said little Abdou with an impish grin.

Suddenly they all laughed together and were up, walking arm in arm down the marketplace. Abdou pirouetting in delight and other young Moroccans coming up, linking arms and smiling as they strolled ahead to the covered mall. Many boutiques still open—and a heavy fragrance in the night air—incense, and hashish floating with the rugs, textiles. Jareeda fending off vendors with a flick of the hand, a fierce glance. They were passing an antique shop—ancient jars, weapons, jewelry. Jareeda saw York looking, grinned, and soon they were all seated in the shop drinking mint tea. A babble of talk, Arabic, French, words of English, Spanish. York couldn't catch much of it, except the rhythm . . . words floating between them in plainsong. York caught up, suddenly realizing what Kebir *did:* Kebir walked the way he walked, smiled the way he smiled, and beheld life with kind eyes. *That* was the answer to his fatuous question. If James made words prance a little, Kebir made life itself a dance. And that being so, Jareeda was right; it didn't matter how you spelled

Kebir's name. What mattered was *Kebir.* He started to laugh. They were all laughing with him, that uncanny Moroccan laughter. It started as mirth in the eyes.

First a silver amulet, then a flat silver hand and a necklace of amber appeared in his lap. His eyes spied a large dagger. And the vendor darted after York's gaze and brought the dagger too. About eighteen inches long, with carved ivory handle. He tried to draw it from its sheath, but it was tied in. The vendor slipped the noose off. "We draw our knives too fast, so we wear a safety cord!"

Jareeda nodded. "Makes a man stop before drawing."

The dagger slithered into York's lap and settled there. York watching it warily. "Do Moroccans still carry daggers like this?"

"In the mountains and the south, often."

He fingered the blade. What sort of man would carry such a weapon?

The vendor laughed. "That dagger has killed more than once! Came from the region of Telouet. It belonged to a khalifa there."

Khalifa?

"A tribal chief, a sheikh."

"I can't afford to buy."

"No need; just for the pleasure of the eyes, m'sieur."

Portable death—for the pleasure of the eyes. York passed the dagger back nervously.

Moments later they strolled on. York had the nagging feeling that all those objets d'art were people, events—not mere objects. And to touch one was to enter a life elsewhere. Like that dagger. He wanted to ask Jareeda about it. But Jareeda was talking to a newcomer, a tall lad in hooded brown djellabah who had turned up after the antique shop. And at the next intersection of lanes Jareeda stopped. "Au revoir, m'sieur York. Abdou will walk you to your hotel."

"Fine. But Jareeda, don't call me m'sieur York. Just York."

"Yes, m'sieur York." Jareeda smiled and was gone.

The new lad walking slightly ahead, hidden in his djellabah; York refreshed by the dinner and walk, looking forward to the mountain jaunt. "Abdou, I think I'll go back to my hotel."

"I'm taking you there." It was the tall lad who spoke up. "The quickest way is down these lanes." Abdou shook his head, but the older one took York by the arm. The alleys growing narrow now, the town above them in looming gables, arcades, fortified walls.

The tall boy pushed ahead, flicking his hood back to see better. His head exposed for the first time. Nose like the curve of that silver knife, tongue flitting over quivering lips, a mane of straight black hair. Almost obscene, such sudden exposure of face. They passed through a lowering archway, high walls, stench of urine. A shadow burst out of the walls, howling around them like a moonlit jackal. Tall boy fell back, grabbed York's arm again, hurling his free arm against the banshee, who sagged away. "M'hashish!" little Abdou whispered, clinging to York. And as they walked on, York caught the sheen of a knife in the tall boy's hand, under his sleeve.

The alleys fled by, another figure tottered past. Where in hell were they? York tried chatting casually to the tall boy, as if just out for a stroll. His name was Mustapha. No, he didn't know Kebir. The lane widened, a few men drifted by, hoods up. A turn in the lane, flare of lights, shrill voices: a small intersection. Group of men carousing by a slatternly café. A body spread in the gutter. The others smoking, spotting them now, and wheeling around them like a pack. Mustapha squeezed York's arm harshly, propelling him on as he smiled, greeting the group in Arabic. Walking as if unconcerned. The pack fell silent, moving closer. And just as the three moved past, man holding a jar leapt at them, tripped in a dizzy arc, shattering jar and spraying the contents over his cohorts. Shouts, fists, flashing knives. . . . Mustapha dragged York and Abdou down a side alley.

They huddled along, pressing together. Tip of Mustapha's knife gleaming beyond his sleeve now, his face sweating, tongue at the corner of his lips. They wheeled around a corner, half tripping over a body. York recoiled against Mustapha, felt the hidden knife.

And now, as they walked on in the shadows, Mustapha took York's hand, fed it through the side vent in his djellabah, thrusting it abruptly onto his cock, which was standing hard under his gown. The silence of two knives, one steel, one flesh. And York clasping the knife of flesh in a spasm of lust that was pure madness.

Mustapha led them on, little Abdou clutching to York, York to Mustapha's cock. Mustapha now strolling with a triumphant grin. Abdou pointed. They had returned to the open market—the floodlit tower of the Koutoubia rising to guide them home. "Good night," Abdou bleated, fleeing. York severed himself from Mustapha's cock. "Your hotel is close by," Mustapha said, voice suddenly milky. "We can go there. I know the manager." But York ran helter-skelter into the square. Footsteps behind him? Tumbling over his own cowardice, glancing back. No one. Just the Koutoubia, upholding a velvet sky. And a single mewling beggar. Seconds later he burst through the glass doors of the Hotel Fauzi. The regal grandfather clock eyed him sternly. The desk clerk chuckled silently—just another tourist fleeing the wonders of Marrakech.

Somewhere in the bottom of the night, York heard the singing voice. Sat up, no one. But still the voice chanting, pulling him up from bed, over to the open window. Voice chanting among the stars, singing out over the dormant town: "Akbarr . . . Allaaahh ak-barrrr. . . ." He stood there naked, immersed in the chant that flowed palpably through the streets, through his window, throughout Marrakech. "Allllaahhh akbar . . . A'laaa," voice booming praise to heaven . . . the priest, muezzin atop the Koutoubia tower, chanting God. He'd heard it with Kebir in the marketplace. Heard it several times these days past. It had seemed a natural part of the din of life, rhythm of the Medina, the ongoing music of all voices here. But now it soared in the silent expectancy of night, song over this city, song all through his room and himself. The man atop that tower, chanting God.

3
LORDS OF THE ATLAS

He was trudging through the snow, up the lane toward the fisherman's house they had rented for the winter. Past Mariam's crazy pink home, Mariam at her door bellowing, "An' where duz ya be goin' to now? Off to yer John, I suppose." Mariam chortling, picking up a tambourine, singing, "John an' Yark, Yark an' John. . . . " York stammered in embarrassment. Mariam was usually so discreet about them. But there she was, clamoring it aloud. He stuck his tongue out at her and scuttled past. But just as he reached Sadie Crocker's home, out popped Sadie banging on a tambourine too, singing along with Mariam. "Yark an' John, our John an' Yark." Sadie laughing and hollering, "An' t' best part of it is, ye never frigs wit our daughters!" And now the whole lane was out in the snow, dancing and wailing, Mariam and Sadie, Polly and Aus', and even old Coo—all out caroling the lane. "John an' Yark, our Yark an' John! Yer *married* now!"

York fled to his house, past the truck and on into the kitchen, slamming the door shut. What had possessed the neighbors to go shouting out their secret to the village like that. But just when he was safely inside, a figure burst out of the cupboard—John stark naked, shaking *their* tambourines and whirling around and around, cock slapping up and down so silly. While Farley ran circles around the pair of them, barking.

And now the alarm was clattering. . . . York lurched up. No Skinner's Lane! No John! Just the sound of goats, strange voices out the window. Kee-rist. He yanked himself from bed; into the coldest shower he could stand, banish the dream. Then sat trying to make notes:

What the hell is going on?

PLACE: Marrakech! Why? A short vacation after finishing my book. Also a vacation from John! But he follows me even in my sleep.

He stopped, mind blank. Dressed slowly, then armed with pipe and notebook made his way to the lobby. He intended to go directly to the Milkbar. But it was still early. He plopped into a leather armchair, determined to assemble his wits. Managed to light his pipe.

Yesterday with Kebir. Incredible lucidity right after. Explains clarity of classic Greek philosophers. Socrates plus mirth.

Marrakech is everything Canada ain't (thank God!). Canada is the world's most successful anaphrodisiac!

I'm currently strung between cock, Christ, and Kebir. Unholy Trinity. Never been a successful Satanist. At best an enfant terrible.

He let out a gurgling sigh, puffed his pipe. The grandfather clock eyeing him sternly. Seven-thirty.

A clock in Marrakech feels so misplaced. Looks at me the way my grandmother used to!

Yesterday with K'bir was *beauty!* Or was it mere *lust?*

Lust *as* beauty?

Maybe the Western world has locked up all *beauty* inside us as *lust.*

Doesn't that explain Johno? All *his* beauty locked inside as lust, needing to be released orgasm by orgasm. Thus each new come a life-&-death battle, a quest for beauty again.

A figure came bounding down the stairs, storming to a halt by York's chair. "You look like Rasputin plotting the doom of the world." York glared, then grinned—the Colonel in morning fettle. "Ready for our jaunt, young fella?"

York nodded. "I'm meeting Kebir in a minute."

"Good-o. James tells me he's splendid."

"What?"

"Oh, you know James; has a fixation with hands. Hands are the implements of the soul, all that tommyrot."

York concluded the Colonel spoke army code. But liked him. The Colonel over at the desk now, cracking out orders. "A call on room 11 at 0800 hours! Goat name of *James Goodison.* Rout him out of bed." The Colonel gone, York jotted again:

> Is it insane to feel joy so strong you become the Burning Bush? That's what I felt yesterday!

He thought of checking out of his room; had the little cell in Kebir's hotel now. But no, he'd keep the room till after the trip—as Insurance.

Then off to the Milkbar, to find Kebir already there. Beside him, his bag for their outing. They were ambling back to the hotel.

A cluster of young Moroccans was milling in front of the hotel. York saw a polished car, battleship-blue—a big Jaguar. The Colonel standing protectively beside it. "Hallooo there, York, I'm under siege! All these fellas want to wash m' car and sell us maps." Colonel in khaki, mustache bristling but eyes laughing. York felt like saluting; he presented Kebir instead. The Colonel nodded briskly. "Glad t' have you aboard. Need a guide in those mountains." Kebir rubbed his nose; how much English *did* he understand?

"For God's sake, Tony, have you invited all Marrakech?" James standing, bleary-eyed, at the top of the hotel steps. Even tired he was elegant, in silk shirt and fresh ascot. Behind him a porter held his alligator bag and two bottles of wine. James nodded to the assembled throng and paraded down the steps, entering the front door of the car as if they were an honor guard drawn up for his benefit. The Colonel shook his head, glanced at York. "Where's *your* luggage, lad?" York had forgotten. He scurried to his room. Where he found an extra shirt, socks, light sweater for cold in the mountains. His binoculars in case of exotic birds. The necklace John had given him, donned as proxy ascot for the occasion. And just as he was leaving, Cedric's red ball as good luck. His talismans. Then ran back to the car, afraid to keep the Colonel waiting.

But the Colonel was at the desk making final arrangements with the hotel. York had time to draw breath, gaze out the glass doors of the lobby. The throng of Moroccans held at bay by James. Kebir, standing near the back of the car, wary, peering inside. No, he'd never ridden in anything like this. Suddenly York saw it through Kebir's eyes—an enormous blue limousine, at least twice the size of Marrakech taxis. A portable English clubroom it was, complete with leather seats, armrests. And James sitting lordly in front, as on the bridge of a ship.

"Kebir looks like he's mounting an elephant hoodah, en route to a tiger hunt!" York opened the rear door, motioned to Kebir, who entered clutching his bundle of clothes. The car rolled silently ahead; the circle of admirers and would-be travelers fell back, waving.

"I'm navigator," James announced, producing a large map.

"Then navigate us out of these carts and donkeys!" The Colonel wheeled the car toward the marketplace.

"The Djema-el-Fna!" James proclaimed. "Turn left!"

They pushed through the morning din. "Koutoubia . . . turn *right!*" The tower glowering above.

"Boulevard Mohammed Cinq." James had a splendid voice. But within minutes he had brought them to a dead end against the city walls.

"You lop-eared goat!" the Colonel bristled.

"Where are you going?" Kebir broke his usual silence.

"Ouarzazate! If we can even get out of Marrakech."

The Colonel reversed the car. Kebir, leaning forward, indicated left, right, left, with a series of nods. They were soon out of the maze of side streets, through the main wall of the town and onto a paved highway. A splash of palm trees around them. The huge medieval walls of Marrakech rolled by, brown-red like Moroccan flesh.

"Used to hang human heads right over these walls," James marveled.

"The good old days, what?" The Colonel laughed.

"Not at all—just recently. The Glaoui was very imaginative in his use of heads." The palm grove waved by, clusters of goats, cattle, carts, and—

OUARZAZATE 197

—a large sign ahead, pointing right. James gave a peevish rattle to his map, folded it away. Kebir nodded and sat back in his seat. The Colonel tapped the accelerator. In minutes they were into a rich golden countryside, strewn with cattle and large white herons, the narrow two-lane highway reaching into the distance.

York was relieved; Marrakech was altogether too much for him. Now he was a comfortable escapee, relaxing in the mobile club land of this Jaguar, watching the land roll by, all picture-postcard. The intermittent geyser of palm trees beyond, and huge trees lining the road, strange with their writhing trunks, tatters of bark. "Eucalyptus," said James.

"Planc trees," the Colonel retorted, "planted under the French regime. . . ."

A grande allée it was.

"Be into the mountains in an hour," the Colonel said. "Ouarzazate in two."

"In three," James murmured, "unless you're planning to drive kamikaze."

York settled deeper into his seat. The trip was going to be fun, these two Englishmen at once old Moroccan hands, and characters.

At the Milkbar, York had asked Kebir what he'd bought for the trip, with the gift from last night. Kebir's smile dissolved slowly—he hadn't bought anything. Why not? "I gave the money to my family. For food." Which silenced York, till he asked what Kebir would have bought. "A pair of pants. I saw them in the Medina last night." York glanced at his watch, jumped up from the divan, out the door, striding down the street, across the market. Kebir in tow, mystified. To the edge of the Medina. "Where did you see the them?" Kebir led him to the boutique. A pair of red pants, burgundy red. Within moments he had the new pants on, the shopkeeper lengthening the cuffs an inch as Kebir stood there. And back they paraded to the Milkbar, for more tea and a milk shake. York glanced at Kebir beside him now, resplendent in his red pants. There was an immense roar, a blast of black smoke. "Hell's kitchen!" the Colonel bellowed, jerking the car off the road as a bus, hurtling past belching black fumes. "Crazy bloody bloke!" the Colonel muttered.

They edged back onto the road, passing a clutch of signs, unpronounceable. Moroccan names. Kebir motioned right. A long bridge over a dry riverbed. A second sign promising Ouarzazate. And York, unnerved, recalled buses in Mexico, used to drive cars right off the road. Mexibuses with their clanging bells, florid motifs—"Jesusito" or "Toro Rabioso" in huge letters. Remembering them from the time there with John.

"Be into the mountains just before the heat!" Only ten o'clock, and already the sun was biting through the windows. Merciless as they sped past cornfields, olive groves. York looked over; yes, the new pants looked good. Kebir caught his glance, grinned.

"Thank you, these, ami." Kebir touched York's arm. "And I see my pants are new, but yours are very old. That makes your gift more gift."

Strange, Kebir's words and way. Courtly somehow, yet intimately perceptive. York turned to look out the window, caught between a chuckle and stupid tears.

"What are you two nattering about back there?" the Colonel barked.

"Don't be antisocial, we can't hear," James added.

York realized they had been almost whispering, off in a separate world. He leaned forward. "I was just wondering—if Morocco is a mirage or a miracle."

Atlas foothills approaching now, and the mountains rising pale blue beyond. And the fragrance billowing in the window with the vista . . . fragrance of field flowers and crops. They were all peering out now, into the sun, up to the mountain tips. As if they weren't driving at all.

"Comin' straight at us!" James yelped. The car swerved, braking to a halt. What was it? York saw nothing, but heard a voice

chanting. And weaving along the center of the road, a yellow robe in the sun, blue shawl fluttering with tufts of red, green. A young woman dancing along the road, up to the front of the car, shaking a tambourine. She flung her head back in a yodel of song, dancing her way around the ambushed car.

"Silly cunt-arsed bitch! Could've killed the lot of us." James snarled. "Just wants her bloody shilling." James waved a handful of money, but she merely rattled her tambourine again, shoving shrill laughter, her stinging eyes, at each in turn. Then, yodeling in wild mirth, danced on down the road.

James drew his hand back, staring at the money. The Colonel shifted into gear, and they drove on in silence. The fields dissolved into foothills. A subtle change in the air: the sharpest scent of the hills, pine trees.

The road swaying now, back and forth, following the contours of the hills. Scrub pine and oak and pink adobe huts flared by the sun. "Stings the eye, it does." James found his voice as he uncorked a bottle of wine.

"Think that'll help your eyes?" the Colonel asked.

"*In vino veritas,*" James answered. "It'll soothe us after that—female attack!" He poured the wine into paper cups, passing one to the Colonel.

"Oh, rightee-o, if you promise it'll improve my driving."

"Wine, York?" No answer. "York, are you asleep?"

"No, just thinking."

"*Thinking!* That can be dangerous for a man." The Colonel chortled.

"Tony, we must do something about our Canadian. He's much too serious."

"What do you propose?"

"Teach him to kick up his heels, what? Kick them up for him, if need be." James was grinning as he tested his wine.

They were already into the first mountains, somber red with slashes of sallow yellow earth, and scrub green. The air had changed, scents as sharp as bird song. A few goats, donkeys grazing along the road.

"Now there's first-class artillery!" James gestured at a donkey, its black hard-on dangling huge in the sun.

"No jealousy on this trip!" the Colonel snorted.

York laughed. . . . Donkey dong: that's what John was always shouting when they were in Mexico, driving south with endless donkeys en route. *"Donkey dong!"* he would blare, gaping at the mighty erections. "I wish mine were black like that."

York gazed out the window. This Moroccan landscape reminded him of the land south of Mexico City toward Oaxaca. Same color-stained rocks, mountains, parched trees, cacti—and same perpetually aroused donkeys. And as the Colonel wheeled around a sharp turn, car lurching, it brought back that wild drive south to Oaxaca with John. Racing just minutes ahead of the police, John's mother had sent after them. John only eighteen then, and his mother hounding them across two continents, criminals for love. They'd driven day and night from Mexico city. And in the first dawn a luminous mountain valley had splurged before them. "It's so *beautiful*, Yo-yo; look at the valley! They can shoot us both if they catch us. But when the bullets hit, we're going to come together!"

Memories seething in York as the road hairpinned around a mountain flank, cluster of pink flowering shrubs, and a rivulet hurtling into the valley below. "Wrong spot to be," James remarked, pointing down the stark drop to huge ribs, a skeleton—remains of a truck. The Colonel wheeling the car over to peer down. The cliff falling sheer to their left, long valley sinking below, foothills fading behind. Among the hills a lush ribbon of green . . . trees, a river.

"Toneee!" The Colonel swung away from the cliff with a skillful flick of his wrist. The car now hugging the rising rock face to the right with inches to spare.

"Ahoy! Our first kasbah," James bleated. The Jaguar swerved to the cliff edge again without slowing, riding the brink. And the Colonel gesturing across James's now rigid body. "Bird's-eye view, what?"

"Tony! There's no *guardrail!"* James squealed.

"Guardrails are for grannies. That kasbah's majestic, what?" Yes, he seemed to ride the cliff edge on a dare, one hand on the wheel, the other saluting valley and kasbah.

And now even James was peering down the vista, waving a camera out the window. York mustered courage, leaned over Kebir to see . . . the castle rising in the valley, like a recumbent lion keeping watch. As they shot around a tight corner, York lurched back to his seat. Kebir biting York on the shoulder as he fell back, grinning mischief because neither the Colonel nor James had seen.

They careened up the hairpin rod, valley unfurling below. The Colonel more agile at each turn, handling the wheel like a race-car driver. Kebir all innocence, nose pressed to the window. And York huddled between his unwanted memories and the threatening majesty of the trip—with Kebir as unexpected mediator.

The car surged around a double turn, forcing the Colonel to slow down. Suddenly the dazzle of flowers and shrubs had turned to rocks, crystal rocks, like giant diamonds and rubies flaunted at the windows. And smiling faces of boys dancing along the road, holding up rocks for sale.

"Stop!" James bleated. The Colonel pulled over to a roadside stand covered with sparkling quartz. The boys running after them, jabbering. All in their late teens, early twenties—flowing in blue burnooses, capes.

"Bargain 'em down!" James jumped out, the others following. The Colonel passed out cigarettes to the boys. Taking advantage of the uproar, York retreated to pee. Stood gazing back down the valley. The kasbah had returned to view with the last twist in the road, presiding over foothills, winding river, mountain steppes. And as he peed, the sound of far-off voices rising . . . was it possible so far?

Kebir was standing off to one side, arms folded, surveying the scene. Like some Shah's guardsman in his red pants, blue shirt. James was hopping around the circle of boys and rocks, snapping quick furtive photos as if he weren't doing so at all. And the Colonel, he was planted like a bluff King Hal in the center of the moving circle. His arm around the shoulder of a big black boy. His other hand inside the lad's robe, caressing a large erection that jutted beneath the garment.

York gaped. But everyone else was laughing, babbling. James snapping more photos. The boys passing the Colonel's cigarettes around.

And as York stood, head spinning at this sight as much as the last, James spotted him. "Hold still, Canajun: I want your *face!*" And laughing, took a quick shot. York stumbled forward. The Colonel now withdrew his hand, the boy rippling with delight and dirhams.

They tumbled back into the car. James scattered coins on the road. The Jaguar swooshed clear of the scrambling boys.

Silence. James sat adjusting his camera, and poured himself a cup of wine. York glanced at Kebir, but Kebir looked as if nothing had even happened. The Colonel driving with a bit more zeal.

The valley climbed alongside them, small fertile steppes carved out of the lower slope on each side. River rumbling now as the valley narrowed to a gorge.

"All the caravans of the Sahara passed through here, Timbuktu to Marrakech," James announced. "Straight into the coffers of the Glaoui. He controlled everything, built immense palaces. . . . We'll pass near Telouet soon: beyond anything in the *Thousand and One Nights!* In the prime years the dungeons held hundreds." James glanced back to see if York was listening. "He ransacked Africa, Europe, for objets d'art, including women. Opulence but with *quality*. That's our man."

James toasted that Glaoui with more wine. "De facto Sultan of southern Morocco. El Hadj T'hami el Glaoui, the Lion of the Atlas, the Black Panther."

The Colonel swerved the car to the cliff edge again. "One more word out of you and the lot of us go for a power drive!"

James stuck out his tongue.

York knew they were just having fun. The Colonel had both hands on the wheel now, the road steeper, every now and then a cluster of huts, mountains stark around them, and the red earth gone sullen black. The car floated through a final turn, clouds close above.

"Look out!" James squeaked. The Colonel swerved, braked. James pointing to the sign—

LOOKOUT

—this time in English.

The Colonel growled, pulled the car over. York grabbed for his binoculars and they lurched out to gaze from high atop the world. The green-black mountains dropping away, the valley, and the winding road they'd left behind.

"On the moon," James muttered.

"Another tot of vino and you *will* be," the Colonel snorted.

Black against the sun a bird—a raven—spiraling down in front of them now. And in its wake, music resounding off the cliff side. Voices singing.

York looked through his binoculars, caught a necklace of trees rising up the far cliff. A group of people in a small field, going around and around, chanting. Floating green fields in the canyon sky. A waterfall spouting out from the wall of rock.

He passed the binoculars to the Colonel, who announced, "They're threshing, a threshing bee."

James took a squint. "Not a spot I'd care to end my days in."

And off again, riding the lunar rock. Derelict stone houses lumbering by. "Abandoned colonial outpost," James declared, his map out again. "We'll soon be at Tichka, the pass."

York shut his eyes. Felt the hand on his arm, Kebir's low voice. "You are nervous." He almost laughed. Kebir was right; they were out on a spree, after all. . . .

COL DU TICHKA
Alt. 2260m

"Good-o," the Colonel said. "From here on it's downhill to the Sahara." And swerved the car through another flurry of sparkling quartz, blue-robed boys dancing the pavement where a smaller road branched to the right.

"*Stop*, Tony!" James rattled his map.

"Not for more of your boys, y'goat!"

"*My* boys? See here, Colonel, Telouet is only a ten-mile detour from here. And it's *the* ancestral kasbah of the Glaoui."

The Colonel tapped the accelerator. "Do we want lunch in Ouarzazate, or don't we?"

James sat forlorn. "Chance of a lifetime, Telouet: eyrie of the Eagle of the Atlas."

"I thought he was Lion of the Atlas." The Colonel snorted.

"He was both; also Viceroy of the South, Protector of the Souss. . . . Well, there's always Tifoultout, in Ouarzazate. Another of his palaces." James took solace in wine, passing a cup to York, who took it this time in sympathy.

They were descending into rock tundra, dwarf pines . . . the oak trees and floral bushes long since gone. Sun harsh as the landscape: rising noon. A hairpin turn revealed the roofs of squat mud homes. "Aguelmous," James announced. A child waved, a voice shouted, "Dirhams," and was gone.

When York opened his eyes again, there was a triumphal stone archway over the road, entry to another village. Scurry of goats, dogs, and—

"Flamin' tank trap!" the Colonel barked, ramming the car to a halt. Yes, giant iron teeth blocking the road. Sten guns swinging at the windshield.

"Passports!"—accusative voice of the officer as they rolled down their windows. "How many days here?" Speaking in halting French.

"Just on a lark, Officer," the Colonel replied in English. James found his passport, stuffed in a large dirham note, passed it out the window. The Colonel surrendered his. York sat frozen; he hadn't brought his passport.

"What is your purpose in the region?" The officer glared at the Colonel, waving three of his men forward. The Colonel looked at James, who said, "Research."

"Tourism," the Colonel barked.

"You haven't got the right stamp!" The officer brandished the Colonel's visa under his nose. The Colonel going red in the face, his scar white.

"Everyone out of the car," the officer shouted. "All luggage out!"

But Kebir leaned forward, began speaking softly in Arabic. The officer seemed startled; had he even noticed him? Kebir flashing his smile, and deference, and a musical flow of words. The officer replying, then Kebir, then the officer, the two in a duet. The officer's face softening till he was grinning, nodding.

One of the men brought a glass of tea to the officer. He passed it to Kebir, who accepted it as if his due. A moment later, tea drunk, the officer waved contemptuously to a soldier. The great iron teeth blocking the road were hauled to one side. The passports returned unexamined. The officer saluted as the car moved ahead. James mopped up some wine he'd spilled on his map. "Bastard still took my money."

The Colonel waited till the Sten guns had dissolved from the mirror. "Rightee-o: I'd been warned. British Consul, Tangiers."

"Warned of what?" York asked, still rattled.

"A hundred tourists a year never come out of Morocco, that's what. Don't even find the bodies—buried in the sand."

"That's what I like to hear." James seemed to be speaking to himself again. They lapsed into silence.

The car sped on through coffered fields, massive boulders eloquent in the sun. Every now and then a huddle of mud or rock huts. And a group of children, dangling small animals on a string. "Squirrels," James said. "Sell 'em for a penny. Sell themselves for a penny!"

What had Kebir said to the officer? Yet instinctively York knew: it was not what was said, but the shared language, the song. So *much* in Morocco felt like song. Suddenly he was in Mexico again, the mountain hamlet of Sola de Vega. Sola, its single dirt road strewn with jacaranda blossoms: "We'll be safe here, Yo-yo, they'll never find us here!"

He'd driven down to the river one night, to pick up some clothes they had washed and left to dry. As he got there a Nazi-style helmet loomed in front of the windshield. A soldier from the mountain garrison, motioning York to get out. He did, the soldier laughing and pointing to an old oil drum close by. York didn't understand. The soldier pointed to his pistol, then to his crotch. . . . York understood: the cock or the pistol.

The soldier bent him over the oil drum, yanked down his pants, and sodomized him for an eternity at gunpoint. "What took you so long, Yo-yo?" John asked when he got back. York never told him.

"Stop, Toneee!" The car yanked to a halt; James gesticulated through the window. The Colonel leaned forward, scar flashing, ready to deal with a new crisis.

"Crikey, you upset a fella! Thought it was more police!" The Colonel grumbled his way out of the car. They were beside a kind of small fortress village, mini-kasbah—red boulders transformed into houses and towers. Patterns embossed in the walls, triangles, circles, lozenges, a visual circus. And atop a tower, fixed against the sun, giant birds with swordlike beaks. Birds standing atop their nest. While below them flapped a barnyard carnival of donkeys, goats, humans.

York gasped in the rabid sun as James skittered around, focusing his camera. But the birds remained imperturbable, scarcely deigning to see him.

"Turn a bit this way," James muttered, beckoning.

The regal birds didn't budge.

"C'mon, I want to immortalize you!" James puckering his lips as he began sneaking toward them.

And still they didn't move. York proud of their dignity as James hopped ahead, kicking up dust like a sparrow. But as he crept close, one of the birds shifted uneasily, raised giant wings to fly. He mustn't—that's what York felt. And as James got set to snap his photo, he dived forward, blocking James, blocking the photo.

"Bonkers!" James spluttered. "You're bleeding bonkers!"

York gaped and mumbled witless apology. What in God's name *was* he doing?

"All aboard, troops!" The Colonel, done peeing, was marching back to the car. "We'll fry standin' out here."

In seconds the breeze was whisking through the car windows. Road angling down into a flamingo-colored plain, jets of green, palm trees. James still muttering about the giant birds, his disrupted photograph.

"They were just storks!" The Colonel snorted.

York sat silent. He reached out, clutched Kebir's arm. Kebir nodded, took his hand.

In half an hour they pulled into Ouarzazate, gasping in the midday heat. "Ask for a place called Dmitri's," the Colonel snapped to no one in particular as they drove down the incongruously modern street of the town.

"Why not ask the Dragon?"

"Dragon?"

"Over there . . . the petrol station!" James pointed. "In case you hadn't noticed, we're nearly out of petrol."

The Colonel wheeled into the station, barking for petrol and Dmitri's. Kebir nodded as the directions were given. York stared at the sign: a six-legged dragon breathing flames. The Colonel laughed. "Believe in dragons, York?"

"No, not yet." But that's what the trip felt like somehow. . . . Yes, bleeding bonkers!

Tank filled, Kebir guided them to Dmitri's, a squat adobe building with protective veranda and a straggle of potted plants.

"Doesn't look too reassuring," James protested.

"It's known for Moroccan cuisine, you lily-livered coot. The rest are tourist spas for the likes of your Lordship." The Colonel nudged James, and they fell out of the car into the smack of sun. York stood in a stupor.

"C'mon, young fella, don't stand there with your expectations drooling." The Colonel grinned, set cap, and boomed into the restaurant.

By the time York drifted inside, James was propped in front of an array of wines, liqueurs, soft drinks: a long primitive bar set amid a long and equally primitive mural of the mountains. The Colonel beside him perusing a guidebook. York plopped into the nearest chair and tried to light his pipe. He opened his diary.

> What was I doing? I literally stopped James from taking a photograph of a stork.

No question: he had given James a sharp shove. Why?

> I felt the birds being violated.

He stared at the note. Something more, but it wouldn't come. And now he realized he had a sore throat too. Yesterday's activities, or the climate change from London? The latter more reassuring.

> Like a *Boy's Own Annual* escapade. Why go reading more into it, just fun?

Suddenly the Colonel recalled the boys, passing out cigarettes he never smoked himself. He blotted that out too. Maybe he hadn't really seen it. Mustn't read his own lunacy into people like the Colonel and James!

A clutch at the back of his neck, strong hand. No one! He glanced around the restaurant. The mural flowing the walls like a review of their trip—kasbah, the lookout, Tichka Pass, storks on a tower. Naive shouting colors of the mural. Morocco as Moroccans see it, primal colors, forms, sunblast, shadows stronger than objects.

"Here he is, writing up his flamin' log!" The Colonel marched over from the bar, glass in hand. York glanced up. James gleaming behind his camera. *Snap snap*—"Got you!" James laughed. York sat up as if vandalized.

"Writing about us?" James pointed to the dairy. "What *do* you think about us?" James smiled encouragingly.

York squirmed. "Frankly, I don't seem able to think about you. But . . ."

"But what?" James persisted.

"But I like you, you're—"

"Admirably put; say no more," the Colonel boomed. "It might do us in."

James lowered the threatening camera. "Where's Kebir?"

"I don't know."

"You don't mean you've lost sight of something as gorgeous as that."

They found Kebir outside, chasing children away from the car. James waved him in and took the table by the front window. But Kebir drew them instead to a table in the far corner—cooler. The Colonel nodded approval. For a moment they sat silent, surveying the restaurant.

Strange place, with its noisy mural enclosing the bar, the bartender lolling there in burnoose and complicit smile—portrait of a man amid mountains. As if they were still in the car, wheeling up the slopes and come to a new vista, new lookout.

The Colonel slapped his knee. "The start of the best kasbah country!"

"Heart of Glaoui-land," James intoned, ordering a bottle of wine.

The Colonel grimaced. "*We* came to Ouarzazate for *food*."

"And what do you propose to eat, mon Colonel?"

"You, if you don't shut up!" James reached for the menu. But the Colonel commandeered it, passing it to Kebir. "He'll choose real Moroccan food." Kebir stared at it, then beckoned a waiter and chattered with him in Arabic. Waiter nodded as Kebir pointed at all four of them, then disappeared.

"What, pray, did you order?" James asked Kebir, who simply grinned. "Doesn't say too damned much, your Kebir."

"No need to," the Colonel snapped. "Says most of it by gesture. Why don't you shut your mouth and open your blinkin' eyes?"

"My dear Colonel," James retorted, "why don't you open your heart and shut your blinkin' army manual?" The two going at each other mercilessly, yet always only at the surface. James brightened as the waiter appeared with wine. "Here's first aid!"

"What I want to know," the Colonel continued, "is what Kebir told the police back there. We might all have ended in the jug: not your wine jug, a jug with bars."

James translated for Kebir, who rubbed his nose, saying, "I saw the officer was Chleuh, that's all."

"All what?" the Colonel asked.

"All that was necessary!" James snorted. "If you really knew Morocco"—he glanced haughtily at the Colonel—"you'd know that once you talk Arabic you're no longer a tourist. But talk Chleuh and you're one of the family . . . at least in Berber country. Isn't that right, Kebir?"

Kebir now turned on James, chattering all lickety-split—York realized it must be Chleuh. James fell silent, while the Colonel bellowed with laughter. "Promote Kebir to lieutenant, instantly!"

Kebir's eyes twinkled. "I also mentioned that you were friends of the Pasha of Marrakech."

"Someone like James a friend of the Pasha?" The Colonel guffawed.

"And that the Pasha asked me to guide you through Berber country. That's when the officer gave me his tea." Kebir looked very pleased.

But James tapped his wineglass. "Wasn't all that a trifle . . . risky?"

"Exactly," the Colonel snapped. "Promote Kebir to *captain!*"

James still didn't approve, but Kebir hadn't finished. "The officer warns us. There was an Algerian border raid south of Zagora. Several deaths."

York wondered if it would be best not to travel any further. But James interrupted him. "Do you know what *Chleuh* means? 'Free men.' And the Chleuh call the Atlas Mountains 'the mountains of the free'!" He raised his glass. "To the *bled es siba!*"

"The what?" James was a gold mine of local lore.

"The country of insolence." James gulped more wine.

The Colonel was preparing to counterattack when a fragrant swirl of steam invaded them, a huge clay platter of food. Kebir rubbed his hands. "Couscous," James announced. "How absoutely right!"

"As officer in charge, I'll begin." The Colonel chortled, digging into the platter and taking enough for two onto his plate. There was still plenty.

"Chicken, with figs and olives and—" James extricated a breast.

Kebir waited till all were fully served, and murmuring "Bismillah," began eating directly from the steaming platter, scooping with bread and fingers.

"Flamin' Beelzebub!" the Colonel shouted, dropping his fork, gulping wine. "This stuff would burn half London down."

While they ate, Moroccans drifted in and out, ordering mint tea. York could feel their glances, though whenever he looked they were gazing elsewhere. And constantly laughing, touching one another, conversation by touch and huddle. So different from his own table, with its sharp repartee. Except for Kebir, of course. Hunched over the edge of the platter as if huddled in a burnoose. Eating so elegantly with his fingers, smacking contented lips as he did so.

What did the Moroccans see as they peered over?

Four men on a spree?

Four men eating more than the dozen Moroccans in the place?

York felt awkward with the Colonel and James, but awkward in a deeper way with Moroccans. As if they possessed secrets of life he could scarcely surmise.

"Salacious secular monks," James piped up. "That's what those Moroccans look like."

But the restaurant fell silent now, a shadow hovering through the door. An old man shuffling in, little boy at his side. The old man started to chant. And sifted toward the bar, the boy holding out his hand and moving among the Moroccans. One gave him a small coin. Another nodded at the barman, who passed over a portion of bread. The old man bowed. "Allah karim." Till one of the Moroccans pushed the boy toward the wealthy corner at the back of the restaurant. And the pair shuffled toward them, all eyes following.

The old man moving across the mural like an Old Testament prophet. The Colonel didn't see them approaching, his back to the bar, nose to the couscous. But James eyed them sharply, patting his wallet pocket as if the wallet might fly out and disappear. The little boy nudged Tony's arm. He looked down as if a dog had nuzzled him. Tony grinned, reached for a dirham. The old man chanted. And they wound around to the other side of the table, where James sat suddenly engrossed in the mural.

Kebir reached into the couscous, found a large drumstick and passed it to the child. The child all eyes as he took it, and the old man sang. York sat dumb; Kebir nodded, and the child led the old man away, his voice quavering in chant, his shadow falling back out the door.

"I told you, York, one of the sights of Morocco—the beggars."

York finally found his tongue. "Moroccans are—they aren't the same as us!"

"My goodness gracious me." James smiled, signaling for another bottle of wine. "You'll have a whole book soon."

"What's this balderdash?" The Colonel surfaced from his couscous but interrupted himself to stare at another foreigner who had just come into the restaurant. A chubby man of uncertain age, great shock of graying hair, followed by three Moroccan lads. Chatting to the barman, who greeted the man with deference.

"Come now, York, you haven't defined Moroccans yet." James again. "Despite your olympic burst of originality."

"I can't. It's the repartee."

"The repartee?" James gazed at York with one eye, his wine with the other.

York hesitated. "Your repartee; it separates us."

"My dear Canajun, repartee is *wit*—higher thought in motion."

York sat silent. Then heard himself blurt, "Wit is simply mirth passed through the mind, which spoils it."

"Not *that's* the best thing you've said all day!" James gurgled. "Do you know what it means?"

"I wish I did. It just popped out."

"Get it down in your notes: another aphorism!" James laughed.

"Why don't you let York eat his food, you young popinjay?" The Colonel had finished his plate, was helping himself to more.

"Popinjay?" James sat bouncing in his chair. "You're the popinjay, all dressed up like a colonel!"

The Colonel bristled. "In Morocco," he said, glowering, "where men are men, and not kewpie dolls—"

Their duel was interrupted by the chubby foreigner, who looked all sympathy and concern. "Gentlemen, I trust your couscous is savory." He spoke in fluent French. The Colonel seemed startled, but James said, "You must be Dmitri."

"That I am! And you—"

"We're up from Marrakech, you see," James began. "Doing research."

"On what?"

"On the—"

"Don't let him get started!" the Colonel bellowed.

"On the Glaoui."

"Ah, fascinating man, the Glaoui. Often here in those days."

"In this restaurant?"

"Indeed. I talked frequently with T'hami el Glaoui. A man of exquisite manners. Unlike his nephew Hammou, I might say, who was known as 'the Vulture.'"

James gaped, stuttering in excitement. By the time the conversation had sorted itself out, they discovered that Dmitri had arrived on foot, Marrakech to Ouarzazate, in 1934. Came up with the French, a provisioner to the army. Had settled in Ouarzazate, and over the years become at once restaurant host, bon vivant and friend to the great, including T'hami el Glaoui.

"He used to arrive with a huge retinue," Dmitri went on. "He'd stroll the street, two men behind him with baskets of money, and pass it out to anyone who asked."

James was so excited, he knocked his glass over. Dmitri waved a little finger. Another bottle appeared.

"He'd stay at the family castle, Telouet. I once got lost there . . . *immense!*"

"I told you, Tony, we should have—"

"Batten your bloody hatches!"

"I used to take food to important prisoners in the dungeons.

Mutilated by torture, usually. But, tell me, how did you get here?" Dmitri asked.

"By car," James replied. "We have a—"

"No, to my restaurant."

"Friends at the Hôtel des Amis in Marrakech," the Colonel explained. "A painter friend recommended you."

"Monsieur Claude?"

"You know him?"

"Been coming here for years. They all come: Claude and that old gentleman."

"Richard."

"Yes. And the beautiful young man, comes with his parrot. Damned bird attacks my guests!"

York sat, amazed. Everyone seemed to know everyone else, and had for years. Dmitri even knew the Glaoui, and James was in ecstasy—not to mention the brandy. "But what kept you *here?*" York managed to ask.

Dmitri paused. "In this region," he finally observed, "it hangs over the walls like an elephant's trunk." James spouted wine and laughter, and the Colonel thumped the table. "Hear, hear!" York was to remain mystified.

For suddenly James was on his feet, clasping a fresh glass of wine. "Gentlemen, this occasion occurs within the shadow of a Titan! The Glaoui paid no taxes, acknowledged no man as master and was host to the lords of the earth." James gargled some wine. "The mountains, the valleys we've traversed were his, and the trade routes funneling from as far afield as Timbuktu."

York squirmed, glanced at Kebir, who was watching James intently.

"His eyes had a strange power. It was said he had the Evil Eye, that one look from the Glaoui would render a strong man impotent." James rolling his words louder with every sentence. The Moroccans by the bar peering over, tugging each other's djellabahs. Dmitri smiling broadly. James was almost on tiptoe now, his face a spasm of handsomeness as he raised his glass higher.

"Until *real* men walk the earth again!

"Until we learn courage again, and the right to laughter and a brave death. . . ."

Even the Colonel was paying attention, thoughts of food cast aside. James poised like a bullfighter about to plunge the sword home: "I give you *El Hadj T'hami Ben Mohammed Mezouari el Glaoui*—

Pasha of Marrakech,
Viceroy of the South,
Lion of the Atlas—

"I give you:

. . . *the Black Panther!*"

Craaash! He smashed his glass to the floor, wine spraying across the restaurant.

"For Christ's sake!" The Colonel pounded the table for James to sit down, but several of the Moroccans were stomping their feet in applause, and Dmitri looked consummately pleased. Whatever James had said, he'd said with panache, virtue enough in their eyes.

James stood quivering amid the debris of glass and words, bowed gravely to the restaurant and sat down. But the Colonel was remonstrating. "Where d'you think you *are*, the Albert Hall?" James was silent, tugging on a glass of brandy again. Wry smile on his face; wistful.

Kebir turned away, nodding. James made his apologies to Dmitri, said he'd been "carried away by the splendor of the occasion and the élan of the company."

"Bally nonsense!" barked the Colonel.

A waiter appeared, the fireworks over. James gestured grandly at the fragments of glass and passed him a ten-dirham note. Dmitri smiled; the waiter smiled. The wine was wiped up, the glass swept away.

Dmitri suggested a proper Moroccan desert to top the occasion. It appeared: sweet honeycake and almonds. "And I'll have a brandy—no, two," the Colonel added.

Now they were all chattering, Dmitri holding forth amiably. Yes, he was Greek . . . had followed the French army as far as the pacification of Rissani. And yes, the Glaoui had a harem of over one hundred and fifty ladies, with additional boys at his disposal for the use of guests.

James, it appeared, had once been a professional photographer—"Doing models," as he put it. He insisted on a photo of their group, including Dmitri's boys. . . . Done!

Dmitri asked where York was from. "Toronto," York said proudly, "one of the pioneer families there." Dmitri was impressed, asking, "And where *is* Toronto?"

Finally Dmitri was saying au revoir; he had a meeting with the Khalifa. Would they care to dine with him tonight? "Marvelous," James said. But the Colonel argued for pressing on. "Catch those kasbahs . . . dine on the way back, what?" Dmitri smiled, asked them to pass fond regards to messrs. Claude, Richard and the baleful parrot at the Hôtel des Amis. And with that he was ambling out the door, followed by his young companions.

Kebir was sitting in bemused delight. James was looking curiously bereft. And the Colonel clucked to himself, "Now there's a book for York to write: Dmitri!" But York was trying to find something to ask James, something that would show his startling knowledge of Morocco to advantage.

"What *is* the Evil Eye, James? I can't seem to find out."

"Now that, my dear Canajun, is an eye that curdles your brain. It's said that Pope Pius XII had the Eye, as did Hitler. . . . Am I right, Kebir?"

Kebir didn't understand. James switched to French; Kebir nodded. "Aisha Kendisha has the Eye."

"Aisha what?" York was out of his depth again.

"Aisha Kendisha. She stalks the land for men to have sex. They go insane afterward. Like that dancing woman, she had the Eye."

"Listening to you goons could drive a man to pee!" The Colonel rose, strode out the back of the restaurant.

Silence. James took the chance to order another brandy.

"Poor Tony just lacks imagination. Too much army in his family! Great military family, though. Finds it hard to live up to all that."

York nodded, wanted to know more about the Colonel.

"You have to prod him a bit," James added. "A sweet old codger under the swagger. As for you, my dear York, you don't really care about any of it. You just sit and spectate! Fodder for the diary."

"What's the Colonel's research on?"

"Ahh, our beloved Colonel is"—James twirled his brandy—"a zebologist."

"A zeb what?"

"*Truant* zebology," James said solemnly. Kebir chuckled, solicitously wiping his fingers with his white handkerchief. James leaned forward conspiratorially. "You saw him at work a while back, very dangerous in this country."

"Yes, yes, I see." But York didn't see at all. Maybe that event with the boys, which York still couldn't believe he'd seen.

And James nodding. "Public handiwork in Morocco is harshly punished, though God knows *anything* goes in private. They're not prudes."

But York was caught in a spasm of coughing. Kebir, after watching an instant, disappeared from the table. And now the Colonel was booming back to their corner. "I have a thought!"

"Don't let it distress you, Tony!"

"If we press on right away, we'll reach Zagora comfortably by six. . . . Splendid material there, you know."

James glanced at his watch. "A little after two. We still have time for another brandy. Protection against the heat."

The Colonel glowered but acquiesced. Brandies all around.

"Besides," James said, "that's the old Glaoui route, we *must* do it."

"Here's to kasbah country." The Colonel raised his glass.

"You mean ksar country," James purred.

"Ksars, kasbahs, all the same thing."

"A ksar is a *fortified* kasbah, my dear Colonel. And in any case, the plural of ksar is ksour!"

The Colonel pivoted in his chair, exploding. "You *are* impossible, James!"

"Thank you." James grinned satisfaction.

The Colonel turned to York. "How about you, young fella? Are you game?"

York coughed, half nodded.

"Fact is, Tony, our little trip is doing York a world of good."

"How do you know?"

"He smiled *twice* during lunch!"

Even York laughed. "This trip with you gentlemen—"

"Please, my dear York, give us our due. Call us the Gentlemen Adventurers!"

"To the escapades of three Gentlemen Adventurers." York raised his glass.

"*Four,*" the Colonel replied, raising his own. "Kebir is a full captain now. No racism here."

"Racism or not, they've changed color," James snapped.

"Changed color?" The Colonel confused.

"Mulatto in Marrakech, full chocolate in Ouarzazate. For a zebologist you're not very observant. And you're supposed to *like* it dark." With which James wobbled off to the washroom.

The Colonel emptied his brandy, winked at York. "A bit silly sometimes. Has an odd notion of what a gentleman should be. But a good sort, really."

York nodded. "He's quite erudite."

"Mmmm. He *was* a bright university man; English literature, languages, that sort."

"That accounts for his use of language," York said.

"Nothing accounts for *his* use of language!" The Colonel growled, then grinned. "Did a thesis on Swinburne. Fell afoul of the authorities over booze. Had a few bad years, been trying to make good ever since. . . . You've got to bully him a wee, needs the discipline."

York understood James now, striving to make a clean start. Gentleman James.

Kebir was back, passing York a small bottle.

"What is it?" The Colonel peered over.

"Dunno." York opened it: cough drops.

"Did you ask for 'em?"

York hadn't. "But I can certainly use them."

"Damned perceptive, your Kebir."

York swallowed two of the cough drops. The Colonel gave him a nudge, pointing through a window onto the veranda. There was Kebir: Kebir in that dark flare of red, plucking fluff from his shirt, rubbing his face, waist—body flowing like a cat, cleaning and preening after a meal.

York went to the door to watch. Kebir strolling up the bright street, jaunty red handkerchief at his throat. Past another sidewalk café. Blue-jean hippies gathered around a single bottle of orange pop which apparently rented the table. Kebir didn't seem to notice them. Then just beyond their table paused pensively, rubbing his thigh, chatting with some young Moroccans.

So casual, this after-lunch promenade. Kebir could have no

idea that York was watching, almost guilty at seeing such a parade—for that's what it was, Kebir as parade!

Kebir was moving toward the Colonel's car, followed by his new Moroccan acquaintances and two of the girl hippies. He now stood by the Jaguar, one hand stroking it. His fingers plucking fluff off his shirt, rubbing his pants, adjusting the crotch without touching it. Such huge hands, strong long deft fingers. And talking of their trip; must be, miming the oratorical stance of James.

Was it all actually there, or just a mirage? York spied Kebir standing utterly still, alert, listening—listening for what? York wanted to shout praise of what he'd just seen. Instead backed away from the door. Didn't want Kebir to see him spying, probing the core of his being. But kept his eyes fixed on Kebir.

And there saw the road, sonorously winding road from Marrakech, great avenue of plane trees, the red and ocher soil of foothills, sprouting green valley, presiding kasbah and soar of eagles over their car, the Colonel gigantic at the wheel . . . their trip now spiraling through Kebir's body, the land as he stood by the car. Like the singing they'd heard at the lookout, chant of the Atlas mountains, the land of "free men."

Chant of Kebir!

York gaping as if Kebir must suddenly dissolve, or leap high across the sky, or . . .

York tottered, clutching at a doorjamb, brain seething from what he'd seen.

Till Kebir strode across the space that separated them, through the door, catching York as he began to fall, shielding him from the hot light.

For a moment York stood shaking, his body an earthquake. Then the surge of calm that was Kebir's smile. It had all happened so fast, no one else noticed. And a moment later they were at the lunch table, sitting quietly with the Colonel, who was settling the bill. York tried to pay for himself and Kebir.

"See here, young fella, let me cover our little luncheon. You pay your shot at dinner. Besides, you've been a great help."

"I have?" York had dismal thoughts about himself just at the moment.

"You certainly have. When James wants some entertainment

now, he takes a swipe at you or ogles Kebir. Takes a weight off *my* shoulders!" The Colonel laughed.

"And there's the gentleman in question." The Colonel pointed out the window. James on the veranda, gazing down his aquiline nose at various stray hippies, dogs, Moroccans, Milord James! A beggar approaching him, beggar on the stumps of his knees, mewling for alms. James looked askance; the beggar waved a short crutch. James waved the man away. But the beggar squatted there like a crushed toad, calling the angels of Allah down on James's head.

York retreated to the washroom. All flies, scattered turds, a boy offering to exhibit the wonder of the Atlas. York, half inclined to see, couldn't pee as a result. By the time he returned, he heard the shout—"Hunt's *awaaa-ay!*" Colonel Tony roaring to the car, waving nonexistent swagger stick.

"Wait, Toneee!" James dodging into the restaurant, while Kebir helped York into the car. The Colonel started the engine, snorting, "*Silleee* James!" as the latter emerged from the restaurant clutching a bottle. Running toward the car . . . and slipping the beggar a large coin.

"*Zagora*—that's our spa!" The Colonel blasted the horn. James toppled into his seat. And as the cluster of Moroccans and hippies jostled in envy around the car, they pulled away. Kebir sat gravely upright, pointing ahead, giving the Colonel directions. In minutes they were clear of Ouarzazate, careening past the usual swarm of goats, donkeys, chickens, walking-bundles-of-laundry. Red land rising furiously around them again, here and there a green slash.

"*There* it is!" James croaked, waving his fingers as a giant kasbah surged out of the palm grove on their right.

"What?"

"Tifoultout!"

"Tiffertit yourself." The Colonel snorted, accelerating.

"The Glaoui's palace. You *promised*. Toneee!" James waving his camera frantically out the window.

But the Colonel just honked, and on they sped, land sallow red under the high sun, road knifing straight at the horizon.

Kebir sat smiling and waved at the land. Yes, waving at the passing landscape, no one in sight now. It was *his* Morocco unfurling around them—something Tony had said at lunch. York remembered Kebir's eyes during that strange oration about the Glaoui. Kebir imbibing James and *knowing* something. York had seen the shift in Kebir's eyes, as if he were gazing over a precipice.

Lunch, the food and the event, had last almost two hours, yet felt like two minutes to York. And how to explain a man like Dmitri, who came to Morocco by accident and stayed thirty years! And what did Dmitri mean? "Morocco never accuses, just kills the fainthearted!"

"Like a ripe fig!" James announced.

"What is?" the Colonel asked.

"Dmitri," James said. "That's who York is annotating now!"

The Colonel laughed. "James can read everyone's mind except his own. And Dmitri looks more like an overripe fig! Now, Kebir is—"

"Not for the likes of you!" James returned. "Whereas our York—"

"Is the Queen Mother in disguise!" The Colonel mimicking James's haughty voice.

"No, York's the Cowardly Lion; he only *looks* ferocious."

"At least he's not the Queen of Oz," Tony replied.

"Nor the Tin Soldier, my dear Colonel."

The Colonel replied by taking a silver flask from the glove compartment, sluicing a shot down and passing the flask to York. There was a crest on it with the motto *Fideliter.* York took a gulp, choked—whiskey! "Cauterize that sore throat for you." The Colonel grinned. James begged a taste, but the Colonel snorted. "You've got your own cellar, right on your lap!" James began to protest. The Colonel started zigzagging the car down the road as if epileptic. James spluttered. Each time he opened his mouth, the Colonel honked the horn and swerved again.

York lurched back and forth expecting quick death.

The Colonel finally resumed driving as if nothing had occurred.

"You leave me speechless!" James bleated.

"Mission accomplished." Tony chortled. And with that pressed a separate horn . . . *tarantarraah!* Hunting horn yodeling and wailing across the road and land . . . *tarrantaaarrraaa-tarraaah!*

Then James began to giggle, clapping his hands in delight. York laughed in sheer relief. The Colonel boomed out a deep-gut guffaw. And Kebir too, because they were all laughing. The car roaring along in a gust of laughter, laughter that digested their wild lunch at Dmitri's, and blessed James for his absurd speech about the Glaoui, and broke York's frown, and installed the Colonel as kindly commandant of their spree.

Kebir was riding like a maharajah now, nodding proudly at the Colonel . . . *their* Colonel. Holding York's hand in the sudden intimacy of the car.

For a while they drove in silence. James opened his bottle. York was too pleased to bother thinking. *This* was what he'd come for: peace of mind, joy of eye, Kebir, and the zany company of the two Englishmen.

It was the Colonel who broke the silence. "Hasn't been a sign of life for miles, not even a tree." Yes, the land barren around them, endless rubble avalanche, red with undertone of black. The belying brilliance of blue sky overhead, like an ocean upside down. The Colonel squinted into the sun, swerved to avoid a boulder in the middle of the road.

"Colonel Tony, you drive like a pro." York praising.

"Well, you know, York, I did drive professionally once." He chuckled. "Drove a truck in Australia a while."

"With the army?"

"No, went off to Australia right after school. The pater gave me passage, enough to live on for a month." The Colonel ready to reminisce. But James gurgled. "Come come, Tony—you fled your bloomin' family!"

"What d'you mean, fled? A Napier never flees, sir!"

"Tony"—James tapped on his wine bottle—"I *heard* the story. In Marrakech." James tapping the bottle, glancing at the Colonel with a sly grin.

"In Marrakech? Not possible!" The Colonel hesitated, fell silent, concentrating on the road, though it was straight for miles.

"Heard it from the bizarre artist friend of yours." James grinned confidently.

"I never have artists as friends; they're contagious!" The Colonel aggressive, yet constrained, now.

"What about Claude, at the Hôtel des Amis?" Tap-tappitytap, James tapped the corkscrew against the bottle. "And that old gossip, Richard." Still no response. "I heard it from all of them, Tony!"

"Christ, you dizzy thing! Just when we're having a darn good time, you want blood!" The Colonel straightened in his seat.

York sat stupefied, wondering how to stop such a cruel game. Too fascinated to try.

Tap-tappity-tappp.

"All right, it was at school. I fell in love. . . ."

"With the school nurse?" James smiled, all innocence, caressing his bottle.

"With the head prefect." The Colonel gulped more whiskey.

"By Jove, you *do* have standards."

The Colonel stared at the road. "Gorgeous fella, captain of rugger."

"Ooh: a *hearty*, rah-rah!"

"He used to write poetry too. On the sly, wouldn't do to have a prefect writing poetry. I was his fag."

"So it seems."

The Colonel stopped, one hand plucking at his mustache. James tap-tapping the bottle again, tap-tappity-tapp.

"I was his batman, kept his room tidy, shoes. One day he showed me his poems. And I showed him some of mine."

"*You* wrote poetry, Colonel Tony?" York blurted.

"Yesss. Dreadful stuff, I'm sure. But I had fallen deeply in love with Robert—"

"Robert Warrender—Warrender of India; *that* family." James nodded approval, glancing at York.

The Colonel silent again, driving into his own long stare. "Flamin' death. . . . *That's* what this landscape is."

"And we're the Charge of the Death Brigade." Tap-tap-tapping on his half-empty bottle.

"I know you won't understand, James." The Colonel growled, staring at the noisy bottle. "It wasn't the usual public-school thing. And stop masturbating that bottle of poison you're holding!" They all laughed nervously.

"It happened after the school match with Harrow. I was polishing his boots. In he came, in his towel; towel dropped before he saw me. And there it was."

"Details." James burped. "*Details!*"

The Colonel glared. "He was strikingly handsome. We did it right on the spot."

"Gory details!"

"When we were *done*, I knew something had happened, something I couldn't go back on."

James sat silent. The Colonel driving more slowly now. They were all staring out the windows, land redder, hotter . . . sun angling right at them. Kebir looked questioningly.

"He loved a young man," York whispered.

James tap-tapping his bottle again. The Colonel tightened his hands on the wheel. "I went to Robert's home for Easter vacation. Old monastery, in the family since Tudor times. Robert's pater an army man like mine, proper martinet. But his mother was divine, liked his poetry. Wanted him to go to Cambridge, read English. Father wanted him to enter Sandhurst, the Guards."

"Which did he do?"

The Colonel paused for a shot of whiskey. James silenced his bottle. Colonel nodded. "One afternoon Robert and I were in their garden, the arbor at the back. Usually very private. He was reading *Lycidas* to me. We both sprang hard; unbuttoned; did the job. And at the climax—"

"There was?"

"There was the bearded face of Jehovah, glaring through the bushes!"

"You mean, God was the third party?"

"I mean, there was Robert's father, face like this landscape: burnin' *death!*"

"Kee-rist, Tony." York hadn't meant to speak.

"Robert and I went back to our rooms. His pater summoned him. By butler. I never learned what was said. His mother came to my room, kept saying 'Tony, oh, Tony.' Wanted to talk, but she couldn't." He looked furiously down the road. "You don't want to hear this rot!"

Their silence said they did.

"We all met for dinner that night: black tie, as usual. I'll never forget the gruesome portrait of Robert's ancestor, the one who joined Cromwell—hanging right over the father. Not a word till the end of the main course, roast grouse. Then Robert's father made his little speech."

The Colonel took a gulp of whiskey, raised his voice to a hoarse, peremptory staccato. "It has been my duty to telephone the Headmaster. Headmaster has been splendid!" Mimicking the father's voice. "Anthony, as junior offender, will be permitted to return to school. Robert will remain at home for final term. Headmaster concurs public reason will be he requires private tuition. On this basis—headmaster and I agreed—nothing further will be said in the affair."

The Colonel sagged, voice dropping. "Idiot *hated* his own son! Made us swear an oath, Robert and me, oath on their enormous family Bible, that we'd never meet again."

The car had slowed to a crawl. Colonel peering out the window. James was silent. York leaned forward, put his hand on the Colonel's shoulder. "What did you do, Tony?"

"What could we do? Robert's pater was General Sir Horace Warrender—a power in England. We swore an oath never to meet again. And for the rest of that evening the father regaled us with stories of Lord Kitchener; he'd served as subaltern under him. Then I was driven home to my family, and they were informed that proper measures had been taken." Tony paused for whiskey, gagged, and gagged again.

"Next morning they found Robert in the stables, hanging from a rafter. He'd used a harness. On the floor was the copy of *Lycidas*."

The car floated down the road for a mile or two. James sat as if impaled. York's eyes fled out the window to . . . fatal yet seductive landscape, how long would a man last there?

The Colonel growled. "Was that what they told you at the Hôtel des Amis?"

James shook his head, unable to look at Tony.

"Well, that's how I went to Australia. If I fled my family, at least I fled forward! And I did drive a truck, to earn my own keep."

James nodded, face drained. "Tony, Claude didn't tell me that much. Just that there was a big scandal, the Warrenders of India. . . ."

"Richard knows, I told him years ago. Hoped he'd forgotten." Tony talking out the window.

James nursed his silent bottle. Bleated, "This horse needs a water stop!"

The car halted, and they burst out like refugees, stupefied in the sun.

"Atlas safari: *take up . . . water stations!*" Tony drawn up to full height, Colonel once again. They dispersed to their work, peeing into the parched rocks. A village simmered on the horizon. Mirage? No sound except the snap of stone underfoot. Yet an eerie beauty to the eye, the crackling laval red, flecks of black.

"Mind if I get a shot?" James ran for his camera.

The Colonel was standing at the prow of the car in khaki, officer's cap, goggles: Field Marshal Sir Anthony Napier, taking the salute. Mustache twitching sternly. "*Step forward*, York, Kebir. Photograph duty!"

York, the Colonel, Kebir—drawn up in array beside the car.

"The Three Musketeers on a spree." James grinned. *Snap-snap.* "Now one more, and smile a bit; not a funeral." *Snap-snap.* The Colonel sagged against the car, goggles falling. They watched as he slumped onto the scorching hood of the car. And jumped to catch him; the three of them around him, sheltering him from the sun. Tony gasping. "You see, he left a note. . . ."

"Yes, Tony."

"Saying he'd always love me. His mother found it."

Kebir massaging Tony's neck. James holding him firm at the waist. "Inside the book. She gave it to me." York propping Tony's shoulders.

"I still have Robert's note!" He roared like a speared bull, then fell silent as they tightened their embrace around him.

A moment later Tony looked across the long valley. "Good place to bury the story once and for all!" He tried to grin. And for the first time York saw his eyes: beautiful, turquoise blue, gentle under the mask of colonel.

James went to pick up his camera; it had fallen on sand, no apparent harm. Car felt cool after direct sun. They drove on, rockscape rolling by relentlessly. Kebir placed his hand on York's. A palpable intimacy in the car as they huddled against the passing land.

4
"CHRIST WITH A HARD-ON"

The Tifernine hills!" James had his map out again.

"Hills?" Tony muttered. "Don't see anything except bloody rocks."

York stared out the window at the heat rising with the very red of the rocks, his fever rising with it.

"What was Tony saying, back there?" Voice flowing from under York's skin: Kebir's whisper.

"That he'll always love a young Englishman who . . . died."

Kebir nodded, had understood before York spoke. And looked out the window, sadness flickering his face. Young Moroccans were always laughing, but there was a silence to Kebir too, like hidden pain. And the very tone of Tony's voice had touched that pain. York had felt it as he had felt his own.

James's voice an excited squeak. "Watch tower!" Leaning forward, York saw a black stab at the sky. And as they wound through the rising strata of rock the tower loomed first in one window, then another, passing from side to side as if following them. Angular it was, separate from the land. Its black stones laid out straight and sharp.

"Good place to incarcerate James," Tony said.

But James squirmed hopefully. "A photo . . . stop for a photo."

"Just French Legion, you know." The Colonel growled. "They built forts all through here."

"Beau Geste country!" James flapped his camera out the window, trying to snap the tower.

York didn't find it romantic at all. He turned away, gazing down the long valley behind, back across the land where Tony's heart had been ripped out.

"Flamin' tower's spying on us," James staring through his camera.

Yes, the tower glaring down again as the car wheeled up the low mountains. Confrontation at every turn.

"That tower separates everything." York as upset as James now.

"Tommyrot!"

"Separation of land from people, brain from body. . . ."

"York's going intellectual on us." Tony snorted. "And it's *your* fault." He poked James, who was bracing himself with wine.

"The Occident invading Morocco." York desperate to explain. "That tower isn't wed to the land."

"Here, York, you need some vino." James passed a tot.

He drank it, shaking. "Tower *watches*, but everything in Morocco *beholds.*"

"Brain damage." The Colonel laughed.

"No, York's using the tower the same way he uses us," James replied. "To make notes."

York shut up. Yes, his fever definitely worse. And as he stared out at the passing lands that horrendous spring in the Mexican mountains lurched up. Broke, stalked by Mexican police, John and York lying together naked one morning. And John's eyes wide and clear. But John couldn't get it up; unusual for him. And abruptly the bottom had fallen out of his eyes. John had ripped himself from bed, saying nothing. Locked himself in the donkey shed. Tap-tap . . . tap-tap-tap, all day the frenetic banging of John's little typewriter. At sundown he reappeared, brandishing the letters he'd written. To his parents, addressed via York's lawyer in Toronto, advising them to call off the police and forward his passport, or he would commit suicide. Because without John's passport they were trapped, certain to be arrested. "I've sent my suicide back to *them*—where it belongs!"

The days passed. They ate tortillas, corn stolen from the fields. The passport arrived, and the telegram from the Canadian embassy in Mexico to York's lawyer: "Police search called off."

That afternoon they had walked out into the countryside, hand in hand. John's eyes whole again. And they embraced, shared love in the cornfield. York would never forget that day. It was the same day he had received the curt letter from his wife, demanding divorce.

"Haven't passed a single car since Ouarzazate." It was the Colonel. James lost in his wine. Kebir reached over, taking York's hand as the car reeled around the curves. On their left, like incision into huge animal thigh, a gorge dropped steeply. And huddling at the bottom, a clot of green palm trees and a few huts.

York closed his eyes. Next he knew, someone was shouting. It was James, leaning forward and shouting. "Land ho! Town ho!" And they were all leaning forward and peering down the rapid incline. Yes, at the foot of the tumbling road a rise of towers, buildings.

"What's it call itself?" Tony asked.

James replied with a belching cough.

"What's its bloomin' name?" Tony repeated.

James repeated a burping cough. The Colonel glared. James grinned, pointing at a looming road sign—

AGDZ

"How would *you* pronounce that, my dear Tony?" The Colonel stared . . . and imitated James's belch. Moments later they pulled into a string of red and yellow clay shops, houses, a towering mosque. A scattering of donkeys trotted across their bow. They nosed their way around a corner, entering the town market. The Colonel wheeling to avoid carts goats vendors. . . .

"Time for a water stop." James announced.

Kebir was leaning left, pointing to a small outdoor café with shaded veranda. They parked nearby and spewed out of the car, into the heat.

"B'god, it *did* follow us!" James spluttered. Above the town, another black-stone fort staring at them. James hesitating with his camera.

"Crikey, *you* think it's romantic, York thinks it's the Evil Eye . . . tommyrot!" The Colonel grabbed James by the arm, propelling him toward the café. Kebir already there, leading them to the shadiest corner of the veranda. For a moment they sat silent, reveling in the shade. Four glasses of orange juice appeared. "Just the ticket." Tony grinned relief, Kebir grinned.

They drank the juice gratefully and took turns disappearing to the washroom.

When York returned from the dark recesses of washroom and café, he suddenly saw them, huge against the sun. The three of them presiding over the market. The billow of robes, turbans, bustle of bargaining and market stalls just beyond. He stopped a moment, perhaps fifteen feet from them, and watched.

James surveying the market, as if in a club window in St. James's. His eyes darting from face to face, assessing and disdainfully dismissing.

Tony with cherubic smile now, shirt unbuttoned, yet always Colonel, always in charge. Scar on his face like a drawn sword. James miming a pasha; Tony *was* a pasha!

York smiled—they hadn't seen him, standing partly behind a pillar. Not even Kebir, who had passed them through a police blockade as if a tea shop. And laughed about it, and no one thought to thank him. Eloquent Kebir, yes! James made impromptu speeches, but Kebir's slightest gesture its own speech.

York ducked farther behind the pillar. James furtively scanning Kebir, glancing away and back again. So James felt Kebir's power too. Something about him drew attention even as he avoided it.

"You're spying on us!" James had spotted York now. "Making notes about us!"

York laughed, came forward. No, he wasn't making motes.

"*Libelous* notes, I could tell!"

"I was just watching you."

"What did you see?" James rapped the table with his long fingers. "What did you see? You must share it."

"I didn't really *see* anything. In Morocco you—"

"Would you two idiots stop!" The Colonel barking. James sat back, took up his monocular position.

Some brochettes arrived. "Already past four. I thought a bite would brace us for Zagora," Tony said. Attention passed from York to brochettes, small pieces of mutton with delicate fatty morsels between them. And another round of juice.

"That's better," the Colonel said, "I can feel my legs again."

"Your legs!" James snorted. "Well, enjoy them. No one else will."

"My legs are an imperial asset," the Colonel retorted.

James laughed. “Your legs are Pooh Bear.”

For an instant Tony looked ferocious, then subsided into a grin. The brochettes were done. Kebir wiped his face with his huge hands, rubbing mouth, cheeks, chin. Taking out his handkerchief, cleaning his hands. “Magnificent hands!” James noted, “but most unusual manners.”

“But, milord James, Kebir’s manners are . . .” The Colonel started.

“Are *what?*” James smirked.

York jumped in. “A courtesy to life, and not”—he glanced at James—“not just a social code he flaunts.”

The Colonel beamed approval. James looked startled. Kebir sat smiling that smile that elevated his body an inch. James finally confessing, “I can’t help liking Kebir,” smile spreading to his own face.

“Quick stroll through the market, anyone?” The Colonel bounced up from his chair, James joining him. York wanted to remain in the shade. Kebir disappeared with the other two, and York opened his notebook, to record what he’d seen a moment ago—that luminous sighting of all three of them. No words came. He concentrated on Kebir.

> The opposite of the Occidental “gay guy” who promises Paradise in a quick orgasm. Such orgasm merely a respite from Occidental hell (& apogee of that hell!)
>
> K. only gives what he already holds. The opposite to debit-loving, expense-account sex (play now, pay later).
>
> Ah—Occidental sex, same as Occidental economics—all mirrored in *national sexual debt!*

He looked at what he’d written, ideas he’d had on seeing that Foreign Legion tower—had clung to them till written. So James was right! But now he’d lost the splendor of that sighting of the Colonel and James and Kebir! Damn!

He sat back and gazed at the plants along the edge of the veranda, geraniums booming the sun. The face of Kebir surging up in the flowers, James and Tony panting their way back to the shade of the veranda, a final orange juice for the road.

James grabbed the *Guide Bleu* from Tony's hands and, sitting erect, began to read.

> AGDZ . . . colorful market town and soukh at the edge of the Anti-Atlas. Beginning of the exotic world of the kasbahs of the fertile Draa Valley.

His voice expanding as he read.

> The drive from Agdz to Zagora is one of the glories of Morocco. The point at which a more ancient black Africa met and married with the Berbers and later invaders speaking the Arabic tongue.

James's face swelling to sensual beauty. Subtle transformation, invading York's eyes as the words his ears.

> A world where magic potions and spells still linger in the hand of local shaman. . . . World where the Evil Eye still lurks. . . .

"Hogwash!" the Colonel protested. "He's making it up!" But James kept on.

> The Grand Hôtel du Sud awaits you in Zagora, built in the style of the mighty kasbahs. And the famous roadsign pointing your way to Timbuctu! You who revere the Glaoui, take a caravan. . . .

James's face now translucent, a shimmering strange beauty, ageless. And springing from James's carefully profiled head, a second head, black . . . long kinky hair, flaring eyes. Cameo of beautiful James and the raging black head beyond! York shifted in his chair, trying to focus. And still that second dancing head, searing black . . . and tall skeletal body jigging up and down like a frantic scream.

James shifted out of profile, licking his lips. "Gentlemen, we are deep in the realm of the immortal Glaoui!"

"You and your immortal Glaoui!" The Colonel snorted. "You long to be incarcerated in one of his dungeons!"

York leapt to his feet, pointing . . . that black dervish head, body weaving a strange pattern around their car. Lurching toward it as if to strike, then away, and back. In ballooning pants, tatter of a shirt, storming his feet at the car. "Sullen sod, must be drunk!" Tony muttered. "So long as he doesn't touch my car." No, wasn't touching it, just snaking his way around it as if to pierce its entrails. Shaking his arms, head high. Black halo like a storm cloud. They didn't know whether to laugh or shout.

York smiled nervously. Morocco played strange tricks with vision. He'd seen that crazy black head bobbing behind James, as if seeing a double James. In fact it was this lunatic silhouetted in the sun by their car. The figure looming around the car was certainly weird, as if weaving a ritual dance.

Kebir returned from the washroom, saw them gaping at the car. He jumped over the veranda rail and bounded toward the Jaguar, flailing his long arms. Black head bowed, leered past Kebir at them . . . and slowly backed away.

"Bloke must be crazy," Tony said.

Kebir came back, beckoning to York.

"Wants to give you a tour of market, I guess. We've got a few minutes." The Colonel nodded and went out to examine his car. York followed Kebir into the square. The lunatic had vanished.

Kebir drew York through the market to a group of stalls, one of which was piled with brass, silver, handmade jewelry. He pushed forward, fingering the smaller objects. Picked one up, holding it in front of York's eyes. "Hand of Fatima," he said, waving the stylized hand across York's eyes. York almost laughed, Kebir so serious. But he didn't want to buy the hand. Kebir looked offended.

The vendor found a larger silver hand on a chain, holding it up, light splashing off it. "Very strong," he said, pointing to a dragon sculpted in the center of the hand. Yes, striking. Kebir nodded vigorously; perhaps he wanted it as a present. York felt foolish that he hadn't realized. He nodded. Kebir bargained the price down by more than half.

Seconds later they were walking toward the car, Kebir carrying the protective hand, content. As they skirted around a cluster of stalls, York lost Kebir in the throng. A camel thrust his head at him, and York panicked, started to run. He caught sight of the car, ran toward it, slowing as he approached, ashamed. And as he stopped, the figure jumped in front of him, waving a piece of fur, like a foxtail, flaunting it at York's face, gibbering. The lunatic again, weaving around York and on around the Jaguar. Rubbing his thighs against the car and pulling away, hips swaying, jabbing at it, mumbling. Then stepping aside, head tilted, scanning the car through something. Other Moroccans gathering around, watching. And the man dancing, scanning the car through a chunk of red glass.

York first wanted to jump forward, protect the car. Then he wanted to flee from crazed car, from Agdz, from Morocco.

"Trying to fuck our car!" An English voice booming. "Intercourse with a car . . . against the law!" The Colonel out at the Jaguar now, checking it as he would a body for broken bones. While James babbled, "Plum crazy, that one!" and reached for money to pay the man into oblivion. But madman had vanished again, dissolving the way everything seemed to dissolve in Morocco. The crowd acting as if nothing had occurred. And York standing as if the top of his head had been sliced open.

"C'mon, you two, before that goon turns you into shish kebab." Tony dusted off his pants, reaching for the car door. "Yeeeowww!" He shook his head in disbelief. "Hot enough to fry an egg!" Then opened the door with his handkerchief, and they all clambered in.

"Which way out of this bedlam?" he asked.

"To the right," James said, brandishing the map.

"To the right, milord James, is a herd of camels!"

James rolled down his window, asking for Zagora. Kebir sat rubbing the new Hand of Fatima. York sat dazed, head burning, Agdz much hotter than Ouarza-what's-it. Heat rising, biting into his neck. He spun around in the seat, glimpsed crazy eyes spitting flames into him. Wild eyes, crinkly hair flaming in the sun, head like black sun . . . that lunatic through the back window of the car, holding up his chunk of glass, sun streaming through the glass, magnified, beaming fire at York's throat. York gagged, Kebir pivoted and saw instantly . . . jamming the Hand of Fatima up against the window, blotting the madman out, as he shoved York away from the window.

The car rolled off through the market, through the milling

crowd, on under that looming black fortress. And a jagged triumphal arch.

ZAGORA

—the sign pointing left. The Colonel wheeled the car past the few remaining shops, a straggle of sheep. Clear of the town, the land surging black rock again and a stutter of palm trees.

"Not exactly *Venice!"* Tony clucked.

"Another ten minutes of that burg and I'd need a brain transplant," James muttered.

"Always did!" Tony added. "And what were you two up to back there, a wrestling match?"

"That screwy Moroccan was *burning* me through the window."

"What with, a bazooka?" The Colonel sounded dubious.

"Piece of glass . . . like a magnifying glass."

The Colonel glanced back as if York might just be going up in flames. Then laughed. "My dear York, you're just as superstitious as old James here!"

The incident dismissed, like everything else odd in Morocco, as if it had never happened. Yet reaching up, York felt his neck still burning and his fever mounting.

Kebir passed the silver Hand to him. York had bought it as gift for Kebir. Kebir whispered no, bought as protection for York. And tried to explain—that's why he'd held his hand up against the madwoman dancing by, the one who had brought the car to a stop. And why he'd held the Hand up against that man, burning York. Kebir urgent. "Protection against the Eye, ami!"

And finally York took the two-headed falcon from around his own neck and gave it to Kebir, then accepted the Hand of Fatima. Kebir content when he saw York wearing it. And they sat arm in arm, as if all was as should be.

"The *Draaaahh* Valley!" James mustered his impresario's voice and waved at the oncoming land. The town well behind now. Palm trees thickening, black rocky land splurting green. The Draa River rising, and beyond, rumbling across the sky like immense prehistoric beast, the mountains flat black with tincture of rose.

But James was holding something in his hand, holding it up. "I picked up your diary, York! You forgot it in the café!" York flinched. Was his brain *that* scattered now?"

Tony glanced over—yes, it was York's notebook.

James asking, "What *this* mean? Tony always looks as if he's wearing gold epaulets and medals, on permanent parade!"

The Colonel chuckled. York leaned forward to grab the book. But James held it away, flipping the page. "And *this?*—'I don't understand silly James. Not sure I even want to!' "

York's head was spinning as he tried to get his diary. But James was holding it like a hostage. "And this gem? 'Kebir's presence judges my entire life!' And *this*—'I hear the wings of Doom fluttering over us!' "

The Colonel gave a sharp toot on the horn and growled. "A gentleman does not read someone else's diary!" And snatched the diary from James, passing it back to York.

James laughed. "Truth is, Colonel, York didn't write any of that. I made it all up."

"You're lying."

"I'm *not!*" James snapped.

"Well, if you made it up, you're brighter than I give you credit for! It sounded like our York!"

"How do you know? Our York doesn't say much!"

The Colonel pondered. "It sounded the way . . . our York looks!"

"Now that *is* bright. For a colonel!"

They all laughed nervously, "The one bit I did see was about the national sexual debt! If 'our York' would kindly explain *that!*"

"I don't know," York spluttered. "I mean, it's correlated to national self-perjury. . . ."

"Ob-fus-ca-tion! Fact is, York's an illiterate in two languages, French *and* English!"

They chuckled, even York who had a splitting headache now. Tony added, "Kebir's the only intellectual here, speaks *three* languages." But their attention passed to red walls, towers, clusters of houses and clay huts springing our of the land around them. Children waving and women singing as bright as their shawls.

"Kasbah country!"—the fait accompli crowned by James's pronouncement.

The Colonel slowed the car through a stream of poultry and donkeys.

"A monument . . . *stop!*" James peremptory. Tony pulled to an obliging halt, peering into the eddies of heat. James pointed his camera at a small triumphal arch, sculpted vases atop.

"It's just the village pump!" Tony gurgled. Yes, the village well, and a young girl drawing water.

Snap-snap—James took the photo, whinnying, "Water is so precious here, they build the Arc de Triomphe around it."

The life of the kasbah teeming around them. Children with goats, sheep, an elder in white turban, dagger at his waist. A nod of donkeys, and overhead, the palm trees like giant fans.

"No sense sittin' here," the Colonel said. "Best get right into it." James was already out, *snap-snap* . . . an orgy of camera. York forced himself out, made for a patch of shade. A little boy ran up, touching his shirt, ogling his shoes. The Colonel was dispensing cigarettes and bonhomie. Young girls drawing water at the monumental well, chasing a goat that upset one of their jars. And Kebir bartering for dates and ambling amid his own in a smile that said he'd come home. The kasbah unfolding all around them—flying balconies, crenellations, turrets. And the elder in white turban, silently surveying—dignitary of the dagger he seemed born to carry. And people flowing in all directions.

York needed a pee, tried to disappear under a tree but the children followed, singing. Finally crossed the road into an orchard and beneath the trees a crop of grain. Peered back at people as he'd never seen them, only read about, ancient peoples, Biblical. All their energy in being.

York tried to grasp what he saw. John would love such a village, why not bring John here, with his flute—John at his best.

He took his pee facing the river below, the near distant mountains charging his eyes. The sound of a horn, wild cry of hunting horn riding the sky. Colonel's hunting horn.

York returned, Tony at the wheel bellowing, "Hunt's *awaa-aayy.*" James covertly snapping picture of Kebir by the well. And a rooster flapping onto the hood of the car. The life of the kasbah going on as if they weren't there at all.

The Jaguar prodded through a final clutch of chickens. James still *snap-snapping* through the window as they pulled clear of the kasbah. "The incredible geometry of those buildings," James said exulting.

"Geometry of the flesh," York murmured.

"An aphorism?" James snorted.

"I m-mean," York stuttered, "it's an intensification of the body . . . those architectural forms."

James protested. "Bosh! They're totally *abstract!*"

"Extrinsically abstract but intrinsically carnal. The body sings."

"My dear York, must you talk in polysyllabics? Are you saying the kasbah was sexy?"

"*More* than that . . . in a way we aren't." Why couldn't he keep his mouth shut and his diary to himself?

"Listen to him! That loony in Agdz put a hex on our York!" York suddenly saw the madman dancing around their car again, hand lunging for a knife. Image burning York's eyes like an incantation, burning his neck, brain. For a moment he wanted to scream.

The kasbah-village dissolved, the screen of palm trees fell away. And rolling beyond, a virulent serenity of blue. "The Draaaah Rivaaaah," James proclaimed, turning their attention to the widening valley on their left. The river much larger now, with running hedge of bright trees willows, poplars surging its banks, like a giant garden. And above the meander of valley, the brooding black mountains.

They drove in silence, every now and then sudden village life spurting around them again. And then that view into the glistening Eden valley. The Colonel stopped once: young woman striding by, a huge collage of amber, silver, bracelets and coins clanking her arms and legs. Carrying a water jar . . . no veil, her face a joyous shout.

"A walking bank vault, all that jewelry." Tony chortled.

"Just another damned virago!" said James.

But York saw the fierce joy of that young woman—could he celebrate life that well?

They were climbing now, several hundred feet above the growing river. The Colonel's excitement growing with the vista, swinging the car over to the edge of the road after each turn for a better view. Till reeling round a sharp bend the entire valley spewed open in a spangle of palm orchards, groves, the river become a flowing lake. And lunging out of the river a turreted castle, kasbah atop and island. Kasbah surmounting the valley. Keeper of the river. . . . *Tarantaran-tarraah,* Tony blasting his hunting horn.

"*Toneee!*" Kebir shouted, hitting the Colonel hard on the shoulder. Tony yanked the emergency brake as the car teetered on the brink of the cliff. The four sitting stunned in the suction of the vista. Stunned at the tottering edge of the cliff they hadn't even noticed.

"Nearly went flamin' over," James whimpered.

They sat paralyzed, York clutching the Hand of Fatima. Tony cautiously eased the car into reverse, backing off to the safe side of the road. They extricated themselves from the car. James gulped wine directly from the bottle as they gasped for breath in the sun.

"Sorry chaps, took it a mite close," the Colonel said. "Raise Kebir to Major!" And examining the cliff—"*There's* the spot, lots o' shade." He pointed to a cluster of bushes, small willows. They almost tiptoed to the point of the cliff giving over the valley. "Best rest here for ten, assemble our wits," he said, setting himself down on an ample boulder.

James gurgled more wine, passed the bottle to York. "It's better than standing there pickin' your nose, Canajun."

"At least he isn't scratchin' his arse, like you are!" The Colonel growled. Kebir produced a bottle of water and shared figs from the kasbah. They just sat gazing at the ground. Tony played with a broken twig, suddenly smiling. "Like England in lilac time . . . oceans of it." Yes, the waves of fragrance they'd followed up to Ouarzazate. Almost palpable, like shifting layers in the air.

Come down to Kew in lilac time,
In lilac time,
Come down to Kew in lilac time,
It isn't far from London.

Tony reciting the lines—"My mother loved that poem." He looked up, gazed into the valley.

"Blitherin' romantic!" James muttered.

"Guess I am," Tony murmured. "Saw too many of my friends killed in the war not to hope for heaven. If only for them . . ." He paused. "Better a romantic than a cynic posing as a romantic!" He squinted at James. "I'm going for a little walk."

"Well, remember you haven't got wings. *As yet!* Don't try flyin' over this damned cliff a second time." But the Colonel ambled on like a country squire out for an afternoon stroll. Kebir had already drifted away.

York went for his binoculars. When he returned, James too had gone—he had their little promontory to himself. A miniature floating eyrie. A few red flowers amids the crushed stones, and improbable willow bushes off to one side. Perching himself on the Colonel's rock, a natural bench. And peered down the valley a bit at a time. Too much to imbibe at once, too much beauty. . . .

Finally he took his binoculars and focused back along the road—stark boulders, scrub, barren land above the valley. And beyond one of the trees, Kebir standing quiet sentinel, Titan in the amplifying sun. Beyond Kebir, the valley surging into York's binoculars . . . blue of river, iridescent green fields. Distant rumble resounding the entire valley, becoming shuddering roar echoed by the wall of mountains. Was it the river moaning such harmonious vehemence? He swept the binoculars down the valley—isthmus of land jutting the river, almost as island and rife with bushes. Cattle looming in and out of roaring bushes, horns gleaming the sun, massive as buffalo. And wandering amid the cattle a tall herdsman, gathering all blue of the river into his single burnoose. Huge birds roving the river edge—ten, twenty, more. Like a great white necklace along the river, a herd of birds, like a herd of cattle.

York closed his eyes, valley surging inside him along with fever. Worth a death to come here, sit with this valley, be seen by such valley he barely dared glimpse.

The binoculars tugged his hands. He opened his eyes, following the gaze of peremptory binoculars . . . upriver, up through the zigzag of fields to the island . . . the jut of turrets, towers, presiding kasbah storming calm above the face of river.

Such a world had always been there inside him, yet forgotten, worse, dismissed by excision of the heart. His body quaking in recognition he feared and needed. He lowered the binoculars, one hand braced on a willow branch. All the land they'd ridden since. Marrakech about to spring at him—like those prehistoric animals carved, painted as blood on caves he'd seen in France years ago.

Binoculars jerked his hands again; his eyes followed. A falcon swooping, playing the air, russet wings in the sun, fantail hovering, dangling the mountains beneath. The binoculars followed, holding their breath as the bird wove the valley into a swoop of song. Then gone, dissolved in the scudding air. He lurched to his feet, adjusted binoculars, questing the sky. Falcon directly above, quizzing him. He took a step, caught the falcon in binoculars—helmet head, white-and-black slash of mask and scimitar beak. Drifting off to the right, gliding slowly down, bringing the sky down and York's gaze with it. That head poised atop a naked body now, body of boy, black youth body. Falcon head and boy body strident in the binoculars, strutting. Ancient god Horus. Black human flesh glistering naked, white hand stroking.

Crazy! York ripped the binoculars from his eyes. But there where the bird had hovered, perhaps twenty yards up the road, Tony and two, three boys. Tony standing bluff king beside the tallest boy. Boy naked, green pants down at his knees. And Tony calmly stroking the boy's hard-on. The other two boys sitting, grinning, sharing Tony's cigarettes. In the background, hidden by bushes, James gleefully snapping photos.

York stood, stuttering disbelief. The falcon head gone, boy's own head instead—eyes swelling. His phallic spear jutting high above the river. Black cock rising to red tip. Tony's white hand caressing and caressing it.

York's body quaked, raging. Red head of that cock swelling; white petals spewing. York groaned as sperm hurtled. He stumbled, grabbed willow branch, groped his way back to the big rock.

He thrust binoculars aside—dangerous, such eyes. Too late—long since the valley as beast, the entire land since Marrakech rampant in him. Demanding he know what he'd always known. He sat clenched over the rock, and saw the eye probing inside him, and great scimitar horns, and flesh shuddering the walls of a cave.

Ten years ago? In southern France, valley of La Dordogne,

with Christine. Chris urging him to visit the caves of Lascaux; see the prehistoric frescoes. He was dubious—what sense in visiting grottoes if one could see Versailles, Chartres? Chris had insisted. There'd be a squabble, silent tears if he didn't go. And there they were, leaving the glorious French sunlight behind and descending into the ground through a squalid tunnel. Dark, musty. Two in a guided group. Didn't know what to expect. The guide presenting his tour prologue: something about Cro-Magnon man. But York hadn't heard, his eyes roving ahead beyond the end of the musky tunnel. On to the cave itself. Disconcerting rumble emanating from the cave. They were ushered into the maw of the cave. Disappointing—it seemed so small. And he couldn't see anything. Then a light slowly ignited the walls, undulating grotto bellying close around them. York felt like Jonah inside the whale. He stepped back. Rough pelt, mane flickering at him from the wall. Portions of animal body erupting in the cave. Imperceptible at first, growing vehement. A haunch, a massive neck, a hump . . . multiple beast lurking in the half-lit walls.

Their guide gesticulating, intoning something about "the worlds's first murals." But the guide himself a shadow, compared with what was gazing out from the wall. Eye probing York, muzzle looming and scimitar horns. Beast amassed on the flank of the cave—seeing right through York and his new Paris suit.

The guide wheeled them on. But York lingered as long as he could, seduced by this bestiary of the Lascaux walls. These shadowy animals like first sunrise flaring the world. *He* the one emerging from a cave to behold this uproar of beasts. As if here the real world, and where he'd come from, the black cave. Yes, the world of Lascaux ominously magnificent—spectral Eden. A tawny rump disappeared into turf on his left, galloping antelopes, horses. And the sharp pang in his flank—shaft of spear jabbing out of the flank of a buffalo beside him. Hurting him as much as buffalo. Roar of this wounded animal joining rumble of cave.

And still he tried simply to *see* these walls. Level after level they clambered down after the prattling guide. "Grotto number three, here you see . . ."

And what York saw was an epochal valley of all beasts, more lovable-ferocious than any he'd ever known. Beasts with omnivorous eyes scanning him. His own body surging forward to touch, stroke a haunch, a mane. Or flee a horn, a randy eye. His body bellowing in such endless life, his eyes prehensile to these eyes.

But the guide always prodding them on—Grotto number five, was it now?

Till they were groping their way back up through the musty tunnel, and standing at his side in the surge of light, palpable in a new and frightening way, his wife Christine. She was smiling as they stood together in the sunlight. Knowing they'd been present at the birth of the world. Beasts, tundra, mountains . . . reborn in their own bodies as he held her hand.

That night, in a small auberge in Chinon, they celebrated the occasion with eel pie and local vin de paille. Discussed the wines of Chinon, the fact that Richard Coeur de Lion had been imprisoned in a castle nearby. But Lascaux seemed undiscussable. York tried once, clumsily, but Christine shied off. And after dinner, York's flesh still rumbling, they almost fucked for keeps. But Christine had just heaved her first moan of release . . . and stopped. Complaining she was sore. My God, she was always sore or dry or cankered. York lay abed, impaled on his own unfulfilled erection. All night his flesh aroar, flesh reborn in that unwitting cave. But Christine's cunt was sore—oh, Jesus, it had been sore for a hundred years or more! Like her mother's and her grandmothers'. Sore since dear Prince Albert died. And York lay insane with impacted potence.

Next morning they had driven on. Visited a medieval cathedral Chris longed to see. Chris losing herself amid the gloom, cooing, delightedly explaining the re-redos, sculptings, iconography of tympanum. But nothing could touch him. . . . Lascaux had transformed and frightened him, threatening his marriage, his sanity.

Some days later Christine did talk about Lascaux. Said it was "indisputably man's first fresco." But York wanted to shout, "Lascaux is hell and heaven born again . . . earth as entrails. Every woman goddess there, every man a bearer of the spear."

Yes, Lascaux the fiery furnace, the flesh of those walls burning York's own flesh, fusing body, brain and being in a new unity. But Chris had continued her academic explanations, hadn't studied art history for nothing. And York, through his pain, *knew* what Lascaux was: the world as its own cathedral, a world men lived embodied in, a world where man's eye was not detached from what it saw. Man no mere observer but part of the tree, bird, beast seen.

York clutched to his rock and willow branch, high above the Draa Valley now. He clenched his eyes shut, to stop the rage from pummeling his body and fevered brain. Only to see those first men: men of the prehistoric cave, racing away from the sight of bison, mammoth, antelope, back to their protective cave, tracing with bloodied fingers onto the cavern walls.

"To see an animal this way is to participate in God!" York's very tumult yanking him to his feet.

He took a step forward, listening. Yes, words seething up. "In Lascaux, animal seen is *our own flesh and blood. . . .* And we seeing it become its dance, eating its very substance with our eye, for joy. And to slaughter such a beast is to tamper with our own life and body, can only be done as sacrament, something offered under God. . . ."

He stood shaking on the brink above the Draa. This valley—Lascaux, as one in him. Lascaux, a piece of the world before the Fall . . . certainly before the Fall we call Western Man. Lascaux, the world when man, beast, eye, body and being are but one. . . .

And if this be so, then all cathedrals built since are shadows mourning a lost reality.

And with this knew that he and his eternally beloved wife went apart over this very reality—the never discussed fact that cathedrals are gray and gloomy. Whereas Lascaux, the flesh alive in the eye of God, alive in a way York had never been, might never be.

York shuddered, traced the sign of the cross. His eye caught now by a sudden stoop, a bird plummeting down toward the river. The falcon back, *his* falcon! His heart leapt, his eyes following the bird as it slowed to an easy spiral over the river. And now, unaided by binoculars, he beheld the sweep of river, the island kasbah, the mountains . . . beheld them as a single sweep in their long drive from Marrakech. This river, this valley, like Marrakech itself, flowing direct from Lascaux. Marrakech: a sign from another route taken over the past ten millennia. And their voyage up into the Atlas Mountains, through some lost Eden, over the burned rocks topping the world . . . their little jaunt smelting York's mind to something else right here in this valley—a garden, stream of life, sheep, kine, herders, kasbah. York suspended within this suspended valley, seen by God. . . .

A tug at his arm: someone hauling him back from tip of cliff where he had been posed unaware. Pushing him firmly back, forcing him down onto the big rock. York saw the red, red pants. Kebir between him and the edge of the cliff where he had been standing, babbling.

Kebir passed him some water. York asked for the Colonel, James. Kebir nodded down the road past the car. There was Tony with another boy. Tony stroking another spear of flesh, the boy glazed in a smile, the first boy lying nearby, smoking a cigarette. James skittered in the open now, gleefully recording Tony and his phallic godchildren. Everyone, Kebir included, acting as if Tony were simply saluting the valley.

A straggle of goats emerged from the bushes, picking their way down the tumbling rocks toward the river. Tony's boys, herders taking their flock to water. Kebir brushed York's arm, pointing to the river . . . river exploding into the air. York focused his binoculars and caught them rising in huge and delicate flight over the shimmer of fields, bridal-white against the green. Up and wavering in line across the flank of mountains. Fifty, a hundred herons, the last of them barely clear of the river and the leader already up into the shout of blue!

Tarantarrah . . . tarraaa—Tony's horn rollicked the vista. James snapped a final photo. Kebir led York to thc car. Thc boys waving, the goats scampering down the cliff side as the car rolled down the road once more.

"*Za-go-rrraaa,* next stop!" James announced as the river dissolved behind them. Tony sucked on his brandy flask. "Remarkable view," James said, patting his camera. "Think I'll develop this roll m'self." And turned to ask, "What were *you* watching so avidly, my dear York?"

"Those birds!"

James and Tony exploded in laughter. "*What* birds? C'mon, Canajun. Can't you just accept what you're here for?" James hectoring. "What were you really watching through those spyglasses?"

York didn't know what to say. That his body had become the

valley? That he'd seen a falcon as Horus, as the falcon-youth? Had walked through Lascaux, with his wife?

He closed his eyes, saw a burning figure . . . figure walking over the river, over the valley, arms outstretched in majesty. "Christ—Christ with a hard-on! That's what I saw." The words bursting out before he could stop them. He sat awaiting more laughter . . . and drowning in the silence.

The river reappeared in the distance. Tony tapped the accelerator. "Get to Zagora by the river, out of this flamin' heat." They zoomed around the curves. York sat in a stupor. At least his crazy words had stopped. And next he knew the car was pulling to a halt past a kasbah. "Need a weewee," Tony said. They trundled into an open stony field.

"Help! Help!" James shouting in mid-pee.

The Colonel marched over, Kebir and York following. "Just a leg!" the Colonel saying.

"Toneee . . . it's a *human* leg!" James clinging to Tony, pointing. Yes, a human leg, dry, most of the flesh gone; leg prodding up from under the rocks. And nearby, more bones, a scalp or two.

Tony gazed around. "Been piddling on graves," he muttered. And pulled James back toward the car, James babbling about peeing on the dead. The Colonel trying to calm him, pointing to his pants. "Would you put that thing away!" James's cock dangling out, half hard. They managed to get James proper, if not calm. And as they approached the car, a gray figure billowed up from the rock, gangrene smile. Tony bundled James, blithering, into the car. Kebir talked with the figure in a gray burnoose, an old man; wanted a lift to his village, a few miles on. Tony mumbled yes. And on they drove, the old man gazing at the landscape passing so swiftly. Another kasbah . . . parade of kasbahs along the route. Two men sitting at roadside working an ancient sewing machine. Gray burnoose was talking across York to Kebir. Had lots of teeth, green and ocher, one in particular wobbly. They must have been talking Berber; York could feel their rapport.

ZAGORA
19
kms.

Sign loomed up, wavering in the heat—no announcement from James. The road descending into a wide rubble plain, more kasbahs.

"Not getting any cooler," James mumbled.

"Where d'you think you are? Garden party at Buckingham Palace?"

The old man shook his arm at the window.

"What's the dervish up to?" James groaned.

Kebir tapped Tony on the shoulder. "His village is here."

The Colonel obligingly stopped the car, peering into the rubble. "What village?" Nothing . . . except a dead goat by the road. But gray burnoose hobbled out, went to Tony's window and shook his hand ceremoniously, then tottered off into the rubble.

"Now there's a gentleman," Tony murmured.

"Gentleman?" James snorted. "He *desperately* needed a bath!"

"Try these," Tony said, passing them to James.

"Bloody hell." James staring at three eggs in his hand, as if hatched there.

"Gave them to me when he shook my hand. Berber thank-you!"

James looked nonplussed, Kebir looked proud. Tony clucked and they drove on. A few moments later a pink-stone triumphal arch soared over them. A small fortress on their left, a straggle of stalls, waving children and a squalid gas station, dragon and all.

"Zaa-gorr-ahh," James squeaked, and passed the eggs to York. "They'll bring you good luck, Canajun!"

They slumped to a halt in front of a second triumphal arch, and a large road sign with a camel caravan painted across it.

TIMBUKTU
52 jours

The others piling out of the car, trotting to a small café on the right, shaded veranda with several young Moroccans drinking Coca-Cola. But York sat numb, clasping three Berber eggs. Sign staring right through him—Timbuktu next stop, end of the world. He staggered out of the car, over to the café, determined they must turn back—crazy to go farther! Bumped into Tony coming out of the café.

"Our luck's in, Yorkers; stay right here for the night!"

"Stay right *where!*" York peered around, seeing only a grubby café, a small grocery shop beside it, and that blaring sign for Timbuktu.

"Right *here!* A real hotel, Moroccan; ten dirhams per night. The gentleman-of-the-eggs told Kebir about it."

"Tony, don't you think—"

"I never think, it's against my conscience. James insists we go to that three-star palace. Yes, the Grand Hôtel du Sud, it's for tour-rrrists! But if we stay here, we see Morocco the way Moroccans see it!" Tony triumphant, clapping York on the back.

York gave up. "Where *is* James . . . Kebir?" They had disappeared. The Colonel chortled, pointing through the open door of the café: James propped happily against the bar, a bottle of wine. "*He's* got what he wants!" Tony disconcertingly jovial as they entered the shade of the bar. York's gaze coming to rest not on James, nor on the handsome black bartender James was encouraging, but on a large lizard directly over the bartender's head. Lizard with almost leonine head snaking up the wall . . . though now York saw it was stuffed and mounted.

"Voilà . . . we have our rooms!" Kebir appeared with a rotund Moroccan, apparent manager of this "hotel."

The Colonel pried James away from the bar. York deposited the eggs surreptitiously on a small table. And they followed the manager out and down a clatter of back stairs to a hallway directly under the café. An underground hotel? York's doubts rose as they descended. Yes, it was clearly a basement hotel, small windows giving out over a sunken courtyard. But the advantage became clear—the temperature dropping rapidly as they descended.

Tony and James chose rooms on the first level down. But Kebir shook his head, leading York down another flight of stairs, down into a nether maze of cubicles. Straw mattresses on planks and small barred windows along a hallway. He peered out. The café-hotel perched on the edge of a slope. And the lower rooms dug into the slope, open-air on one side. Kebir nodded, pulling York to a cubicle at the far end. A human stable, with a door, window. The door with a scrawled design on the inside, finger painting, like worn bloodstains.

York flopped onto the straw pallet, aware his throat was very sore. He swallowed four flu pills and closed his eyes, grateful . . . this cubicle a few degrees cooler than the floor above.

The leonine roar, ebbing to a slit-throated sob, woke him. He lurched up, glimpsed the prison bars of the window, blood on the door, shimmer of flames outside. Sat stark upright, trying to remember: The trip into the Moroccan mountains, see the kasbahs.

He fumbled off the bed. Where's Kebir? Groped his way into the narrow hall, past other underground cells, stench of piss, and up the maze of stairs. Bursting into the flaming street. The town showered in red, blue-red, brilliant orange. Entire town, sky, trip—going up in flames.

He stood gasping in the sunset.

Sound of laughter, the bar. He stumbled along, peering in. Billow of robes there, giant lizard on the wall. Lizard snaking the shimmering light—booming blond head right beneath, the Colonel. York made the sign of the cross and looked around for Kebir. No Kebir. He backed into the flaring street. Neither night nor day, world in apocalypse, sun storming huge into palm trees. He groped his way along the road, past their car.

TIMBUKTU
52 jours

Damned sign again—camel caravan painted on it, three camels and a man in blue across the desert. Caravan flickering in the burning light, blue man waving, beckoning York into the desert. York's eyes followed the road past the sign. The bellowing was coming from there, the roar that awoke him moments ago.

He sheered off, walking past the sign, past a pair of Sten guns, soldiers standing guard there. A small fort. He pretended he hadn't seen, hadn't been spying. Just on an evening stroll.

On his left, the giant rooster crest crowing the sky: palm trees. A clutch of houses, clay huts. Past huge kasbah. Yes, Grand Hôtel du Sud. James was right about that.

Follow red sky.

Small ridge past hotel calling. Vista over town, a lot of gardens, orchards, bananas, date palms, all writhing under sunset.

Mountains over there, a pair of 'em—hello. Larger one rises to big knob on top, like the Old Man in Osprey Cove, wind-sculpted rock. See it every day from our living room window.

The world follows me everywhere I go. All I have to do is see. . . . My eye is my brain, my body my eye. And I only me insofar as I dare see sunset shouting at me.

Lucky to come here—sunset world of Morocco! World seen in lightning bolt, aflame.

World seen at instant of orgasm.

World as monstrance, showing body of God as endless normal.

Only way to see.

John always sees this way. Alleluia!

Could never get Chris to see the same, tried. She always said, "You go too far, York," and fled to her art books. Truth is, I never went far enough. Never lived up to what I knew, sensed. Afraid. *Is here far enough, Lord?*

He was sitting on the ridge, cross-legged, hands spread to the sky. Sunset dying, moon rising, moon of dark eyes, moon of *Kebir's face!* Kebir's face looming in the dusk, eyes gazing warning. He motioned for York to follow and loped back across the huddled town.

"How did you find me?"

"Télégraphe arabe," Kebir murmured. "Never go off alone, ami, *never!* You will never return." He glanced around. "Or you'll return in a different body!"

What nonsense Kebir was muttering! York would have laughed but for the flames in Kebir's eyes.

TIMBUKTU
52 jours

The sign heaved. York tiptoed up, touched it. Weird, a sign with camels on it, palm trees! Just like the Colonel and James to press on to Timbuktu—by camel.

Kebir pulled him away from the sign and toward the café, laughter, music. Boys milling in front of the café, waving large tambourines, skin drums. They were dancing, burnooses flowing—whaaa-yeeeaayy, the slow, rolling chant. Spontaneous festival for full moon.

And up on the veranda, two figures in wicker armchairs. The one tall and burly, crisp in khaki and pith helmet. The other willowy in tropical shirt, white ducks and a straw boater. Colonial governor and aide-de-camp, presiding over the populace dancing at their feet.

Out of a Kipling story, the Colonel and James, sipping aperitifs in the Moroccan moonscape. A table laid out between them: white cloth, wineglasses, bottles. James waving metronomic hand in time with the boys' chant. The Colonel beaming approval at the dancers.

Vision from a world whose nostalgia had cradled York's childhood. He wanted to laugh. Couldn't—they were *his* Colonel, *his* James now. These two loony Englishmen who'd brought him on safari to the ends of the world.

"Ahoy there! Who were you chasin'?" The Colonel saluted York's return.

"Chasing?" York scrambled up the steps. "A Moroccan sunset—"

"Ye gods, first the bloomin' birds, now the sunset! Had us worried. Thought you'd wandered off into the *Sahararrrah!*" The Colonel waved a hand. A boy brought chairs. Kebir and York took their appointed places at table.

"Apero, York?" James motioned, and the waiter produced a bottle marked "Gentleman's Port." "Don't be fooled, it's a Moroccan port, but adequate as aperitif."

York nodded—if James had produced vintage champagne, he'd have nodded.

"To our gentleman's safari!" The Colonel raised his glass.

"And to Moroccan youth," James added, gazing at the dancers. "Pour le plaisir des yeux, what?" But York was gazing at Kebir.

The waiter passed hors d'oeuvres: olives, anchovies, almonds, pickled corn. "As fine as Raffles," the Colonel stated.

"Raffles?" York mumbled.

"Raffles, in Sing-ing-apore," the Colonel bellowed, began singing—

On the road to Manda-laa-aay,
Where the flying fishes play-aay

James joined in, their creaky voices riding the chant from the street—

And the dawn comes up like thunder
Out of China, 'cross the bay!

Then sat listening to the drums, plainsong-in-the-flesh, right there swaying in the street. Blue robes and jeans flowing silver in the opalescent light of the moon.

"We're planning tomorrow's excursion." The Colonel tapped York's arm. "Toot across to Foum Zguid, maybe Tata—sniff a bit o' the Saharrrarraah." York barely making out the words. Dizzy.

"Or Tamgroute," James shouted. "Minutes away! See the old Koranic manuscripts!" The drums getting louder, the dancing shifting closer.

The Colonel leaned over to Kebir, passed him ten dirhams and pointed to the dancers. Kebir nodded, descended to the street. The music ebbed, and Tony grinned. "Told 'em to switch to dinner music." Yes, the drums muted, conversation possible again.

"*When* do we return to Marrakech, Tony?" York popped out.

"Return? To Marr-arr-akech?" The Colonel whimsical.

"Marrakech?" York repeated. "When?"

"Never." James laughed.

"Tomorrow afternoon," the Colonel said. "We'll be driving out of the sun that way."

Relieved, York sat back to enjoy the evening.

"Dinner on the edge of the Sahara," James raised his glass.

"We've ordered something special," Tony added.

"Must maintain standards," James said. York tried to smile, but his eye pestered by the sign to Timbuktu.

"That's the ticket." The Colonel emphatic. "Standards, tradition!"

"Now when Tony's father was governor of Gibraltar." James intoning the words.

"My grandfather, not my father!" the Colonel snapped. "And neither one of 'em would've condoned the like's o' you!"

"I was about to apprise York that your *grandfather* was a friend of Maréchal Lyautey."

"Ah. . . . Now Lyautey, there was a *man!"* Tony adjusted his pith helmet sternly.

"Boys' man," James snapped. "Moroccans loved the fact he loved their boys!"

The moon cascading in and out of small clouds. Kebir swaying with the music from the street.

"Time for a sniff o' vino." The Colonel pounded the table. The waiter-boy returned with red wine, uncorked the bottle, pouring from a height of two feet. Not a drop spilled. Colonel congratulated him, a black lad with glittering teeth, elegant hands. And slipped him some coins.

James chuckled, surveying the bottle. "Even the wine merchants are buggers in Morocco!" He pointed to the label. "Sidi Bugari."

"Here's to our Kebir—guide plenipotentiary!" James wavered to his feet, lifting his glass.

The Colonel followed. "Captain Kebir—saved our skins from the damned police."

"You forget, Colonel; you've already raised Kebir to full major."

"Major?"

"Yes . . . after you nearly drove us over that cliff!"

"Aha. *Major* Kebir, of the cliffs and all Zagora." The Colonel bowed, James emptied his glass, and Kebir stood nodding time with the music.

They regained their seats, the Colonel saying a word to the waiter, who disappeared. "Now for our Moroccan specialité. A gold guinea if you can guess, Yorkers." York couldn't guess anything at this juncture; if Tony had said "broiled Moroccan," he would have believed.

The boy reappeared, bearing a massive platter with tall conical cover. Set it in the center of the table. The Colonel nodded, the boy raised the cover with a flourish; a laval burst of steam swept the table. James was bouncing with delight. "Do that again, Tony!"

"Do what?"

"Make him bring that platter in again, raise the cover." James bobbed up from the table, producing a camera.

"Ninny!"

But the waiter was commandeered, platter covered again, while James marshaled Tony, Kebir and York to one side of the table. *"Now!"* James said. Waiter marched in again, raised the cover . . . . another blast of steam and drums from the street. *Snap-snap.* James gleamed satisfaction as they settled down around the platter.

"Are we permitted to eat yet?" the Colonel asked. James nodded, wriggling over his camera. Waiter-boy poured another cascade of wine, pausing with care at the Colonel's corner of the table. Boy smiling, Tony smiling. Boy busying himself with nothing as Tony fondled him, caress almost hidden by the table, wisps of steam and the chortle of tambourines from the street.

"Magnificent, simply magnificent!" James said. For a dizzy moment York thought he was referring to the waiter-boy, the ongoing caress at the corner of the table. But James was bouncing in his chair. *"Look!"* He held up a postcard, passing it to York, who gazed at it, befuddled. A silver view, yes: grinning Friar Tuck of a face, mustache; and another face, bearded, half-scowling . . . and Kebir! Photo of them, faces floating above the whirling steam of platter.

"I'm using the Polaroid—*instant* results!" James bounced triumphant. York realized that the splash of light with the photo hadn't been moon splurge, but Polaroid flashbulb.

The Colonel finally relinquished wine and boy, and leaned over to look. "Crikey Moses, it's us!" And started to laugh. "York looks so serious!"

"And Kebir so relaxed . . . his secret smile!" James up, peering over their shoulders in satisfaction.

"Damned dangerous machine, that! Might catch anything."

"Including your handiwork, my dear Colonel!"

"C'mon; food's getting cold." Tony took a piece of flat Moroccan bread, jammed it into the platter of rice, meat. "C'mon, York, see if you can guess."

York imitated Tony, dipping the bread into the vegetables and sauce at the edge of the platter, tasting it cautiously. Mouth puckering, a musky savor, like garlic with rabies! The waiter emerged with an extra bowl of the sauce, taking it to the Colonel's corner. Colonel again slipping his hand under the convenient apron; boy smiling, holding the bowl as if sacred duty. "Like it?" the Colonel boomed.

"Like what?" York's eyes following Tony's hand.

"That sauce, y'goat."

"Oh." York hesitated. "Armpits, tastes like *armpits!*"

James lifted an eye. "Didn't know you went in for that?"

"I—" York's eyes fixed on the Colonel's caressing hand.

"Smen!" the Colonel boomed, removing hand from boy and gulping a spoonful of sauce.

"*Semen?*" York blurted as the fragrance of dead flesh floated from the bowl.

"*Smen!*" Tony bellowed, burying his wrist in the waiter's crotch again. "Made from rancid butter . . . vintage butter."

"Like the Colonel himself." James squirming in delight.

And Kebir set the improbable Polaroid photo aside, and with deft flick of bread into sauce was tasting, smacking his lips in loud approval.

"Kebir knows it's the *real* Morocco." The Colonel held the sauce out to James. But James busy with his camera, bobbing in time with the music. The Colonel still holding the precious sauce forward. James gave a final defiant wiggle in his chair and took to his wine.

"You dizzy bitch," the Colonel roared. "Stop fuckin' that chair of yours!"

James froze.

"Fuckin' your chair like a nannygoat, you are!"

James sat rigid, butt immobilized. "And who are you to talk, Colonel—with your crotch connoisseurship, right at dinner!"

"A gentleman must keep his hand in," Tony boomed.

"Told you, York: our Colonel *is* a zebologist!"

"A what?" York spluttered.

"Zeb! Arab word for—penisss!" James hissed.

Kebir laughing as James raised his glass. "To our beloved Colonel, perambulating zebophile . . . cocksman extraordinaire!"

The Colonel froze, then exploded into laughter. And now they were all laughing, and the Colonel lurching to his feet, waving for silence. "I propose a serious toast: to Morocco, *the land of zeb and plenty.*"

They clinked glasses, even Kebir with his untouched wine, as the street music rose to rhythmic din and the moon stared down and the sign surveyed them silently.

TIMBUKTU
52 jours

Flash-snap. James's camera again. "Got you!"

"Got what?" the Colonel growled.

"The Three Zeboleers!" James prancing around, developing his shot. Tony refusing to look at the photo.

"If you take more damned photos, York'll start takin' notes. Narcissistic ninnies!"

"But we're here to look," James protested.

"We're here to enjoy ourselves," the Colonel barked, and tapped York's arm in mock ferocity. "You haven't touched the meat yet!" York reached into the platter for his first chunk of meat. Like musky veal it was, succulent. Maybe goat?

"Camel," Tony roared triumphantly. "*Suckling* camel!"

"What you'll be doin' next, mon Colonel, sucking camels!" James hissed.

"I warned you, York. Not *quite* a gentleman!"

James coiled, preparing a retort, but Kebir smiled at York, saying, "You're a Berber now. Eating camel couscous and smen!"

James shifted target. "That's the first thing Kebir has said in two weeks!"

"Keep your malice away from Kebir! Has no need to blab like us. He's an *omnipresence,*" the Colonel stated, pleased with his word.

James snorted. "Next thing, you'll be describing him as the Real Presence, all that Catholic hogwash of yours."

The Colonel flinched. "Keep your nasty wit off my religious beliefs."

"Just because your sister's a nun, *you* think you have religious beliefs. . . . A proxy Catholic!" James smirked. The Colonel silent. How little York knew about either Tony or James.

"Why don't *you* say something, York?" James jabbed his eyes across the table.

"Sin is man's last chance."

"*What?*" James leered.

"Of knowing God. We've lost access to grace . . . leaves sin." York sat, stuck in his own words. The Colonel belched, closed his eyes.

"Our York only says something interesting by accident, then doesn't know what it means!" James raised his glass. "To our *Archbishop of York!*"

York flinched.

"Saintly sinner . . . sinning his weary way to Jesus!" James held his glass raised. "But York hasn't got the courage of his sins!"

The Colonel growled. "Have *you*, Milord James?"

"You'll see," James snapped. "But what does our Archbishop mean by 'sssin'?"

"Sin," York murmured, "is the thwarting of grace, for the sake of lesser gain."

"That definition is brighter than you, my dear York."

Suddenly York leaned toward James. "Thank you. You've just helped me define my nation."

"Your nation?"

"The thwarting of grace, for the sake of secular gain."

"Thwarting?" James taunted.

"By act of will," York replied, his ears catching the music. It was as if he didn't see James at all, though James was bobbing up and down right in front of his face.

"A religious loony!" James snorted.

"York's different, that's all!" The Colonel banged his fist on the table.

"And how d'you know *that*, mon Colonel?"

But James had already switched his attention to the street, the chanting boys. Clapping in time to their serpentine rhythm. And some of the boys began clapping hands in time with his, glancing up, flashing moonbright smiles . . . *whaa-yyeeay*.

James tottered down the steps into the street to dance alongside the young Moroccans. They in their billowing robes, a few tattered jeans, and James jaunty in boater and white ducks. At first they paid little attention to him, bobbing awkwardly beside them. Then gradually swallowed him into their group, only his boater floating into view.

"Dance himself sober, I hope!" The Colonel grinned. "Are you a dancer?"

York shook his head. "I can't seem to move right."

"The Draa Valley, the Souss . . . famous for its dancing," the Colonel noted. "They say everything through dance."

"Tony, what made you come into the mountains—this trip?" York surprised by his own question.

Tony fingered his glass, looking solemn.

"Well, you see, York, if you're going to flame out . . . you might just as well do it in style!"

"Do you mean that?"

"Of course not! But it's the answer you wanted, isn't it?" The Colonel chuckled.

York busied himself with camel stew. Finally said, "Colonel Tony, you're a lovely man." The Colonel's turn to lose himself in the stew. The tambourines clamored louder with the drums. And somewhere beyond a low rumbling of night, like distant roar of lions.

"C'mon you louts!" James minus boater. "Time to enter the *real* Morocco. Up and dance!"

The Colonel glanced up to retort, flashed a sheepish grin. "Rightee-o, help digest this camel. Up and at it, troops!"

Now they were all out under the tumbling moon. James possessing himself of a larger tambourine, waving it wildly out of time with the drums. The Colonel jigging knee-high, escapee from an English May dance. York forced his body into the winding rhythms—resulting in instant hiccups. And for a moment he stood stock-still in the swaying street, trying to locate Kebir. Couldn't find him. Just that goddamn sign to Timbuktu. Then he noticed a young lad, the youngest of the group, dancing as if in a trance. Dancing with head back, hips rolling, as if the boy were ogling the dancer on the far side, the tall dancer there—Kebir! Dancing as part of the group, yet partly aloof, as if holding secret. Dancing with scarcely any movement at all, rhythms simply flowing his body, his eyes half closed.

By the time York realized his hiccups were gone, the Colonel was pulling him by the arm back up to the veranda. Back to the high safety of presiding table, Tony beaming satisfaction. " 'Three jolly farmers once bet a pound/Each dance the other would, off the ground.' Remember that, York? Schoolbook poem . . . early memory work!"

York shook his head.

"I knew your education was incomplete!"

But James sat, mournful. "They're so *elegant!*"

"Who?"

"Moroccans: do everything so elegantly!" James immobile, prodding his glass. It was empty and York took the bottle, pouring wine all around. Spilling some as he did. James sneered. "*Canajuns* . . . never suffer from elegance."

"Lay off York! What's *he* done to molest you?"

"He's a disaster," James spouted. "The worst disaster of all."

"Explain yourself," the Colonel shouted.

"I mean"—James smirked—"he's a *boring* disaster."

"If that's the case, why are you always trying to extort something from him?"

"Because he doesn't give!" James snapped.

"He just gave you a glass o' wine you don't deserve, and mustn't drink!" The Colonel removed the wine from in front of James.

"York doesn't share!" James sat back, jaw clenched, one eye a-squint, appraising the world to disadvantage. Yes, miming York. The Colonel laughed.

"Nothing to laugh about. Our fellow traveler is a bird-watcher, religious nut, nose-picker, and closet gay!"

"No harm in bird-watchin', Milord James. At least he doesn't pick his arse!" The Colonel ready for the fray.

"A dud, a sort of epic slug," James shouted over the drums. "A voyeur!"

"You're the voyeur!" The Colonel snorted.

"Through his diary York sits in judgment on the world."

"I doubt that," the Colonel replied. "And if he does, I doubt he's aware of it."

"Precisely. A portable rebuke and doesn't even know it. Christ with a flamin' hard-on, that's how York sees himself."

"Leave Christ out of it," the Colonel barked.

"As for *you*, Brigadier Napier, your hobby's pickin' up waifs and strays and coddling 'em."

"I presume that includes yourself." The Colonel glared.

"York *must* have some lofty pronouncement!" James rapping the glass with a fork. But York sat in a daze, one ear clinging to the flow of music.

"Speak up, York."

"You're ferociously perceptive."

"Aha, our Archbishop just said something."

The Colonel banged the table. "Our York's pondering good stuff!"

And York still caught in the ebb and flow. Finally saying, "What I'm experiencing on this trip lies beyond—"

"Beyond your snotty priggishness." James waved his glass across York's face. "He can't even pee without goin' forty feet away; saw him. . . ."

"What did you want—a photo of York peeing?" The Colonel stared.

"All he has is his arrogance!"

"York is not arrogant."

"How do you know that, Colonel?"

"Because he's lost. No one who's lost is arrogant."

James turned to the Colonel and raised his glass. "To the intelligence of that comment, Tony. Quite beyond you. But York would be arrogant if he could. Just hasn't the courage."

The two Englishmen apparently doing battle over the remains of York's soul. Was it mostly wit and wine? Or an aura of doom floating over all of them? "It's all I can do just to be here, that's my one truth." Looked up at James, then glanced away. His eyes falling back on the boys dancing such joy in the mud street. If any remnants of his sanity lay there, with the chant of Morocco.

"York's just here to write about us." James talking at Tony but still taunting York. "You may be a success as a writer, but you're a failure as a human being."

York tried to pull his eyes away, away from James's fractured, stinging eyes. "You're only half right."

"Only half?"

"I'm a failure as both." And with that, able to rescue his eyes from James.

"False modesty ill becomes you, my dear York. You see yourself as a hero."

"Hero?" the Colonel asked. "He's just a bird-watcher."

"As an epic hero—for his next book," James stated, refilling his glass. "But the verity is, he's on the run from something. Or is it someone?"

The Colonel poked irritably at his cold food. "What makes you so sure our York's a failure?"

"He wouldn't be with the likes of us if he weren't!"

Suddenly James pointed to the street. Kebir dancing with a ponderous dignity. Chest puffed out, swaggering, as if wearing a row of medals. The other dancers laughing, stamping their feet in time with his outlandish dance. Kebir unaware they were watching from the veranda now as he mimed the Colonel.

It was bare minutes since they'd all been out there dancing. Suddenly James on his feet, focusing camera as Kebir broke away from the circle, marching with bravado toward their table. And laughing—yes, he knew they were watching, had waited for his moment. *Snap-snap*, the camera flared, halting Kebir in mid-swagger. He stood abashed. But the Colonel chuckling and clapping vigorously. Kebir nodded his way up the steps.

"Stop!" James shouted.

They all looked. But James just wanted another shot of Kebir.

"Bally fool," the Colonel growled. "Whole world's gotta wait on his camera." While James maneuvered Kebir to the right angle, on the right side, right tilt of his head. But Kebir was looking uncomfortable, the Moroccans in the street all laughing; the music had stopped. And one of them was mimicking Kebir, posed as tourist for the camera. James muttering, "It's no good." But the Colonel waved a hand and the music started up again. And just as Kebir relaxed, grinned . . . *snap-flash*, James got his photo.

James was timing his camera, and in seconds flaunted his prize. Kebir didn't want to see. But the Colonel did, musing, "Kebir is somebody . . . tells us things we forgot a thousand years ago." He passed the photo to York, who took it warily. But this was Kebir of the thousand years, caught between the Moroccan world of the dancing street and theirs. Looking as if he must flee, or simply vanish upon being seen by pagan eyes.

James gloated at his instant trophy. "Kebir always looks like a visitor, always just arrived. Those magnificent *lips!*"

York thrust the photo at him and turned to his wine, violated. The music and dance floated up again, quieter now. After all, the visiting dignitaries had departed the dance, all back on the veranda whence they had come. The two worlds separate now, as if *snap-flash,* James's camera a barrier between them.

"York's *mesmerized* by Kebir!" James pronounced.

"Maybe," the Colonel said, "but I admire the way Kebir cares about York. All the small ways he shows he *cares.*"

"York's mesmerized," James repeated.

"And the big ways. When York almost fainted, by the doorway in Ouarzazate. No—*keep quiet,* York! Kebir was over in a flash to catch him! And York was smiling in seconds. And at the cliff—"

York sat shuddering. "You care too, Tony. About everything!"

And James silent, fiddling his camera. Finally saying, "You're lucky, York."

"Lucky?"

"Lucy to have Keb." James gazing wistfully at the photograph.

"So that's the problem. You're *jealous!*" Tony stared at James, reached over and took his wine away. "Moreover, not even York refers to him as 'Keb'!"

"I'll have you know, Colonel *Zeb*. . . . "

"All that nastiness about York because you're flamin' jealous. And don't call me Colonel Zeb!" Tony slammed his fist on the table.

James rigid in his chair. "I'll have you know, Colonel Napier—"

"Stop all that 'Colonel' nonsense! A figment of your aspirations." Tony going red in the face.

"And *yours,* my dear Tony," James purred, drinking copiously from York's glass.

The Colonel took an abrupt gulp of wine and turned to York. "Fact is, I'm not a Colonel! Never was."

"Pay no attention, York. He's flat drunk!" James protested.

"I did fight in the Desert War, El Alamein, Tobruk . . . as a sergeant. They wouldn't grant me a commission because of the scandal. I enlisted as an ordinary soldier." Tony paused, eyes imploring.

York longed to say something. Nothing came.

"But your father was a general, Tony, and governor in Gibraltar. You *always* have that." James leaned forward, pleading.

"Keep your genealogical ambitions to yourself, Lady James. Besides, it was my grandfather, I told you." Tony caught between tears and pride. "And as for your hoity-toity job in 'communications,' as you like to put it, why not say you're a personnel manager in a telephone office? Since that's the truth."

James crumpled over his glass. The sound of tambourines and drums rolled over the table as Tony threw his helmet on the floor. Kebir watching wide-eyed, York sat paralyzed. Tony's face sad, regretful now. And James dismantled. York wanted to go over and embrace them, tell James's he'd always be elegant, tell Tony he'd always be Colonel Tony. But sat frozen in his chair.

James found the practical solution; he ordered more wine. And they sat watching the performance in the street.

"There's the *real* rebuke," James murmured. "The way they dance and make song, out of nothing!"

They retreated inside to the bar. James propped up under the watchful lizard, adjusting his Polaroid to snap the dancers who trickled in from the street. Tony found his waiter-boy and produced his silver brandy flask, telling the boy to fill it up "against contingencies." And flask filled, he held it up to York. "This was my grandfather's, then my father's. It's about all I inherited when the old man passed on. He *was* a full general, and my grandfather ambassador to Spain. James had part of it right." Tony shaking York's shoulder. "Gran'pater was a friend of Lyautey."

"Lyautey?" York clutching at something to say.

Snap-flash. James catching one of the boys by the bar.

"Lyautey—first of the French pro-consuls in Morocco," Tony shouted above rising din. "Le grand Maréchal, friend of the Glaoui, friend of every Moroccan who ever met him."

Snap-flash—another target taken. And James . . .

"Lyautey"—Tony shouting—"was destroyed by the French government . . . too sympathetic with the Moroccans. Moroccans wept when they heard." Tony brandishing his flask like a sword. James flaunting his instant photos like black magic in front of the boys.

"Grandfather found out Lyautey was returning to France on just another commercial steamer after he was sacked." Tony's silver flask flaring bright. "Gran'pater put in a word with the admiral commanding British fleet in the Mediterranean. And when Lyautey's steamer passed Gibraltar, there they were!"

"Who?"

"Pair o' British destroyers, all crew assembled on deck. A signal sent . . ."

Snap-flash: James going after the big black with the drum.

"Signal asking if Maréchal Lyautey was aboard the steamer. The answer—yes!" Tony leaning down into York's face. "And the pair o' destroyers fired a full-gun salute. Crews cheered . . . full honors for the fallen pro-consul, d'you see?" Tony crashed a fist onto the bar, his eyes raging with his words. "It was the right thing to do, York . . . *grant a man his honor!* Even if his own people wouldn't. No member of the French government met Lyautey when he landed home in France."

Snap-flaash—the boys now clamoring for photos. James the center of them. Wine flowing; glasses crashing. Kebir trying to catch York's eye.

A sudden hush took the room. "Bloody gawd," James croaked, peering at the door. They all swiveled to look. Bull of an army officer blocking the door behind him. A trio of soldiers in bullet-shaped helmets. The boys huddled against the bar, hiding the wine. James wobbling, holding his camera aloft as if that might explain the fracas, the wine bottles scattered around, the wine spilled on the floor. The officer stepped across the threshold, motioning for his backup men to follow. Two of the boys dissolved under the bar, one into the toilet. The pudgy manager appeared, smiling obsequiously, patting the officer's arm, plucking fluff from his uniform. Officer nodded grudgingly. Manager said something in his ear. The officer scowled. And withdrew.

Kebir pulled York aside—time for bed. They left James displaying his shiny photos and commandeering more wine. Tony standing silently, holding his only heirloom.

Out into the street. York tried not to see—

Timbuktu . . .
Tombeau-too . . .
Tomb-for-you.

Down the maze of stairs to their little cell. Stripping naked for cool sleep, and tumbling exhausted onto straw pallets on either side of the cubicle. York's head gyrating with Tony's words. "Grant a man his honor!" Would he ever be able to say what he knew, live what he knew?

"I like Tonee!" York heard as he verged on sleep, heard it before he felt the weight on the edge of his bed and saw the black body burnished silver by moonlight. Kebir sitting in the hot silence, stroking his knees. "I had a friend too. . . . He was—" A hidden shudder in Kebir's voice.

"He was from Sweden . . . a painter. I was his friend." Kebir sitting up proud, sad. "He asked me to live with him. He rented a farm, outside Marrakech. An orange grove." Kebir paused, staring out the small barred window. "We kept goats, too. . . . I left school to live with my friend." He stopped, always spoke so little. Would York ever hear the rest of the story? He squeezed Kebir's hand, grateful for this much.

Kebir blinked, gazed down at York, eyes probing. "I was seventeen, my friend was twenty-five. He stayed with me over a year." Keb nodding, proud of this. "He painted a picture of me." Keb raising himself higher. "A picture of me holding my dagger. The dagger my grandfather always used, to sacrifice the ram for the Aid el K'bir!"

Silence. Kebir nodding into space, seeing something.

"I came home from market one day after selling some goats. My grandfather's dagger was gone. . . . Gone off the wall where we had it hanging. My picture was gone too. My friend was gone." Keb quivering in the silver light. York tightened his grip on Keb's hand.

Now he sensed why Kebir never sold his body in Marrakech as so many others did. Keb often standing aloof, off to one side. A proud pain lurking in his eyes, waiting for the other. Responding to affection first given.

York's final energy shuddered into Kebir. Keb staring at the wall, eyes blinking. "I had to pay rent owing on the farm. . . . I worked for a year to earn the money. I couldn't return to school." He squeezed York's sweating hand and rose like silver panther, crossing their cell in a single stride to his own pallet. York heard a rattling sigh, then still breathing deepened into gentle sleep.

York lay turbulently on the prickly mattress. Dry heat of the night rasping his throat. Aftertaste of that sauce coming up in a hiccup, rancid. And with it the din of their dinner. James saying, "York would rather be a martyr than helpful." So many sentences James had tossed like fireworks in the night. "*Sillee* James," as Tony had started calling him.

"*Sillee* James" is right. I'm lucky to have Kebir!

He rolled on the pallet, trying to find a position at once comfortable and cool. Spun by Kebir's story. "The dagger was gone. The picture was gone. My friend was gone!" Keb's story—the roaring he had heard earlier. Coming from the desert below. Louder now, deep sobbing roar, like slaughtered lion. Flinging him onto his back, gasping for air, impossible to sleep.

He glanced at Kebir. Keb lying naked on the straw, elongated in sleep. So virile, yet innocent, a touch of madonna adding to his presence. And his zeb afloat with the moon, coasting across his belly. Male flower glistening the night. The phallic auto-da-fé of the past five hundred years, crucified in public cause. For what? After all, Keb's zeb his instrument of song, of dance. And gazing now, York beheld the black mountains, the herons a rising alleluia against the sky, and Kebir standing at cliff edge, that red handkerchief he always wore expanding, gesticulating, displacing Kebir—John, Big Red, waving . . . jumping up and down, shouting. . . .

York leaned forward to hear what John was shouting. "You just want to be crucified, Yo-yo!" John always a shout, even when silent. Always grabbing. York sat up, John's shout dissolving as he did so. He looked again—it was Kebir lying over there, serene in sleep.

Kebir as silent presence York always felt if rarely saw. John erupting York's mind, clawing for his attention. Kebir materializing out of nowhere when York most needed, bearing touch and his healing smile. But John yanking York's wounded mind. Ongoing battle from the very beginning of their trip—*Kebir* vs. *John!*

York perched on the edge of the bed, assuring himself it was Kebir he saw there, not John. Wondering why he'd seen Kebir so little on their trip. Yet he saw everything through Kebir's very presence, Keb as his real binoculars. But when he was with John, saw only John, or saw anything else despite John.

He sat shivering in the heat. How could he love Keb and be John's mate? Fact was, his love for Kebir lay beyond anything he could comprehend. Came from another world long since abolished by his own society.

The night bellowed again. He fell back, longing to embrace Kebir. Hoping the desire would die into sleep, in the safety of Marrakech tomorrow. But his hard-on burned like a torch in the night.

He felt a cool glow on this back. Turned with half a cry. Kebir's eyes, pain gone from them now. Kebir standing by the bed, smiling. "You called, ami?"

"Called?"

"I heard you calling me." Kebir swaying as he stood, cock rising slowly as their eyes met. Cock rising in salute as York drew Keb down beside him in mutual embrace. Straw crackling under their weight, their bodies chanting praise in the night. Shouts perforating the door of their cell. *"Help!"* reverberating from the hall. Keb leapt up, pulled on pants, producing a knife from his bundle of clothes. York grabbed shirt, trousers.

"Help!"

Kebir already out into the hall groping his way, York following behind. Sounds of a scuffle, shouts from upstairs. *Craa-aash!*

Silence.

They crept barefoot up the stairs. A bottle smashing. Someone yelping. Footsteps fleeing up the hall.

"You dizzy goddamned bitch!" The Colonel's voice.

They entered James's room. York peering bravely from behind Kebir. "Four of them!" Tony in his underwear shouting at James, who was tottering around naked, with the remains of a hard-on. Tony spotting Kebir, York. "Got here, did you? Well, it's all over, just threw the buggers out! They were tyin' him to the bed!"

"Just havin' some vino, givin' the boys a spot o' wine." James, unable to get underwear on, was struggling with his socks. York stared at a spreading pool of blood beside the bed.

"Just giving 'em wine, were you, with no clothes on? And shouting for help? Look at the ass on you!" Yes, James's buttocks raw red. Tony began straightening up the room, pushed the bed back against the wall while Kebir mopped up blood with a towel. York picked several photos off the floor, and the Polaroid camera lying amid broken glass.

"Just what were you up to?" The Colonel muttered, picking up a pair of clamps on the end of a chain. "What's this?"

"I like rough trade now an' then. Braces a fella right up." James babbling his own lingo, BBC accent long gone as he hid some rubber object under the sheets. "Give a girl a chance, wot?"

"Chance to be murdered, that's what!" Tony tossed James's trousers to him. And stood growling, still the Colonel in his underpants, blue silk underpants.

York glanced at the photos. Young Moroccans sitting on James's bed, big smiles, bigger erections. James on his knees gazing devoutly on the grandest of cocks as he caressed his own. Recognizing the boy from the bar with huge hands.

Tony picked up James's wallet. "Tyin' him to the bed and fightin' over his wallet, that's what they were doing."

"I just give 'im a bit o' money fer the work they was at." James like a flayed cat. "Went a bit too far, thought they was stealin' me wallet and me camera. . . . Just playin', like."

"Just playing? And what happens if your play pals go to the police?"

"Never will, 'cause the police is worse than they is."

Tony grabbed photos and camera, took one glance and bellowed, "You goddamned lop-eared goat. These *are* a jail sentence in Morocco. You know that!" He suddenly stopped, eyed the door. York didn't dare turn around. Voices . . . Tony hitching his underpants up. Kebir stood up, eyes bulging.

The officer stomped into the room, pistol at waist. And one of the boys, the one with the big hands.

The pudgy manager entered with another of the boys. York got halfway through the sign of the cross. The officer surveyed the room, smiling knowingly. James still trying to do up his trousers. The officer stared at Tony, who drew himself up to full height—underpants and all. Holding the Polaroid in one hand, photos in the other. Officer scrutinized Tony and camera. The photos mostly covered by Tony's ample hand.

Tony took a step forward, smiling with great dignity. Held the camera out for the officer. Officer startled, taking camera, examining it as criminal proof. Tony explained in bad French how it worked. Kebir babbled it into Arabic. Officer shook his head. Tony stating, "Yes . . . *look!*" He took the camera and stepped back, focused. *"Here!"* The officer glared up. *Snap-flash.* The officer fell back. Tony yanked the undeveloped photo out of the camera, barking at James to time it. The officer looked enraged. Tony passed the camera back to him, explaining how flashbulb and timer worked. Officer wary.

"*Now*, Tony!" James squeaked.

Tony pulled the developed photo out, glanced at it, passed it to the officer. Officer gaping at instant color shot of himself looking ferociously military. *Impressive!* He started to grin. Tony adjusted underpants, gave a slight formal bow. "A present for you, m'sieur le Commandant!" He pointed at the flashy camera, "A *present* to mark our visit to your hospitable city!" Kebir translating and bowing. Tony slipping the compromising photos under a sheet. The officer smiled politely and asked if film for such a camera was expensive. The Colonel didn't know, glanced at James, who went over and returned with several packages of film. Also a large dirham note placed between the packages. The Commandant was grateful for "the consideration they had shown to Zagora."

A moment later they were all sitting on stools and the bed, sharing a glass of vino. The manager was smiling benevolently. Kebir continued translating in two or three languages. The officer and Tony referring to each other as "mon Commandant . . . mon Colonel" with ever greater insistency. The two boys were beginning to look worried. The Commandant asking "the Colonel" if the boys had been bothering them in any way. Tony assured him the boys had been as hospitable as Zagora itself. The Commandant nodded approval and extended his smile to the boys, who looked relieved. James, his fly still undone, and with no shirt, continued pouring wine. York, squatting on the floor, gaped at the Colonel. Tony in his underpants, managing to act and look like a full general.

The officer patted his presentation camera and film, spewed advice. "You must watch out for thieves, I regret to say! Best to travel early mornings, until this heat wave passes. Yes, worst in years. Even the goats are suffering. Yes, a Hamadja group in M'hamid now, special rites." The Colonel inquired delicately about "border incidents." The officer looked wary. "A bit of trouble, south of M'hamid, Algerian brigands." They all nodded gravely. The Colonel tucked an unruly testicle back into his underwear.

The officer rose, saluting Tony. Tony bowed impressively, holding underpants in place. Officer paraded out, followed by cowed boys and manager. Two soldiers stationed just outside the door clicked heels.

Moments later they dispersed for sleep, Tony insisting that James lock his door. And as Kebir and York groped their way back down the hall, York saw the face. Face of the waiter-boy from dinner peering out of Tony's room. Caught between chuckle and scream, York followed Kebir back to their cell. Keb was soon snoring again. York lay sleepless, the confrontation between Commandant and Colonel toppling his mind. But even more, that initial sight of James's room—the bedding hurled across the floor, the broken glass, the wine spilled like blood. And James sobbing over what he wanted—a beaten ass and a threatened life.

5
WAR IN THE DESERT

"You're my life mate, Yo-yo!" John bending over the bed to him, whispering, "Life mate, life mate." York laughed, sat up. No John! Just the red of the pants folded on a straw bed across the cubicle. Tiny cubicle with barred window. . . . York stared at Keb's new pants. But no Keb. He stumbled up, dressed, and out the door, down the passage. And as he went, saw the black figure out the corner of his eye, through a small window onto a courtyard. Black figure bobbing up and down, hands outstretched.

Strange sight, man bobbing up and down like that. But it was Kebir, praying. That Muslim way of praying, bobbing up and down on a mat. Out there in the courtyard on his knees, facing the dawn, his towel as a prayer mat.

York was startled, didn't know Keb prayed, mumbling as he bowed to the ground . . . his face so intent.

York stood absolutely still. Foolish, staring like that; yet Keb saluting God first thing made him so happy he wanted to weep.

Suddenly he ducked away from the window—spying on a man at prayer! He tiptoed back to their little cell. Rummaging in his bag—pulling a shirt, Cedric's ball, *binoculars*—that's what he wanted. He slung them around his neck and set out again creeping up the stairs, past James's locked door, past the Colonel's snoring, out into the street. Yes, just in time, the sun barely breaking the horizon. And just that damned sign staring at him—TIMBUKTU. He scurried past it, fortified by knowing they'd return to Marrakech today. He'd come as far as he could.

He was just following his nose. A fragrance from a small house ahead. Vines around it, small trumpet flowers acclaiming dawn. A puff of smoke, diffuse smell of resin with mint. He turned and followed the smoke to a sputtering fire outside a small mud home. Woman huddling over the twig fire brewing fresh mint tea. York wanting to join her, but the woman held her face down, cajoling her little fire. Another woman passed by, carrying a bundle of fresh mint and flowers. She was veiled, eloquent, but excluding him. He broke free of the billows of mint, into a wave of morning air. Following an odor of fresh straw, newly drawn milk, the first droppings of bird and beast. Sweet mingled musk of farmyards flowing around him.

Halfway across the crouching town, approaching that kasbah of all creature comforts where James had wanted to stay, the Grand Hôtel de Sud. Idiotic luxury, it seemed, remant of the French raj. He almost ran past it to the ridge beyond where last night he had marked sunset and the first moon. He scrambled over and down to a small embankment, a dike with rivulet gurgling alongside, feeding into a patchwork of small gardens. And stood hushed lest he molest the morning peace.

Whisss-whisss-whistle—jerking his binoculars up, yellow-black-brown bird dissolving into clusters of dates, date palms. Whisstling, the small bird whispering into the golden dangle of dates. Lost the bird but heard now the date clusters singing, the palm trees seething in the morning breeze. Huge banana leaves rustling. Sitting now amid the extravaganza of greens, oasis here at the edge of encroaching desert. White butterflies, a bob of blue sprouting from a banana bunch, quizzing him. His eyes floating to the bird, swaying with it in this lush greenery. Palm trees expanding with the rising sun, blithe as willows now. Stabbing down into the lilies of the pond, a kingfisher. And the familiar strut of green heron into the rushes. Scurry of a sora rail into the nearby alder patch.

The world was back, as if he could reach out and take her hand. But there was no Christine. This orchard grove and rivulet was not their farm, not the pond they so loved—but a palm grove in southern Morocco. And this wasn't a morning walk with Christine, nor even a stroll with John across the heather of Osprey Cove.

A sun ray exploded gold. A bird soaring up, swooping. So lucid there, gold and iridescent green and russet, hovering in the sun. Seeing it pluck a large black bug in mid-flight. Then dissolving back into the palm trees.

The surging chorale of myriad birds in the morning oasis. The two mountains of last night in uprising beyond the trees. That knob-topped mountain there, like Osprey Cove's Old Man. And the sun thrusting up behind now.

For a moment he sat in alleluia. Then stood up, nodding to the spot where the golden bird had been. He walked on silent feet through the waking town, eager to return before the others had missed him.

As he rounded the corner of the mud homes and saw their café-hotel, he half expected the Colonel and James to be sitting on the veranda, as if they'd been there all night. But they weren't. The café so dingy, squalid, perched over the edge of the road. How could it have been so regal last night for their wild banquet of camel and wines? Morocco seemed all sleight-of-eye, sleight-of-mind. But there it was, sad little café, its identity confirmed by TIMBUKTU.

"Crikey Moses, York, hurry. We're off!" Tony spotting York and saluting in high fettle.

"Already? Marrakech?" York's hopes soared.

"Off to the wedding!"

"Wedding?" York gaped.

"Nothing less! Down in M'hamid!" Tony pointed to a boy in blue burnous cleaning the back window of the car. "This young chap has a family wedding there this very afternoon. He's invited the lot of us—if we'll drive him there." The Colonel brisk in khaki shorts, safari shirt, pith helmet at jaunty angle. York walked up slowly, trying to grasp the situation. "Come now, young Yorkers, you'll love it! Desert oasis . . . the real thing . . . once in a lifetime."

York, feeling well beyond his lifetime already, babbled protest.

"If we don't drive this splendid fella to M'hamid, he'll miss his sister's wedding. Can't let that happen, can we?" Irrefutable reasoning.

York went up to sit on the café veranda. He closed his eyes a moment. He jumped up, dashed into the café and grabbed the manager. Yes . . . a bus! When? Thursday! What's today? Tuesday! He returned to the veranda and sat staring at the sign staring at him—TIMBUKTU. That's where these idiots were really headed. He was about to remonstrate with the Colonel when he saw a tall Moroccan striding up the street. He came directly to York. Kebir—glowing over York's chair, eyes demanding to know where he'd been.

Keb ordered juice for both of them. Told York he'd already put his bag in the car. Then produced a small ball. Was it York's? No. But Keb had found it in their cubicle. York looked again. Yes, it was his, or rather his son's. He couldn't explain it to Keb. Couldn't explain it to himself—his talismans.

"Now here's our archbishop looking his usual cheerful self!" James emerging from the bar with a brace of bottles. Gleaming in white shirt, blue shorts and suede loafers, as if nothing had ever happened. Deposited his wine on the table and shook Kebir's hand. Kebir wiping his hand with handkerchief. James took no notice, seating himself at the table and surveying York expectantly. York finally asking, "How do you always manage to look like the Immaculate Conception?" James waved a dismissive hand and asked, "But where did you disappear to this morning, my dear York?"

"I went out bird-watching."

"Bird-watching. Are you sure it was just bird?" James rapped his fingers on the table.

"Yes, just birds! My wife and I used to go on morning bird-walks."

"Wife?" James paused, as if savoring an indiscretion. "And pray tell, what's his name?"

"Troops will muster for departure!" The Colonel marched to the veranda in full verbal regalia. The Colonel and James taking up station in front of the car. York sitting between Kebir and burnoose boy in the back. Feeling that he'd gone for a bird-walk with Christine this morning. Just the same as five years ago at their farm. John rarely joined York for bird-walks. "I've got a cock you can watch, Yo-yo." That's what John said. John and Christine endlessly present in him, virtually interchangeable. And here he was on a trip with Kebir. . . . Was it all brain fever? Yet he felt so lucid, as if on rendezvous . . . but with what?

Pulling ahead slowly, the manager still bowing and the Colonel saluting grandly. James waving at some boys who were following the car.

TIMBUKTU
52 jours

They rolled past the ever present sign, York determined not to notice it. A final triumphal arch passed over their heads. They were nosing down the uncertain road toward an open plain of sand and rocks. Tony chortled. "Giving the Commandant that camera saved our skins!"

James snapped, "Just remember, my dear Colonel, it was *my* camera you generously gave away!"

Their excursion into the Sahara had begun. York sat clenched to his seat. He could feel the endless subterranean bellow of Morocco.

Safely beyond the town, the sand rising to meet them, sluggish under the wheels. And the strange land coming closer, shaking the car. Same throaty roar that had troubled York's sleep the previous night.

"Looks like a giant sea serpent!" James said.

Yes, giant sea serpent out the front window—a caravan of camels bellowing and snaking its way across the road. Several hundred camels floating up, and every now and then a rider peering down from high above the car. Dark men in blue togas, black turbans. Rifles slung nonchalantly across their knees, their smiles flung nonchalantly at the stranded car.

York leaned forward to see. The riders silhouetted against the rising sun, dark skin gleaming with their robes. Dark blue flames atop the lofty camels. One of them waved, beckoning toward the desert with disdainful smile. Then a white camel, a young boy atop on a red leather saddle . . . proud as a drum major, handsome. "Now you just stay in your seat!" Tony flung out an arm to retain the excited James.

"But he wants it!" James blurted.

"He may well want it, but he doesn't want *you!*" The Colonel was adamant. "All you'll get out there is a knife in the ribs."

"Just my flamin' luck!"

"Luck?" Tony gurgled.

"To be travelin' with sexual amateurs!" And with that he leaned out the window—*snap-snap*. "Got 'im!" And waving at the departing boy.

One of the camels had halted right by the car, entrails spewing out its mouth, a ballooning slather of gut. James wanted that too, furiously focusing his camera. "A damned slaughterhouse, that's what!"

"They store their water in that," Tony replied. "Large inner pouch in the throat." The camel standing there, sucking its dangled throat back in as it cast a jaundiced eye upon them.

The end of the caravan trailed off to their right into a giant corral. Camels with their pole-vaulting strides, bodies somehow immobile above those elongated legs. A moving frieze of them like a single giant beast across the bow of the car.

The sand and dust subsided, the road visible again. Road? Just tire tracks across the rubble and sand. Tracks stretching ahead like a half-visible railway on out past the last hump of land. James rustled his map. "Tony, are you sure that . . . ?"

"Not going lily-livered, are you?" the Colonel snapped.

"Certainly not! It's just that the road seems . . . undeveloped."

"I told our Blue Boy here that I'd get him to his wedding. When a Napier says he'll do something, by God, he does it!'

And with that James folded his map. The car lurched ahead, gathering slow momentum through the rocks and sand, following the feeble tracks. Every now and then an upright rock set as marker. Kebir sat nervously erect. York in a daze but grateful to have identified the low, rumbling roar of a herd of camels. He hadn't been hearing things after all. Besides, the trip past Zagora would be memorable for that caravan. The seething power of it. He'd send a postcard to Osprey Cove, of a caravan. Say he'd gone on one! John would rage with envy.

The car rolled on in silence. The sand had melted with a crushed rock surface that sparkled black and gold. The sun climbing implacably, freshness of dawn long since gone. A huge hawk soared in front as pathfinder for several miles. What was there to prey on out here? The last of the black mountains was sinking slowly at the outer edge of the massive cauldron they were riding.

"Which way?" Tony asked at a barely visible fork in the trail. An obelisk marking the spot wordlessly. The Blue Boy gesturing right. York wondered where the other trail went. Either way felt nowhere.

The Colonel gave a toot to the horn, the sound ricocheting across the bleak rock face, pockets of blown sand. York glanced at Blue Boy, who was sitting in taut wonder as the car surged ahead. Sitting erect, fingering the plush upholstery. The boy feeling York's glance, returning it. His eyes reaching out, his leg pressing against York. No, it couldn't be so. Yet there it was again, boy pressing York's thigh, glancing over. York felt his hackles rise as he wondered if he was going cock-crazy. Or did the boy simply want reassurance, inclusion in their little group?

York sank bank in the seat. Where in God's name were they going? A wedding, out here in the sand? A hoax, an ambush? Yet Tony always seemed to know what he was doing. Tony puzzled him. Was Tony a bogus colonel who was a genuine colonel on mission? Certainly accounted for Tony's efficiency, honor, all hidden under casual bonhomie.

And James?

All a hoax for real—that was the truth.

He opened his eyes. More sand, glittering sand stinging his eyes. Face rising out of that cauldron. Silver-gray eyes, face of Christine surveying him across the sand. Moon-beauty of her face, world seen through the shuddering blue of autumn chicory. Face of endless imploring.

Rammed his eyes shut again. "I didn't abandon you, didn't. You drove me out!" He peered out at the desert. The face gone in the blown sand. The haunting sense of Christine. Why hadn't they lived up to their dream? They'd seen it all that day in Lascaux. And she'd fled to her chapels of repose. And he raging out into the world . . . for what?

"What are we so damned silent for, you sullen sods?" Tony bellowed into life. They'd all been silent since the roar of camels. "Chance of a lifetime!"

"Jolly old pleasure excursion, what?" James wiped his face with a silk handkerchief, opening a bottle of wine. A light wind scuffed the sand into shifting puffs like sudden golden bushes. Only the shimmer of desert—the rocky cauldron dissolving into sand. And the implacable blue overhead.

"Someone here before us." The Colonel pointed. A massive skeleton looming out of the sand. Car skeleton, plucked clean.

James swigged his wine. "Just where the hell are we, Colonel Napier?"

"En route to a Moroccan wedding, that's where." Tony clutching the steering wheel with both hands as the wind tossed a cloud of sand across the car. When it blew clear, Blue Boy leaned forward, waving to the left. Yes, in just those few seconds the car had strayed well off the trail. The Colonel muscled the car back on track. Silence again, except for the car, which seemed to cough with each gust of wind. Blue Boy sat erect, eyes held to the path across the sands. Kebir rubbed his nose attentively.

"A *cone!*" James shouted, pointing off their left bow. About a hundred yards away, sand sprouting up from the desert, rising in high, dizzy cone. "Tornado!" James dipped deeper into his wine.

"You're the tornado, my dear James. That's just a low-pressure area, funnels the sand and wind."

"You're a *high*-pressure area, Tony. This excursion into the Sahara is loony. One flat tire—"

"No danger of a flat tire!" Tony chuckled.

"Why not?"

"I don't have a spare!"

York watched the spinning sand cone dissolve in the distance. It was beautiful, wavering up and up into the sky like a genie. But the car was moving slower now as Tony concentrated on the trail. James putting more film in his camera. "If we're going to die in a tornado, might as well get a shot of it."

Another stone marker. Tony glanced back at Blue Boy, who gazed an instant, nodded right. The car spluttered, picking up speed again. But the trail less clear. Blue Boy was leaning forward to make sure the Colonel kept on track. A shadow lurched up over the bow of the car, a pair. Giant birds flopping up into the sky, black against the sun. "Rotten!" Tony jerked the car to a halt, rolling his window up frantically. Pungent smell spewing into the car. "Smen!" James said as they peered out. Dead camel rotting there. Overhead, the vultures dangled the entrails.

"Good place not to stop," the Colonel noted, revving up. The engine coughed in the heat. York watched the vultures—the sun doubling their size, so to see these birds was to see giant rocs of ancient times, carrying men off whole.

The car surged on, shuddering in a gust of wind as Tony wrestled to hold it to the trail. Blue Boy was speaking with Kebir, who relayed it. "He says a big war film was made here. Lots of tanks, guns."

"One of those Rommel–Montgomery things, I suppose, war in the desert." Tony chatty, determined to appear unconcerned. Yet the road tracks were virtually invisible now, save to Blue Boy. And the car had been coughing for some time, though no one mentioned it lest it be so. Another buffet of wind hit the car, blinding the windshield. The car halted dead.

"What are you stopping for now?" James moaned.

"I didn't stop . . . the car did!" Tony hunched over the wheel, gazing at the sand.

For a moment they all sat as Tony tried the starter—a coughing splutter. They clambered gingerly out into the sun, James clutching his bottle of wine as he would a first-aid kit. For a few seconds they milled around the car, blinking. Stranded tourists wondering where the bar had gone.

Kebir stared at the car as he might at a camel with a broken leg. York was too upset to take the pee he needed. Then Blue Boy flipped the hood of his burnoose up, instant shade. James nodded and wrapped an ascot around his head. Tony put his pith helmet on and tried to look efficient. York stood hatless.

"This is no place for a wedding!" James glared at Tony. Tony glared at the car, finally stepping forward to open the hood. "Yeeeowww!" And fell back, waving his hand.

The Colonel adjusted his helmet, yanked the ascot off James's head and approached the hood warily. Wrapping the ascot around his hand, he pried the hood up in a flood of steam, like their camel couscous. After the steam had ebbed, they peered in.

"It's still there!" James noted.

"What's still there?"

"The engine, my dear Colonel!"

Indeed it was; sizzling, impossible to touch. York peered beyond the steaming car. Eddies of heat rising visibly from the sand. And the sand itself burning underfoot. How long could they last here? Couldn't walk back to Zagora. No water.

"Try starting the car, James. I'll watch the engine." What did the Colonel know about engines? James hunched gratefully in the shade of the car, pressed the starter. Engine turned with a racking cough. Died.

York closed his eyes. There she was again, Christine. She was saying something. York trying not to hear. He forced his eyes open. No Christine. But Tony bending over the car, pointing to a translucent line in the engine, liquid foaming inside.

"Even the gas is boiling."

Silence and a whirl of wind, sand blistering their faces.

James emerged from the car wearing his boater and brandishing the map. "About twenty-five miles to Tagounite, I reckon."

"Never make it on foot," Tony muttered. And, still using James's ascot, began undoing the radiator cap. Another blast of steam, followed by trickle of frothy water. "Dry!" He looked around uneasily. There might be a camel caravan tomorrow.

York blinked—she was there again. Christine . . . staring at him now. Her cold eyes saying "I told you so." It was like that with Chris: one minute hot, next minute dry ice! You never knew. And then John erupting behind Christine and shouting, "It's pussy whip, York, that's what it is!" York stared, John jumping up and down in the sand. And Christine smiling, as if she'd known all along.

Kebir returned from the car with his little bundle of clothes. He pulled a small bottle of water from the bundle, offering it to York. York about to drink.

"Stop!" Tony snatched the bottle, strode over to the radiator, pouring the water in slowly. Engine hissing, spewing vapor. "A tithe of what we need," Tony muttered. Kebir watched, went back to the car and emerged with another bottle. "That's my *wine!*" James bleated. Kebir began pouring it into the radiator. The engine hissed, gurgled. Alcohol fumes eddied all around them. Kebir, muttering "N'shalla," kept right on pouring. The Colonel clapped hands in approval. "Better than standing here like a batch of jilted spinsters. Go fetch the second bottle. *Now!*" The second bottle was duly opened. The Colonel took a quick gulp, then carefully poured the rest into the steaming radiator.

James was aghast. "Cars don't run on wine, Colonel Napier!"

"This one does! Club car . . . likes wine!"

The gurgling in the engine was subsiding. The alcohol fumes

wafted away. Tony closed radiator and hood. "Troops will muster in car!"

They stumbled into the car. Tony passed his brandy flask around. "One for the road." Pressed the starter. The motor whined. Died. Silence.

Tony sat up, adjusted his helmet and goggles, pressed the starter again. The engine turned over, ebbed . . . then coughed into life. The Colonel let the car idle a moment, then moved it slowly into gear. The car rolling unsteadily ahead.

"Tagounite, for chrissake, get us to Tagounite," James said, whimpering.

The Colonel paid no attention, his eyes fixed on the trail. Car spluttering but moving faster now. The desert sifting by serenely, as if just waiting.

York's eyes were fixed on the sand: he saw a truck there, an armored one. A man sitting on top, above the hood. Man huge in the sun, sitting like a figurehead, waving. "Crikey Moses, young York, it was a close thing." The voice rumbling in York's ear. "We set out at the edge of dawn, d'you see. The sun our best weapon, the only real weapon we had."

York closed his eyes. Voice didn't stop. "Drove right into the eyes of Rommel's panzers. Reckoned if the Germans spotted us, they'd assume we were attacking in strength. Coming straight at 'em that way. And they did. They fell back, waiting for our full attack to declare itself."

York shifted in his seat. Not only seeing things but hearing things. The voice went right on. "It was at Tobruk. Rommel's boys had us surrounded, forced the Eighth Army to surrender. But the Coldstream Guards have never surrendered in their history. Group of us went to our commanding general, requested permission to fight our way out through the German lines. That way no Guardsman would be taken prisoner, d'you see. . . ."

York opened his eyes, staring into the glare of the desert. Yes, that familiar if forgotten voice . . . his uncle. Uncle Bartle sitting up on the prow of his armored car. Leading his little contingent of heroes into the toughest panzer divisions in the world. Uncle B.—waving to his men. Suddenly his smile gone, the red spurting out of his shirt. "You see, they nicked me. But we came through, we fought again . . ."

"What did you say, York?" York glanced up—it was Tony. York replied by coughing, blowing his nose, as if it had been that which Tony overheard. But yes, he'd been talking to himself, talking half aloud. York closed his eyes, felt the hand on his knee, Keb's hand . . . like a spurt of lucidity.

The car swerved in a sudden blast of sand, Tony yanking it back onto the trail as a wind cone blistered past. Car rocketing ahead in the vacuum left by the passing cone.

"Tony, what if we break down again?" James whinnying in the front seat.

"You'll have to learn to ride camel, that's what," the Colonel said, bluffing.

"Right to Timbuktu," James muttered, swigging more wine.

York took the hand on his knee, held it hard.

He peered out the swaying window. Burned sand seething by. And superimposed over it, black on gold, Keb's immobile face. Keb gazing ahead, leaving York his privacy. York startled by that remembrance of Uncle Bartle, long dead now. "Grant a man his honor," yes.

He looked up. The car dragging through a drift of sand across the trail. Tony adjusting his goggles, and James, "Lady James," whimpering beside him. Wake up, York! This ain't the world of the British raj. Much less of Kipling and *Captains Courageous*. All that romantic hogwash is long since dead. You're here in the Sahara with a pair of English gay goons!

"Land ho!" Tony bellowed. Everyone peered ahead, straining to see.

"A tower, mosque," James echoed. Tower rising brilliant white from the sand.

"They'd best be praying for us." Tony revved the car faster. Another moment and they saw the walls of a town floating beside the mosque.

TAGOUNITE
Zegdou Foum-Zguid
M'hamid
TIMBUKTU 50 jours

The sign jumped out of the sand, mercifully confirming tower and town.

"We've come two full camel days," James announced proudly.

"Not bad, given that you're a goat," Tony muttered.

They nosed through a high arch toward the mosque, the center of whatever town it was.

"Judor." James pointed at a small battered sign beyond the mosque. Small arcade, bazaar, a café. Tony wheeled the car through a battalion of yelping dogs into the shade of the mosque. For an instant they sat staring at mosque, café. Kebir and Blue Boy moved first, loping into the café.

"C'mon, you sods!" Tony next. Finally they were all seated in the reassuring shade of the café.

"Four Judors for starters!" Tony barked at the waiter. No one said a word till they'd been drunk. "Four more, and a round of shish-kebab." And in minutes they were assaulting a large plate of kebabs, the meat interspersed with slices of roast fat, tasty as the meat itself. The Colonel ordering more. "Gives a fellow an appetite!" What does? "A breakdown in the desert!" The second round of meat activated the Blue Boy, who announced to Kebir, who announced to the table that "M'hamid is only twenty-seven kilometers away."

"M'hamid?" James muttered.

"That's where we're going, bonehead!" the Colonel snapped, cleaning an entire skewer of meat into his mouth.

"You and your ruddy Berber weddings, invitation to a funeral!"

The Colonel gagged, swallowed his meat. "Nearly had yours in Zagora. Besides, the wedding is Bedoui, not Berber."

James sat rigid, finally turned to York. "Why aren't you taking notes?" The thought hadn't crossed York's mind. "You mean you've dropped your dismal diary? Congratulations!" Silence. The Colonel ordered more judors. Kebir mopped his hands with satisfaction. Blue Boy sat watching the Colonel—were they or weren't they going on to M'hamid?

"Damned good thing I thought of putting wine in the engine back there," James declared.

Tony gaped, finally said, "I'll confess I half thought we were for it. Don't even have a tool kit in my car. Damned stupid of me."

"We *know* you're stupid, just didn't know you were suicidal." James smirked.

Tony glared. "I never dreamed we'd be touring the Sahara, that's all. It was your idea."

"*My* idea? Now see here!"

"The whole trip was your idea. Scout the natives!" The Colonel suddenly brightened. "Raise Kebir to major immediately."

"You've already breveted him as major, remember?"

"Raise Kebir to Colonel . . . for putting your wine to proper use in the radiator."

"Demote him for abusing wine in that fashion." But James was grinning, patting Kebir's arm.

York wondered at the preposterous English banter. He loved it, just couldn't make sense of it. Had they all just risked death back there, or hadn't they? In either case, he was convinced they were traveling under a hex now. Kabir had said about the Evil Eye.

"He's at it again," James announced.

"At what?"

"Thinking!" James brandished a kebab skewer in front of York's eyes.

"Stop molesting the boy. He's harmless."

"His Grace hasn't told us what he thinks of us," James persisted.

"Why should he?" the Colonel thumped the table. "Besides, he never says that much."

James smirked. "Precisely. It's what he doesn't say that tells. Our Canadian friend is an *ontological snob!*"

The Colonel blinked. "Where did that unholy phrase come from?"

"York's own essay, my dear." James turned to York. "You're gay too, York! And a Johnny-come-lately sodomite into the bargain. Ask your boyfriend there."

York sat stupefied. The Colonel, enraged, finally said, "A little dignity, a touch of class, wouldn't hurt the occasion, my dear James."

"Who are you to talk, Colonel Napier? You act like a fallen angel when you're just a fallen gentleman!"

"At least I'm not an *imitation* gentleman!"

James smirked, turned to York. "Our mighty Colonel, you should realize, is a grocer. Runs a shop in London!"

Silence. The Colonel's scar flashing red. York closed his eyes, clinging to his chair. The breakdown of the car seemed nothing compared to this. When he looked up, Tony was ignoring James and calling Kebir and Blue Boy. They came over, had been discussing the poisonous snakes of M'hamid—vipers, the desert cobra . . . they fall asleep in the sun, buried in the sand. Stumble over one and it strikes in fright. Tony listened with interest, James with alarm.

"That settles it!" Tony banged the table.

"Settles what?" James asked.

"We continue on to M'hamid!" Tony glared down his specs at James. "First-class chance to expore cobra territory." He rose in a grim smile and trotted off to the car.

James sat like a drained turnip. And when York finally gathered his wits, he saw the Colonel was changing water in the car radiator. "He's good at that!" James snapped, nodding toward the Colonel.

"Good at what?"

"Changing wine into water!"

York glanced around the café. Impeccably clean, yet squalid. Suddenly asked, "How long have you known Tony?" Yes, at least change the conversation.

James appraised the question. "In fact, I've only met him on a few visits to Marrakech."

"I thought you were old friends."

"Of course not. I do have standards, you know." James paused. "Let's just say we share common pursuits, a few unsavory friends."

"But how do you know so much about him?"

James toyed with his skewer. "We old Marrakech hands know most everything about one another. And what we don't know, we invent."

"Is it true—" York hesitated.

"That your Colonel runs a grocery shop? In fact, he runs the meat counter in a grocery shop. In the West End. His father left him destitute. *That's* all he has." He pointed to the car.

Startled, York looked direct at James. James nodded, tongue

flickering across his lower lip. "You're like me, my dear York. You wanted him to be the real thing."

"C'mon, you sods, we'll miss our wedding." Tony stuck his face in the door.

James picked up the bill. York protested. "You shouldn't have to pay for us all." James laughed. "I'll end up paying for the whole schmozzle, anyway."

There was only one route out of Tagounite. Toward Timbuktu, as James noted. They wheeled through the squat village, waving children, cringing dogs, out onto the trail. Tony followed the tracks like a hunter following spoor. A partly graveled trail now, pure sand on either side. No scattered rocks, just the tawny dunes cresting and ebbing around them.

Tony chuckled. "How I managed to put you out of Tagou-what's-it without your taking a single photo, I'll never know."

"Truth is, Colonel, you've ceased to be worth the trouble." James sniffed. "As for our retreaded madonna back there . . ."

"Retreaded what?"

"A retreaded virgin in disguise, that's our York." James seemed tickled by this, but York heard nothing, fighting to quell the faces rising out of the sand. Christine's above John's, the pair of them out past the second dune. Her eyes buzzing as she watched the careening car. John gone. The car becoming sluggish, slowed by a sand drift. Then sputtering ahead onto gravel. Deep into the world of caravans now, nothing else could survive here. It was after eleven, sun near its zenith, heat rabid. York sat dazed, was it the engine coughing, or him? Yes, James was right, he was no hero . . . no Uncle Bartle rallying his men. He was on the lam without knowing it. And why in the Sahara, if he loved John? Just another gay blade off on a spree?

Was he really there by accident? After four goofy years with John. Divorced from the wife he loved . . . all family ties lost . . . forbidden to see his son. Christine had the law, the money . . . sold their antiques by public auction in his absence. Psychic death sentence. Why not give in to their silly spree?

Run out into the sands, naked . . . they'd never catch him. Yes, if his love for John worth all losses, why was he here without him? At least he knew how they saw him, his family, friends, society—a cocksucker gone nuts. Too polite to say it that way, of course.

The sand whirled by, puffs of gold skittering in the wind. "Breeding counts," Tony said, praising the car as it skidded through another drift. James produced yet another bottle of wine. Where does he keep them, in his shoes? He leaned back, head throbbing. Clamped his eyes shut . . . there she was again. Standing out front on the sidewalk. Standing stock-still, face taut as she confronted the house. Her body all angles . . . gray-flannel silhouette. Christine: that afternoon in Yorkville, the year *Media Madhouse* came out. Huge uproar, libel suits, Chris's parents urging divorce. And there she was in her tight town suit and high heels, glaring at him from the sidewalk. Behind her, groups of hippies drifting by, tinkling tambourines. Rhythms of Yorkville on a bright June day. . . .

James was testing his wine, a happy gurgle. "The Glaoui visited Paris, have I told you?" York mumbled yes . . . no. "He was walking down the Champs Elysées in retinue and saw a Rolls-Royce in one of the big salesroom windows. He couldn't resist; went in and asked the price. Do you know what happened?"

York hearing James but still under the glare of Christine. Back in old Yorkville, hippie center of Toronto in the 1960s. He and John had taken lair there after their flight from Mexico. "Where we should be," John said. "Besides, that's how you got your name: York of Yorkville." So they felt at home. Till that day Christine came to visit him in the little room they'd rented. And refused to accept his long letter of outpouring to her. Demanded that her lover read it too.

Another gurgle from James. Was York listening? "The salesman looked at the Glaoui's Arab dress and asked where he was from. Marrakech! 'Marrakech?' the man said disdainfully, 'this Rolls-Royce is worth more than the whole of Marrakech!' And abruptly turned his back. . . ."

But York still seeing Christine. Christine staring, tapping the toes of her blue-leather shoes on the sidewalk. York wanted to retreat to his room, his rejected letter. Forget it all. Christine jerked her hand. Holding the small blond boy by the hand. Jerking his hand because he moved. Never move! My God . . . my son! York lunged out the door, down the steps. Christine frowned, tapped her shoe a final time. Cedric leaning forward, eyes agape, Daddy, about to shout, "Daddy's here!" Words forming on his lips. She jerked his hand again. The boy stiffened, words dying. . . .

"The Glaoui left in a rage," James waving his bottle to mark this historic fact. "But a while later he dispatched a properly dressed French friend to the salesroom, with instructions to buy the car for cash. . . ."

York nodded, but his real attention on Christine, and his six-year-old son. "Don't let him wander off by himself," she said. "I'm taking him to my parents at six o'clock, and I don't want him . . . *dirty.*" Their son stood taut.

James tapped the wine bottle to emphasize his point. "The salesman paid all due respect to the Frenchman in his proper suit. But was startled when the man paid the full price in cash: large bills! And asked said salesman to park the car just outside the shop, immediately. He did so, and handed over the keys. It was then that the Glaoui stepped majestically forward. . . ."

Christine: "I'll be back at five-thirty sharp." Words crackling at York like a memo. He nodded, not much time. "Where will you be?" she asked. York blinked, pointed across the street to the café. She nodded. "Fine!" Her eyes staring right at York, even as she overlooked his scruffy presence.

"The Glaoui had been waiting outside for the salesman to emerge with the Rolls. . . . And the salesman was startled to see this Arab back. Do you know what the Glaoui did then?" Silence, which James took as interest.

While Christine gave a final jerk to Cedric's hand and executed a precise right-angle turn, grinding her heels into the sidewalk. Perfect. She paused, then was gone . . . clickety-click along the pavement, heels poising her above all mortal danger.

James chortled delight. "He summoned several men who had been waiting in a truck nearby. They immediately carried several cans of petrol over to the Rolls-Royce. The Glaoui instructed them to pour the petrol all over the new car. The salesman protested—"

For a moment York and his son remained disabled. Standing several feet from each other like complete strangers. York glanced over at a hippie sitting in battered jeans, bare feet, serenely accompanying the rhythms of Yorkville on a little African drum. And winking, grinning at York. York grinned back awkwardly and turning, saw his son in bluebird-bright shirt, flannel shorts.

Cedric's eyes in a frozen stare. Sultry blond hair brushed and parted in a precise line. Yes, Cedric standing as if Christine had relayed the message through his nerves forever. "Daddy is evil; *beware of Daddy!*"

"The Glaoui then lit the gasoline . . . the Rolls rose in instant flames, consumed in a matter of minutes." James looking so proud as he said this, nodding his head in satisfaction. "The Glaoui bowed to the stupefied salesman, saying, 'If you ever visit my city, please ask for me.' Ask for who? 'The Pasha of Marrakech!' " James turned triumphantly to York. "Did you get all that, Archbishop?"

York nodded, mumbled reply. Yes, he'd heard, or, more truthfully, overheard James's oration. Couldn't really avoid it.

"A superb example of the Glaoui's style, you see. Write it down, York. We'll do a book together on the man."

But Tony, who had been curiously silent, turned and gazed at James. "There is absolutely no need to write it down."

"And why not?"

"It's all in that book, *Lords of the Atlas*, by that chap who loved otters."

Silence.

James swigged his wine. "I'm doing *original* research!"

"Everything you've recounted about the Glaoui is in that book and you know it. Why pose as an expert? To impress poor old York?"

James's face slowly fell. And his wine bottle rose. . . . Blue Boy meeting each rising dune as if he recognized it. Scarcely possible; the dunes must shift from week to week, hour to hour, wind to wind. Kebir had unbuttoned his shirt to the belt and was peering out into the desert. And York trying to quell that scene in Yorkville, that final encounter with his wife, his son. He'd done everything in his power to forget it in the intervening years. Placed a continent, a lover, between the event and himself. Had fled to the mountains of Mexico, the forests of British Columbia, the winds of Osprey Cove. To forget and find a new life. Yet it had all followed him here . . . why?

"Stop!" James bleated.

The Colonel slowed to a halt. "What now?"

"Photo," James muttered.

"Of what?" Tony growled.

"Sand dune over there: like a shark's back, fins and all." James had mustered his camera, was already shunting out into the sand. Uncertain, the others followed. The Colonel rammed his helmet down over his eyes, frowning into the dunes. Blue Boy seemed to drift over the sand in his big sandals. And Kebir with his long strides. But York sliding and sinking. And the Colonel almost falling down the face of a hummock of sand. Yes, slippery underfoot, solid one instant, giving way the next. Like dry quicksand. As they made their way toward James's shark dune. And James turning to take a quick shot as the Colonel stumbled again. "That's it, hit a fella when he's down," Tony said. James grinning delight.

They were out atop a ridge, gazing into the desert. . . . Nothing. Just glaring, golden, dunes cascading, rolling—yet ominously still. "See any birds, York?" the Colonel asked. And Blue Boy was gesturing past where the trail disappeared. "M'hamid-el-Chislaine"—was that what he said?

Kebir took the chance to move off to one side to pee. James seemed too preoccupied with his Hasselblad to notice. York half noticed out the corner of his eyes, sharp silhouette of Kebir against the afternoon sun, black on gold, all color dissolving.

Blue Boy was standing, apparently staring straight ahead, but his whole body listening, as if transfixed. York followed the line of his sidelong gaze to Kebir. For an instant York saw as Blue Boy saw: Keb limned in the flare of sun, at once hunter and dance and spear of flesh.

"Troops will fall in for photo duty!" James mimicking the Colonel.

They fell into line, Tony muttering, "C'mon, we'd best cheer him up a bit." Kebir beside the Colonel, then York and Blue Boy. All holding hands. *Snap-snap.* "Ohh, you all look so sexy!" Then the Colonel was scuttling for the car. But James shouting, "Wait, I want one with *me* in it." And suddenly York was doing camera duty. The other four lined up, arm in arm. The car in the background. York focusing, trying to find all four faces. Tony's cherubic grin, yes; and James with face slightly turned so pockmarks didn't show; Blue Boy all eager; and Keb all smiles. But flames were exploding around Tony and James, around all of them! And around the car.

"What are you doin', Canajun?"

And for an instant York wanting to shout, "Turn back, we must turn back!" But he got the shot—*snap-snap*. And another, James ecstatic. "Immortal," he said, "among the gods!"

"Immortal be damned," the Colonel said grumpily as they clambered into the car.

"Just because you," James started.

Taranta-raaah-arraah, the Colonel blasted the hunting horn, cutting James dead. The car churned ahead, rolling across the sand. York was gazing out the window, oblivious to his own thoughts. His entire being invaded by the desert. No postcard, no quickie snapshot, that desert. It was a viper, inside of him as well as out there. Coiling, recoiling, in the vestiges of his brain. And still those flames around James's head—halo gone amok.

Nearly an hour since they'd left Tagounite. James mustered the guidebook again. "It's called *M'hamid of the Gazelles.*" The what? "Famous for its gazelles, or was. They're apparently extinct. So are the cheetahs."

"But not the cobras!" the Colonel added, glancing at James. "They're for you!"

James replied by sticking his tongue out.

Kebir was sitting twiddling his long fingers, glancing at Tony, James, and York, though York didn't notice. Kebir with an intent look on his face, as if listening to something none of them heard.

Blue Boy was leaning forward, face glowing, blue robe billowing with breeze through the window. A vivid expectancy flushing his face. Yes, they must be getting close to his home village. And what would M'hamid of the Gazelles be like? Calm, York prayed—peace after the bedlam of Zagora, the chaos of their voyage.

As York glanced over, Blue Boy led his gaze down to his robe. The robe had risen, projecting at his groin. Hard-on part of the boy's excitement. Sculpted through the dazzle of robe. But a sign rearing up from the sands, shouting—

FOR GOD'S SAKE,
TOUCH!

Exhortation repeated by the boy's eyes, flowing mane of hair. For God's sake, *touch!* As natural as shaking hands. Homage to the lord of the land, of the Atlas Mountains, the rage of desert. *Touch!* Boy shifting in the seat, exposing entry pocket to his robe. Hard cock eloquent under the blue. Silent hum of car, wind over sand.

York saw his hand slide to that point of entry. And stop midway. Stop as Kebir moved forward. And Blue Boy glancing over, wondering—why no touch, no dance? Why was York sitting frozen there? Failure to touch . . . life failure. York slumped back in his seat, clenching his truant hand. When he opened his eyes a moment later, the sign had sunk back into the sands. And Blue Boy had subsided, gleam gone with his homecoming hard-on.

"Geysers, like bloomin' geysers," James shouted.

"Flamin' orchard." Tony chortled. "A date grove!"

Yes, orchard of towering palm trees soaring over them as they rounded a ridge of sand. The car moving like a panther in the sudden sensuality of shade. The Colonel stopped. James waved his camera through the window, *snap-snap*. "Those trunks are just the right shape and size!"

"For elephants!" Tony laughed.

But York sat shivering, hot-cold shiver. The thick dark palm trunks rioting on all sides. One more push and he'd be over the brink. . . .

"So M'hamid of the Gazelles does exist." James chortled.

Trantarrahhh-aaah-rrraah, the horn rollicking through the maze of trees. Kebir taking York's hand. And Blue Boy smiling again. Home for the wedding!

6
THE FIERY FURNACE

"M'hamid! Three huzzahs for M'hamid!" the Colonel bellowed as they shot out of the palm grove into a clearing surrounded by mud huts, a few small shops.

Tony coaxed the car into the scant shade of the buildings, the sun directly overhead. A scatter of people popping out of the boutiques to appraise the arrival. James, Tony and Kebir bundled out of the car. Blue Boy paused a moment in his seat, long enough to be seen and envied by other young Moroccans. And York sat, dizzy from the throb of his own head. Just what and who was M'hamid? A moment ago they had been surrounded by the majesty of the palm grove. Now he stared out at the abode shacks, yelping dogs, a single donkey. And young men, boys, peering in wonder at such a windfall as this car. What in God's own name did Tony and James expect to find here? He scowled—why the hell couldn't he be a good traveler like the others? James and Tony always spoofing . . . even when serious. And the more serious they seemed, or even bitchy, nasty, the more they laughed. That crazy banter of theirs kept things going. And Kebir, always smiling, radiating serenity, quiet joy. York pried himself out, following the boom of the Colonel's voice into the nearest shop. Shade closing over him, his eyes blinded by the shade. Skitter of voices all around him, Moroccan voices and the whinny of James asking for gin and Judor. And slowly the colors, iridescent greens, yellows, blues began to appear. York's eyes swimming to slow focus on the slashing teeth, bobbing colors. String of beads, multicolor glass, bones. And those teeth, slashing off the end of the beads, necklaces. The angle of sun highlighting them in the gloom of the little shop.

A dance of the polychromatic beads. York fingered the necklaces, strident as he touched them. His eyes dilating, flowing to the largest, deep amber—eyes of a young Moroccan, behind the counter. Their gaze meshing as York rubbed his thumb along one of the ivory tusks. Moroccan smiling through an aureole of blond hair. Can a Moroccan have blond hair? Does . . . and a copper face. Moroccan smiling silently as if they'd just embraced. York's thumb touching the tip of the ivory tooth.

"Crikey Moses, our York is drugged on Goulimine beads!" Tony's laugh boomed across the little shop, pulling it into momentary focus. James already negotiating purchase of a rug with Kebir's help.

"C'mon, York, there's more than beads here," Tony said. "I smell the real thing!"

"Actually, what I need is a shit." He heard his own reply with surprise, his eyes seeking the door. One of the boys clustered in the door understood, if not the words, at least the glance. He beckoned. York followed him out into the blitz of heat. "Wait!" Tony striding after, thrusting something into York's hand. A piece of scrunched newspaper. "May need it. Morocco doesn't provide the amenities." York nodded, followed the tall ebony lad across the empty plaza. The sand squeaking underfoot. They were approaching a high mud wall, an open doorway. The youth's face pointing through the doorway. York entered. Nothing. No roof, piles of dry turds scattered in the corners.

He poked further into the ruins, found a small room at the far end with the remains of a lattice roof. A cat perched under the lattice yowled at the intrusion and withdrew to rooftop peering down on him. He quickly lowered his pants, put his hands on the floor, heaved. A single turd shunted out . . . thud. Earth tremoring beneath him now, mounting his spine. And overhead the face of cat through the slats, cat overseeing the invasion of his lair. And returning to perch just under the lattice. Yellow and black spots like ocelot, this cat.

Slight scuffle behind him. He glanced back, saw the tall ebony lad standing at the entry to the room, his robe pulled up. Peeing. York felt vulnerable, like Blue Boy squatting in the desert. The ebony lad standing, sunlight catching his cock in sharp silhouette as he peed. Standing so relaxed as York crouched to the trembling earth. Distant drums touching York's spine. Cat's eyes blaring wide, tail twitching—what were they doing in his lair? York's eyes wide on the towering boy squeezing last drops from cock. Boy grinning, cock head grinning . . . surveying York. Cat mewled, sifted over to the edge of roof, watching. Boy on display.

York stumbled, fell onto all fours. Cat blinked. Black cock swelling in boy's hand. Cat eyeing twitching cock.

He lurched up again, hand braced against the wall. Black boy shook red knob, his lips parting. York grabbed his pants, got them half up. Black boy gliding forward. York yanked pants up to butt. Boy touching York, hand on his shoulder, black cock hard against his buttocks. York froze. Cock nuzzling his bare flesh, cock hot yet cool, burrowing into his open butt. Burrowing into open York, climbing up inside his spine. The sound of drums rising as they stood together swaying. Ebony boy ferociously calm. York dropping his head against the wall.

Boy stamped his foot, stamped twice, dropping his head onto York's shoulder. Cat yowled and fled.

They walked slowly back across the burning plaza. The town seared under the beating sun. Seared into a single huddle of houses, leaning tower, panoply of nearby palms.

A dog barked, a pair of dogs, hurtling at them like rabid hyenas, bristling. The ebony boy picked up a stone, waiting . . . waiting till the dogs bore in again, and *crack*, smashed the biggest on the side of the head. *Craack* . . . York saw it! They were walking beside the river, late afternoon. A dog in the nearby field had found a buried bone. And was making off in triumph. *Craaack* . . . the man hurled a large rock, smashing the dog's thigh, dog screaming—back leg shattered and dangling at abrupt right angle from its body. The Mexican sneering content as the dog straggled off. "But it's a death sentence, Yo-yo. . . . He just *murdered* that dog." Mexicans cruel that way, with dogs, with each other.

He felt the hand on his shoulder. Turned . . . not John, and this not the mountains of Mexico. The hand black, an ebony lad, tall, smiling, his face familiar. Where had they met? Yes, the lad and a cat, but where? Ebony lad drew York across the unfamiliar space. Past the car toward a little shop. But as they approached, the ebony boy dropped discreetly back, York entering alone, the blond Moroccan behind the counter.

He gazed around the shop, hearing the singing again. The voice—"Your friends have gone to the wedding. I will bring you there now." Voice of the blond boy in halting French. York smiled, fondling one of the necklaces, the giant tusk-tooth dangling at the end. "It's from the wild boar, up in the mountains. They are very dangerous." The tooth nearly six inches long, curved like a saber. York nodded. He just wanted to stay and listen to the song.

But the blond Moroccan installed another boy behind the counter, beckoning for York to follow him. Out the door . . . all but bumping into the ebony lad as they went. York recognizing the feet, toes. Ebony lad wanting to come with them. But blond boy dismissed him. They walked past a string of mud homes, the sand sliding under York's feet, but blond boy floating across it with his big sandals. "How come you're blond?" York wanted to ask. But surely there were blond Moroccans? Like redheaded Mexicans, result of a mixed marriage, a mixed night.

And as they walked, "Your friends ask about a hotel," blond boy was saying. He had such sultry eyes, honeycomb brown, like the sultry blondness of his hair. "But the hotel is closed now. There's a big room behind the shop, you can spend the night there." The boy slowed down, watching York fumble along the sand. Boy glancing at York's city shoes. Silly shoes for sand, silly feet. York caught up, grateful for the offer of a room. "I could go back there in a while and rest. Exhausted from the trip. Our car broke down. We fed it wine. . . ." He lurched ahead, sand burning through the thin soles of his shoes. Blond boy nodded. "I'll make you a special drink, with gtran. Foreigners see strange in the desert. The real desert starts in M'hamid!" Blond boy proud of this. "We have a saying. . . . The desert bites!" They were skirting a long wall now, drums thudding louder. "For the wedding, they drum all day, all night. There's other people here too . . . Hamadja."

They turned through a break in the wall, another small clearing. Drums flaring close, a flash of burnooses, black turbans. A small crowd gathered in front of one of the houses, under the shade of palm trees. A figure in a straw boater, standing like a large heron: James. And Kebir swaying as if in a trance. They were watching a giant black drummer who was pummeling a trio of drums. Several feet high, the biggest drum. And others beating time with small clay drum-pots. Some banging large spoons together . . . *clackety-clack* and *boom!*

"Really marvelous, no?" James clutching York's arm, trying to stamp time with his feet. Kebir turned, saw York and broke into a smile, smile spiraling up through his torso to emerge in his eyes.

"Winged Victory of Samothrace!" James nodding at Kebir.

"Where's Tony?"

"Beloved Colonel went for a tour."

"A what?"

"With our Blue Boy." James nodded. "Have you noted the hands?"

"Hands?"

"On that big drummer fella!"

York glanced at the largest drum. Huge black hands caressing, beating the drum.

"Best ever!" James slapping his thighs out of time with the drums. And for a flaring instant York saw him naked, ass raw, blubbering with joyous terror—James, in that little room in Zagora.

He glanced at Kebir, but Keb was talking with Blond Boy. The drumming increased. York wheeled around. Why was everyone staring at him? *"Whaaa-yyyeaay."* The drummers wailing. *"Whaaa-yyyeaaay."* York's head whirling.

He needed to calm down. Saw a small courtyard, thatched with palm leaves, beyond the pummeling crowd. York shoved through the swaying people. They seemed to give way, not even noticing him. The tall ebony boy grinning as York stumbled by.

He got into the courtyard, and sank onto a small stool, eyes closed. There was a chittering hiss like large birds, geese. He looked up, the courtyard a pandemonium of women scurrying, throwing up walls of color, a flail of shawls. Women in blue, red gauze hissing as they bundled something up and out of York's sight. Something they rushed from York's eyes to the protection of the house at the far end of the courtyard. Like a flock of giant birds protecting their nest, the older women rusing toward York now, flapping arms, falling back in a violent hiss. . . .

He hadn't seen them when he entered, too busy seeking shade and haven. It was too hot for all those layers of clothes, must tell them that. One of the older women darted at York, shawl flailing, and out the door of the courtyard. York upset now, something deranged here. He was about to go find Kebir when a Moroccan burst into the court, waving his arms, shouting. Two more right behind . . . kicking the stool out from under York. A knife flashed . . . shouting melee over York. Kebir and Blond Boy barging in, Keb butting his head against the man with the knife, butting like an enraged goat. Blond Boy grabbed York, Blond Boy and Keb pushing York out of that lunatic courtyard, out into the pelting sun.

The drumming had stopped. Everything had stopped, save the hullabaloo from inside the little courtyard. And the circle of men forming slowly around York. Circle of Blue Men drawing closer to York . . . their eyes piercing him with accusation. What had he done?

An older man in a white robe, large dagger slung at his side, walked slowly forward, gazing at York as at transgression absolute. Began speaking to him in what sounded like Arabic. And gesturing toward the courtyard. The crowd murmuring, nodding as a single head. White Robe nodding. And a figure pushing through the circle . . . wearing a boater. James in his idiotic boater. The crowd watching York. And White Robe still talking. James wobbled his way over, tapping White Robe on the arm. But White Robe disdained even to notice him. James stepped back, sweeping his boater off in a tipsy bow. "We must have more drums!" Glaring at White Robe. "Who stopped my drums?" And York vaguely aware he had, just by sitting on a stool. And they were all staring at him again.

The crowd parted again. Burly figure parading through, pith helmet at rakish angle. "What the hell's going on here, a murder?" The Colonel arriving in full array. With his Blue Boy and Kebir. Blue Boy's eyes going wide as he turned and bowed to the man in the white robe, murmuring something. Then ran into the little courtyard, arms aflail.

James turned on the Colonel. "High time *you* showed up! York went into the barnyard there . . . and the music stopped." James stamping a foot. Tony glared and assumed his most official stance. Kebir went up to White Robe, giving a slight bow. White Robe nodded with one eye. Kebir pointed to Tony. "Colonel Tonee, *Colonel* Tonee!" And something which ended with "Marrakech . . . Pasha." Tony nodding, smiling for White Robe, who acknowledged him by flickering the other eye. Blue Boy reappeared now, accompanied by another elder. The hubbub in the courtyard ceasing. Silence.

White Robe conferred with the arriving elder. Tony stood doing his fervent best to look like Henry VIII. But White Robe effortlessly looking like Genghis Khan. James squatted on the sand, fanning himself with his boater.

Finally White Robe nodded. The elder nodded. Blue Boy then presented Tony to the elder, his father. And father presented the Colonel to White Robe . . . Caid of M'hamid-el-Ghislaine, repeated several times. What was a caid? No matter. Everyone bowed each time it was said. Finally the Caid held out both hands in formal welcome to the Colonel. The crowd murmured. The Caid smiled approbation. Blue Boy's father found stray fluff on the Caid's sleeve, plucking it off with a diligence bordering on reverence. And the circle of Moroccans were talking again. The Caid strode off with the elder. James staggered to his feet as the drums started up warily.

"C'mon, York!" Tony grabbed him by the arm. Keb and Blond Boy joined them. James wavered, then turned back to his beloved drums, wobbling with the renewed rhythm. They were walking toward a cluster of palm trees, Tony guiding York there for shelter. The sand almost cool underfoot, sound of a waterfall overhead: the dry rustling of palm leaves.

Under the trees, well away from the crowd, Blond Boy started talking animatedly with Kebir. Kebir translating for Tony. York paying no attention, his mind adrift amid the palm leaves. Till Tony's voice caught him, urgent voice. "You broke Islamic law! You entered the women's compound . . . on the wedding day, you coot!" York nodded. "You entered when they were dressing the bride: a sacred moment." Tony shaking York's arm. "No man must see the bride before the ceremony. The man who drew the knife was the husband-to-be. . . . You committed rape!"

"Rape?" York staring at the camels.

"You saw his bride!" Tony drawing York over to sit on a palm log. Tony put his arm protectively around York's shoulder. "As a foreigner, you didn't know their customs. Blue Boy explained that to his father, and the father explained it to the Caid."

Blond Boy's eyes wide on York as Tony spoke. And Kebir nodding. York had to understand. "C'mon, let's stroll a bit farther,

I'll take some sense into you," Tony drawing York on. And York blurting, "They wanted blood . . . blood!"

They were approaching the last palm trees, the Colonel still talking. "We got off because we're Blue Boy's guests. Moroccan laws of hospitality are very strong. When the Caid understood what had happened, he ruled that you had never entered the bridal courtyard. He ruled you'd never entered, therefore there was no transgression. Moroccan logic, d'you see?" They were climbing a ridge of sand under the final palm trees. A pair of dogs shot up, growling. Blond Boy plucked some stones, hurled them at the dogs. Dogs falling back, snarling, Keb positioning himself between dogs and York. The Colonel saying, "Be double careful, Yorkers, there's some religious group here, fanatics."

They were nearing the top of the ridge. York stumbling, Kebir catching him. Spread before them the open desert, like a great golden tide. And off to one side a cluster of giant grounded birds, wings spread like ravens across the sand. And beyond the tents, the rising din, camels lying like stranded ships in the sand. Men carrying fodder. And gunshots. Fight or festival?

Blond Boy said something. "A caravan just in from the south." The Colonel holding York's arm as they slid through the sand to the tents, bombarded by fragrances: sharp, bittersweet, mint and leather and smen. That underlying odor of a caravan, a race of men. And more dogs hurtling from the tents. Barking as they approached, then attacking from behind. Blond Boy and Keb throwing more rocks. And boys playing amid the camels. And a large dog scurrying out from under the flap of the closest tent, huge chunk of meat in its mouth. And York laughing, clapping his hands. Then the dog catapulted into the air, spinning so gracefully, meat floating out of its jaws. Spiraling nose-first into the sand, a shrieking animal wail. A young man strolled out of the tent, jamming a long pistol into his belt. Nonchalantly picking up the meat, not deigning to see the dying dog. The pistol shot, lost amid the uproar of the camp.

"Crikey, they shoot fast!" But York was stumbling toward the writhing dog. Kneeling and holding the dog's head as it died. Keb chasing after him, urgently pulling him away. The young man at the tent laughed, proud laugh, and fired a shot over their heads.

They pushed on along the line of tents, York gazing at the

blood on his hands. . . . Kebir gazing apprehensively at the tents. But Blond Boy pointing ahead, to the camels. Yes, entire caravan bivouacked there. The desert men in their blue robes and turbans, tending them. A young boy goaded one of the camels into a run. Riding atop a rope-work saddle, waving—go for a camel ride? Yes, why not take a camel ride, ride into the sun, the rippling sands? Ride just once, laughing, waving . . . to Timbuktu.

York tottered, spiraled facedown into the sand, vomiting. Entrails spread from Marrakech to M'hamid. Keb kneeling, sheltering him from the sun, Tony massaging his back.

They stumbled back toward the clutch of palms, the sound of drums. "A touch too much sun," Tony was saying. "They'll take you back to a room behind that shop. Get some rest, Yorkers. I'll go cope with the elders a bit and find James." Tony nodded at Kebir, and Blond Boy and turned toward the wedding party.

Before York knew it, they were in the bead shop. Blond Boy leading them to a large room at the rear. A tiny window, straw mats on the floor. Blond Boy unrolling a thick rug, opulent, like an orchard in full bloom. Then brought some cushions and pointed to the rug. York refused to lie on anything so beautiful. But soon he was stretched out on a large sheepskin atop the rug. Cool, comfortable. Keb whispering with the boy, going out. Blond Boy lighting a candle. Room flickering. Figures on the wall—a winged horse, head of a woman wearing a crown. Riding high over birds and flowers, over temples. Queen of the World. Blond Boy going out. Keb back with York's little bag and binoculars. Who's that woman on the wall, Keb?

"The spirit of the night."

Spirit of the night?

"She's in the Koran. She is the speed of the light in the stars."

Wonderful: picture of the speed of . . .

Blond Boy back with jug and glass, talking with Keb. Mixing something black in the glass, adding water. Pungent smell, harsh.

"It's gtran" Blond Boy holding up the glass.

Gtran?

"Made from tree roots," Keb murmured. "Cures the sun. You had too much sun."

Blond Boy pushed the glass at him. "Drink it quick. It will bite."

York took the glass, hand shaking, spilling. Blond Boy took it back, held York's head, pouring the drink into his mouth. York spluttered, drink biting his dry throat. Winged Woman laughing, watching the drink shake York's body. Alarm in Keb's eyes. "I'll find Tonee, ami. I think we should leave." Kebir dissolved. York coughed from the drink, acrid. Blond Boy sitting cross-legged beyond the candle, eyes aglow like a great black-and-gold cat, watching.

York closed his eyes, flopped back . . . and back. Yes, there he was, his son standing at the edge of the sidewalk. Right where Christine had left him.

How could he break through to his son? In less than an hour Christine would be back. He glanced at the hippie drumming nearby. And beside the hippie a red rubber ball. "May I borrow that?" Drummer nodded. York reached for the ball, looked around. Yes, Cedric still there motionless. York tossed the ball in the air. His son's eyes widened. Tossed the ball up again, playing with it, pretending it was two, three balls. Cedric's eyes following Daddy dancing up and down with the ball. . . . Ball floating up and York catching it, passing it behind his back. Cedric craning his neck to see. As York carried on with his little jig, oblivious to the world walking by. And Cedric enthralled—never seen Daddy do anything like this before.

"Here!" York lobbed the ball to his son, who spurted forward, catching it awkwardly with two hands. Both still now. York smiling. Cedric clutched the ball to his chest, eyes gleaming.

Holding up his hand. "Put it there!" Ball shot out of Cedric's hand, back to York, who caught it, bounced it right back to his son with a little whoop. He fumbled, then caught it, nearly smiling. York calling out. "Bet I can catch it better than you did!" And Cedric, looking wily, suddenly bounced the ball back to York, bouncing it high over his head. The ball dissolved into the flower bed behind him. Cedric laughed. "You ca-an't catch it, you ca-an't catch it!" And scooted triumphantly after the ball into the flowers.

"Here it is, Daddy!" He emerged from the flower bed clinging to the ball. York crouched, Cedric running right into his open arms. Both of them silent now. Ced turning the ball over and over, his head down.

"Where did you go, Daddy?" Silence. "Mommy said you were having a holiday." Cedric examining the red ball as if it held the secret.

"I went to Mexico, Ced."

"Is Mexico fun?"

"Fun . . . ?"

"Mommy cried when you were away." Blurting it out, his fingers twisting the red ball. "She cried at Christmas!"

York stood up. "Would you like a lemonade?" Cedric nodded. They wove their way across the street through hippies, cars and sightseers, Ced clutching the ball in one hand, York's hand in the other. "Where are we going, Daddy?" York pointed at the old house. "That's a funny place for a lemonade." Yes it was: old Victorian home—high, pinched gables, narrow windows. All angles, gawking primly above the crowd. But on the ground floor the Penny Farthing, café with large sunny windows and terrace. "And funny people, Daddy!" Ced pulling York's hand while he gazed at the blue-jeaned kids in their gaudy tops.

York quickly steered into the café and its barn-board decor, coffee bar hung with swaying glass beads. A corner table available near the door: privacy, but with a window onto the parade outside. Ced perched on the chair like a bird, eyes wide, clasping the red ball.

"Two lemonades." York to a waitress arriving in a swoop of hips. "Large, please."

"May I have ginger ale, Daddy? Mommy always makes me have lemonade."

"One ginger ale, and a lemonade for me." Waitress receding with a wink. York's ear catching. "Hey, Mr. Tambourine Man." And beyond that the echo of Christine's high heels. She'd be back in—what, half an hour? His son's golden hair loose around his forehead now. Ced peering around the café as at a circus. He dropped the ball. Both watching it bounce under a table where a shaggy German shepherd lay. Ball rolling under their table. Cedric looked up at York, eyes asking. York nodded, and Ced scurried after the ball. Stopping short, testing the dog. Dog wagging its tail. Hippies at the table with their dominoes. Ced looked back; Daddy nodded. He crawled under the table after the ball. And sat there patting the dog. Looking up at Daddy.

Lemonade and ginger ale arrived. The flow of kids along the street, their walk flowing like their long hair. No Christines there. And if I leave, go with John, then Ced'll be caught in that strait-jacket—for life.

He looked back. Cedric had patted his way up the dog, standing now watching the dominoes. Glancing in Daddy's direction. York nodded, eyeing the blue and gold of his son. Hippie at the next table grinning, catching Ced's eye. Ced tossed the ball to him. Hippie laughed, catching the ball. And bounced the ball on into the next room, under more tables. Cedric skittering after his ball. Holding the ball like a newfound prize. Tossing it in the air, trying to juggle like silly Daddy. Dropping it. Ending in front of a girl in a rainbow shawl. Holding ball as bright as apple, displaying it to pretty girl. What would Chris say? But the girl smiled, stroking his son's ruffled hair. And Cedric wide-eyed, bounced his ball into the front room, following it all flibbertigibbet like a blue-gold bird back to Daddy's chair.

Ced standing close to York now, eyes shining. And dropping the ball right under Daddy's chair. Scooting down to get it. And up again, leaning against York's legs, clutching his hand. "You are my Daddy, aren't you?" Whispered shriek. And just as York was about to ruffle that golden hair, stricken, Cedric whispered again. "Mommy's always kissing Peter!" And stood examining his red ball as if for the first time. It popped out of his hand, bouncing across the floor. Gold head in frantic pursuit.

When he looked up, Ced was engaged with another hippie fingering the colored beads around his neck. Hippie smiling, playing with Ced's dancing fingers. York slouched over his lemonade. "York! I must protect Cedric from you." Christine hissing at him over the phone yesterday.

Cry of glee catching his ear. He glanced up. Ced playing a game with hippie's hands. Frolicking with those long fingers. No, never did that at home.

York sat torn—joy at this sight of his son, pain in his body. The minutes danced by. Cedric warbled into action again. York staring down at his own clenched fingers. How could he leave his son now? Yet if he stayed, he'd be false, propped up as a portrait of a father painted by Christine. He'd remain stillborn, and his son too. *That's* what he must tell Ced. But how?

He looked over. His son peering at him from beside the hippie. Like a little rabbit, nose a-twitch, peering at Daddy. Their eyes meeting—Ced bouncing back into play.

York tasted his lemonade. Christine hated what he was doing, while asserting that she herself had driven him to it. That gave her satisfaction. Love me or I'll kill you; love me and I will kill you.

A shove at his knee, small hand, blue sleeve. Ced standing shy, his hand there. "Daddy, you're very sad."

"I can't explain, Ced—"

Ced's fierce whisper as he leaned against York. "You *are* my daddy!"

"Yess. I *am* your daddy."

"Then you like me?"

"I love you, Cedric." He put his arm around his son. And felt a presence beyond them. A pair of eyes, naked, dilated. Waves of long brown hair. Hippy-of-the-red-ball crouching on haunches gazing at them.

The sound of high heels grinding on the doorstep. Yes, Christine was back, reared up on those high heels, there in the café doorway. Glaring down at them.

Precisely, her eyes said, precisely why I did not want Cedric to go up to your room. An orgy . . . a public orgy!

Ced shifted uneasily, though he hadn't yet seen Christine. York stood up, guilty.

"We were playing ball, Mommy." Ced taking the ball, about to toss it to Mommy.

"Time to stop playing ball, Cedric!" She tapped out the words with her toe on the step.

"You're back early, aren't you?" York hoping to deflect the rage.

"I knew there'd be something . . . odd!" She clattered forward to rescue Ced. Ced becoming Cedric as he clutched the ball.

"Can't we sit, Chris? A few minutes?"

"Ten minutes! I'm due at my parents'." Christine tightened her grip on her purse. Was *not* going to sit at that odious table. She glanced toward the inner room—they would sit there, in the least visible corner. Marching across the Penny Farthing, seeing no one. To the farthest corner, sitting down. Back wedged to the wall, in sure defense. York facing her. Cedric floating uncertain between. Christine straightened his sweater. . . . "His hair is a *mess!*"

"They have mint tea, Chris," York ventured as she brushed flecks of dirt from Cedric's pants.

"Fine. We have a minute!" Buzz-buzz. Cedric looked at the floor, truant ball behind his back. No waitress. Christine erect in her chair, looking past York's shoulder. Lips zipped tight. No, he couldn't talk with her now. Not in this state. They'd never talk again. She had already told him over the phone, "I'm not going to give you any satisfaction, York!" He got up, angled off to find a waitress, find some tea, find anything. As he reached the bar, the tug at his pants. Ced had followed in his wake, out of Mommy's glare.

"May I go and play in the garden, Daddy?" Cedric whispering, pointing out the back door, more tables, hippies out there.

"Yes, but for God's sake don't go into the flower bed, don't get dirty, don't . . ."

"I'll be very good, Daddy." Ced whisking out the door. York leaned against the coffee bar. Buzz-buzz. "And some honey, my wife likes honey." He carried the tray toward the table, seeing her out the edge of his eyes. Still rearing tall, yet expectation in her glance.

"You always like honey, Chris." He passed her the pot, sat down. Stirring his tea in the wary silence. Finally looked up. Her eyes wide on him, their sting gone. . . . He dropped his eyes back, stirring. Each diligently stirring. Glanced up again. Yes, her eyes wide with expectation. But he had nothing left to give her. "So how was your winter, Chris?" Inane.

"Brrr . . . freezing. You know how bad the heating is at the farm. It was so cold, Touc died!"

"The toucan died?" York looked up again, caught the dimple of her chin, the peal brooch at her throat. Single black pearl, belonged to her grandmother.

"Yes, dead on his perch." Her throat trembling. "I buried him out on the terrace, beside the spruce. Thérèse howled and howled, wouldn't eat for days." The black pearl once belonged to the Empress Eugenie, at least that's what grandmother said. "I saved all our plants, though. Put them in the kitchen and kept one burner of the stove on at low." She was leaning forward, shoulders relenting with her eyes. "I even saved your big prayer plant. Thought I was going to lose him." He caught her look. Proud. His eyes fell back to the brooch. "And I managed to save the big turtle. He cracked his shell falling down the stairs, during a storm." She waited.

York sat numb as her picture of their farm poured in on him. Her voice that complicit purr it always was when they talked of home.

"I wanted to send you money, Chris." Absurd; he'd been so broke in Mexico, he'd swapped his watch for a turkey. He and John ate turkey stew for a week.

"Oh, I knew you had no money. I found a job interior decorating. But my father stopped it."

"Stopped you?" York saw her mouth twitch open.

"Father said I should be looking after Ced."

"Damn your father. He always stops you—always did." York spilled his tea, started wiping it up.

"You know what he's like, always disapproves. But whenever he stops me, he gives me money. So I moved out of the farm. Rented a small house in the Annex. It has an enclosed porch for the dogs." She prattled on, black pearl bobbing.

"And our cats, the marmalade one is pregnant now." Chris chatting on, sipping her tea. "And your favorite, the Abyssinian, is courting next door. And poor Astrid . . ."

He looked up, past the bobbing pearl. Her face glowing now, silver moon afloat in the purr of domestic talk. The divine Christine, as his friends called her; her beauty brought men to their feet in an age when no one acknowledged anything. A holy beauty almost, as she burbled on about their farm, their pets and plants. Yes, they'd been married a thousand years. Had he ever fled to Mexico? Been John's lover?

"I gave your mother the biggest of the succulents at Christmas, easy for her to keep." She was looking over at York now, lower lips starting to swell, as always when she was excited. Her finger moving around and around the rim of her cup.

York looked away. "When did you start seeing Peter?" Question blurting out. She blinked. "Oh, him." Raising her forefinger to her lower lip. "I suppose around the end of February. The cold spell . . ." York silent. End of February, that's when he had planned to return to Toronto. But John's parents had sent the Mexican police.

"Peter's the seal man. He's leading the crusade to save the seals. The methods of killing baby seals are so cruel." She daubed more honey into her tea. "Peter showed me pictures of how they kill them . . . terrible cruelty." She sipped the tea, tongue flickering at the corner of her mouth.

Cruelty? To baby seals? York wanting to shout, "But what of *your* cruelty to your own son—or even your husband? You're an expert at it."

"Chris, I couldn't write you, I was on the run. Couldn't phone. My lawyer told me the call might be traced." York leaned across the table, eyeing her directly. "I was in Mexico."

She fell back. "I thought you were here."

"I had to run. John's parents sent the police here *and* in Mexico. They're as crazy as your parents." York finally focused now.

"Was he that red-haired one I met?"

"Yes. He fled *his* parents, came to Mexico after I got there. To join me."

She rubbed the edge of her cup, eyes falling. "So it was him; you brought him to the farm for dinner once. We talked about our families, how they wouldn't let us live our own lives." Her finger twisting the handle of the cup. "He was handsome."

"Chris, you told me to bring anyone I wanted. You said it was the best way." He paused. "You told me . . . to find a man, if I wanted."

"I know, I just didn't . . ." Her voice small now, forefinger pressing her lips like a wound. "Didn't want you to find another woman, really."

"I couldn't take you with me, Chris. Remember, you asked me to take you with me. Said you'd go anywhere. . . ." Chris nodding as he fought to explain—explain what? Her finger probing into the flesh of her lips. Yes, she had wanted to come, face shouting to come, as York had walked out the door of their farm. Yet she'd fought him all the way, day after day sabotaging his writing with a flick of her eyelid or a hopeful smile.

"Chris, I wanted to come back to Toronto in February to see you. But there was a warrant out for my arrest, so I wrote that letter."

She sat silent, fingers probing swollen lips.

"Then I got the advance for my book, enough to come home. . . . That's when I got your note about the divorce. I phoned you right away, and I asked you to wait!" She nodded, eyes saying her worst and her best hopes confirmed by his words. "You said, 'Yes, I still love you, York. Yes, I'll wait.' "

She was blowing her nose, tears bubbling down her cheeks. He was dumbstruck. An hour ago she'd slaughtered his last hope, and now she was leaning forward, silent pleading. A word and she was his. Chris leaning forward, open. For a paralyzed instant he felt that his love for John, all his efforts to write, were gross perversions. She swayed toward him, blurting, "Someone always had to die, York . . . in our love."

He felt cold. His clothes wet, clinging to his body. A pair of hands massaging his shoulders. Big hands rubbing his neck, forehead. Candle flickering. Shivering he tried to sit up. He wasn't on a bed at all. On the floor, on thick rugs and a sheepskin. And that regal lady on the wall riding triumph across flowers, birds, towers. She was talking again, her hooves clattering the sky. He glanced around. Silhouette entering, carrying a teapot.

"Fresh tea, ami." Dark face gleaming in the candlelight. "You slept long. We must change your clothes."

Dark face smiling, stripping York's clothes off. Rubbing him with a damp cloth, dry towel. Finally he was sitting, warm and dry, on the rug. Sitting in a light brown djellabah, drinking mint tea.

Kebir nodded, putting extra sugar in York's glass and grinning.

"The wedding. You went into the house, remember? The bride's home." Kebir whispering. York nodding, almost remembering. "It's forbidden to see the bride before the marriage, ami. The husband has a right to kill you."

"Me?"

Keb nodding. "It was fortunate that the father of the bride is a friend of Caid." York vaguely remembered a hullabaloo, all those hissing women.

Kebir silent a moment, finally saying, "When you slept, you were wrestling with a demon. I could hear—"

"Hear what?"

"A djinn in your body. It was buzzing all the time, like a bee. You were talking. Someone was crying."

York shivered. "Someone always had to die." Yorkville, that's where he'd been. And his head whirling. "Chris, I tried to tell you. I wrote that enormous letter just to tell you. You refused to read it."

"I couldn't, didn't want you harmed, didn't—"

Kebir had taken York's glass, holding it as York babbled. And the Winged Lady nodded serenely. "You must be a strong man, York. Anyone who lived through what I've put you through would be dead by now!"

York shuddered. Yes, Christine said that, out at the farm on her birthday.

"The Evil Eye, ami—it bit you. That shaman!"

Who?

"That man dancing around the car in Agdz. He cast a spell on Tonee's car." Kebir taking York's hand, whispering now. "That's why you had a demon in you."

York looked—there was Christine. Why was she weeping? And for a moment York utterly still. The verdict that afternoon in Yorkville—end of his marriage! He'd longed to forget—never written of it in his diary or talked about it, even to John. But it had remained etched in his nervous system. And now, here, it had all flooded back, word for word. He turned. She'd gone. Just the lady gazing down imperturbably, as if she'd known all along.

"Drink your tea, ami." Kebir passed him the glass. York's hand trembling. Silence. Running his fingers through the rug. Suddenly laughing. "It's like flying, sitting on a rug as beautiful as this." Kebir nodded. "In Morocco, each rug a story; some are magic."

Magic?

"Genies live in certain rugs, djnoun. On certain days we see them rise. You're feeling better now, ami?"

Better? York looked around. "Keb, I've got to get out of this room. It's . . ."

"There's dancing now."

"Dancing . . . the wedding?"

"No, religious dancing. The Hamadja. . . ." Keb paused. "James was dancing with them."

"James?"

"He was out there with Tonee, dancing!"

"Well, good for James!"

"No, dangerous. They use cobras . . . they dance with scorpions. They dance in fire. They—"

"Keb, we must see this."

"Then put this on." Keb passed him the silver Hand of Fatima.

"Must find Tony and James." York lunged to shaky feet. Keb gave him a pair of pointed yellow slippers. "Better for the sand." What? "In djellabah and babouches the night will hide you, ami."

They made their way out into the street. For an instant York swayed at the sight of luminious white tusks. Longed to see one of those animals. See as it sees. And Blond Boy? Where was he? He wanted to thank him.

"Don't speak, and follow me!" Kebir pulled him out of the shop. It seemed cold now, full moon across scudding clouds. Clouds in the Sahara. Odd being here at all. Sand a silver gold in front of them, town erupting under the moon. Keb drew the djellabah hood up over York's head. He saw his shadow following Keb across the sands. He glanced at his watch. After ten; had he slept that long? Strange, almost never looked at the time anymore.

Thudding of drums growing louder under their feet. His slippers kept falling off. Keb stopped, showing him how to lean forward into the slippers. Like skiing, crossing the sand in these slippers. Though hard to keep up with Kebir, who floated over the sand. Houses unfurling around them, bone-white like Bethlehem.

Keb beckoned him on, skirting by the taboo wedding house—no one.

"The others are dancing by the tents, out beyond the palms," Keb whispered. A stray dog yapped close. Keb threw a stone, and dog disappeared in its own snarl. They reached the first palm trees, drumbeat rising above the sand. Soon after, a pond like a mirage. And a figure rising over the pond. They stood silent. Figure rising on the far side, naked from the waist up, silver flames around his head, torso. Figure walking slowly around the pond, approaching them. His ribs projecting like naked bones. Within feet of them now, his face contused, facial flesh floating out, prehensile. Totally silent, yet close now, eyes wide on them. One hand held across his chest, a knife cutting *through* his hand. But no blood. The man passed, not even seeing them. Kebir waited till he was gone, then put his own hand down . . . the entire time had held his hand up against the man, protective hand. Keb drawing York on through the sailing palms. Drums rising, *boom-ka-boom,* as they emerged from the palm oasis into the edge of a seething crowd.

Keb motioned for him to keep his hood up and they merged with the crowd. Grasping York's hand, weaving a path through the swaying mass toward the drums. "*Aaa-yyyeeayy . . . whaaa-yaaayyy,*" howl of drummers, four, five of them pummeling drums with long hooked sticks. Where did crowd end and musicians begin? Figures in the crowd with their own drums. And all pounding time with their feet. A flute, whining, snarling voice of a big flute. And a long moaning horn. Vortex of sound, the drums, the chant of the crowd. York hiding under the djellabah, standing behind Kebir, invisible in the tumult. A man just beyond Kebir clutching a cactus, large cactus, squeezing it to his chest . . . blood dripping from hands and chest. The huge drummer, the one from the wedding, slamming on the largest drum. Ferocious silhouette against a fire behind. And the crowd swaying in a big circle around drummer and fire. Man with the cactus smiling, eyes rolling.

Keb clutched York's arm, nodding left. Figure stumbling out of the circling crowd toward big drummer. Figure in white shirt, flannels, waving ascot like a flag. James!—tottering forward, trying to keep the rhythm, sinking into the sand, stumbling to his knees. Up again, crowd weaving the circle around him as if he didn't exist. But James ecstatic, face flushed and handsome.

Kebir pulled York sideways, zigzagged toward James. The long horn blasted. A turbaned figure fell into the sand, facedown, feet in spasms. *Clatter-di-clack . . . booomm.* They had nearly reached him. James bobbing like a yo-yo amid the flowing bodies. Kebir grabbing him, pulling him away from the drums and the crowd. James shouting, hitting at Kebir. "How dare you? I'm dancing, goddamn *dancing.*"

"Where's *Toneee?*" Keb shouting in James's ear. James waved a detached arm toward the tents beyond. "Beloved Colonel on maneuvers—with Blue Boy." James giggled, fondling Kebir's crotch.

York tried not to see, Keb unable to move and James thrusting his face at York. "Now what d'you see, boyo? What do you see?"

York closed his eyes. *Slaaap*. James slapping York's face hard. York's eyes spurting open to see James's face flush with his own, eyes without center, without core. "Never looked at me, did you, York? You're *cruel;* never really looked at Jimmy," he hissed point-blank. "Have a good look nowww!" James's face with lips swollen, eyelids. "Can't bear to see silly James, can you, York? Don't want to know . . . about yourself!" James turned, kissing Keb's hand, licking his wrist and up his arm. Then lurched back into the rage of crowd.

York stumbled after him, but Keb yanked him back. "Find Tonee . . . find the Colonel." Propelling them both toward the tents, the drums pursuing them. Two burnooses, boys, rising excitedly out of the sand. Keb shouting something, the boys pointing to the largest tent, the last one. York and Kebir pushed on past more tents. Suddenly a billow of robes, turban, a black-ivory face ferociously gazing down on them. A man high above their heads, rifle across his knees . . . on a huge camel . . . floating out of the sky. Beyond him, heads and humps of hundreds of camels silhouetted in the roaring night. The blue man exterminating them with his eyes as he might an insect.

Kebir pulled York beyond that gaze of lethal majesty. York glanced back to see if such a high rider was really there. He was, laughing with the moon, cradled rifle pointing to the final tent. York stumbled, fell out of a slipper, couldn't seem to keep his feet on. But they were nearly there. Hidden laughter crackling around them as they climbed a final ridge of sand. Male laughter from other tents and a pungence in the air. Suddenly Keb stopped, stamped his foot. York colliding with him. Blue Boy an elegant wraith, absent from his own body as he drifted past, silent.

Kebir stared. "Tonee . . . Tonee was with him!" No sound from the final tent. The ebbing tide of drums behind them, seething roar of camels all around. Kebir hesitated, holding up palm of his right hand again, muttering. Suddenly stamped his foot. Large flap on the side of ten exploding open, solitary figure hurtling out, spinning across the sand . . . spiraling into the air, and down, nose-down in the moaning dune. "Tonee!" Sharp fragrance billowing through the open flap in the wake of the flying body. And a single pistol shot.

Keb dragged York toward the figure slumped over the sand.

Oozing cough, blood from the face. "Tonee," Keb whispered, kneeling beside the man, grasping his shoulder. They turned the body over, propping it up. It coughed again, blood dripping from face, shirt ripped.

"You found me." Tony lifting his head, eyes empty. "Didn't want you to find me." Voice distant as Kebir wrestled him to his knees. "Didn't want anyone now—" Eyes beading, then vacant. Kebir feeling Tony's body for wounds. York sure the Colonel done for, waiting for a final pistol shot. But the Colonel threw their hands off, lurched to his feet, standing like a bloody bull, swaying. Wiping clots of blood from his face, neck. What had happened? What was Tony muttering?

York glanced at the tent. Not a sound. As Tony pulled his shirt together, Keb pushed him over the top of the first dune, away from the tent. Colonel protesting. "I've got to go back!" He motioned to the tent, turning. They grabbed him. "I left it there," Tony muttering again. Left what? York expecting the tent flap to explode in pistol shots. "My brandy flask, my father's, all I had . . . in that . . ." He waved an arm at the tent. Silence. "No, no . . . mustn't go back there!" He stared at the sand, about to fall. They caught him, propelling him toward the palm trees, the three of them wobbling across the dunes. Tony babbling something about "honor . . . lost." But he was still alive. And as they reached the first protective trees, he stopped, straightened up. "Where's James?"

"He's dancing with the Hamadja." Keb peered in the direction of the thudding music. The Colonel wiped blood from his dripping nose, mouth. "Got to get him out of here!" He brushed his clothes, fixing his belt. They pushed past the pond, solitary camel drinking. Drums rising. Would they ever know what had happened?

"And you!" Tony suddenly turned on York, grabbing him around the neck with both hands, one eye on his face, the other drooping. "Don't you ever do this. D'you understand?" Shaking York bodily in the air. "You don't need to!" York unable to breathe, much less think. "Don't ever become like James and me!" Words raging out of the Colonel. "D'you promise?" His fingers gouging York's neck. "*Promise* me!" York nodded frantically.

Tony's scar flashed white in his bloody face. York gulped

breath. Kebir glancing at the Colonel like a djinn come to life. Tony asking, "D'you have a son, York?" York nodded. "I have no children. D'you understand now?" York didn't. But the Colonel had his arm around him, and they were strolling as if nothing particular had happened.

The Colonel turned to Kebir. "The dance? James?" Kebir had deliberately steered them into the palm trees, avoiding the Hamadja.

"Whaaa-yeeeayyy"—chant and drum roar flooding toward them. Turbans bobbing black above the dunes like heads rolling across the sands. Bodies emerging as they mounted the final dune beyond the palms . . . bodies swaying, blue, black, white robes flying by moonlight. Smoke billowing from the far end of the crowd, deep horn rasping. Colonel eyed the thudding mass, barked, *"Find him!"*

They ran through the crowds, Keb in the lead. Crowd rapt in its own rhythms, hands clapping, feet pummeling the sand. The strange musk of throng: flesh, sand. Men and boys clapping, probing, flowing one into one another. Eyes a thousand miles from the palpitating bodies. A man grappling a boy by the throat, biting. Boy rotating his thighs—

They were approaching the fire, swarming up to mesh with moonlight. Crackling up from the bed of sand, sparks shooting, fragrant smoke hovering over rolling head. Sweet wood smell mingling with the musk of men. *Clappety-clap.* Figure hurtling over the fire, dancing among the upper flames. Crowd wailing, yodeling as black figures treaded the flames. Another, and another. Young men spiraling through viper tongues of flame. Boys, men, in an open circle around the fire, swaying with the dance. Eyes fixed on sizzling dancers. Flesh fused to flame in a single groaning dance.

A wan figure staggered out from behind the drums, clapping floppy hands, gleeful, pirouetting. "James!" Tony plunged forward, stopped as James hopped barefoot to the very edge of the fire. James sniffing the flames like wine . . . and fell back, hands covering his singed face. In no danger; could barely stand. Wiping his face there with yellow silk handkerchief. Tony laughing crazed relief.

Drums rolling faster now, the huge black leading, head back, hammering his relentless drum. And serpentine curl of flute, coiling, recoiling, with the beat of drums. A knife flashing. *Clap-clap-clappety clap* . . . and *booom*, another figure flying shoulder-high over the flames, hovering between fire and moon. And slowly arching across—and down, in a scatter of embers at fireside, laughing. *Whaaaayyeee-aay*. And *booom*, another! Colonel clapping time with crowd as black feet taunted flames, walking the scattered embers. James backing up, crouching, toes dug into the sand, eyes fixed on the flames, face aglow, flickering with sudden hope of jumping, soaring like gazelle, just once. Tony thrust forward to stop him. *Kaa-booom*—three dancers hurtling over James, tumbling him facedown into the sand as they soared in unison over the fire. *Whaaaayyyee-ayyy*. Trio held in the eye of fire, then gliding down the far edge in yodeling wail. Tony beating time, pounding his feet. James lurching up again, staring at the flames.

York wanting to save him from the dance. Wanting to turn, run screaming. But he was hostage to the flying dance. Bonded in musk and chant and the singe of flesh. He must escape. But his body caught in the whirl of sound. *Clap-clappety-clap*. The crowd swaying in open circle around the fire. Vortex of flesh thudding time with the drums.

Kaa-booom—blue figure whirling out of the crowd, whirling toward flames, catapulting up over fire, spiraling over grasping flames, high, higher than the others . . . head back, hair flaring gold against the night. Crowd yelping, legs storming time with his flight. Blond Boy cascading down the flames, whirling clear of the fire. The crowd surging back. Other bodies now dancing with, whirling with the flames. Blond Boy in the lead, leaping the dizzy flames—black figures, blue, writhing atop the fire, cascading over, gliding down the flank of heat. And whirling before the fire.

The Colonel pointed . . . James! James tottering into the arena again. Clapping elegant hands at Blond Boy, waving his handkerchief, trying to follow Blond Boy's dervish dance. Stumbling shimmying . . . lips swollen in yodel, face with desire to dance. Blond Boy doesn't deign to see him! *Whaaaayyeee-aaay*. James executes his broken pirouette, eyes yoked to spinning feet of Blond Boy. *Clap-clap-clappety-clap*. Blond Boy leaps to edge of circle, pulling at a man's waist. Tall man, laughing teeth, black turban. Blond Boy pulling at the man's waist, and in single bound back dancing, blade shimmering in his hand. Knife dancing with his hand, with the eyes of crowd, slicing over his blond head. James skittering in glee, following the dancing blade. Blond Boy whirls under knife. James claps eager hands, eyes wed to knife. Blond Boy draws slow tip of knife across forehead, blood flower spurting out head, down cheeks. Boy shivering as he flows red, shivering as the drums resume. . . .

James drops to his knees, eyes wide on the blood-flower. Drops with wild scream of belief. *Whaaayyyyeeayy* . . . drums surge up, feet surging with. Blond Boy suspended in *boom-boom-kabooom* . . . dancing the spray of his own blood, spraying the trampling sand. Blond Boy surging with everyone's blood-dance, tongue lolling out, catching his own blood, all their blood. Circling, circling in fast-slow dance. Circling around the fallen James as if not seeing him. And James gazing up, lips swollen red, face flushed ripe, the beauteous face, white under the dropping blood. Madonna James. Struggling to rise, each time sinking farther, down into the sucking sand. Blond Boy skeins his dance around the James no one deigns to see. James of the seraphic face now, eyelids tremoring, tongue at tip of lips . . . milady's face, full-born at last. Face praising knife overhead, adoration of blood and the singing blade.

Blond Boy quivers to a halt. Directly above James. Music stops, chanting dies. Tall black turban claps hands once again. Knife descends slowly, cutting the silence.

"Christ!" Tony lurched from his stupor, lurching toward immobile James. But Kebir blocked him, blocking Tony with his body, his eyes hissing. "Don't move, or we die!"

7
LE TOUT HÔTEL DES AMIS

He awoke in a room swimming in blue—mixture of oasis, sky and dancing robes. The shimmering face of James floating across the ceiling. James the dandy, James the choirboy—*faces* of James floating there. James the clubman, James the orator, James the—York shut his eyes to shut him out. "Don't want to know about yourself!"

He hoisted himself up in bed. Large comfortable bed. Already daylight, cool. Sound of birds outside the window, song of birds excited by morning. Today it was back to Marrakech! Colonel had promised. Crazy Tony might easily go straight on to Timbuktu. If so, York would simply walk back to Marrakech.

Knock at the door. York slumped back. Door swung open. A floppy red hat, yellow cape and droopy white pantaloons swept into the room. Must be James. James being funny. York didn't laugh. The apparition settled on the bed, a secret waiting to be divined. Pure James. York about to tell him to go to hell. Sweeping off hat, swarthy face looking forth, dangling goatee, and eyes announcing, "Voilà, I'm here again!"

Not James at all. For York knew he was already in Timbuktu. He gazed at the newcomer, but newcomer merely nodded approval of York's astonished gaze. His straggly Manchu goatee bobbing in gratitude. James would have been easier to take, when goatee broke into a torrent of French. "You see, you are safely home now. A most spacious room, the most discreet of friends, and all the tranquillities." Who was this man? "Lest you missed your passport, it is downstairs for security. One never knows." York hadn't missed it, but yes, would like it back. Goatee waved an understanding hand, a massive ruby ring. "The dear Tony brought everything, your pipe, your notebook and binoculars; he thought of everything on your behalf. Even extra money in case of . . ."

York propped himself up. The Colonel, that's what he really wanted to know—where was the Colonel? Couldn't get his words out. A commiserative smile from the gentleman. "Tony requested us to keep a close eye on you. Intimated you were inclined to do unwise things. . . . A bit rash, are you?" York shook his head. Goatee nodded. "Such a distinguished man, our Colonel. That air of breeding, like a gallop of fine horses, no?" York had almost mustered a reply when Monsieur Goatee tossed his cape aside, revealing a scarlet waistcoat matching his hat and ring. Hat and flare of waistcoat silencing York. "Also I am happy to inform you that that splendor, Kebir, came to visit yesterday. Alas, you were asleep. You slept all day, you know. But quite the best thing under the . . . *circumstances.*" The man paused, then smiled reassuringly. "But he will undoubtedly appear again tomorrow." York nodded; Tony or Kebir, he must see one or the other. "You see, m'sieur York, I promised the Colonel I would keep you safely horizontal until your hallucinations—if you'll forgive the word—decline, dissolve, disappear!"

Of course; only, where was Tony now? But the question interrupted by a peremptory scratching at the door. "Teeno-feeno!" York's visitor dashed to open the door. "I forgot Teeno-feeno!" York saw no one. Just this lunatic rushing at the door and bowing as a long black object hurtled at the bed. With a grunt. Sniffing at his legs. A black dachshund. "You'll like Orestes. He's chaperon to our . . . cénacle." York nodded again, as if a flying dachshund were no surprise, while Orestes calmly sneezed upon his face. "M'sieur York is a *friend*, Orestes! We must treat him with courtesy." Orestes retreated to the foot of the bed and curled up. The man smiled proudly, gave a toss to his cape as York spluttered, "*Where* is Colonel Tony?"

"En route to England, of course. He invited you to accompany him, thought it the wisest solution. But you categorically refused. Had work to do."

"What work?"

"Ah . . . you said it was urgent. But, my friend, you wouldn't divulge what work it was . . . very secretive. Kept jotting notes. In bed, in my room, in the *commode.* Out there"—the man gestured to the hall—"on the toilet, the door wide open, taking endless notes. We were most concerned. There's only one toilet on this floor. But when we examined your notes"—goatee gazed into York an instant with broiling black eyes—"they were about birds."

"Where *is* here?"

"The Hôtel des Amis. Very quiet, very distinguée; more like a private club. That's why Tony felt—"

"But where is the Hôtel des . . . what *town?*"

"But, Marrakech, of course." The man waved a casual hand. Orestes gave a little bark. "My dear Orestes, m'sieur York needs repose!" Orestes scratched his ear. The man stood up, adjusting his hat into more prominent view. "And lest it should have slipped your mind: *I* am monsieur Claude!" York nodded gratefully. Monsieur Claude bowed. "The hour is late. Shall I have your breakfast sent up?" Without waiting, he clicked his heels and, followed by Orestes, swept out of the room.

York lay stupefied a moment.

Couldn't think. It was Claude's eyes. Had only seen them an instant—burning. But Claude was a friend of Tony's. Tony *had* mentioned a friend in Marrakech, hadn't he? An artist. Or was it James . . . ? The Colonel and James and their idiotic trip. A little jaunt, they'd said, into the mountains. York shut his eyes. Couldn't cope with that right now. And saw them again. Boys dancing through flames, *whaaaayyeee-ayyy*. And James shuffling out to dance, estatic, till— *What happened to James?*

Another knock. York propped himself up, braced for yellow cape and flying dog. It was breakfast. And a smiling face, Moroccan, cross-eyed. "M'sieur Claude says you're ready for coffee." The Moroccan placed the tray on the bed. A slit-throat scream from outside.

"What's *that?*"

"Brigitte." The man nodded. "Our parrot. She always screeches at the dog." He glanced around the room, one eye on the cupboard, one on the ceiling. "Shall I open the window more?" York nodded. The man moved over to the windows, a pair of French doors onto a balcony. The sun shot in, revealing a large palm tree just beyond. The man juggled his eyes toward York. "This way you get a little view." York managed a smile, suddenly asked, "Is this Marrakech?"

"Yes, it's always Marrakech."

York looked at the tray—coffee, hot milk, croissant. But couldn't eat. He went over to the balcony, peered out. He was on the second floor, at the height of the palm leaves. A small red bird popped out of the crown of the tree, quizzing him. The leaves brushing against his balcony. Below, a lush tropical garden splashing around a large enclosed courtyard. For a dizzy instant York felt hidden like a bird in a nest, high over the secret oasis. Then the cry, someone else being strangled amid the plants. The parrot again. York fell back into the room, scream slicing his brain like a murder. He slammed the windows shut, dropped back into bed, covering his ears with the pillow. But the room resounded, figures leaping through the fire, *boom-ka-boom* of the drums, Tony shouting, "Don't ever become like us, York!"

He lay shaking, hands clutched to head. Suddenly out of bed, dressing as fast as he could. Checking for his wallet, groping his way downstairs, out the front door, out through the screaming garden into the street, stopping passersby, demanding the post office.

The post office was cool. High ceilings, a huge portrait of the king. He stood in the main hall panting, trying to gather his wits. Made his way to a window on the right: LONG DISTANCE TELEPHONE. An impassive face. Could he phone Osprey Cove? Never heard of Osprey Cove. In Newfoundland! Never heard of— So he couldn't phone John. Besides, Ma Snook had the phone, not John. Had to phone someone, talk to someone sane, someone who was not Marrakech. Yes, they could reach London. He had Stephen's number. He entered a booth, pulled the door shut. The phone was ringing now. He'd tell Stephen exactly what had happened. A human sacrifice. . . . What could Stephen do? At least he'd commiserate. And maybe he'd have news from John. They'd arranged that. Phone ringing, then a voice. Did he want Zurich? Damn, no! London. "We'll try again, m'sieur, the lines have been switched." Fucking switched! What was James doing, dancing like that? Dancing with those maniac dervishes. Phone ringing again. Why didn't Stephen answer? Please answer! Got to talk to *someone, now*. A voice. "We're not getting through, m'sieur. Do you want any other number in London?" York stared at the phone. He tried to get out of the booth. Door wouldn't open. Trapped, always knew he'd end up trapped. The door pulled open from the outside. York stumbled out, gasping for air.

"M'sieur, you owe us for those calls." Woman shouting from the window.

"But I didn't get through!"

"Service charges, m'sieur, the time."

He paid, then stood there, unwilling to face the Marrakech sun. Suddenly remembered—Stephen said he'd forward any mail to the central post office, general delivery. He got on line. Maybe a letter from John. Yes, a letter from John!

"You have your passport, m'sieur?" He was at the window again. No, he didn't have his passport. "Other identification?" His driver's license in his wallet. Yes, that would do. And no, there was no mail for him. "Do you have any other name, m'sieur?" Any other name? These people were crazy! He grabbed his license back and ran out of the post office, into the blare of midday. Stood trying to remember from what direction he'd come. Saw red waving in front of his eyes. An arm, red stump of an arm brandished in his face. A beggar crouching on the pavement, no legs, and waving a raw end of arm inches from York's face, shoving it into his eyes like a saber. York dumping all his change over the beggar. Then running down the burning street, past chic French shops, across the mall, about to vomit. Running till he found shade, under an arcade. Leaning against a pillar there.

He hauled himself together, puzzling his route back to the hotel. Walked right by it at first. Then heard murder again—screaming cry of the parrot. And looking back saw the garden splashing up over stone walls. Bushes and vines and wall hiding hotel's facade. He backtracked—an ancient sign:

HÔTEL DES AMIS
PENSION COMPLÈTE
PISCINE
REPOS ET
TRANQUILLITÉ

Faded sign with flowers painted around it. He pushed through the wobbly iron gate. Geraniums amid surging cacti and vines . . . plants tumbling and leaping up, onto and over each other. And a tier of trees, shade. One big palm tree geysering up to a small balcony where his room must be. He almost laughed—daft oasis of a garden, with grass poking up through cracked tiles and deck chairs lurching like forgotten guests. The hotel itself peering through the garden as if in dismay. Only two stories high; might hold fifty guests. Moroccan version of an old French manor, like an aging dowager. Colonial relic hidden here in the back streets of Marrakech.

York taking it in when a dog exploded, barking savagely, backing him into a clench of cacti. "Mathilde, shut up—it's our guest!" Cross-eyed Moroccan of the breakfast tray padding up to rescue York from dog and cacti. The dog drooped away, fat mangy creature half the size of its bark. Did m'sieur want a cup of tea? No, he wanted to flee to his room. Cookies? No, he needed to lie down. Dog barking again. "Mathilde, *shut up!* M'sieur York, this is Mathilde." Mathilde sniffed, waved a dubious tail. York inched his way toward the hotel entrance. "M'sieur Claude was asking for you. He was upset when you . . ." Cross Eyes darted ahead, knocking on the door of the first room. Door opened a crack, black goatee protruding. "Khalid, how often must I tell you—" Claude, goatee quivering, "Aha, my quixotic friend. Where did you go, running off like that?" He gathered York into the room.

"I went to the post office."

"But you ran out in the high sun like a dervish! I saw. So did Khalid. We were distressed." Claude's voice undulating around York. "I promised our Colonel to keep you out of the sun. He said you suffered sunstroke."

The room gradually emerged into focus. Large bed on a dais; extended headboard an ornate gilt mirror, stretching from bed to ceiling like a massive high altar. And matching it, a massive armoire with carved crown pediment. And bombé bureau with baroque pilasters. A room of high ceilings, deep cornices, swaying silks. Claude pirouetting around York, waving a large baton as if conducting a symphony. And off the end of the baton another face . . . floating there beside the window. Dark face, long Apache hair and all eyes, engulfing eyes. "You like it?" Claude watching York watch those eyes.

"Like it?"

"My portrait of Alainie!"

"I didn't realize it was a painting."

"Aha . . . then it is a success, my dear Alainie." Claude waved his baton, in fact a cluster of paintbrushes. As he talked to someone emerging from the corner, same dark face, hair and eyes as in the portrait. Young Moroccan poised serene, silent, in the mottled light. His blue robe enfolded by curtains.

"Sit down, my dear friend. I'll just add a touch or two." Claude dancing up to the portrait, stroking the canvas. Alainie's eyes bathed the room in a warm glow. York settled in a bamboo chair, the room parading around him. Over the bureau an old photo of the Kaiser in full military array, spiked helmet, sword. And another of Czar Nicholas meeting with the Kaiser aboard a warship. Along with a shelfload of books in French, English and Spanish.

"Very Third Empire, no?"

"Third what?" York had caught Claude's eyes contemplating him in the mirror.

"You were studying my room. The style is Third Empire, don't you feel? A retired French cavalry officer created it."

"French? With photos of the Kaiser?"

"Ah, he was a Teutonophile. Kaiserophiliac. Lived here for years, then disappeared into the Sahara. In deference, they left the room intact. And I've fallen heir to it." Claude brandishing explanatory brush.

York gazed around. A salon dedicated to the ancien régime, with its drapes and tassels and massive gilt mirror catching smaller mirrors placed on side walls. So that to look anywhere was to see several rooms. "It's a bit . . . improbable. In Marrakech, I mean."

"Nothing in Marrakech is improbable, my dear fellow." Claude poised on tiptoe, goatee quivering with precision, and executed a final touch to his canvas. Then wheeled toward York, paintbrushes conducting conversation again.

"You must rest. You look wan. Here." Claude wafted to the bureau, selected a pair of sunglasses. "An extra pair."

York tried them on.

"But how dare you come to Marrakech without sunglasses? My dear, that is like visiting the North Pole without gloves."

York faltered. "I—I don't know how I came to Marrakech in the first place. Let alone that trip—"

"Ah, the voluptuous valley of the Draa. The land of the ksar and the kasbah, sublime invitation to—"

"And I certainly don't understand how I got here."

"The Colonel, my dear; you drove back with the Colonel and Kebir and—" Claude's brushes waving in about four mirrors. "Tony assured us the return trip was even more magnificent."

"But I remember nothing. Nothing after—" York stopped.

"After what?" Claude peering through the mirrors.

"After that insane dance in someplace in the desert."

"M'hamid, yes. An exquisite setting; the palm trees are a rapture."

"But they were dancing—and then Kebir warned us not to move! James was . . ."

"You had a little sunstroke, that's all. Often happens. That Sahara sun bites like a viper."

"James. What happened to James?"

"To dear James?" Claude's brushes dipped. "But he departed with the Colonel, for Tangier."

"Departed? When?"

"Yesterday. Sent you his love and prayed you would join them again next year."

"Back here? Again?"

"And why not? Where else do you encounter such splendors?" Claude smiling at Alainie. "Ah, Morocco invades the seeing eye, no?"

"Invades everything," York murmured, now seeing several Claudes reflected in the large mirror.

"Eh bien. Tonight you join us for dinner, here in my humble salon." York glanced up, Claude waving the baton-brushes. "After all, we must celebrate your recovery. Alainie will be here. And Richard, Bertrand . . . one or two other illuminati." Claude smiled expectantly.

"Who are Richard and Bertrand?"

"Aha!" Claude raised a brush as if summoning the gentlemen in question. "Rrrichard is . . . a connoisseur of life, of books, of angels! A onetime friend of Proust." Pause. "And Bertrand is . . . ah, but you will *behold* Bertrand. Did you know that the aging Marquis de Lur-Hanoult himself experienced a heart attack upon first seeing Bertrand?" Claude erect as he pronounced this mystery. A strangling cry broke the moment. York blurted, "Who *owns* that parrot?"

"Ahh, the parrot! Now, that belongs to Bertrand. He's having an affair with it."

"An affair?"

"A fanatic for macaws, my dear. *Red* macaws." Claude looked unhappy, brush dropping. "Bertrand keeps *strange* pets." Claude beaming at York.

"Claude, I must rest . . . if I'm to enjoy the evening."

Seconds later York upstairs in his room, locking the door behind him carefully. He slumped onto the bed, fumbling for his notebook.

> *So James didn't die!* He & Tony en route to London. Why didn't I go with them? Why here in this loony-bin hotel?

He lay back. Words seemed useless. Longing for sleep. But eyes no sooner closed than he saw them: Kebir sentinel over the endless valley, Tony in underwear offering camera to Moroccan commandant, James on his knees in the sand, blubbering with fear—or satisfaction? He grabbed his notebook.

> It's burned in behind my eyes. The sight of them. James *flirting* with death, a final fling. Claude says nothing happened. *But I saw it!*

He paused, trying to focus.

> What was the whole lunatic expedition about?
> When I'm stronger. Ask Kebir.

And collapsed into sleep.

When he awoke, drums were pounding close. No, someone hammering at the door. He lurched from bed, opening the door to disjunct eyes: Khalid. Grinning at York standing sleepy in underwear. "M'sieur Claude expects you." York grimaced. "I'll be down shortly." He quickly dressed, toppled down the stairs, along the hall. And knocked. The door swung wide, music leaping out, then Claude, embracing him. "Our honored guest!" York entered the music, visual stutter of candles, rich-sweet scent. So opulent now, the room. Candles igniting cornices, moldings, shimmering over the faces of ornate plates and guests. Claude clapped hands, pranced to the center of the salon. "Our friend from . . . *Canada!*" Claude balanced at the end of long ivory cigarette holder, blue silk kimono rippling. Around his waist a wide scarlet belt. "Richard, this is m'sieur York, in the risen flesh. York, m'sieur Rrrichard. Alainie you've already met." Claude announcing York to guests, guests to York, a flourish of cigarette holder for each, so that all York saw was the whirling ivory holder and Claude himself. And only after Claude had placed him in a chair by the bed could he start sorting bodies, faces, floating smiles.

Yes, there in the corner, as if never having moved, was Alainie. Alainie of the omnivorous eyes and hopeful smile. And his portrait beside him, his double poised on an easel. And the elderly, fragile dumpling of a man perched on the edge of the bed . . . that was Richard, friend of Proust.

Beyond Richard, lolling on an ample cushion, a tall young Moroccan smoking a pipe, eyes closed. And below the giant mirror, lying on a silk pouffe, another long black form, the dachshund of strange name—Osiris was it?

But it was a figure by the wall that commanded York's eye—elongated figure in a bamboo armchair, head a splash of gold, eyes turquoise, lips of secrets. And immobile on this young god's shoulder, the vehement red of the parrot. Macaw scornfully surveying the crowd.

"You require wine, my dear!" The cigarette holder dancing at York's nose, a glass, wine pouring forth in candlelight. York took the glass, saw it moving to his own lips. . . . The mirror, huge mirror over the bed. It was there that he beheld the silent blond god with flaming bird—gazing out of the mirror, appraising the room. The dapper old man at bedside, hunched in a permanent grin of appreciation. . . . Mirror capturing the room, doubling it, trebling it. So that York couldn't tell who was where in room or mirrors. All palace now, crown over the armoire illuminated by candle from behind. Figure of the Kaiser reviewing his troops. And in his ear the coiling Moroccan music, insinuating its way through smoke and musk and quizzing eyes.

"But can't you see, he's an *angel!*" Claude addressing the portrait of Alainie.

"But you can't touch angels." Voice behind York in sultry objection. Voice like an oboe.

"Ah, but you can! Only first they must be seen for what they are: messengers from the gods!" Claude waving ivory holder imperiously; oboe voice protesting from behind York's left ear. Golden head talking, inclining into the mirror. The parrot slowly spreading a wing as if to emphasize the voice. Bertrand, it must be—the one who caused a heart attack to some aging marquis or other.

And as York confronted this vision, Claude glided away from the portrait toward him. Tapping the little old man sitting on the edge of the bed with that ivory baton. "Rrrichard is arbiter elegans; *he* will pronounce!" The wrinkled face of Richard igniting as Claude asked, "Is Alainie a true angel? Or what Bertrand says, a mere echo of desire?" Richard grinned in glee, but a crash of glass interrupted his verdict.

York sat, dizzy, a voice in his ear now. "Claude flaunts this absurd belief, about boys as *angels!* Finds one in Taroudant, in Ouarzazate, in Essaouira . . . but they're merely boys. Pretty teenage boys. And they always turn out to be onions; peel them and eat them!" Woodwind voice in York's ear, golden face in mirror. "He likes them with Greek noses, giant apparati. And spies on them for weeks before he even speaks to them. Won't touch them till after he's painted their portrait . . . calls it 'the necessary adoration.' " York nodded, as if it all made sense. And found himself staring at Alainie's portrait.

A hand reached up from the floor, passing a pipe to York. He took it unquestioningly. Thrust it away; he never smoked hashish. Or marijuana. Enough troubles as it was. Pipe disappeared into the smoke, another hand. "We're told you had a fling in the mountains." York hesitated. Gold Head smiled. "The mountains are always an adventure." Shaking that splendor of hair to great advantage. And now Richard murmured, "Claude told us you went as far as Zagora, where the ancient library is. . . ." York couldn't remember any library. Only Tony and James on the café veranda by moonlight, eternal pashas, boys dancing at their feet. Wasn't that Zagora?

"Splendid spot for stargazing!" Gold Head again, gleaming at York through the mirror.

"Stargazing?" York trying to banish the image of James waving, shouting something at him.

"Gazers make special trips from Zagora into the desert . . . since the twelfth century. . . . The dryness, a remarkable clarity by night. Averroes said the same. And the Koranic manuscripts! Camel caravans out beyond M'hamid." Both Richard and Gold Head talking at once, parrot pecking Bertrand's cheek with affection. The figure in the large candle by the mirror, jumping through the flame. James yelping barefoot through the flames.

A knock at the door. Claude, who had been arranging the dinner table, soared across the mirror and swooshed the door wide. Kebir, serene and tall, entering as if always there. Bowing slightly to Claude, even as he stepped past the impresario cigarette holder to take up his station at York's chair. His presence rising silently in his spine. And Claude, catching up, announcing, "Our little surprise, York. Your Kebir has arrived, as you see." Claude dancing around the pair, making presentations. "Richard, this is the renowned "Kebir of the Draa Valley and all Zagora." Richard grinning appreciation. "We heard of your exploits." Bertrand adding, "And of your talents." And presenting his macaw. "You must meet Brigitte, she's our chaperon tonight." And Kebir bowing as faces, smiles and parrot were paraded for mutual delectation. Grinning at Alainie, whom he clearly knew. And the Moroccan of the hashish. York sat dazed, making sure it truly was Kebir, and not another fiction of mirror or mind. Yes, definitely Kebir, in blue burnoose with leather belt and pouch, and sandals, two-headed falcon at his throat. Richard murmuring in York's ear. "We all hoped your friend would be able to join us for our little soiree." But York scarcely hearing. Claude laughing and pointing his cigarette holder, declaring, "York is undergoing an ecstasy." Everyone delighted, except Bertrand, who looked strangely petulant as all eyes focused on Kebir.

But before York could say anything, Claude had whirled to the door again, clapping his hands in summons. "The tagine—tagine à la Marrr-akech!" And the cross-eyed Moroccan was bearing in a large platter that smelled like distillate of hashish. "*Another* surprise for you, my dear York: tagine à la Khalid."

And before York knew it, they were gathered around the low table, the platter fuming in its center. A kind of stew, lamb tagine with black olives, raisins and a blast of spice. Khalid sniffing the fragrance in approval. And Claude urging him to join them, partake in his own cuisine. But Khalid, saying, "Minbad," withdrew.

"Such a dear sweet man, Khalid," Claude pronounced, waving them into the tagine. And for a moment there was silence and the slurp of sauce. York hoping for a few quick words with Keb, Richard was talking with Kebir. And Bertrand at York. And Claude at everyone. And when a momentary lull occurred, Claude mustered his cigarette holder once again, waving it at Richard. "You *must* finish telling us about Eulalie, must initiate York into the wonders of Marrakech."

Richard wiping a finger over the tagine. "You know that she has a male harem, black boys; nicknames them Monday, Tuesday, Wednesday, depending . . ."

"Depending on the day she uses them," observed Bertrand tartly.

"Please allow Richard to finish. *He* tells it exquisitely." The parrot squawked, propelled an eye at Claude. Richard wiped a second finger. "When Eulalie first came to Marrakech, aeons ago, she had herself carried around on a litter with a canopy. A large black marched in front bearing a red baton." Richard paused for effect. York murmured, "Oh, who was she?"

"The Countess Eulalie de la Manche, a légitimiste. Never acknowledged the Comte de Paris! She's quite divine. Holds court twice a month. Le tout Marrakech, except for the Auk. She refuses to see the Auk ever since he apprised her that all people are equal and brought his chauffeur to dinner."

The Auk?"

"Field Marshal Sir Claude Auchinleck."

He lives here?

"My dear, you'd be amazed at the people who live—"

"Or hide out!" snapped Bertrand.

"—in Marrakech!" Richard now pivoting on his stool, elegant little man in his seventies, waxed mustache, twinkly eyes.

"Rrrichard knows *everyone* in Marrakech." Claude then lowering his voice. "Even better, he knows everything *about* them!"

Only Kebir was making headway with the tagine. Alainie was admiring his portrait. The Moroccan of the hashish, after rummaging the tagine once, was on the floor again, sucking his pipe.

There seemed to be two of them there. At least there were three bare feet visible, and presumably a fourth under the bed. York glanced into the mirror. And Kebir on his right, catching York's glance in the mirror and laughing—better than conversation. Now he could see Bertrand in the mirror, shaking his head, shimmer of long gold hair to emphasize a point. He wasn't a beauty in the classic Greek sense, more a Nordic god of the paler sun—Baldur, Baldur the Beautiful. Perhaps that's why he kept the flaming parrot astride. Parrot's vivid red making him Viking. York felt happier—he'd placed Bertrand the Beauteous. The situation more controllable.

"Don't you agree, York? Richard *must* write his memoirs!" Of course. Richard had been telling more Marrakech stories, for York's benefit. They were awaiting his response. He tried to think of some Canadian stories. But his mind a blank. Finally, "Canadians only tell dirty jokes. All talk but no action." They laughed politely.

"Tony tells us you are a well-known Canadian author."

So that was it; York there on false pretenses. "No, I'm not well known," he muttered. Claude looked displeased. "I'm just infamous!" They all perked up.

"My dear, you've come to the right place. Marrakech!" Richard pivoting with glee. "Pray tell us, for what are you infamous?" Claude nodded, waving his ivory vigorously. Richard continued. "Any fool can be famous, but *infamy*—that requires courage, audacity, cunning."

York closed his eyes. He could sense them looking at him. Yes, when he opened his eyes, they were all peering expectantly. Finally said, "I've never really known why; I'm infamous without effort." He was being serious, but they took it as being clever. York sipped his wine. "You must confide in us, York. We are friends, and friends of friends. I think it's because I'm not a Methodist." Richard tooted. "I mean it. In Canada, you have to be a psychic Methodist to belong, though you mustn't believe in God!"

Richard bailed him out. "I once knew a Canadian family; the husband sold insurance. Their sole point of pride seemed to be that none of them had ever been in prison or in debt."

The chitchat whirled on: Bertrand on Richard; Claude on Bertrand and macaw; and all on Marrakech. At last York had a moment to talk with Kebir. He was anxious to discuss their trip; but impossible now. At least he could catch up on Kebir himself. Keb had found work. What work? Laying tar on a road outside the city walls. Wouldn't be able to see York for a couple of days. York silent, trying to imagine Keb laying tar. Why? Till he saw Keb wiping his long fingers with white handkerchief, smiling his post-tagine smile, blessing the world. Yes, Keb's task in life still was . . . to be Kebir. To be the person he was: the splendor of their voyage through the mountains, song of that high valley, endless dance of Morocco. The door swung open again. Khalid entering with another tagine, though they hadn't finished the first. Khalid smiling enormously through steam and praise of his cuisine. And behind him that dog wagging its fat stomach. . . . Explosion of barks. Black sausage attacking fat dog. "Orestes . . . *Oresss-tes!*" Claude shouting as his dachshund assaulted Khalid's dog. Bertrand launching pillows at both.

The furor of dogs subsided, Mathilde was expelled from the room and Orestes given tagine on a silver saucer. Khalid was persuaded to stay. "For some of your exquisite tagine, my dear Khaa-Khaa." Claude beckoning Khalid to a stool. "He's part of our family—la famille des amis." York liked the phrase.

Khalid grinned and begged to report. "A new couple has just checked in."

All heads leaned forward to hear. "What gender are they?" Bertrand asked.

"They're from England, a man and his wife. In their sixties."

"No use at all." Bertrand sniffed.

"They wear such hot clothes, all prickly," Khalid continued, "as if it were freezing."

"Tweed," Richard affirmed, "the tweedy country-style."

"I told them to take off their clothes."

"Take their clothes off?" Claude murmured.

"It's a heat wave!" Khalid said. "I suggested a cold shower. She said showers were for soldiers and sigh-kotts."

"Sigh-kotts?" asked Bertrand.

"Psychotics?" Claude suggested.

"Yes, that's what she said."

"She's absolutely right," Richard mused. "Cold showers *are* for soldiers and psychotics. I want to meet the lady."

"But how did they find their way here?" Claude asked. "We usually have cognoscenti."

"It is no problem," said Khalid. "I've put them in the other wing. They won't get in your way."

"Under quarantine," Bertrand added.

"Also, I should warn you a German tour is due in."

"Put them under quarantine too." Claude waved his holder. Khalid promised he would.

York about to laugh, it was all so presposterous, when the parrot shot forward, grabbed Claude's ivory cigarette holder. Grabbed it in a quick claw, and as quick again was back in place on Bertrand's shoulder. Claude froze, goatee quaking. Richard chortled. Macaw chortled in imitation of Richard. Bertrand refused to intervene with macaw, who was flaunting the holder. York watching in the mirrors the look of cold disdain on Bertrand's face, mirth on Kebir's. As macaw flaunted the precious holder, and then in a single bite snapped through the thick carved stem.

Claude shaking, then asking, "But why did your parrot do that, Bertrand. *Why?*"

And Bertrand replying through the lethal smile. "Because he *likes* you, dear!"

Claude quivering as if violated.

"But I forgot, my dear friend." Claude rising, adjusting his shawl and his dignity, and going to the bureau. "I forgot this!" He returned with an envelope, passing it across the table. York opened it—a photograph. Photo of a man out hunting, a squire, puckish grin.

"He signed it on the back." Claude pointed.

For York, in memory of our safari. *Keep your promise!*
Love from "Colonel Tony"

Sweet picture of Tony younger, arrayed as full British gentleman. York silent. Like a salute from beyond the grave, this photo.

"That bogus Colonel, thinks he's so grand." Bertrand snorted. "Travels around like a sultan, and all the while he's masturbating young boys."

York passed the photo to Kebir, stunned.

"Pompous English prick. Still thinks the British rule the world!"

York picked up his wineglass, and turning looked directly at Bertrand for the first time. Bertrand nodded, as if York had done the right thing at last, had finally been convoked to the beauty of Bertrand. But York raised his glass higher, long-stemmed wineglass, and with calm precision smashed it over Bertrand's head. Wine and glass spraying over that golden aureole, as over the startled parrot. Richard clucked approval. Kebir spurted laughter. As Bertrand shook the shower of wine and glass from shining hair and smiled with satisfaction.

York longing to retire to bed. But felt he must stay, make amends. God knows he'd never smashed a glass over anyone's head before. Suddenly everyone was making amends for him. Claude passing a plate of cakes as peace offering, and brandishing another cigarette holder, a silver one even longer than the ivory. Richard diligently engaged with Alainie and another young Moroccan—they clearly liked him, called him "notre sage Richard." Kebir protecting the photo of Tony. And Bertrand complimenting Claude on his portrait of Alainie. "This time you've caught the eyes, that infernal innocence!" Which delighted Claude. "Shall I do one of Kebir, his smile?" But York didn't like the idea.

Music on the cassette resolved the evening. Like the music in M'hamid York longed to forget. Claude began undulating rhythmically, opening doors onto a tiled patio off the far end of the room. And dancing out onto the tiles, swaying serpentine beneath his silk robe. And joined by Alainie and another of the boys; a weaving flow of flesh through the candles. Claude repeating over and over, "C'est une extase."

Would Baldur dance too? But Bertrand stretched out on the bed, legs spread, an arm dangled to the floor. A cossack shirt, black, and white baggy pants. And dark gold belt. Striking . . . like a god dreaming there, his arm caressing a dark body lolling on the floor beside. As Bertrand gazed up into the mirror, at himself and the lolling boy's blue-robed body.

Suddenly Bertrand was up, depositing macaw atop the cupboard and disappearing from the room. Kebir, giving a gentle touch to York's shoulder, had gone to join the dancers. And Richard? He'd fallen out of view of the mirror. But York located him in a bamboo chair, gazing in beatitude at the boys dancing. "The Gnaoua," he said. The what? "The music; it's Gnaoua. They dance you into a trance." York nodded, had just seen Bertrand's trance.

Bertrand was back, carrying a round wicker basket and a large flute. He placed the basket on table, himself at the foot of the bed, and began accompanying music and dance. Flute weaving its song through cheeks puffed round, face flushing as he piped. York closed his eyes, swaying with the music. And when he opened them moments later, saw the figure in the mirror. Face in profile, ears pointing high into the flow of hair. And eyes fluttering shut, eyelids quivering. Face fallen from a classic Greek vase, face of a god of dance, ecstasy.

York stared. Face floating in the silent mirror, the shock of golden hair. Pan, playing on his pipes, and all the world a dance. *Bertrand* . . . Bertrand plying his flute, feet dancing in song, face transformed from one beauty to another.

Richard leaned forward, whispering, "You see? We must allow ourselves to be seduced by life!"

But York heard just the music. And the face of a lost god in the mirror.

"Here's Amelia!" Claude tapping York with his cigarette holder as he danced toward the round table. "Amelia wants to join us," pointing into the wicker basket on the table. A black, triangular face jabbing up and swaying, tongue darting out irate. Cobra coiling up coldly, eyes hissing. Bertrand plying the pipes.

"Do you like Amelia? Our hotel mascot!" Claude so pleased. But York rigid, staring at the swaying cobra only feet away. Never entertained a cobra face-to-face before, not sure he liked them under any conditions. Bertrand on his feet now, weaving his flute around Amelia's bobbing head. Bertrand dancing around table and snake, black and gold, his head thrown back. Satyrling incarnate.

Claude pushed his cigarette holder at Amelia, and Amelia struck at it, and Claude laughed and pushed again and Amelia was striking and striking at the bobbing silver holder. And Bertrand shouting at Claude, and Alainie shouting at the snake. Richard stood up to impose order, Bertrand trying to hit Claude with his flute. "Claude things he's a jettatore . . . thinks he's got the Evil Eye!" And Richard: "The Evil Eye is no joking matter!"

Amelia's basket had been knocked on its side, and Amelia slithering across the table, black coils slapping cutlery, glasses. One of the Moroccans poured wine on its head, and macaw, from atop the cupboard, screamed bloody hell.

Kebir pulled York to the door. Claude spied them departing, and with a whirl reached their side. York endeavoring to thank him for the evening. "In your honor, dear Canadian, to salute your recovery." Claude insisting Kebir come again to "our family of friends." Kebir smiled, saying, "N'shallah," a word he'd often used; York asked what it meant. Claude huffed. *"God willing*, you know nothing of Morocco if you don't know *that!"* Bertrand coaxed Amelia back to her basket, and Richard, smiling as guardian of divine secrets, waved good night.

Kebir led York back to his room. And was soon administering a massage. Then undressing him gently. And they lay naked together. Kebir with a hard-on, but York with none, though his entire body aflame from music and wine and the floating smoke of hashish. And glimpsing Kebir's regal erection—the unbidden, yet real guest at their feast. And feeling there must be a way to salute such a guest of honor. Beyond thanks, beyond mere sex. But Kebir made no move toward sex, simply holding York in his arms, massaging him with hands and eyes till York was drowned in sleep.

> *19th, Sunday:* I asked the manager of this café, asked him twice, & he said "absolutely Sept. 18, & it's Sunday everywhere, even in Tel Aviv." Looked at me a bit odd.
>
> *Hôtel des Amis:* Richard calls it "a spa for the cognoscenti." I can't figure out what it is. Claude is clearly Grand Master of All Ceremonies.
>
> Bertrand is an illegality!
>
> Richard is . . . sweet. He said, "You've just been through hell and seen orchids! And that's what matters."

He finished his mint tea, ordered a second, and a croissant. It was already four in the afternoon. He had slept fourteen hours.

> The way Kebir danced. Can't help comparing him with John. Keb all flow & John all flaunt.

He was pleased to be taking notes again. Pondering this when he felt a pair of eyes on him. Young Moroccan in the corner of the café—twenty-two, perhaps. Handsome, gazing unabashedly at York as if naked. Couldn't cope with that. For a moment he just let his eyes wander amid the jacaranda leaves, the trees shading the café, the chitter of sheltering birds. Yes, a whole world, the leaves shimmering. His pen starting in again, almost on its own.

> He was moving like a bird, tall willowy bird, head and neck arching forward as if seeing something. Yet not looking at all. And seeing everything with the very movements of his body. As he turned amid the candles, drifting smoke and chant. I almost shouted out, "You're so beautiful, the way you move . . . only birds do that, birds in mating dance." Even Claude looked effortful beside. Keb in that trance of dance that's so Morocco—as if life a dance, and words only accompaniment.
>
> It was the way he danced in Zagora (?), out in the moonlight street, as if a palace, that young boy ogling him . . .

Yes. This was what he wanted, the way he wanted to see, *did* see.

> Keb dancing all alleluia . . . like those herons rising the sky in the river valley. If I could have danced like that then Chris & I would still be what she wanted us to be. & Ced wouldn't have lost his Dad.

There was a crash a few tables down, someone knocking cup and saucer onto the sidewalk, some glasses. York's pen stopped. Trying to recapture the flow. Couldn't. Finally jotted.

> The Occident sees with the eye of the mind. Moroccans see with the mind of the eye.

But it wasn't the same. His damned diary too often a case of looking at, and not of being with.

Yes, his dance—it was for me. Why didn't I realize? His eyes said—

But another clatter: a pair of tourists descending two tables away. Knocking a chair over. Goddamned tourists parasite a culture. Should be a law against them! Such flaunt and visual clatter, one couldn't concentrate. A pair of white hippie girls, jeans meticulously faded and patched, with noisy look-at-me smiles. No, Moroccans never made a noise. Always singing and dancing, yet never making a noise.

Fact: You rarely see women in Morocco. They're kept under wraps. But in Canada, America, all you see is women.

The two girls now addressing the waiter in loud American, giggling convulsively. Waiter spoke no English, they no French. Waiter bowed, the girls jangled their wrists—

Whatever they do they're on display, the Misses America! Another waiter. Ice cream and coffee. Everyone within twenty feet has to know. . . . Yes, fingers poised. Eating like ladies, dear! Ladies of the Immaculate Conception. Chittering. Neither listening, but the eyes cantering the café. Sweeping up that Moroccan stud in the corner. Feasting on him.

Stud glancing over. Blond girl jerks her head aside, *in contempt*. Ain't gonna admit *she* wants cock!

York slammed his notebook down. Tried looking away, but the clatter and chatter of the ice-cream girls could not be overlooked, no intention of being overlooked.

She's groping that Moroccan but pretending to talk to her friend, nose airborne. One eye on the White House—the other on the next available penis.

Summoning the waiter now like a slave. Christ, they act like they own the world. Well, they do!

They're getting up to leave. Thrusting a bill into the waiter's hand—but they don't even see him!

The penis is following them down the street.

For some minutes York sat wordless, as if a short-circuit, as if static blasting all around him.

> But that's what's wonderful about Marrakech! No Wasp torture here—
>
> Torture by WASPs is gynarchical, cunt-rule getting its way & thereby never getting what it wants.
>
> Women having ruled (invisibly) for years, are now rioting for their freedom . . . because when they ruled they never *got* what they wanted.
>
> And the gynarchy engenders the gay world.
>
> But Marrakech is the opposite of gayness. Phallicity here a predicate of virility.
>
> Gay world is a predicate of phallic failure!
>
> Therefore . . .

He picked at his nose, waiting. Yes, one of his syllogisms about to surface. He'd almost forgotten his endless sensibility syllogisms and sightings. He waited, but nothing more came. A stray thought: his trip with Tony and James, hadn't that been gay?

> Gay world is Mommy's revenge, passed through Sonny-boy. Mommy's cunt-rule passed up dear Sonny's ass.
>
> All those prim, regnant ladies contemplating the verity of their favorite son as the neighborhood cocksucker, secretly driving Mommy wild with envy!

He paused, pondering. That was it—

> At the very moment the women broke out . . . they were bound to kill! Willy-nilly.

> That's when I got out and ran for my life! My own one-man Male Liberation Squad.

He stopped and examined his notes, reading with a mixture of triumph and apprehension. Suddenly ripped the pages out, crumpled them up and set off down the street. It was a little after five, but his day was already done.

The shutters flew open to a burst of sun and the silhouette of the big palm tree. So beautiful that morning palm, it shocked York. Khalid's eyes shocked him, too, and the sweetness of his smile as he set the breakfast tray on the bed. So did Claude, who had followed Khalid in with sun and tray and was already ensconced on the edge of the bed. "You'll never guess. Richard was locked up all yesterday!" Locked up? "In his room, with that boy, the one at our soiree who tried to drown Amelia in wine."

Khalid winked a free eye. Did York want anything? York wanted Khalid to cart Claude away. Mustn't say that. And Khalid was gone in the aftermath of his smile.

"You see, our ancient Richard still performs!" York contemplated what ancient Richard's performance might be.

"But why won't you let me do it?" Claude's voice suddenly sharp.

"Do what?" York's eyes back to Claude, his hands pulling breakfast tray carefully up over his lap.

"Paint a portrait of Kebir."

York glanced back at the palm tree; couldn't think why Claude shouldn't paint Kebir's portrait.

"You implied it would be downright perilous if I painted him!"

"Did I?" York hesitated. "I'm glad."

"You're jealous, that's all." Claude rose from the bed, striding across York's view of the palm tree.

"Yes, I'm jealous. About anybody with Keb." York dallied with his croissant.

"Don't be so honest! Honesty is boring." Claude coming to a halt right in front of York. York staring up. Claude dressed in suede and leather—black waistcoat, tight white pants, knee-high black boots. Beaming at York.

"You slept well again, eleven hours!" Yes, York had slept very well. "You are feeling stronger, are you not?" Yes, stronger, thank you. "So you must finish your breakfast and come with me to the market."

Twenty minutes later they were parading out through the hotel garden to a nearby market. Kaleidoscope of vegetables, fruit, cheeses, flowers, and Moroccans. As they entered, Claude announced, "Life, my dear friend, is an adventure of light and ecstasy!"

> *Monday Sept. 20.* 10:40 a.m.—This café is my convalescent ward. I like the wicker armchairs, the shade of jacaranda over the sidewalk. It's almost cool.
>
> Claude exhausting. He takes the market by storm, sails through the vendors, drawing the eyes of all boys.
>
> Heat remains unbearable (how does C. survive in his various outfits?). Keb told me I should go back to the mountains, an inexpensive tourist place he knows: cooler and safe. Does he mean he'd come too? What about his tar?
>
> *Roof-terrace* of the café now—eight floors up. Cooler up here. Panoramic view of Marrakech & mountains beyond. City afloat in a *sea* of palm trees.
>
> Kee-rrrist! Walked over to the parapet to see better. Suddenly about to fly over it, like one of the swallows. Mustn't get agitated like yesterday. *Keep out of the sun!*
>
> Magnificent view of the Koutoubia Tower lunging up into sky. To see truly is to believe, to have faith.
>
> The terrible game our society plays *against* faith of any kind.

He leaned back, watching the swallows interweave the sky. And a pair of storks booming by. The swallows swooping around them, chasing. Birds important: they articulate the sky, they raise our heads. York's eyes following the swallows and the realization that the sighting of a rare bird always presaged a major event in his life. That emerald-colored bird he and Christine saw just before Lascaux, or the ospreys that helped John and him decide on Osprey Cove.

And now two majestic storks, like airborne kings, trailing the city in their wake. What did that herald? He pondered the chasing swallows diving, stabbing at the eyes of the storks. The storks changing direction now, coming right at him, almost at eye level, panorama level. He felt a wild stab of joy, giant birds looming straight at him. And an urge to rush over, stand again by the parapet. Stand and raise his arms in salute to such kings of the sky.

> Fact is, I'm a goof for birds. Part of my system of sightings, omens, oraculations. Birds are messengers. Joy in the eye. And if I ever lose that, I'm a goner.
>
> I get these crazy ideas. And I act on them. Or them on me! I have a lover's rendezvous with God. Petitioner reaching out for holiness. Isn't the whole of medieval mysticism just that—a lover's rendezvous with God?

But the sun sizzling now, even in the shade, even high above the street on this mirador. He took the elevator down, soon trundling along the boulevard toward the hotel. Avoiding beggars, calèches, and a boy peddling hashish. He passed the market of his morning with Claude. Well, he'd simply avoid Claude and his oddball friends tonight, stay put in his room. Unless Keb had left a message.

He knew he was approaching the hotel when he heard the jabber of macaw. It no longer sounded like murder absolute, just a friendly strangling. Almost laughing as he pushed through the gate . . . Hôtel des Amis indeed. He paused part way up the winding walk. The garden as old and overrun as the hotel. Geraniums over vines over cacti over trees. Claude claimed it was Khalid's pride and joy. Of course—Khalid was cross-eyed; so was his garden. So, for that matter, was the hotel itself—curious hybrid of French château and Moroccan arcades, pillars, arabesqued windows. It only looked majestic; in fact, was quite compact, its wings running into each other like Siamese twins. Yes, a large pension, really.

York fell back. The English couple passing, strolling en route to their room on the second floor. He looked so proper with his flannels, suede shoes, cane. What would *he* have made of Claude's soiree? And she was still wearing tweed. Tweed in a Marrakech heat wave! And one of those *Country Life* hats, like an inverted chamber pot. They paused an instant. She was examining a cactus through a magnifying glass. "Sabra superba illuminata," she commented. "Its barbs are mildly eczematic. But it's flora superba!" He was poking at the underbrush with his cane. "Lizards!" he muttered. "Shouldn't stay in a hotel with lizards." York watched them meander up to their room. Yes, it was in the left-hand wing, so Khalid did deserve the right side for the inmates, the cognoscenti!

"We see everyone, and no one sees us!" Voice sibilant in York's ear. He spun around—Claude, standing right behind him, grinning in triumph. Had he been there all the time, hidden in the swag of vines? "They once ruled the world," he said. Who? "The English, my dear. And look at them, they're unimaginable!" Claude grinned in complicit malice. York laughed. "But so are you, out in the high sun again! Come, a cup of tea to relax." Claude clapped his hands, and Khalid suddenly materialized. Had he been watching Claude watch York watch the tweedy English couple?

They sat in front of Claude's room under the arcade. A boy appeared with mint tea and cookies with honey inside. Luxurious in this garden; the three of them just sitting, sniffing tea and the shade. "You can always tell when Khalid has had a good night. He has that *seraphic* grin. His assistant, you see, is. . . ." Khalid put his head down, a little shy. But with a wave of the hand Claude shifted subject. "This hotel was founded by a Frenchman in the days of Lyautey. He came here because he liked the fauna. His various boys ran the hotel." A shout—goddamned macaw screaming blue murder again! But Khalid was suddenly on his feet, eyes careening. Another shout, which died halfway. Khalid running into the hotel, Claude and York following.

The uproar was coming from a bathroom on the second floor, just past Bertrand's room. Someone inside pounding on the door. Stout old door standing a few inches off the floor, top open for ventilation. Claude knocked discreetly. Another battering from inside, someone kicking on the door. "Let me out!" The Englishman. "But the door opens from your side," Claude replied. Fortunately his wife had arrived, asking what the rumpus was all about. It was all about her husband. "In there!" Claude pointed.

"Herbert, what's wrong?" she croaked.

"Is it still there?"

"What, dear?"

Richard arrived breathless to know. They couldn't explain. Claude got down on all fours to peer under the toilet door. The wife expostulated at this, but Claude was back up immediately, whispering, "He's standing on the toilet. Hanging on to the water pipe above his head."

"Herbert, is this one of your silly jokes?"

Khalid made the sign of the Hand of Fatima.

The door finally opened and Herbert emerged, pale, pants undone, eyes sweeping the floor. "Where did it go?"

"What go, dear?"

"The cobra—in the bathroom."

"Herbert, there are no snakes here. We asked about that at the travel agency."

He stood looking at them all as if it were a plot. "Lizards in the garden, and a cobra was wrapped around the base of the commode. I saw it . . . just as I got settled. Raised its head, hissed!"

"Herbert, you know what the doctor said. How much have you had today?"

Silence. Till Richard stated, "M'sieur, there are sometimes small snakes in the garden, but never the biting kind. Besides, snakes don't climb stairs." This seemed irrefutable to everyone except Herbert. York translated, and Khalid nodded energetically.

"Herbert, you need a little lie-down, dear."

"Rebecca, I need a drink!"

"No more drinks today!"

Herbert glared. "Either I saw a cobra, in which case I must have a drink; or else I imagined the damned thing in which case a drink can do no harm. Where's the bar in this place?"

"Bar? In the Hôtel des Amis?" Richard asked. Yes. "The bar is closed, like the swimming pool." When did they open?" "They've both been closed since 1966. For renovations." Herbert blinked. "But I happen to have a Calvados in my room, if that is of any interest. I'll fetch it immediately," Richard said, and disappeared downstairs.

"Herbert, for heaven's sake, do up your pants!"

Herbert did, then turned and plunged after Richard.

Rebecca stood dismayed. "He's been out in the sun, you know." They all nodded. "And he does have a problem with snakes. His closest friend was killed by a snake. In Hyderabad."

"Hyderabad is noted for its snakes—the striking kind," Claude pronounced.

She was grateful for his understanding. "You people seem to live here."

"In face, madame, we do. Our spa, if I may so call it."

She nodded. Claude presented Khalid and York, "our resident Canadian." More nods as she congratulated Khalid on the hotel garden. Claude becoming very grand. Rebecca emerging as the Queen Mother. "I must thank you all for your kindness today. This dreadful mistake; of course there are no snakes." Of course not. "I'll tell Herbert we must all dine together; you'll be our guests for dinner." Of course. And with that she swept off down the hall.

As soon as she'd gone, Claude hissed, "Where's Bertrand?" Khalid tapped on Bertrand's door. Silence. He took out his master key and unlocked it. They entered the room gingerly. Yes, Bertrand lying spread-eagle, tummy up, on the bed. Naked. His eyes open, gaping into a large mirror propped beside the bed. Mirror propped so Bertrand could view himself full-length, gently dallying with his resplendent self. Khalid snapped the door shut behind them.

"Where's Amelia?" Claude belligerent. But Bertrand oblivious to their presence. "Heroin," Claude muttered to York. "He disappears now and then." Claude peered warily under Bertrand's bed, hissing at Khalid, "Look in the closet." York couldn't take his eyes off Bertrand, fallen satyrling. And Claude snorting over York's shoulder. "Spanish lace, I told them!" *Spanish lace?* Claude pointed an accusative finger at Bertrand's penis. "Uncircumcised." Khalid found Amelia's basket, kicked on its side, top off, but no Amelia! Then looked out on the veranda. "Here she is." Coiled tranquil around a water jar, Amelia cooling herself.

York, incapable of anything, retreated to his room. His last sight Khalid sneaking downstairs with Amelia's wicker basket. "I'll hide her in the toolshed. She'll be safer there."

> I've had enough of this loony place. Want to be back with Big Red. I just need Johnsex. Kee-rrist, our long carnal battle! Convert John's lust to love, my own love to "honorable lust." Is John right when he says, "There *is* such a thing as honorable lust"?

He paused. Knew that he was on to something again; he could feel it.

> John was a sexual cacophony when he came to me, all his mother's blocked orgasms tied into his spine . . . matriarchal murder-system; slaughter Daddy by slaughtering sonny-boy!

He lay back, staring at the ceiling. The hotel was definitely quiet now. No screams, shouts, explosions. Ominous. Something was about to erupt.

> Something Claude said at that Mad Hatter's soiree—the phallus the earliest known protection against the Evil Eye. Signs in the form of erect phallus, sometimes with wings.

Yes, these were real clues surfacing. Meant he'd have to stay in Marrakech a few more days. Finish the job. Had the same feeling of mission as traveling with the Colonel, in the mountains, the Sahara. On mission!

> Aha—must be why I reacted that way to the Misses America, at the café. They treat cock as beyond the pale, even as they hunt it. And maim it.

He lay on his bed twisting and turning, following the urges of his diary, the proddings of his oracle. Yet even after two hours of pondering and jotting, his notes would have made no sense to anyone short of a phallic cabbalist.

> I *know* there's a syllogism lurking—the big one. Once I get it, I'll get the hell out of this loony hotel, out of Marrakech, I promise me!

He sat straight up, farted loudly, always a sign of determination.

> CLUES:
> a.) one wandering cobra! (and errant master)
> b.) the Phallic Liturgy of Marrakech (good phrase)

c.) those girl-hippie alias Misses Amurrica!
d.) the Evil Eye (& something in Claude—ah, eyes that hiss!)

Yes, this was the big one all right: the Syllogism of the Last Chance. He couldn't hang on in Marrakech much longer. So it was now or never. Ah—

e.) The fact that something in John terrifies me. But what?

Thank God. Had it all down at last. First time he'd admitted that something in John *did* terrify him. He contemplated his list. Yes, it was major. Maybe a sighting. He often had them at moments like this. A sighting would surface the syllogism now, had to.

He closed his eyes, expectant. Nothing. He opened his eyes, stared at the diary, certain it held the key to his life. And for that matter, to his paralyzed nation. Weren't his problems those of the nation at large? And if he could solve these personal conundrums, would he not redeem the nation? It was clear.

Equally clear was that after another half hour of contemplation, he could make nothing of it. Must be something missing, a final clue. Yes, he'd damned well have to stay in Marrakech to find it.

He drifted toward sleep, still clutching his notes. And at sleep's edge saw it: the Koutoubia rearing like a verdict against the sky, the two storks thundering by, storks pursued by a melee of swallows. And the entire city lying beneath, as a single castle. . . . His sighting, the sighting he'd been waiting for! But it was too late; he was already asleep.

8
THE MAGIC CARPET

When he awoke it was cooler; the sun had already fallen low. He felt hungry and fresh, his body aglow. The strange, high effect of the Hôtel des Amis. Probably loony, the hotel made him nervous. He needed to get away from it, go for a stroll. And presto, he was tiptoeing downstairs, eager to evade Claude, Rrrichard, Bertrand, Mathilde, macaw, the English couple, and above all Amelia. He made it, right to the gate.

"And where are you off to, like an escaped convict?" Claude's singsong voice lassoing him as he scooted around the gate into the anonymity of the street. He glanced back. Claude's hand floating above a cluster of geraniums, goatee thrusting like an accusative finger. York grimaced, backtracked, saw the easel there. A watercolor, in myriad shades of green. Claude likewise green pants, gossamer shawl of green. No wonder York hadn't spotted him among the plants. Claude jabbing at his painting. "I came from my siesta and saw the light had changed, pale veridian. I said to myself, '*Green*—must do something about green!' " York nodded. Claude's smile engaging as he glanced up. One must *obey* the light of each day. We forget to obey the light!" York had to admit he sometimes forgot. Just seeing Claude like that, bobbing Peter Pan of the flowers—laughable, yet so much more as well. As Claude obeyed the light, dancing the light of the day onto his easel. York felt rebuked as he leaned into the green of garden, green of painting, green of exquisite Claude, suddenly standing back, taking another brush, poised for an instant, then abruptly stabbing a dash of red into the symphony of green. Claude's furious chuckle as he rammed the red in. And more. York backing off, keeping his gaze on Claude as he backtracked to the gate.

"Why are you running away?" Claude's brush pointing in judgment. As York turned to escape, a strange panic rising in him.

"Why don't you want to talk?" Claude jabbed more of the harsh red into the green.

"I'm just going for a walk."

"But we *should* talk—Tony, James, your little voyage into the mountains."

"Later." York backing out of Claude's aura.

"But why are you afraid?" The words stinging like the red as York fled out the gate, churning down the street. Pausing as he reached the mall, watching a small boy polish large shoes. Shoe-shine boys and men at every intersection; one older man, down toward York's favorite café, even had his shoe-repair shop spread all over the sidewalk. Always struck York, the man had only one ear. . . .

An older boy was eyeing York now, sidling up. And a calèche passing slowly. York leapt in, slumped into the worn leather seat. Calèche bumped along the mall; mobile haven against traffic, marauding boys, and Claude's taunt. "Why are you afraid?"

They were passing a park of palm trees, geyser of palms, regal in the slanting light. This was the right way to see Marrakech, not by taxi at all. Taxi hurtled you through the city. Calèche wheedled you in. The driver turned his head, eyes asking directions. York pointed to the Koutoubia. One of Claude's kinder suggestions. "Sit by the Koutoubia at sunset!"

For a few trundling moments York watched the world passing. Couples out strolling, a donkey blocking traffic, a cart whose wheel had dropped off. The ancient fortress walls loomed up, ferocious pink in the angling sun. A medieval dream, Marrakech. As the tower rose high over the ambling calèche, and the words returned: "Why are you afraid?" The driver held out his hand for dirhams. York paid. Driver gestured for more. York didn't care.

He settled in a small café across the mall from the Koutoubia, ordered a milk shake. Gazing at the tower in fine vista across the road. Squadrons of birds skittering around its top. Their aerial play heightening the tower, pulling York's eye up and up. . . . "Why are you afraid?" Claude so indignant. York sucked on his milk shake. Was Claude mad, a "jettatore," able to cast the Evil Eye? Or just a failed artist marooned in Marrakech, as Bertrand had said? Sky shimmering pink now, tower catching the light. Conundrum of Claude tumbling the edges of his mind like those birds around the tower. Swallows careening, mewing as the sun edged below the canopy of palms. Koutoubia booming the final sky, birds looping, racing around it, agitated at loss of sun, lamenting the end of day.

The tower stood giant. Suddenly birds gone. Sun gone. Only the silhouette of the Koutoubia, solitary in the dusk. York felt an urge to stand, acknowledge the event.

He stood up, intending to return to the hotel, haven after this outing. But his feet going in the opposite direction, toward the market. His pace quickened as the music closed in on him. The flickering lights of the Djema-el-Fna, "place of the Apocalypse" someone had said. The sound of distant flute, calls of the last vendors, soft rustle of djellabahs flowing by, Keb's dinner stand. Yes, been hoping to find Keb. . . . But no Kebir. Nor his friends. Just a ram's head staring at him from a platter.

"*Hasheeesh*, you want hasheeessh?" Tall lad thrusting into him, pushing packet at him. York moved ahead silently, into the dark. The boy followed. "I got more than hash." Boy running alongside, arching crotch at York. "You wanna make sex?" Rolling his eyes with body. Insisting, "You *like* zeb! You know you like. . . ." Boy hopping along beside, words growing louder. "Why you come to Marrakech if you no like zeb?" Two others racing up, leering. One of them hissing, "You're a homo!" And the other chanting, "Homo, dirty homo!" Boys prancing around and around, York pressing his way through them. "Homo!" As he fled down the market: "Homo! Homo!" Drums of the square echoing the accusation like gongs in the night. Till the boys fell away and he slowed to a walk at the far end of the Djema-el-Fna.

And soon was funneled into the Medina, along the alleyways of boutiques, submerged in aromas of tea, fruit, hashish. Stalls chirping, chortling like birds, a giant aviary. He paused, saw the red, blue and yellow plates, jars, cups, jugs, ceramics and pottery stalls. Wares of the market, the vendors swooping out, flaunting their goods. "For the pleasure of the eye." No need to buy, just delight the eye! York drifted on.

In the central alley now: splash of textiles, dresses, rugs, hanging over counters, up walls, off ceilings. Old man squatting barefoot, puffing content on hash pipe. Urchin making tea. Handsome youth beckoning to the back of his shop.

He slowed again as textiles changed to bronze, silver, clangor of fierce jewelry: massive arm bands, earrings, armor-plate necklaces. He floated toward a display. "M'sieur." Boy lunging out the door, pulling him in, plopping him onto a stool. A small shop, walls a-clatter with silver, brass, ormolu. Embossed and filigreed and chased. Orbs of amber resonant between. Heard the rhythmic hands . . . hands hammering, ancient hands kneading, working such power of jewelry. His eyes resting on a dagger, silver dagger dangling from the wall. Boy following his gaze and bringing the dagger unbidden. And York caressing the sculpted handle, tingling his fingers. Boy laughing. "That dagger has killed men." Words lurking in the back of York's memory? Words from that earlier visit with Kebir's friends—months ago, it seemed. And was this the very shop where they'd sat over tea, dagger popping off the wall, then as now?

"You seem afraid of it," the boy saying as York fingered the dagger. "Why is that?" York silent, eyeing the knife, abruptly thrusting it aside, running out the door, down the lane. Where was Kebir? For a wild moment thought he saw him entering a side alley ahead. And followed, followed those eyes floating above the milling heads. Eyes like deep orbs of amber. Following his Kebir. Or was he?

Music drew him on. Down an alley with flare of colors overhead, pendant greens, reds, purples. Weaving through the hectic skeins, expecting Keb to soar out of these flames and claim him. No Kebir. Only the rage of colors—dangling bundles of fresh-dyed wool.

Where was he? Another alley, floating patterns. A shining metal door on his left, courtyard beyond. He was about to pass when two boys lunged toward him. He turned, ducked through the golden door. The boys didn't follow.

He was in a large enclosed court, gallery above. And all around him dancing patterns, chanting, proclaiming. He stood dizzy, feeling somehow naked. His eyes slowly drawn to a swaying pattern. He put his head down, resisting—listening. Sure he was being seen . . . by whom? And all the time drawn forward as if in a current. He raised his eyes. Who sees me?

A rug.

Blue, yellow, green . . . and red, points of red. Large rug hanging directly in front of him, from a beam. As if the whole Djema-el-Fna were dancing down the alleyways into this one face of carpet with its canary tassels. Flying tassels, hooking York's eye. He slowly returned the gaze of carpet, eyes flowing through the fringe, on through intricate border, blue-red maze. And deeper into green, core of green and flowering yellow. His hands rising toward the rug, palms open, receiving the sun.

He glimpsed around. Other rugs, smaller, hanging nearby, but he was caught in its vortex. Didn't want to get out, but must. Seeking an exit, path out through the winding contours of color. But points of red blocking, reversing him. Flares of red surrounding the calm green. Tried again to escape, his eyes riding the dare of rug right to the edge of the cliff, to see kasbah presiding the valley, their first kasbah. And the valley winding on, Colonel wheeling the car up the flank of the mountain.

York's body flung around and around as the rug still gazed serene. He yanked his head to one side, stepping back from crazy rug, muttering, "Lascaux."

A second step back. "Morocco, locked into a rug!"

Another step. "A hex, like that lunatic put on our car!"

Another step and he was all but clear. He glanced up, assessing such an insane adversary. He fell back into the carpet. Their car hurtling on to M'hamid.

"Don't be afraid." Voice from the carpet. "Morocco likes you."

York gaping, staring into the rug, like staring into the sun.

"It likes you." The rug speaking so clearly. York turning away to assemble his wits. A face floating toward him, black-gold face of a young Moroccan appearing from one side of the hanging carpet.

"I was just . . . admiring your rug."

"You were in a trace, m'sieur. Like a dream of hashish."

York spluttered. "That damned rug did it!"

The Moroccan fingered the tassels of the swaying rug. Like a giant cat he was, gold-black cheetah. "Where are you from?"

"The Hôtel des Amis."

"What country, I mean."

"Canada."

"You've come a long way to be frightened by a rug." Moroccan's eyes laughing as his fingers dallied with the tassels. Yes, absurd. York stepped forward to touch it, his fingers tracing the patterns running in from the edge of the carpet. Fingers plying the golden run of rug. Current tingling his hand, up his arm—he glanced over, saw big black fingers furrowing across from the other side of the rug, lithe arm glistening. The Moroccan silent, eyes fixed on the flow of the rug.

"I'm Karim. . . . And you?"

"I'm York."

"Do you always get high on rugs?" Karim's eyes dancing as he toyed with one of the tassels, twirling it. Suddenly they were both laughing and moving to a bench at the edge of the courtyard. Karim talking of the rugs. "The one that caught your eye is from Rabat. Like a peacock it is." York nodded. "And the one beside it, the long yellow one, from Ouarzazate. It's like a field of flowers. The red and silver one with the large diamonds is from Rissani, the Souss . . . Berber, like me." Karim talking of his rugs like friends, relatives. "And the black-and-green there, with gold, is from the Draa Valley, near Zagora. It's Berber too. You can always tell: the real Morocco." Yes, like an ebony rainbow it was. "Land of the free men." Was that what James had said? James making that speech about the Glaoui.

"Do you want some tea?" Yes, tea would calm things down. Even if York knew the big rug came from Rabat it still troubled him, seducing his eye. And he didn't really know where Rabat was.

"Or come to my home. It's close. You will meet the best rug of all." Why not? And in no time Karim had closed shop and they were strolling back through the fiery lane of textiles, wools.

"It's like a floating garden." York peering up at the swaying skeins of color on both sides of them. Karim reached up and stroked them like ponytails . . . Karim soaring like a giant blue bird in his burnoose. York trotted beside, feeling like a displaced sparrow in his brown T-shirt, dingy flannels. Yes, Karim so tall, his wave of hair brushed the hanging wool as he surged along the lanes. Yet he himself serene above his stride, like Keb. . . .

York's stocky body gradually adjusting to Karim's flow, the boutiques swimming by.

They wheeled down a smaller alley into a maze of lanes and dimming lights. Now passing a bundled figure lying behind a stool, oblivious. And just as York began wondering where he was, Karim drew up before a wooden door studded with brass nails. Pulled out a large iron key, swung the door open, and ushered York in as if to a palace. But they were in a cramped, dingy halllway. Door clanked shut. Karim bolted it. York quailed.

Karim led him up a narrow stairwell, toward fluttering lights. Lights becoming turrets, domes, castellations as they approached. A large lantern of perforated metal and glass spinning reds and greens onto ceiling and walls.

For a moment York couldn't quite see the room they were in. But Karim gestured to the far end, to a long low divan covered with leopard pelt. York groped toward it—and stopped. He glanced down, the yellow carpet writhing underfoot. He'd already walked roughshod over green, then red arabesque, and now was standing on yellow. The pelt of the rug, the lilt of yellow, protesting his shoes, their clumsy bulk. He'd scarcely even noticed the rug. But here he was invading it, its lucid yellow trampled. He glanced back. Karim was taking off his sandals and socks. York retreated and removed his own shoes, feeling guilty of trespass. Ridiculous. . . . Yet when he followed Karim across the purring rug-face now, it was different; he felt upheld, airborne as they floated to the divan.

Karim sat smiling, impish grin as he twiddled his toes. And pointed at York's socks. York removed them too, resting bare feet gingerly on the carpet. His feet starting to twitch, toes sneaking forward into the caressing ruff of the carpet. Furrowing into a run of golden yellow against blue. Truant toes, he almost pulled them back. But the rug held them, inviting them to remain. His wan feet sucking up the color, and his eyes ferreting on into the heart of the carpet. But the center of the rug kept eluding him. His eyes traveling around and back and around . . . the colors swaying, refusing to rest. Whole room swaying under floating lantern, colors cascading down through shelves, plates, curtains, to merge in the winding roads and byways of the carpet.

"You like voyaging in rugs." Karim's laughing voice. York had never thought of it that way—voyaging in rugs! Yet that's what he had just been doing. "I have many American friends who come year after year. They come to see my rugs, to buy." Karim cocking a big toe in pleasure. "Would you like to see them?"

"Your rugs?"

"No, my friends." He reached into a small coffer by the divan. And emptied a large envelope beside York. A sudden spray of faces, jeans, bright eyes, women, young men: photographs. Karim in several, overtopping friends by a head, a rage of curly hair. He picked one up, grinning. "She liked the gold-and-black ones. In Telouet."

"Liked who?"

"The rugs . . . Glaoua rugs. We went there together." Yes, photo of Karim with an American girl, blond. She was leaning against him happily, in the Djema-el-Fna. "And this one was from New York, a model. She said, 'Karim, you're more beautiful than your rugs.' She didn't buy any." Yes, there she was, statuesque, holding his hand. "This one comes every winter." York looked, photo of a youth in dapper white suit, boutonniere, handsome. And signed. "For K., who knows all the sights." Karim chuckling, leafing through more photos, his toes wriggling with delight as the faces and memories rose. Several of himself, sometimes serious, yet the eyes always bubbling, body always moving, even when still. The lantern spinning its color onto the photos, spinning York's head. And Karim laughing as the photos whirled by, and taking something else from the coffer. A cigarette, lighting it as he pointed to a photo of a man, all muscles and mustache. "He asked me to go back to Chicago to work for him, in a gymnasium. Said I'd have huge muscles within a year."

"What did you tell him?"

"I said I have enough already; lots of exercise." Karim passed the cigarette to York, who puffed without thinking. Karim produced a photo of two young girls, one on each side of him over tea. Adoring glances. Karim lighting another cigarette. And only several photos later, as the smoke and faces coiled around them, did York say, "But it's marijuana."

"Of course. It's good?" And York, dizzily enveloped in rug, photos and smoke, kept right on. The room never seemed to sit still. Shelves prancing the walls and ceiling, dissolving into arabesqued panels. Pattern of rug surging and looping and dissolving. And York suddenly bursting out, "That's it!"

"That's what?"

"The way the lanes in the market move, the way you walk, the rhythms of the music. . . ." York sitting upright, eyes passing from Karim to lantern to rug.

And Karim laughed, thrusting his feet deeper into the carpet. "Is that what you were thinking all this time?"

York stared at the rug. "I don't know. Something back at the shop . . . and in those photos. Something about you."

Karim sat back, face flickering in the lantern light, puckish.

"There's a rhythm in it—in you! It's regal, it's . . ." York feeling idiotic. "It's all part of the same thing, like the rug back in the shop, that rug I saw."

"Rug that saw you, my friend." Karim's face impassive now.

"The w-way you walk—" York stammering. "It's like flowing water, it's—"

"Ah, but the way you Americans walk! It hurts to see."

"So sensual, you're all so sensual, that's what!" York babbling.

Karim dallying the rug with his toes, uncertain.

"It's like your pictures; they're not just sexy, but sensual—"

"But that's normal."

York paused; what the hell *was* he trying to say? "It's as if you'd slept with them all, and. . ."

Karim ruffling the leopard pelt; puzzled.

"But is . . . is everyone bisexual here?"

"Bisexual?" No, Karim really *didn't* understand.

How on earth could he ask more clearly? "Look, these photos. They're of you and boys, and you and girls, and they all look so . . . pleased."

"You mean, do we sleep with men and women?"

York nodded.

"But of course. Don't *you*?" Karim holding the big tassel between his toes and gazing intently at the rug. And nodding to himself. Finally turning to York. "So *that's* what they were asking, all the Americans. I could never understand." He laughed. "But the question is so strange, no? Women, boys, rugs, they're all part of the garden of Allah. This rug you see, it's from Zagora."

Silence, but for a sound emanating from Karim as he sat, his face that black-gold mask once again. York turned away. He glanced at the carpet. Same sound, muted drums, so maybe the sound wasn't Karim. Maybe . . .

"But don't you feel a difference . . . when you sleep with Americans?"

Karim nodded, big toes jousting with a tassel of rug again. "The women can't wait. And the men are all afraid."

York winced. "Afraid of what?"

"But I hoped you could tell me. The men don't talk; they run away all the time. They say they are staying, but they run away inside themselves."

Silence. Karim nodding at the rug, as if it were the rug he'd been talking to. "They want to buy me when they buy my rugs. All the same, someday I want to go to America. I'll come to visit you. . . ."

York nodded. "You're like your rugs—everything you do. The way you say things."

Karim smiled. "You see, friend, rugs are alive."

"Rugs know a person by the way he walks on them."

"How did *I* walk on it—this rug?"

"Ah, you crushed him. But he stopped you."

York nodded.

"And you kneeled to remove your shoes, as if you'd never done that before." Karim so impassive now, as if in a trance. "Then he accepted you."

"Oh?"

"He likes you." Karim serene, unblinking. "How do you feel now, with your shoes off?"

York gazed at his feet, floating on the rug. "Naked."

A gurgle of laughter. "It's hard to run away when you're naked."

"Why would I—"

"You have wanted to run away three times, since the rug in my shop caught you." York should never have smoked that marijuana. "In Morocco, rugs are our garden, our friends, our companions in prayer." Like soft thunder, his words. York wanted to reach out, touch him. Reached out and caressed the rug instead.

"So you're no longer afraid, friend." Karim relenting, harlequin in dance again.

And for a moment they were quiet. Karim reclining on the

cushion at the head of the divan. Blue robe spread over leopard pelt. And York gazing at the carpet before them. He picked up a photo—a young man, imploring. And another, girl in expensive sweater and jeans. Out of place in her jeans, as if worn by act of will. He closed his eyes, then looked again. Yes, her body all angles, though bending so concertedly for the camera. And clinging to Karim as if for dear life. Winsomely handsome face but aloof.

"You like her?"

York studied the girl's face.

"She wanted to stay. Said she would never go back to her family." Karim eyeing York as he stared at the photo. "Her brother came to find her, a long way."

Without thinking, York flipped the photo over. Toronto, a Toronto address on the back. He thrust the photo aside.

"What has stung you?"

"Stung?"

"Your body has been stung."

And glancing down, York saw his arms crossed in front of him, tense. "Yes, that photo hurts."

"She has pain, that one. She was afraid of her parents."

"We all were."

The room shunting forward under York's eyes, a shudder of shelves, plates, objects he couldn't define.

"I promised you tea, special mint. You'll smile again." Karim gazing over. "And I'll put music on for you, Berber music, to bring the dance." He reached down beside the divan, touching a hidden radio. Music spiraled out over the leopard pelt, over their knees, feet, and across the carpet. Igniting the yellow of carpet. The yellow winding like sun into the carpet's core. And Karim rising inside the coil of music and color, towering over the rug. Blue-black column of Karim towering there. "Please honor my tea as you did my rug." Was that what he said? But Karim gone.

For a moment York saw him there still, looming out of the rug. His jade-black eyes and wild nimbus of hair. And invisible majesty of walk, gait soaring beyond laughter, making alleyways ring. Karim had majesty.

He drew back on the divan, nervous. Strange sound of Karim—a chanting? No, a rumbling in him. It was in Kebir that he heard chanting. He glanced up as if Keb might appear, out of the rug, like Karim.

No Kebir. No Karim. No one.

Where was he? Somewhere in the Medina, the old quarter. What had they been talking about? Rugs, sex, photos, the way Karim walked. It all went around in circles—Arabesque, like that rug. Must've been the damned marijuana.

Yet it wasn't. He had always seen things that way, felt them that way. Just couldn't express them as Karim did, his own mind and tongue not equipped. As if Karim took it all for granted. Karim a child of something more than sex. York no longer knew anything except that Karim, this rug, the one in the shop, that Moroccan music, their conversation—all felt one and the same, interchangeable. And all had a kind of majesty that York could barely grasp.

He grabbed for the photos, wanting to see Karim again. Yes, there he was, clowning in the Djema-el-Fna, posing as sultan, proud clown in a cape. And always that smile. Beyond mockery, closer to mirth. Another shot, Karim surrounded by tourist girls, like the ones in the café. Girls appraising Karim with their smile. He paused—why had he been so harsh about the girls in the café? Why shouldn't they hunger for a Karim? There were no Karims in America, much less in Canada. Anyone as alive, as sensual, as Karim would be illegal in North America. No kings allowed!

He stared at Karim in the photo, trying to comprehend. My God, just those lips—he felt embarrassed just noticing them. But in North America, men not supposed to have lips at all . . . just oral zippers. Karim's lips a vocation, to celebrate life, sing and kiss. He flipped to the next: Karim on a camel, gazing down, high potentate. Yet that laughter on the lips so much more than mere laughter. A holy uproar.

A final photo, just to be sure. There she was: the Toronto girl. Karim beside her, looking curiously stern. As if the girl had transferred her tensions into him. She must have let go in Marrakech. The gleam in her eyes said that too. York felt envious . . . not for the girl but for Karim—because he'd succeeded. York knew that girl all too well. The kind that gives promises of Mona Lisa in heat, yet once married, enters upon a life of denial.

He stared at the girl. He didn't know her, but knew dozens like her. Yes, knew those marble madonnas along the very lines of his own smashed nervous system. About to toss the photo aside, but a voice welling up inside him. "We were *all* damaged. And she was damaged too—all of us, caught in the same straitjacket."

He opened his eyes to an empty room. And the music slowly probing its way back into his ears. Chant existing only between the notes, never as melody. He leaned into the sound of his toes coiling into the rug, furrowing a curve of blue, gold, in time with the music. His body starting to sway, ebbing and flowing in the breath of the room.

He dropped back on the divan, peering into the room. Just a plain white room. But a splurge of colors thrown out by castellate lantern never still. Colors refracted over old plates hanging from the walls. Large plates, patterns spinning through them and from them. And those tiered shelves with arches, arcades, buttresses—like a floating carnival. And between the shelves and pendant plates, daggerlike black carvings, staccato phalli dancing the walls. The room no longer white but a liquid gold and black, blue-black.

He shifted on the divan, determined to assimilate the room. His toes working the rug, eyes swimming amid the majestic black carvings, the shelves. An enormous eye to the left of the lantern, watching him. He leaned forward. Same blues, yellows, turquoise green as carpet. And stabs of black. A plate drew him into a spinning circle, a center, where a beast lay hidden. The music of the room more insistent as he tried to see. Rug seething there, rumbling . . . no safer than the plate. And the music churning as his toes furrowed the carpet. Majesty and mirth lurking in everything, till he was overwhelmed by furious urge to dance, strip off all his clothes, *dance*.

He clamped his eyes shut. And when he opened them, he was in the *flow* of the room. His eyes swimming around the room, and always back to the carpet. Yes, everything led to the carpet. He wanted to bow to its magic, its hidden commands. Kneel and give thanks. York's eyes followed the dance of rug down through riot of yellow and red to black at the far end. Black of carpet rising as a huge foot. Rising, hovering as black knee, pair of naked legs. And York's eyes rising with, up to bulge of buttocks, blue-black buttocks. . . .

York blinked to focus, control the fantasy. But his eyes fell into unblinking eyes across the room, jade eyes, face an impassive gold mask. Those lips . . . Karim, must be! He heard the silent laughter.

He fixed on the rage of colors, reds-blues-greens on the naked chest floating before him. Enormous tattoo of a dragon on that chest. A pair of hands clasped across. Looked again—no tattoo at all. But brass, enamel, large teapot, shimmering atop a tray of canisters, glasses, like a floating city. Domes, towers, minarets, amplified by lantern light. City of hospitality, upheld by Karim's hands.

Karim shining naked there, like some regal priest at presentation holding the tray of office. And the motion beneath . . . shudder of Karim's cock shifting its head, snouting slowly forward and up to see.

Cock glaring right through York.

He yanked his hand across his eyes. Wake up back in Osprey Cove, back in London, back anywhere but here. Dragon looming closer, that russet helmet of flesh, too. Karim moving slowly to the center of the carpet and the whole room moving with him . . . music, colors, walls and plates in pageant. The city upheld in his enormous hands. . . . Marrakech on a gleaming tray, and the snorting beast beneath. York heard his own chopped breathing. He lurched forward. Dragon head shunted closer, and lantern splashing fire. Fire down the long, hard body. And York poised at the edge of divan, caught in the energy of a scream that wouldn't rise. Closed his eyes again but could not blot out the sight of the risen Karim.

He looked again. Karim standing serenely potentate, and slowly moving forward along the line of their mutual gaze. Flowing with the carpet.

He paused one step in front of York. Tower of flesh in the gathered room. York felt the pressure rising in his spine. And Karim expectant, holding the brass tray above York's head. Pressure rising through York's neck as the tray tilted slightly, flashing light across his face. And the bellow of that helmet of flesh in front of his eyes. York fell forward, onto his knees. As he reached out, clasping the black dragon rod, pressing it to his forehead. Fully expecting the city to come crashing down on his skull.

He relinquished the dragon rod, gazed up. Karim standing in a black-gold glister of thigh, belly, chest . . . still holding the city in his hands. Karim drew back slowly, set the tray on the rug, motioning York back onto the divan. Then strode from the room.

Karim was soon back, bearing a plate of cakes, a hand towel. Back in a dancing smile. Naked, shimmering naked, but subsiding now. Golden mask of his face dimpling as he sat beside York, busying himself with the tray. Raising the ornate teapot, cascading the tea through the air into blue glasses. And opening one of the copper jars, taking a sprinkle of white petals, scattering them into the tea. Sharp fragrance of mint and flowers billowing up. York followed, fragrance of the high mountain slopes, he recognized it.

They savored their tea silently. As if nothing had happened. York glanced over—Karim cross-legged over his slurping tea, naked. His cock like a domestic pet, relaxed, dozing. No dragon there. Yet moments before he'd been a Pharaoh, at once king and priest in his own temple. And now sitting there, playing with his toes, happy clown.

York felt stunned. Suddenly he stood up, peeled off T-shirt, pants. And sat down in his underwear, his own startling hard-on also gone. Karim sat sniffing his tea. "So you like it?"

"Like—?"

"Our tea."

York nodded. "It's like the mountain flowers."

"You've been in our mountains?"

"As far as Zaroga, M'hamid."

"Za-go-ra."

"Yes, at the edge of the Sahara. And farther."

"Mountain mint has a sharper bouquet."

Words flowing back and forth like the fragrance of the tea. Karim nodding and shifting from the divan onto the carpet. His head at the same height as York's now. Giant imp he was, toes wriggling in time with the music. When York had his clothes on, Karim saw him naked. Yet even when he saw Karim naked, he understood nothing about him. He gazed around the room—it was quiescent now, intimate. The warmth of the rug, the vivacity of the plates on the wall. Moments ago it had been a palace. As that big lantern still was its own hanging palace.

"My friends call it the room of the magic carpet." Karim grinning as he followed York's eyes around the room. "They write me from New York, Chicago . . . all over America. They write and say, Karim, please take so-and-so to your room of the magic carpet. *You were paying homage, friend—to the magic carpet.*"

York glanced over, Karim slurping loudly on his tea. Had Karim really said that? York peered around the room again.

"A fine rug is Allah's garden!" Karim scattered more petals into the teapot, as if he'd said nothing. But grinning—wild, sweet harlequin. "You asked to see the genie of the rug."

York gaped.

"Your eyes asked." Karim picked up the teapot, arched a further shot of tea into his glass, chuckling. "You Americans have much money but no eyes."

Stupefaction.

"Outlines only; no substance, no flesh. But there are rugs."

Silence.

"You see the world in silhouette, no?" Karim's words grave, but his eyes laughing as he cupped his hand over the glass. "You ask me many questions; you ask yourself more, I hear them." He paused, savoring his tea. "You no longer see the room, no? No longer hear the music?"

York glanced up. Karim was right. His babble of questions, real or imagined, had banished the room, the rug, the play of music.

"We must give homage to Allah every day."

York didn't dare say anything.

"That way we are able to dance, to hear, to see." Karim rubbing his bony knees, eyes rolling through the rug and over to York. "You've let your tea get cold." He took a fresh glass, filled it, passing it to York. The rumble of the room returned with the dance, the mirth of yellow. York heaved a sigh, sank back on the cushions. Karim with his head against the divan, smiling. The pageant all around. Plates, shelves, the black carvings in exhortation. And the red flower swelling, rising firm but gentle from Karim's naked lap. No dragon now, but orchid of the carpet. Karim risen again. York cradling his tea, Karim swaying in his silent mirth. And only when he burbled into open laughter did York see his own cock had risen, too, standing hard inside his underwear, prodding to be let free.

He removed his underwear and joined Karim naked on the rug. The room at one with their delight. And Karim gazing full into York's eyes, but York sensing that to open farther was to be locked into this rite of room and tea forever. He reached across and took Karim's cock, fingering it till it swelled shuddering full, black scepter over rug. Karim reached for a bowl on the tray. A fragrant oil; he rubbed it on their fingers, their cocks. And together they lay, the only conversation that of their stroking fingers. Till York felt Karim's flower swell further and saw that red head burst and the swoop of petals out the top. . . . Karim's eyes reeling, a warble of laughter deep from his throat. And petals spurting white onto his belly, outrageously white on the dripping black skin. And York laughing, sudden whoop of laughter. The mirth of each resounding the room. York saw they had flowered together.

With their laughter still echoing the room, Karim served more tea. For some moments they sat in silence, as if they'd known each other a lifetime. Karim sprinkling more flowers into the teapot, floating the fragrance through the room. "It belonged to my grandfather's family." Karim talking of the teapot. "A sheikh up in the mountains, beyond Ouarzazate." And now York listening to a distant sound. "A ksar on an island in the river." York heard it again, the rumbling, subterranean bellow. "My grandfather's father was sheikh of that valley. And his people before him came from the south, the deep Sahara." York hearing the sound of that valley, flow of the river, soar of falcon . . . Keb standing high over the valley, and Tony giant in the sun. "And this rug, these plates, these carvings, all come from the valley of my ancestors." Karim then saying proudly, "We are the people of the Souss, Berber and African!"

York nodding, heart bursting.

"But what are you hearing?"

York looked askance.

"I see you hearing something; your whole body is hearing."

Then York knew. "It's the sound of the oxen, the birds, on the river where your ancestors' home is. I've been there, Karim."

"It is so. The valley roars with the cattle, the animals; it's like a giant cave. . . . You know the world was born there."

Karim sat serene and proud, his face a king's.

9
THE MAN WHO CAME TO DIE

He was sitting so silent: a little old button of a man, in green silk dressing gown, cravat and slippers. Perched on the edge of the chair, flirting with something in mind or memory more than anything present. His face seemed all memory, events that had distilled into a sweet map of wrinkles. York catching him out of the corner of his eye. Catching Richard like some dapper leprechaun engaged in meditation. And unwilling to interrupt, though they were in York's own bedroom.

Fact was, York was barely awake, trying to gather the wreckage of his mind together. He'd been awakened by that morning murder, macaw in full voice. Then the birds caroling from the palm tree. And when he finally opened his eyes, there it was—the figure rising over the end of his bed like black smoke. York had sat up. Just a knock at the door. He'd flung a towel around himself and gone to answer, expecting breakfast. It was Richard instead, scurrying all twinkle and courtesy to take up his station on the chair beside the bed.

York had retreated to the horizontal again. Had he heard the news about dear Eulalie? York couldn't remember any Eulalie. No matter; Countess Eulalie had given a party the previous night, and the police had raided. And you know how harsh Moroccan laws are on sexual variations, especially between Moroccans and foreigners. The police chief had dismissed his men and joined the party; yes, dear Eulalie had seen him eyeing Tuesday . . . Tuesday, the pretty black from Rissani. And immediately offered his services to the chief. You know. . . . York never knew anything this early in the morning. But Richard had looked pleased, about to provide further details. Another knock. "That will be Claude; he was upset you were out so late last night."

It was Khalid, with breakfast. Did York want his veranda doors opened farther? Yes, maybe, no. The sun had sliced in with louder bird song, and Khalid had taken the chair on the other side of the bed. Might he report? Report what? "Amelia's still safe. In the garden shed. She tried to escape, but I caught her under the palm tree." At which Richard had leaned forward. "That Englishman admitted he sees things; he actually imagined a cobra! He's very bright, though. Says Marrakech is Chaucerian. I told him Rabelais."

But York hadn't been listening. Seeing those eyes again, hovering over the foot of his bed, naked black body shimmering. Yes: Karim a rising spectre there.

Another knock—and the door had swung open to Claude, in red smock and shawl. York had wished it another color; barely nine-thirty, difficult hour for red. But Claude whirling in to stand at the foot of the bed. Karim dissolving from view as Claude asked, "Have you heard the news?" They had not. "A *stabbing*—in the Medina! That pretentious American who claims he's an artist . . . been living here for years." York tried drinking his coffee. Claude pirouetting around the news of "this especially bloody stabbing."

By the time York had coped with coffee and croissant and was almost awake, Bertrand had arrived to arrange himself across the end of the bed, in dressing gown and little else. Claude announcing proudly, "Le tout Hôtel des Amis is now in plenary morning session." And the news of the day and various nights had been paraded, amplified, duly savored. Khalid rolling his eyes in pleasure. Richard keeping a hopeful eye on Bertrand's scant dressing gown, in case of exposure. And Claude endeavoring to find out where York had been the night before.

Each time York started to speak of it, those black eyes reappeared over the end of the bed, warning him not to. York had fallen silent, at which the face had nodded approval and finally disappeared.

"Very well," Claude had said. "But you must behave yourself for the duration. We promised to care for your well-being."

Of course.

"Besides, Kebir came looking for you last night, and we couldn't tell him where you had gone."

Keb?

"He left a message. Would you join him at his home, tomorrow night, for dinner? I myself will drive you there."

And before York could untangle any more of it, all except Richard had left. Sitting mercifully silent now, lost in his own meditation. Bird song from the garden flowed through the window, repossessing the room. And for a moment York just lay, the cataclysm with Karim last night crashing inside him like cymbals. And *le tout Hôtel*, and Kebir. Just churned inside him in fragments, demented fragments tormenting him. Till he turned and gazed at Richard, elegant little man; what was it Claude had said? "Rrrichard is an endless subjunctive clause out of Proust."

"I fear we're rather much for you." Richard breaking his silence. "A good deal to assimilate all at once."

York nodded.

"But we felt it might give you a boost if we dropped by for coffee."

York ashamed; it hadn't crossed his mind they were mounting this improbable levee to help him.

"We know you've been through a somewhat"—Richard paused, plucking fluff off his gown—"exacerbating time here. Tony did tell us some of it. Morocco can be a shock your first time." Richard leaning forward, apparently gleeful.

York propped himself up, determined to speak about the previous night. "Richard, a crazy thing happened. . . ." But no sooner started than the eyes were back again, sentry over the end of the bed. He must be imagining it. Yet each time he tried to speak, the figure rose higher in warning. Till it was standing naked, erect, regal. York flopped back on the pillows. Richard watched, saying gently, "Whatever it is, don't try to explain. It can wait till you're ready."

York startled; had Richard seen . . . ? No, impossible. And now the figure dissolving, ebbing away from the end of the bed. York suddenly wanting to ask Richard about majesty. Something in Moroccans *was* majesty; safe to discuss that, wasn't it? "I can't make head nor tail of this hotel." Not what he'd intended to say at all.

"I'm so glad."

"What?"

"I'm glad you don't understand the hotel. If you did, I'd think you were completely crazy." Richard grinning delight. "I call it the Hotel Rabiosa. Which is why I like it."

York stared.

"It's so surreal, it incurs love."

Richard sitting in a flicker of a smile, like a visual giggle. And York about to give up.

"Life beyond its limits. Where you see best." Richard rocking back and forth in the chair. "You see, our little hotel seduces in so many interesting ways."

York didn't need seduction. But Richard tittered and went on. "I mean, so many different people, all on display. Some are here for a day or two, but some stay for years, like me."

"How long have you been here?"

"Over a decade."

"And Claude?"

Richard mused. "About four years. Bertrand comes and goes. Mostly goes, but leaves macaw and Amelia in our care."

Silence. Richard gazing out the window now, listening to birds in the palm tree.

"You're a bizarre crew."

"I hope so," Richard chuckled. "That's what fascinates you."

York laughed, sat further up. "One minute you seem so loony, if you'll forgive me. And the next you're all so brilliant, le tout Hôtel. I can't decide which is real."

Richard grinned happily. "You don't need to."

"Claude is Merlin. And Bertrand is—"

"If you pigeonhole us that way, you'll never see us, and never really know us." Richard tittering to himself. "But maybe that's safest for you."

York nodded absently. "But what makes you all friends?"

"Feelings, emotions, betrayals—the desperate need to share." Richard giggling to himself.

York looked again. He couldn't place, pigeonhole, nor even locate the man in any recognizable way.

"And the need to share in adventures. Remember, privacy is reality."

"I beg your pardon?"

"The res publica is void, a banquet of wind." Richard gazing at the palm tree now.

"It's like a great green cockatoo." Richard gurgling into laughter and pointing to the palm tree. . . . And yes, it *was* like a—what had Richard said?

"I've spent years trying to decide. And now I know—it's like an aroused green cockatoo!"

And suddenly York was laughing too. Sharing Richard's sheer merriment, of palm tree and life.

But Richard gazing back at York. "I say the res publica is empty because in public we merely exist. Which is sheer evasion of life."

York tried his cold coffee. It might prevent further vertigo. "What made you stay in this—?"

"Ah. In the world we live in, most people want to *have* more. But I wanted more time to be." Silence. "I found that despite appearances, the Hôtel des Amis is a good place to find more being."

York sat straight up.

"I stayed for a week. Then a month. Then ten years. And now I am waiting."

"For what?"

"For death."

Further silence.

"I am preparing myself for death. That's all I own now."

"I'm sorry, I didn't realize—"

"No, no; what's terrible is that people no longer own their own death. They want to forget death. Worse, they want to overlook it." Richard twinkling on the chair. "Death, you see, is my best protector."

York wanted to grab for his notebook, wanted to lean over and kiss this magic little man.

"Don't bother writing it down," Richard murmured. "It's what you've come for."

York gaped.

"What you came to Morocco for. Like your adventure last night . . . a revelation!"

How could he know? York hadn't said a word, hadn't been able to.

Richard giggled happily. "We'll come to that, my friend. The important thing is this: You barely have time to *live* it. And if you start writing notes about it, you never will. At least, not the way you lived it last night!

"No blood!" Richard paused. It was as if he'd been talking to himself. Though his eyes flickering all around York. Were *those* eyes back? No. Just an aura floating around the room. York slumped, not daring to ask.

"You may wonder why I talk to you this way."

York nodded.

"Before Tony left, he asked me to be with you a little. Do you know what he said?"

No.

"York is like a troubadour monk without a song."

Silence.

"Are you a religious person?"

"No; I mean, I never was. Hated it—brought up Presbyterian. You know, Sunday hymns and clean underwear. But . . ." York faltered. "But then I became a journalist, to find out what the world's about."

Richard nodded. "And what did you find?"

"All about journalism. The slickness and sleaze. The plausibility."

Richard grinned. "Of course. Journalism is the voice of existence, not of being. Clearly you were a failure."

"Not at all; I had a lot of success"—York vehement—"which cured me of journalism."

"But not of yourself," Richard murmured, glancing out at the palm tree again.

"Well, I found myself moving towards . . ." York hesitated.

"Things of the spirit?" Richard studying the palm tree.

"I couldn't admit it, but yes. I was exploring emotions, passion, spirit—"

Richard leaned forward. "While trying to sustain a plausible facade. Why not say it? But what did you find?"

A sudden scream from the garden; York covered his ears. And when Macaw was done, knew. "What everyone finds: death; and the chance for heaven. And hell, daily hell."

Richard sat back, a-twinkle again. "Final things. Heaven and hell; the day of judgment; death." His words so easy, but felt like doomsday inside York. Drink your cold coffee, York Mackenzie. Richard crooning himself. And when York reappeared from behind the coffee cup, asked, "So what did you do?"

York laughed ruefully. "I ran away."

"A wise beginning!" Richard so pleased somehow. Twirling immobile in his chair. "No one confronts such matters anymore; you *have* to run away."

Silence. York had to ask. Sat up. And stopped. The eyes at the end of the bed again.

A delectable laugh from Richard. "You want to ask about love."

"Well, yes, but—how did you . . . ?"

"Dear friend, you just balked at final things. Then you sat up all eager—to discuss first things. What else but love? But which love? Love as sex, love as eros, love platonic, or love romantic?" Richard rattling them off like beads on a sudden rosary.

"*Not* platonic!" York clear about that much.

"And not romantic. 'Romanticism is cynicism on a bank holiday.' " Richard waving at a blue-and-yellow bird on the veranda. "Oscar Wilde."

"And not just sex." York clear about that too.

"No, it's very tiring. Worse"—Richard giggled—"it's dreadfully messy."

York stared at the remains of his croissant. "Then it's Eros."

Richard mused on the word, as if this were a new thought. "Yes, Eros is the taboo god. Only sex survived the steam engine." He twittered to himself.

What? York couldn't follow the half of it.

"That's why Tony knew you needed protection."

York peered over. Who *was* this dapper little man, prattling along with death as crony? Richard chortled. "You see, at Claude's soiree I noticed a few things. You didn't talk much. And you certainly weren't watching crotch. Though there was plenty present and offered. Like the other cockatoo."

"I beg your pardon?"

'The golden cockatoo was there, and avid. He rarely produces Amelia except as foreplay."

What in God's own name . . . ?

"Bertrand, of course." Richard twittering in glee. He was wearing his bracelet of love.

York's vertigo was on the rise again.

"His skull bracelet, he always wears it when campaigning." Richard gurgling in delight. "He was testing you, my dear. But your attention was all on Kebir; you were mesmerized when he danced. And most striking of all, you were afraid."

Silence.

"Afraid of your own trajectory." Richard laughed aloud, as if their morning merriment had reached its apogee. "You see, one false move now and you're dead."

"Dead." York testing the word.

"Of course—extinct, perdido! You're so fragile now. Very dependent—on Tony, on Kebir, even on our famille des amis." Richard chuckled.

York propped himself up. "You say I can't cope. Then you tell me all this—and laugh!"

"Ahhh," Richard raised his hands. "Because you're ready to start fighting back now." He gazed at York. "Up to this point you've been entering sacred ground like a trespasser. No? Your courage has all been passive. Courage by default, so to speak; Morocco has overwhelmed you." Richard visibly delighted with his own words. "You can't believe it's all happening, though you keep praying it is."

York certainly couldn't believe it was happening.

"But now you must move forward: face whatever has brought you here. *Face* it—with open eyes instead of a squint and a notebook. And then you'll be strong again."

York gazed at Richard. Only half an hour ago this man had been babbling about a Countess Oolala.

Richard chuckled. "Never judge people by their gossip, my friend."

York fell back against the pillows. Was Richard clairvoyant?

"And as for pigeonholing people, which we all enjoy now and then, would you allow me to situate *you*?"

York stared, nodded.

"*Erotic eschatologist*—in search of final things, mediated here and now through Eros. You've been announcing it all morning."

"But I've said nothing at all!" York spluttered.

"Exactly. Consider last night."

"I said *nothing* about last night. I couldn't; I tried."

"Several times, and it died on your lips. Eros always dies if talked about. You saw the god last night. And you watch for him this morning." Richard a ferment of pleasure now. "With that look on your face."

"What look?"

"Ah, my dear York." Richard cuddled his thighs. "Do you really not know? The look of holy terror—fearful ecstasy."

York closed his eyes, hearing Richard's words, yet not. And when York looked up, Richard was leaning forward, eyes pouring into him. "That's what Tony wanted me to tell you. He didn't have the words; he knew I would."

"What did he—"

"In our flesh there is an ecstasy of spirit." Richard gazing into York, then sitting back, all grin and winsomeness. His effort completed; message given. And his face suddenly smooth, as if all wrinkles dissolved. And Richard so radiant, clucking to himself. Then he was gone.

York lay with the remains of his breakfast, bird song and sun pouring in from the veranda. A mangled cry from the parrot. And Bertrand shouting from next door, shouting at Claude in the garden. Something about that absurd Englishman "complaining about all those brazen boys who accost him in the street!" And Claude in a shouting whisper back, "We'll set up a special protection squad for vagrant Englishmen." York then began to laugh, laughing till the tears were spent. And a ray of intelligence flickered across his mind. Capture what Richard had said. He reached for his diary.

He clenched his pen. Not a thing. Just Richard passing him a message he couldn't remember. Nothing but "green cockatoo."

The black form burgeoning beyond the foot of the bed again. Wide resounding eyes. Rising there and slowly parading in naked pageant around the room. And the dragon risen. Karim nodding, smiling, as if this room were part of the Magic Carpet now. Smiling, bowing . . . dissolved.

York stared. The aura pervading the room, a shimmer. He fell back. Desperate for something to straighten his beleaguered brain. Suddenly out of bed, rummaging through his valise. There it was, the file with his essay and dust jacket. Reading—

> What I have tried to show is that our current national literature is not a literature of love, nor celebration, nor heart. It is a willed literature of people on the make. Secular suc-

> cess is the engine. Social status the goal. Snobbery the hidden key—the snobbery of a people who vehemently claim to be antisnob. . . .

That's what it said. He stared at it. And the dust jacket. His new book: three years of work, ten years of rant.

> YORK MACKENZIE is one of Canada's most fearless and controversial new spokesmen. His 1968 first novel, *Media Madhouse* . . .

He turned, walked to the wastebasket, and dropped the whole file in.

> *It's Wednesday now,* (date?)—10:46 a.m.
>
> Dreamed of John again. John rising naked from the Magic Carpet! That freckled light skin, smoky eyes. John in majesty, smiling, bowing. John's dragon wasn't a dragon, but a red hammer. And Kebir bursting into the room, shouting at me, "Don't move or you're dead!"
>
> Last night thought I'd have to flee Morocco. Virtual nervous collapse. I still feel half drugged, half nuts, half fevered, & half growing, despite myself.
>
> Hoped Keb would come by last night. Where *is* he? With someone?
>
> At least I managed to keep out the golden horde this morning. Promised to join them for lunch.

And yes, shortly after noon they were assembled on the patio outside Claude's room: Claude in full regalia, Bertrand and ominous macaw, York, Richard and the English couple. They were suddenly all friends, the foreshortened friendships of tourism. At least Rebecca was no longer in tweed. In fact, in a startling ensemble of silk and gauze: half Morocco and half Edith Sitwell, as Richard observed, managing to make it sound like a compliment. Though not even Richard could cope with her hat—an enormous machine of straw and what appeared to be picture wire hung with strawberries. "Bloomsbury on a fête galante," as Herbert remarked.

The conversation was brilliant. Led by Rebecca herself, who was clearly something of a horticultural expert. She had found some rare species of cactus in Khalid's garden, which they all had to go and view. An elongated carbuncular thing; Bertrand in a quick aside thought it might prove advantageous as a dildo. Even Herbert revealed an avuncular wit—which till then, Claude noted, had been "heroically concealed."

York followed little of it. Just sat as far in the shade as he could, looking forward to dinner at Kebir's. What would it be like? And for the rest, York sat staring at the assembled Hôtel des Amis. He was trying to reconcile their celebratory brio, with the suspicion that they were life's rejects, modern versions of remittance men, when Rebecca erupted in his direction. "But you *must* regale us with your Sahara odyssey, dear boy!" Herbert adding, "Yes, we hear it was one of a kind!"

Fortunately Richard intervened. "York hasn't really assimilated it yet. An impasse of imagery, if you see what I mean. But give him another day or so and we'll all be dazzled."

York nodded gratefully—an "impasse of imagery," to say the least. And Rebecca turned her attention to Bertrand. What *was* that curious bracelet he was wearing? Silver wrist bracelet with small gold balls dangling from it. "But they're not balls," Rebecca trilled, leaning over to look, "they're skulls!" Yes, miniature skulls, golden skulls. "Has them made right here in Marrakech," Richard noted with pride. "But why skulls?" Rebecca asked. "Mementos of successful loves," Claude replied. Which Rebecca thought a splendid joke, if a trifle macabre. "For Bertrand," Claude added, "a successful love ends in one of three ways: the beloved has a nervous breakdown, gets clapped in a madhouse, or commits suicide." Renewed hilarity.

Bertrand himself adoring the attention, his tongue darting in and out as each skull was discussed. A long juicy tongue. Keerrist, I'm on to tongues now, York thought. Tongues, hands, lips . . . where would it end? Seeing the dragon again, teapot and tray and majestic black body parading again in the rising flesh. A sighting, but it felt more like holocaust. To see the dragon was to see their entire trip. And York could neither discuss that, nor rid himself of it.

York was ready to excuse himself and retreat to the calm of his room. His escape was stopped by the arrival of a desiccated figure in a buttercup-yellow suit, perforated polychromatic shoes and a carved bamboo cane. Face from an Egyptian tomb, a mop of auburn hair streaked with fiery red. Claude rose grandly to make the presentation. York didn't catch the name, just the fact that this was another Canadian—from Montreal. A clothing and costume designer. Had once done some costumes for Balanchine. Conversation swirled on. York trying to digest this apparition: Resident in Marrakech for years now, but definitely a fellow countryman. In York's addled mind they simply didn't make Canadians like this. Including the wig the man was wearing. Somehow the whole thing disturbed him almost as much as Bertrand's skulls. An impression confirmed when the man leaped over and wheezed. "I understand you had a very special trip into the mountains—big fat cocks!" York froze. And when a moment later he took York's hand and said, "We're all hoping you'll settle in at the hotel, become a permanent resident," York exploded. "I'm not looking for a death sentence!" And fled to his room.

> *Mid-afternoon* abed. The only safe place in all Marrakech. An ongoing Mad Hatter's tea party, that's what this hotel is.
>
> Rebecca & Herbert, I conclude, are volubly normal. She now refers to us as "you boys."
>
> But that Canadian: a terminal freak show! That's when it hit home. *Am I going gay?* What's to prevent it? Be better to cut my cock right off; right now.

The mere thought made York sit up. It would never do to cut off his oracle. Find some other solution. Immediately.

> R. was just being kind—but he's right! I *am* at an impasse. Can't remember half of what happened.

> Can't cope with the Magic Carpet. The majesty of that young Moroccan—breathtaking. Soul-taking!

He examined his notes. Clearly le tout Hôtel was frightening him into lucidity.

> I've lived the mad odyssey. Received the love of a woman, & of a man.
>
> CHRISTINE: Loved me absolutely. Maybe *that's* why she wanted to murder me. Fulfillment of her love was psychic murder.
>
> & JOHN: Something perverted, no? Inversion-perversion? Yes, must admit this. Some weird desire to cause pain. Like the time he spilled boiling water on my leg by accident. Said he was sorry, then laughed! Yes, but he left everything to live our life.

He dropped his pen, discouraged. Such notes lucid, maybe—but so little for the heart. Like his books.

Suddenly filching in his valise. The photos of Osprey Cove, that's what he was after: John's photos of their beloved cove. And the fisher folk who had adopted them. Spreading the pictures over the bed. There she was, all gussied up in Sally Ann uniform: Katherine Snook—the mighty "Ma Snook," as she was called by all the village—standing at the podium in the Citadel, her words belting out. "Ye got ter pray to our Lord or ye'll rot!" And another photo of Mariam, feisty Mariam, holding a basket of fresh berries; must've been the day they all went berry picking. Because there was Sadie with her basket, too, and the little Snooks. And a picture of old Jim in his battered leather hat. "Fixin' up wit' a lobster pot," as he said.

And as he shuffled through the photos he wondered why he hadn't looked at them sooner. Because something about the cove had entered his heart as no other place in the world. Wild, austere joy of Osprey Cove and its folk, tumbling down the coast of Newfoundland to a windy ocean. Giving lair to John and York. How could he forget?

* * *

By seven o'clock Claude was pounding at the door, storming over the end of the bed. "Why did you spurn our luncheon party? Just pull yourself together! Half the town is pursuing your Kebir, and all you do is sleep." And shortly York was dumping down the stairs, Claude expostulating behind. "Do you realize Kebir is faithful? He comes or leaves a message every day!" Claude arrayed in lunar blue for the evening's occasion: blue kimono, pantaloons and sash. Ushering York toward a battered little Deux Chevaux, whose door half fell off as York stumbled in. "Here, hold it with this!" Claude handed him a rope with a noose at the end. "Put it around the handle and hold tight." York desperately holding the door shut as they clattered away from the hotel, toward the mall. Claude fierce over the steering wheel, goatee thrust forward, gesticulating at all in his way. "Idiots—they're as stupid as their donkeys!"

And as they swung into the mall, and on around the busy traffic circle, York's door kept threatening to fly open, rope or no rope. Claude suddenly leaning over. "And what were you really doing two nights ago?"

York couldn't remember, clutching the rope and door handle for dear life.

"You refused to stay and talk with me." Claude honked loud at an errant calèche. "Went racing out the gate like a banshee! Didn't come back till *very* late."

York realizing that was the night of the Magic Carpet. Mustn't talk about that. The door handle had just fallen off.

"I told you, use the rope!" Claude leaning over, wrapping rope around flapping doorpost. "And next morning when I was telling my exquisite story of the stabbing, you weren't even watching." He finished tying the door with one hand, navigating wildly with the other. "Your mind was on something else."

"Claude! For chrissake, slow down, this door will fly right off."

Claude swerved again, scattering a huddle of pedestrians. "Your eyes were transfixed!"

"When?" York determined to avoid discussion of the Carpet.

"At our session, yesterday morning." Claude slowed the car. But York remained silent. Claude jerked left; York's door fell open. Claude reaching across to yank it shut, foot on the accelerator . . . *zooom!* York's jaw still clenched shut.

"Ah, so be it. Some are afraid of Morocco." Another swerve of the car.

And suddenly York was talking; talking of the Magic Carpet, the teapot. "I tell you, he was standing stark naked with a magnificent tray."

Claude slowing the car as soon as York started, driving at a comfortable crawl now, the Koutoubia rising majestically before them.

"It was the rug in the shop. I heard it talking, like a drug on my eyes. I—" York stopped short. But Claude speeding ahead, swerving past a clutch of bicycles. And York clutching the flapping door. "He invited me home for tea. And the rug in his home was the same. Like a sleeping dragon."

"Dragon? You mean the design?"

"No, it *felt* like a dragon. Inside the rug."

Claude eyeing York dubiously. "The gentleman standing in front of you, *naked?*"

The car at a crawl now, ambling through the Djema-el-Fna. Music of the last snake charmers winding through the window. Memory of "homo . . . homo!" winding out of York with his story. "The rug, the teapot, they all had the same sound as Karim."

"Sound of a *teapot?*" Claude swerving abruptly to avoid a donkey cart. Door heaving open.

"Claude, please! Yes, Karim had a definite sound, like his hard-on."

"Ahhh."

"He stood there with an immense hard-on, right under the tray with the teapot."

Claude tooting the horn. "Magnificent."

"Fiery, like the head of a dragon, rising out of the rug, out of Karim." York feeling idiotic, yet eager to finish now. "Do you understand? A dragon!"

"Sacré dieu, if you can't see the dragon in a fine hard-on, you can't see at all!"

York grateful someone understood. "And it was beautiful when he came."

Claude glaring at a passing beggar. "Tell me!"

"The sperm, shooting like white flowers onto his jet-black skin."

Claude honking furiously, pedestrians scattering.

"And he threw his head back and warbled, like a great night bird."

"A *large* penisss?"

"Gigantic, I told you."

"Very Moroccan; they've been influenced by their donkeys." Claude accelerated, his horn blasting the twilight, car careening through side streets, alleys, children. York clinging to his vagrant door. Claude gave a final honk, slowed to a kindly crawl. "Don't you understand?"

York shook his head.

"You saw an angel!"

Claude eyeing York as he would a doomed idiot. "You are one of the privileged." They were heading down another alleyway, in what was clearly a slum. "You've been here only a few days, yet you're blessed with one of the Angels of Marrakech!" Claude honking again, honking and zigzagging the car through the lane, scattering vendors, beggars, dogs. And York catching a glimpse of Claude, eyes glinting through half-shut lids, lips thrust out, rounded in satisfaction. Unmistakable—face of a man who has just drunk blood. York had seen such a face before, vampire face. He slumped back in his seat. Clutching the rope on the door. Bereaved of the Magic Carpet, of Karim, of what had passed between them. As if in telling the story he'd betrayed a secret, a trust, and sealed his own impasse.

When he next looked up they had stopped in a sudden open space. Sand, mud and garbage strewn everywhere. Cement blockhouses in the center like squalid barracks. This couldn't be where Kebir lived! But Claude already out, hands on hips, surveying the blockhouses. "It's that one." He bustled ahead, winding a path through refuse and the dark. York trailing in misery. Into the second of the buildings, up barren cement stairs. Like a barracks—or a prison. Claude talking with a young man at the head of the stairs, who pointed along the corridor to the end.

Claude knocked. The door opened a crack, then wider, to Kebir's proud smile. "Allah karim. Come in." Apartment closing around them like compartments of a ship. Tiny rooms, cubbyholes. Faces popping out at waist level, children's eager eyes.

Kebir ushered them to a door at the far end. Sweeping it open . . . to a small room, low divans, cushions and a worn rug. Seating them low around the single round table, under a swaying light bulb suspended from the ceiling. Claude sat with a flourish that acknowledged a palace in disguise. York's eyes averted, but couldn't avoid the light from that lonely bulb, revealing the room, declaring its poverty.

A small bunny-face bobbed around the door, was waved back by Kebir. The largest statement Kebir's smile. Claude finally commenting on the elegance of a cushion. Garish velveteen red, with splashy picture of the Koutoubia: "Bienvenu à Marrakech."

"But I have never seen one so raffiné." Claude plucking up the cushion, appraising it, passing it to York with sweep of hand. York wanting to weep, to smash Claude in the face.

A massive figure arrived in the doorway. Swathed in shawls, mantles, belts, gaudy cloth, layers upon layers of them. Standing behind Kebir, only her face revealed through the carnival of dress—warm face, large nose, heavy-lidded eyes. Ampler version of Kebir's face floating above him there, gazing with an imperturbable benevolence upon them. Claude rose in elegant salaam as Kebir moved to one side and Mother bundled into the room, down onto the teetering end of a divan. Everyone smiling, nodding, endless litany of Moroccan greetings.

Another Kebir-face appeared with tea tray, a teenage girl in worn burnoose. She placed tray on table and disappeared without a sound. Kebir contemplating the teapot of special occasion, freshly polished, embossed, stained and dented.

Claude nodded delight. "*Magnificent* today! The blue, I've rarely seen such blue. Canaletto blue, really." Claude's words flounced off the cement walls. "Of course, we have dear m'sieur York with us now. He's already part of the family of the Hôtel des Amis." Claude pirouetting a hand. Mother sat like a crowd, attentive to his words. "He is enjoying an impromptu vacation with us, a period of repose after completing yet another of his admirable books. Aren't you, my dear?" York nodded, grateful that Claude was filling a void—"But, he has a tendency to gallivant, an inclination to adventure. Off on the Magic Carpet; Ali Baba without the thieves." Mother nodded appreciation of such delicate information. Kebir smiled politely. While York sat in unexpected turmoil, half wondering if the eyes, the dragon head, might reappear here. But they did not, and he knew they never would again.

Claude paused in the after-ripple of his words. Rearranging himself on the divan, the long elegance of his body striking a pose like a scimitar. A little boy wriggled into the room at rug level, almost hidden off the end of the divan. He crouched there, staring at Claude as at a blue genie. York staring too. As if in York's innermost eye Claude had replaced the specter of Karim. And Kebir as well. Claude sitting as preening pageant within the echo of his words. His own Blue Angel now, social angel, filling and dazzling this squat cement room.

Kebir poured tea, a cascade of green-gold. The little boy passed the glasses. Mother sniffed the tea. Claude coddled his as if an exquisite brandy. York burned his fingers on his. From a window, music coiled in like hidden incense from the dark. And the little boy hid his leg because York had spotted it. Leg that twisted oddly at the knee, ending in a stump foot. Claude raised his glass, savored. "Ahh, mountain mint. From beyond l'Ourika, no?" Mother wobbled an appreciative chin. Kebir grinned, settled on the divan opposite York, nursing his glass. A serenity of silence inside the coiling music. York bumped into the little boy's glance, boy suddenly hiding his misshapen knee with both hands, his bowed head seeking benediction.

"But this abysmal heat wave is nearly over now. Our hottest September in nineteen years!" Claude's words drawing all to him. Mother nodded, accepted Claude's statement as significant. She solicitiously adjusted the third layer of her clothing, a glint of bright mauve peeping forth. At which Claude shifted slightly on the divan to expose the deeper blue of the pantaloons under his kimono. Mother blinked, revealing a layer of gold beneath the mauve. Another face in the doorway, another flickering Kebir-nose. "I see that Providence has blessed Kebir with many brothers and sisters." Claude tossed a smile at the hovering face. Kebir nodded proudly. "I have another brother, in the army, the tank corps." Mother turned up the palm of her hand as approval. Hand all painted in dots and lozenges. Sienna and ocher-red splashed around her fingers, across the open palm. In the wake of such largesse the little cripple was following York's smile across the floor, scrambling over to take up station between York's knees. At which Mother turned her other hand up, revealed messages of delight. "Alas, my friends, it's time for me to leave you." Claude rising to go. But Mother raised both hands, fingers flashing, as if bespeaking treasures yet to come. And Kebir said, "You will join us for bstilla?"

"Ahhh, bstilla!" Claude cried. "Such temptation! But alas, I have a rendezvous in the Djema-el-Fna." Claude embracing the room in a wide gesture of both arms. Bowing gracefully to Mother, picked his way to the door. Pausing only to eye Kebir en route. "You must care for our dear York. Show him le tout Marrakech. And escort him safely to the hotel!" Kebir nodded politely, his eyes imperceptibly elsewhere. Claude shot a wink at York and departed.

They sat for some moments after Claude's grand exit. Gradually the music filtered its way back. The soothing silence. And Kebir's eyes. . . .

Late the next afternoon, after dodging the hotel menagerie and checking the post office, York found himself wandering aimlessly down the boulevard. Found himself at the outdoor café across from the Koutoubia, seated as far from the sun as possible, guzzling banana milk shakes against the heat. Yes, had come to be near the Koutoubia. Something about the tower mesmerized York. Maybe it was the sky, the swallows dizzying around its upper reaches, and its colors, endlessly changing with the sun. . . . And as he gazed, found himself writing.

> It was Mother who was the monument last night, catching the flicker of colors with her every breath. She was so serene, almost mockingly aware there was no need for words. As if waiting for the last echo of Claude's words to die after his departure. Then Kebir disappeared. And Mother moved her hands again. The room tilting toward her painted hands, a spangle of reflections. And Keb back bearing a rug, slowly unrolling it across the floor in a splash of colors. All eyes & breathing swam to meet the rug. Little brother eyeing me to see if I felt the honor—the rug of honor for their guest.

York sat back. An evening of transformations. Later Kebir's father had turned up, in time for supper. A small, vibrant man with one ear missing. York kept thinking he'd seen him somewhere before. But then the silence had turned to chatter. Father said the Glaoui was the real hero of the south. A Berber, like their own family. The Arabs being the money men of Morocco, and the Berbers the farmers, the folk, and the warriors.

> Yes, when Father popped up, the brighter colors of the rug starting to jig and dance. Then Father flicked an eye to Mother, & Mother to Kebir. And Keb disappeared again. The little boy so excited he was clutching my leg. And Keb returned bearing a platter. All eyes turned & followed the platter to the table, and everyone nodding as Father said, "Bstilla." I felt the same, sudden honor, as when the rug was brought as Father served the bstilla. "A pie made from pigeons," he said. "My friend brought them fresh-killed yesterday." And everyone seemed to bow to pie as Father intoned, "Bismillah . . . bismillah."

He paused, ordered another milk shake. And gazed across at the Koutoubia swaying with the sky.

> The bstilla itself was part of the majesty of Marrakech. All talk ceased. And before I knew it, it was done. Father gone in a final salute. "We receive you as our son." And Mother dissolving from the room in a final flotilla of robes & color.

As if to see Kebir and family at their dinner was to see the Koutoubia before him, part of the same millennial mystery.

> After, Keb and I sat alone, listening to music on a small cassette. No need to talk, the room so beautiful. Electric light doused, two candles on. The Magic Carpet was back; that's what I felt.

And later they had walked to York's room at the hotel. Talked awhile. Though Keb wouldn't say much about the trip; just that Tony and James had been unwise, and that he'd known there was trouble from the moment James made his speech about the Glaoui, in that restaurant in Ouarzazate. From that time on he'd kept a double watch.

> He said even less about our time in the Sahara, except James was wrong to dance with that religious group. I asked, "Was James in the car with us, coming back?" Keb just nodded, wouldn't say any more.
>
> Toward midnight we ended up abed, naked. But each time I got a hard-on I'd see that face—Claude's vampire face in the car as he drove me, demonic. Evil Eye? In effect, C *stole* an orgasm from Keb & me

He abruptly stood up, bowed to the Koutoubia and hurried off down the street in the slanting sun. But after fifteen minutes of stumbling down honking streets, he still hadn't fully absorbed the evening with Kebir and his family. A shoeshine boy flagging him down; did he want a shine? Why not? And as he sat on the wooden box, watching his dismal shoes brighten, it struck him. The little man down near the café, with his entire shoe-repair store spread across the sidewalk, little man with one ear—was Kebir's father! That's why his face had been familiar. He overpaid the shoe-repair boy wildly, and fled down the street. Bursting through the gates to the hotel garden. "Nobility! Nobility!"

That evening Richard, Claude and York were rolling down the boulevard in the Deux Chevaux. "Adventure in the Medina by starlight!" That's what Claude had said. At least he was driving more carefully this time.

When they reached the market, Claude led them to an outdoor café that jutted over the street. Bertrand and an enormous black boy were already there, awaiting their arrival. Claude stationed Richard beside York and promptly ordered a bottle of rosé. Another dark boy cast up and sat beside him, as if his rightful place. Claude barely deigned to see him; too busy scanning the open square, like a hawk for passing prey.

Yes, it was a splendid spot for observation: the entire market square unfolding before them. The veranda of the café full—young Moroccan lads and tourists, almost all men. Including a table of macho beer drinkers who were celebrating the night. But York registered little of this, caught in another of his sightings—Kebir naked, Keb walking toward him from a burning window. York remembered; it was here they had come, after the cubicle in the little hotel. Yes, had ended at this very café with

James and made final arrangements for their "jaunt into the mountains." James would research the Glaoui, the Colonel would "find specimens."

Suddenly Claude was introducing a trio of Englishmen from the next table. A Dr. John Russell, little bantam cock of a man in his sixties. And his cronies, one always prodding his nose, the other with a memorable ass. A beautiful Moroccan boy with them. The doctor smiled sweetly as York was introduced. "So pleased to meet you, dear. We've heard it's your maiden voyage to marvelous Morocco!" York nodded. Clearly the doctor was an old acquaintance of Claude and Richard. Soon both groups had drawn their tables together and were gossiping at an enormous rate over more wine. Till the doctor turned to York. "And just what has captivated you the most? You know: the advantage of fresh eyes in foreign parts." York took the question seriously, pondering.

"I think it's their majesty. They do the smallest things with such grace. Like tea. They make it into a ceremony, a ritual. . . ." York sitting and eyeing the Koutoubia across the square as he pronounced this. It was the evening at Kebir's home he was seeing now.

"But they're so squalid, really. Such dirt and poverty!" The little doctor grinning at his two companions.

York was determined. "No, there's a nobility that transcends any of that."

"Precisely," Richard said.

"Oh, tut, their only majesty is in their hard-ons, though that"—the doctor smiled—"is of international quality. After all, pretty boyos are the biggest single industry in the whole of Morocco."

York stared at the doctor, who seemed delighted with himself. While Claude tried to divert attention to the macho table two down, the doctor leaned over and tapped York affectionately on the arm. "Do tell us about your trip into the mountains. It's the talk of Marrakech, you know."

York squirmed.

"Oh, come now, don't be so shy, darling; *everyone* knows about it. You took that lovely tall boy as your guide. Now please tell me, just what *was* James doing in Zagora? That extraordinary episode downstairs."

Richard was trying to silence the doctor, but he went right on. "Automatic jail sentence, you know; group sex is definitely taboo here. Not to mention a fling at S and M." York sat aghast. Claude telling the doctor it was merely hearsay, but the man was bouncing gleefully in his chair. "James was looking for it; yes, *looking* for it! We've all known that since the little incident in Goulimine, four years ago. . . . Come now, what happened in M'hamid? No one's seen James since! What do you—"

The explosion came two tables away. The macho table: tourists and Moroccans in melee. Knives, chairs flying into the street. And a brawny tourist crashing their table over, cursing in English and hitting out. Striking Richard in the face. And abruptly possessed by gods not his own, York was up and shouting. Smashing at the tourist with a bottle, goddamn tourist hitting Richard like that! Two more bodies thrashing across their capsized table, chairs. York clouting another flying body, and now at the little doctor. His arms windmilling. His face ecstatic as he roared, "Bismillah! Bismillah!" And joined the Moroccans, battering away at any tourists he could reach. A big one behind him, arm raised with a broken table leg as cudgel, aiming a lethal blow at York's bobbing skull. But before it could descend, the patron of the café had turned a large fire extinguisher on the group. Dousing York, the man with the cudgel, and several groaning figures on the floor. Claude had retreated inside the restaurant for a clearer view of proceedings. While the little doctor, drenched in wine, danced up and down in glee, shouting, "Bravo, bravo!" And York, spluttering and gagging from the extinguisher, abandoned the scene.

There was an impatient knock at his door. Breakfast? But it was nearly eleven, he'd slept late again. The door swung open: Claude in his original garb—yellow robe, shawl, white pantaloons. Billowing into the room, glaring at York. "You were on the Magic Carpet *again* last night!" No, no. York plopped back into bed. "But you disappeared." York admitted he'd fled the garrulous little doctor, the brawl and, for that matter, Claude.

"Well, yes, he *is* the worst gossip; tongue like an adder. But better to keep him on your side, it's less damaging." Claude installed himself in the chair. "I will say, my dear, you were a splendor during the brawl. A true fighting dervish! But didn't you realize, you were waging war against your fellow tourists!"

"I'm not a tourist."

Claude doodled a foot, nodding. "You mean you're already a faithful Marrakshi: an apprentice sultan, bellowing your own Moroccan battle cry."

York sputtered.

"But you should be more cautious; you easily could have been killed. There were several knife wounds, and one of the tourists was taken to the hospital. Besides, you have more the air of a human sacrifice than a hero." Claude smiled sweetly.

York propped himself up. "What was that little doctor saying about James? Something about not being seen since our trip?"

"Oo-la-la, you mustn't take the dear man seriously. He was just baiting you. He did say you make a charming Sir Galahad, albeit in reverse. He and his friends—"

York lunged out of bed, shouting. "I don't give a sweet fuck what people like that say about anything! They take something beautiful and turn it into shit. They . . ." York bellowing around the room like a stuck bull. "They take the best music we have and turn it into cheap disco. The same as they do with sex—turn a symphony into a fucking caterwaul!" Claude laughing, but York shaking his fist. "They trade God for cock, and then we all lose both!"

He lunged back into bed.

"Never underestimate the little doctor, my dear. He's seen you with Kebir, and he's been chasing that one for years. Wanted to know how you hooked him."

"Hooked? Kebir?"

"Of course. If Kebir's not an Angel of Marrakech, he's certainly one of the seraphs." Claude doodling his foot lazily.

"Keb? He wouldn't play that doctor's shitty game. He's not—"

Claude tapped his foot. "He's not gay, you mean."

"No, he's *not* gay!"

"What is he, then?" Claude purred.

"He's—"

"He's like you, is that what you mean?" Claude purring his words. "And *you're* not gay, of course not; you're simply what the doctor says."

"Which is?" York shut his eyes, seething.

"One more self-deceiving cocksucker, posing as Galahad to titillate yourself."

York stared up bleakly. "Claude, I've never been part of the gay world. I know nothing about it. And I certainly don't understand the Hôtel des Amis, let alone someone like that doctor."

"We're just a gaggle of bitchy gays, is that it?"

"I didn't say that."

"What are we, then?" Claude doodling his foot again, a leisurely figure eight.

"I damned well don't know! Some combination of demonism, genius and utter debauch."

"Thank you, dear friend, for your splendid tolerance." Claude smiled. "Beware of the good Dr. Russell. He's one of the Marrakech regulars, like Tony and dear James. Comes every year, knows everyone and spreads the most vicious lies about us all." As if finishing some mission of mercy.

York groaned.

"Now, if you'll just shed that air of living sacrifice and tell me where you went last night . . ."

"Where was I?"

"Yes—*where?* After your holy war in the café we were worried you'd been hurt. Couldn't find you anywhere."

York pondered. "If you really must know, I went and sat with the Koutoubia."

"*With* the Koutoubia?"

"In front of it. Cross-legged. We were talking."

"But *who* was? Who went with you?"

"I was talking with the tower."

York remembering clearly now. Yes, he'd fled the café, the fight, the little doctor's taunting words. Fled pell-mell across the market, to come to earth in front of the tower. And then sat, gazing at the Koutoubia as if it had always been part of him. And suddenly floating up in front of the tower—a rug. Someone unfurling a rug. Kebir and his family, floating in front of the tower, having tea. Yes, Mother sitting as majestically as the Koutoubia itself. Father squatting on his haunches, chattering away. And little brother with his maimed leg. "We receive you as our son." Words he could hear distinctly, followed by—

"And what did the Koutoubia have to say?" Claude leaning forward.

"That's our business!" York vehement; then, seeing Claude's disappointment, "But it ended by telling me, 'Women, boys, rugs. . . . There will be music, too, and dancing.' " York irate at having revealed even this much. "I then rose, bowed and strolled home. And yes, I was propositioned on the way. A fine boyo; a 'pretty' boyo, to quote the unspeakable doctor. I gave him twenty dirhams and sent him home to bed. There, are you satisfied?"

Claude sat back, chuckling. "I do like you when you're angry, York."

"Why?"

"You lose some of your celestial smugness. In fact, you become almost human."

York looked up, but Claude was sitting curiously still now, huddled inside his shawl as if chilly.

"Something wrong?"

Claude shuffled a foot on the floor. "Don't you see how ludicrously unfair it all is! Here you bumble your way to Marrakech, all wide-eyed and stupid. And"—Claude twining and untwining his bony fingers—"and everything just happens for you."

York did not understand.

"You are a completely unadventurous soul. You quail at a teapot, yet adventures explode all around you, accost you, make off with you—in spite of yourself." He contemplated his own words ruefully. "You soar into the Thousand and One Nights without even noticing you've left home. Moreover, you are escorted like a pasha—by someone you meet by chance, who forthwith becomes your deeply devoted friend." Claude rolled his eyes, nodding. "What's more, you emerge from a cascade of the most delectable dangers, unaware there even were any!" He plucked his goatee unhappily, as York tried to protest. "Look, you don't even have to find a Kebir—*he* finds you! And several of us have been chasing him for months."

York sat up.

"And then one night, because you happen to miss your Kebir for an hour, you wind up, presto, on the Magic Carpet. But you don't have to chase that, either; it comes looking for you and invites you home for tea. And there again, presto"—Claude snapped his fingers—"one of the Angels of Marrakech is before you, dragon and all at your bidding."

"It wasn't my bidding! I was—"

"Or you cast up at our hotel, the inner center of the Marrakech cognoscenti. The one place where someone who's been through all this could be truly understood."

"Are you saying—"

"We have *all* watched over you, night and day—though you never once realized it. Did you know that on one of your trips to the Mirador, Khalid sent his boy to keep watch?"

"What the hell for?"

"Ahh . . . people have soared like birds from the top of the Mirador." Claude paused, hunched inside the shawl. "And then when a fight breaks out at the Café du Glacier—violà, you become Richard Coeur de Lion, no? And we all adore it. And then you drift off absentmindedly to the Koutoubia for a little chat."

York shook his head. "But what's wrong with that?"

"What's wrong? What's *wrong? I've never done that,* don't you see? And I should have! That's Morocco; that's what Morocco *asks* of us!" Claude pulled his shawl tighter. "I simply don't understand. "I've lived in Marrakech over four years. I quest for Angels, but all I end up with is onions. That's what's wrong. And that onion stole my wallet last night, during the fight." Claude paused. "Three wallets since I came here . . . and one passport. And that is the reward for all *my* adventures of light and ecstasy." Gone his Merlin look, his Mad Hatter air. Gone the shimmer and dance that was Claude. And what York beheld was big sad eyes, a tattered goatee and a balding head.

York about to reach out, but suddenly Claude was up, wafting around the room, shawl whirling, in one of his finest pirouettes. Claude in full swoop again, as if all Marrakech dangling from his fingertips. "You see, dear friend, I know your secrets!"

Secrets? Kee-rrist. "Look, Claude, I have no secrets. And this picture of me walking across a mine field picking daisies—that's not what's going on! The truth is, I'm at a total fucking impasse!"

Claude bowed.

"I can't figure out *what's* happening. Anywhere in my life. I came here to sort things out, and it's only made them worse. Ten times worse!"

"Ahh—you see, dear friend, Morocco breaks down the barriers."

"Breaks down my mind, you mean. I feel like a truck that's stuck in the snow, and my tires keep spinning. All gas and no traction."

"How very Canadian." He paused, his eyes piercing York. "But I suspect I have the solution to your impasse—right here!"

Claude performed another pirouette around the room and, reaching into his blouse, whipped out a large brown envelope. "As I said . . . I know your secrets, dear friend!" Claude whirling to a halt by York's feet, dropping the envelope on his knees.

York stared at it. "Where did you get this?"

Claude smiled. "You were expecting important mail; we all knew that. So this morning I asked at general delivery again."

York watching the envelope as if it must bite. "But how did you get it? Didn't you need my passport?"

Claude shook his head at such naïveté. "I know the boys there. They'll get anything I wish, for a consideration."

York still watching the envelope, untouched on his knees.

"What are you afraid of?" Claude eyeing York like a hawk. "You'd think your life depended on this letter."

York finally plucked it up, pried the brown envelope open, peered at the smaller one inside. Claude leaned forward, peering too. York turned the brown envelope upside down, the white one swooping out like a gull to his lap. White envelope with a bright sun painted across one end, and flowers. The scrawl of green ink so familiar. "Good news!" Claude grinned.

York opened this second envelope, unfolded the pages. A sunflower exploding across the first, sunflower in red, green, gold. He laughed nervously.

"I told you it was good news!" Claude on tiptoe, pointing. York nodded. Claude was right: a chain of flowering phalli drawn up through the sunflower. And Claude executing a dance around the end of the bed. "I'm so glad. You had to have this!"

"What do you mean? You don't even know who it's from."

Claude paused. "I think I do!"

"Or what's in it."

Claude stood, hands on hips. "My dear friend, you treat us like absolute idiots! You've been waiting for this letter for days. That's what you've really been doing here! The whole hotel has known—ever since you went running out to the post office, the very first day you could walk. And checked at general delivery at least four times since."

"I didn't realize I was—"

"Khalid did; he had to give you your passport every time. And reported you must be expecting something important, you were so nervous. That's when we suspected the real situation."

"But I didn't know that myself."

Claude laughed. "Maybe you really *are* an innocent. But we knew. You had that Damocles look, even with Kebir. And it wasn't Marrakech or Kebir." Claude gazed at him searchingly. "Your mind was somewhere else, no?"

"My mind was right here, in this furnace of a city. What's left of it."

"Ahh, but you see, you were quite delirious when you first arrived. You were talking of someone called John."

York flinched, covering the letter.

"Precisely. Talking of John, and a flame-out, and a place called Osprey, no?"

"Osprey Cove."

"Yes. That's where your letter is from?"

York nodded.

"So I sat and listened. And all you talked of was this John. Though you've never mentioned him to us since. As if you've been hiding him, or hiding from him, no? And then we pieced it together, Richard and your devoted slave." Claude bowed with a flourish of shawl. "But Richard said not to mention it till you were stronger. And now there's no need."

York gaped. "I've been *here*—"

"Because of John." Claude grinned.

"—on a personal mission." York dubious at his own phrase. "On a quest, if you will."

"Perhaps. The holy fool; a good disguise for a sacrificed heart. But the truth is, your so-called quest involves a young man called John. Who has red hair, a flying zeb, and who holds you hostage.

"*That's* why you haven't been paying attention to Kebir lately.

Kebir is just a stopgap." York winced. "And it's been a life-or-death matter, despite what you think. Richard agrees about that. Or you wouldn't have done all the childish things you have. Wandering half crazy through the Medina at night, going off with the first pretty rug merchant you meet, confounding quick sex with Divine Service." York babbled protest, but Claude stamped his foot. "Conducting séances with moldy old buildings, attacking tourists."

York was stupefied.

"And not least, my dear Canadian, treating your distinguished friends at this hotel as if"—he bowed again—"they weren't worth knowing in the first place!" Claude chuckled. "But I must thank you on behalf of us. Just watching you, my dear. Like seeing a murder mystery unfold. All the elements, with only the exquisite corpse to come. Claude tilted his head, appraising York. "But why aren't you reading your letter?"

York glanced at the pages in his hand.

"You *must* read it! End of your beloved impasse, no?"

"I can't now."

"But you've been waiting for it. We've all been waiting for it! Hurry up, we're short of gossip."

They both laughed, but York's laugh hurt.

"Come now, dear friend, your sun has risen again—right there on the envelope."

Claude winked. "But what does that make Kebir?"

Silence.

"Maybe he's your moon. The other side of your universe."

York groaned. "How do I know what Keb is? And I'm here because I don't know what John is, either."

Claude bowed. "But now you do: he's a flying zeb, right there! And flying zebs are always good news!" And with that Claude danced out the door.

For a short while York rested, listening to the song: birds in the palm tree beyond his veranda. Get over the session with Claude. Every time he went to pick up the letter he heard his tumble of words. . . . He got up, tiptoed to the door, locked and bolted it. Had to cope with John's letter himself, without an audience thank-you.

Back in bed, he was about to start in when bloody murder broke out in the garden. When macaw had finally ceased, York was still holding the letter, wondering. Would it be song or murder? Inane question; Claude had already pointed out the sun, the flying flowers and zebs. "I told you it was good news!" But the truth was, he never knew with John; could never guess from one day to the next. *That* was why he was hiding in Marrakech; Claude had forced him to realize.

York had to admit it; he hadn't dared look at a single photo of John since he'd left. Barely looked at the pictures of Osprey Cove, because to remember the Cove was to remember John. He lifted the letter slowly.

> Ospreycove (*our* Cove!)
> Goofy Newfie,
> Tuesday, Sept. 7, '71
>
> Dearest Yo-yo—
>
> I've just finished playing "Greensleeves" on my clarinet. And am off to bed thinking of you. It seems that the old adage, "Absence makes the heart grow fonder," is true. Because every day you've been away I've grown fonder of you.

York closed his eyes—yes, it *was* the sun!

> I want to thank you for setting up evening meals for me at Mariam's. They've been a boon to me—keeping me on schedule and giving my days some center point to work from. As well as being a real delight in themselves. Mariam is incredible! It's a real joy just to sit in her home at dinner, night after night. And I ask myself why we never arranged to have our evening meals with her when we were together? I suppose we cherished them too much to ourselves to share them with others. And I think that is part of the heavy discipline we've been keeping. However, I hope that is done with now—and we can relax somewhat in our living.

One of John's flying flowers broke through the letter at this point. Sunflower starting at the lower edge of the page, climbing up the side of the letter, then surging across the typed words. York grinned.

> Mariam has been incredibly kind to me—feeding me, mothering me, brothering and sistering me. She has the potence of life. So many evenings I've gone there, tired and exhausted, bound (and bonded) to my writing. And left joyful, alert to the stars and wind and rain.

And Mariam's great pumpkin of a face and knowing little smile, as if lewdness could be holy. "Maid Mariam," they called her, all two hundred and more pounds of her. "An which o' yer tricks is yez up to t'day?" she'd shout out. And suddenly he saw it: that time just before his departure, Mariam and her clan gathered around the kitchen. And Mariam cleaning up, not seeing John sneaking in on all fours, right under the table. Sneaking up to her big fat ankle and giving it a quick bite. And Mariam stomping. "By the flamin' Divil, an' what's it be?" Mariam jumping back to look under the table. "An' it's Red Beard hisself . . . an' I'sll fix wit ya!" While everyone roared with laughter.

> And you will be happy to know that my clarinet sounds a lot fuller, crisper, less squeaky, just because of my time in Mariam's home. And we must get you a smaller accordion. An accordion you can play, and not one so big it plays you.

Another flying flower, a phallus, bursting across the page. And York seeing John's face, John's cheeks all puffed out, blowing on his clarinet. John nodding and swaying as he played, his eyes dancing across to York. Whenever they traveled in their little house trailer and were tired, John would say, "Time for the pipes, Yo-yo!" They'd stop and John would take out his clarinet—till his song turned wherever they'd landed into a garden. Like their little shack in Osprey Cove, rented after the winter had made the trailer too cold.

> I preface my days with a brief bird-walk. The Yellow Fellows are migrating now, and there's almost always one near Mariam's potato patch. A lot of species, too, but I avoid the Bird Guide, just trying to see the birds themselves. You'll want to know that the Sea Eagles are overhead most days now.

York smiled; for three years he'd been coaxing John out bird-watching. "Beauty flies into your eyes, John, with birds!" And now he'd won. This next year they'd do their book celebrating the yellow warbler. Follow its migration from Osprey Cove to Mexico and back; follow in their trailer, John doing the photos and York the text.

> My novel progresses well. I get about five pages a day. Next piece is the Yorkville section, my mother and Crustine, that whole horror scene! It's the bleak, black Protestant ethic for sure. Progress depends on my sanity, and that seems to grow as I work ahead. But I'll stop as soon as I see the hair on the palms of my hands. I'm committed to *not* working on the book when we're back together.

Something ominous in the fact that John was writing about Yorkville now. They had never talked about any of that, just buried it in its own pain. And now John was coping with it. That maniacal drive with John's mother. She'd been driving her car as if to smash it, immolate York. Shouting at him, "You're public enemy number one! Give me back my son!" But John had refused.

And "Crustine"—how long since he'd heard that name? Nickname his family had given her. "Crusty," they'd say. . . . Her face changing so unexpectedly from ice, dry ice to hope that day in the Penny Farthing. And as she drove Cedric away, he'd shouted, "Daddy, Daddy!" and thrown him the red ball to keep. York had never seen his son again. Christine applying for the court order the very next day.

York had tried to write about that and failed. But John said *he* damned well would. Said it the day after York was beaten up in a back alley in Yorkville. No one York knew, no pretext, just a savage, methodical thrashing. And John saying it was his own family; they'd warned him they would "have that man beaten impotent!" John had sworn right then and there to write it all. "I don't want others to go through what we have, Yo-yo, just to love!"

> This letter is short. I miss getting letters from you. And was grateful to get your card about the vacation in Mo-

rocco. I realize you don't write a letter unless it's an epistle, as you once said. Still.

If you do get as far as Marrakech (I found it on a school map here), send Ma Snook and Mariam a postcard of a camel. They'sll die a-marvelin' at it. Ma Snook says, "Tell that varmint York thet Hosprey Cuv hain't got no law ginst camels. But it might git shot fer a moose on a foggy night."

Yes, Ma Snook was impossible. Her English a modern version of Chaucer, her temper a national hazard. He could see her grabbing John by the ear and shouting, "You jes' tell that varmint Yark. . . ." He hadn't even sent a postcard to the Snooks, nor to Maid Mariam. Just one short letter, a couple of cards to John from London. In fact, barely thought of Osprey Cove at all. Why? Osprey Cove was their real home now, the Snooks their family.

That's all for now, you old yo-Yo!

Except that I think of you often, that your spirit permeates the air wherever I go in the Cove, and especially at Mariam's, and in our hanging flower garden here in the trailer.

Except that I love you, and I keep on loving you, and I will love you as long as I live (for if I stop it's sure death anyways).

Except that I see how not having completed my Mexinovel has held me up in my affections for you, Yorklove.

Except that I can see clearly in myself days that will be lived around birds and walks and flowers. Rather than around books and trips and ego and sex.

Except that I still want you, after over four years together. And learn to want you more, and more joyfully, and more sanely, each day.

Except that—I know you love me, and it gives richness and fullness and peace to almost every moment of my day—

is all,
Love,

thyJohn

He set the letter down and lay gazing at the huge sunflower drawn beside John's signature. Sunflower cavorting up the body of the letter in green and gold, its head spreading across the top of the page . . . "Here comes the sun!" And the signature in green ink: "thyJohn." Always signed their letters that way: "thyJohn . . . thyYork."

He lay back, head reeling in joy. As if some immense weight passing from him, some debilitating weight. And the bird song from the garden spiraling in. As if it had ceased from the moment Claude had arrived—ceased, till the letter read and known. And the palm tree bursting into his eye again. Yes, a green cockatoo, as Richard had said. York chuckling—how kind the hotel had been, all les amis. And patient. Putting up with his nonsense, his glowering, his outbursts. He must tell them, thank them. How brilliant they truly were! And kiss Khalid, on both eyes. He clutched the letter, laughing. How could he have been so wrong about the Hôtel des Amis, le tout Hôtel? They were guilty of nothing but friendship and the desire to help.

And mind still spinning, he gazed at the letter, the splashes of yellow, green, red across the page. The flying zebs, like sudden cherubs. John, of Osprey Cove! And with that sat up again, reading the letter through from the beginning. The quiet joy of it from the start, the singing joy as he came to the long ending, almost a coda, like John on his clarinet. "I will love you as long as I live. . . ."

Suddenly he stopped, and wondered why. Till he looked again.

> I will love you as long as I live (for if I stop it's sure death anyways).

something about that line throwing York to a halt. Was it that John *knew?* It was certain death if they ceased their love? York had always known their lives were fully wagered. And had sensed John aware of it too. It was after a particularly long fuck. And John smiling, prancing around the trailer, still naked. And playing on his clarinet. But he had stopped in mid-note, saying, "If you ever leave me, Yo-yo, *I'll kill you!* D'you understand? *Kill you!*" York had understood; hadn't been able to get an erection for days after, still avoiding John's eyes. But that was only negative proof, and sinister somehow. Now John knew positively—their lives were staked to their love!

York fell back, joyous at the letter. And boggled by that line, almost a throwaway in the body of the letter. Worth coming to Marrakech for this letter. Worth coming just for that single line. Yes, York had always sensed he'd come for reasons deeper than vacation or sun. And that's what Claude had said; he was here to wait for this letter.

For a moment he lay clutching it. Crazed by joy, as he pondered his entire time in Morocco. The madhouse of Marrakech . . . sure death *here,* come to think of it. Claude had said that too. "It's a life-or-death matter!" Yes, York wandering oblivious through danger; death lurking in the mountains, the desert. Now, with John's letter in hand, he knew how true it was. Death all around him, ever since his careening arrival.

Death riding the car with the Colonel and James. In Zagora, the Sahara, M'hamid. He had sensed it so often—at the brink of a cliff, in the sands, at the edge of a dance of fire.

Like an aroma, the scent of flowers, death always present. A smile away, a knife away, the flick of a car wheel away. Palpable. The look on James's face—death by ecstasy, was that what he'd been seeking? And all but found?

And Tony's death when they drove the infernal valley. Tony's living death after the suicide of his lover. And his other death, out in that tent. "Don't ever become like us, York."

Or death whispering by in a walk through the Medina. A clap on your back, a knife through your lungs—meat for passing gossip.

Or simply the death of the mind in the oven of southern Morocco. Till you ran laughing into the sand, ripe for the ride to Timbuktu.

York urgent to catch it—death dancing daily, like sunbeams in Marrakech. Like the Hôtel des Amis. Parrots, wisdom, snakes and high laughter. Richard here to own his own death, and why not? And jettatore Claude whirling in a dance of life as dervish as any in M'hamid. Daily dance, magnifying life yet flirting with the elegant suicide of the soul. And Bertrand the Beautiful, a sordid wreck at twenty-five . . . here in Marrakech to finish the job? Hôtel des Amis as much a death as any moment on their mountain trip. Death their best protector, Richard's very credo.

Death for York Mackenzie, because of what he'd seen. And felt. How not? The Carpet, the Koutoubia in carnal trance, return of the gods, Pan, Christ, the battle joy of Galahad amok. Death as expiation! Blessed death, anyway.

He lunged up, grabbing for the letter—it had saved him from all that! And if his time in Morocco had been a dance of death, it was because he'd fled from John, fled their love. He laughed, churning laugh. And collapsed into merciful sleep.

10
JOHN OF OSPREY COVE

He was awakened by knocking. Two o'clock! He jumbled the litter of pages together as Khalid set the tray on the end of the bed. "You slept past breakfast, but I've brought you lunch. M'sieur Claude said you received good news." Khalid grinning toward the letter. Yes, thank you, it was good news. "Very good news?" Khalid sat down. Yes, very good news. Khalid grinned delight. "Does this mean you'll be leaving us?" Yes, it did. "That's not good news, m'sieur York." Khalid laughed. "But you'll be back." Silence. "So I can tell m'sieur Claude and m'sieur Richard that you are happy?"

"Khalid, please inform messieurs Claude and Richard, also m'sieur Bertrand, in fact, *le tout Hôtel*, that m'sieur York is in ecstasy!"

Khalid's eyes rotated with pleasure as he departed. York sat in bed, gazing at lunch and letter, chuckling—this hotel was definitely preposterous. He nibbled on the lunch, cold chicken and salad. But the letter—flowers and flying zebs twinkling up from the pages. And the sound of birds. Lunch, breakfast, whatever it was, would have to wait.

He picked up the letter again, skimming it. His finger tracing the signature, the wildflower surging up from "thyJohn." Like touching John's body, like touching his zeb, York's finger tracing from page to page, the names of Mariam and Ma Snook and all Osprey Cove, their voices singing from the letter. And suddenly over to his valise for the photos. John shoving them into his luggage at the last moment. "You might want to take a peek now and then, Yo-yo, 'cause we all loves ya!" He fished the envelope out and scurried back to bed. Pouring the photos over his knees.

There they were: the head of Farley peeping up, a giant smirk from Mariam, the sharp eyes of old Jim Snook, and a pony cantering across a beach of dories. Photos flaring an instant collage of Osprey Cove. Ma Snook at her front door, arm raised, brandishing a soup ladle like a truncheon. York chuckled, closed his eyes, not wanting to see it all at once. And heard them chattering and shouting—voices he had locked out these past two weeks, drowned in the din of Marrakech.

Eyes still shut, he reached for one of the pictures, opened a squint to see . . . who? Outrageous flamingo pink, with yellow trim—the home of Ma and Jim Snook. Perched at the foot of a glowering gray cliff. He could hear music from the radio floating out the open window, fiddle and accordion music, folk songs. "I like the accordeen," she'd say, clapping her hands in time. Daft little house, crouched amid the armies of potato plants, tomatoes, piles of manure. The Snookery: that's what they called it. Hearth of reigning elders of the clan.

York opened his eyes full. There she was, standing right at the front door. Ma Snook and her militant soup ladle. Standing and shouting, "I wants more space fer me flowirrrs!" Bellowing it out and waving her ladle. Must have been the morning John and York went to borrow Jim's dory for the day. And before they got to the door there was Ma, marching out and flailing her largest soup ladle. "I wants more space fer me pretties!" And John quickly snapping a photo. "Ye kin plant yer 'taties up past t'creek some!" Grabbing Jim's shovel like a broadsword, she was banging a hole right through the old picket fence, rooting up rows of young potatoes. Jim shaking his head, his 'taties jilted like that. "Yeeess, an she's gone plum varmint agin. Cain't do nuttin wit her whin she's loike that." As Ma Snook hurled dirt and 'taties and fence up and out, till she had her flower seeds all planted. And when done, all sweet as a daisy, as if she'd just negotiated a small adjustment in life. Standing by the white and orange and pink picket fence, patting the plastic statuette of Snow White that stood atop the fence post. The statuettes of Donald Duck and Winston Churchill nearby. As Ma grinned a bit sheepishly, saying, "Well, an' I guess it be time to sarve a spot o' tea t'the lot of ye. C'mon in."

But John was jumping with laughter, snapping another photo and shouting, "Yer garden is a marvel, Ma Snook, sure an' it's a wonder of the world!" At which Ma brandished her shovel, retorting, "An' ye'll be a marvel when I fixes wit ya! I'sll jes stick ye roight up atop o' me fence, along wit milady 'ere." And with that she ducked behind the fence and came up hurling a clod of dung at the gang of them. Because by now her menfolk were standing around in silent support of Jim during the destruction of his beloved potato patch. Sammy Snook whispering to Jim, "Now look 'ere, Pa, I'sll jes give ya some of me own garden fer yer 'taties!" York secretly applauding her flower rampage, an act of genuine floral imperialism if ever there was one.

"An' it's *you* who's the marvel, Ma Snook!" York blurted aloud as he lay in bed with the letter. And reached down to pluck another picture. Saw the woebegone face, small black head bowed . . . Farley, their little mongrel Labrador looking so sad there, beside John's rocking chair, as if betrayed. Usually all cavorting and affection . . . adopted by the village, with food stations in all Snook homes and the butcher shop. "An' 'ere comes Farlee, John an' Yark will be followin' on." Farley had the rights of the Cove, including most of the bigger male dogs, who felt the little black dog was a succulent number.

But here was Farley, looking woeful and weighted down. Till York saw the white wings strung around her neck and started to laugh; the wings were Valentine cards! Valentine's Day, and Farley had gone off on her daily rounds in the Cove. Gone off a-visiting friends and allies, with no sense of anything out of the ordinary. Scurried home earlier than her wont, howling to be let in. And John upset as he rushed to the door to rescue her. Scuttled in all woebegone, trailing the white objects. As if she had tin cans tied to her tail; that bad. And John angry, till he calmed Farley down and got at the things around her neck. "Come and look, Yo-yo . . . *hurry!*" John stomping his feet in glee. Showing York the envelopes tied around Farley's neck. And inside each a Valentine's card. So John had given Farley a moose bone to solace her dignity and taken a quick photo. Then they'd sat down to read the cards.

All the rhymes and riddles and notes written in the peculiar Osprey Cove hand, nearly indecipherable. One from Ma and Jim Snook, with a note: "The two of you beter git on down here for a Valintine supper, or we'll cut yor doreys off!" A command invitation.

And one from Maid Mariam, a postcard of a giant red lobster with a big heart painted on. Which York felt was mostly for John. But John laughed, saying, "We'll share it anyway, Yo-yo!"

And one from Jed and Marie saying, "Your mitey odd neiburs and we love you, so never stop. xoxxo."

John chortling away, reading each one aloud, while Farley chomped on her windfall moose rib. And York sat between tears and laughter, sign of rare happiness. Because all the cards were addressed to "John and Yark" or "Yark and John" . . . the way the kids would chant each time they walked down along the beach to the Snookery. Daily chorale atop the waves, singing them home.

But most of the cards seemed to be from Ma Snook's granddaughters, Molly and Grace, a pair of pretty teenagers who played blithe tambourines each Sunday at the Citadel. Cove gossip said they were playing for John and York, because whenever John or York went up to the Mercy Seat to pray, Molly and Gracie would break into a special spangle of tambourine playing. And Mariam said, "Git ready fer a twin weddin' . . . 'cause Ma Snook is plannin' t'marry off Mally an Gracie t'John an' Yark!"

So that evening, when they went to Ma Snook's for the Valentine supper, John said, "But we couldn't marry both Molly and Gracie, Ma! That would be too greedy, like. We'sll just marry one of them between us, York and me."

"Marry jes t'one of 'em, ya say? Now that's a hard ticket!"

"Well," said John, "we'sll share her!"

There was a hush as Ma pondered this special offer. The assembled members of Snookdom awaiting her word. "Naw, thet'd be lean meat fer the poor girrl!"

"But Ma Snook . . ." John paused, clapping his hands. "That way she'll get twice as much, not half!" At which the Snook clan shouted in laughter, pushing Molly and Grace toward John. The two girls shrieking in mock alarm and fleeing Ma's kitchen as far as the door, hoping to be followed. Old Jim Snook restored order, saying his "wimminfolk was actin' up agin." And it wasn't till days later they realized that all the Valentine cards purporting to be from Molly and Grace were written in different hands. Probably by Mariam, and young Sammy Snook, and Jed. Didn't matter; York carefully kept them as joyous memory.

He gazed at the romp of photos—old Jim Snook! Jim, alias Pa Snook, standing outside the Snookery fishing shed, working his nets. Jim in his forever worn blue sweater with the flowers woven into it. And his forever leather peak cap. And forever cigarette butt dipping from his mouth. It never seemed to be lit; just there, like sweater and cap.

York held by those Celtic eyes now. Jim saying something, York leaning forward to hear. "I s'pose ye'll be comin' by tonight, la. It's our bach'lir night." Yes, their bachelor evening, a custom by now. The first had been nearly a year before, a few weeks after they'd arrived. York had dropped by the Snookery, found Jim alone. "Me wimminfolk 'as gone out gal'vantin'." Which meant that Ma Snook was out with one of the family, or down at Mae Hann's store. And Jim was "bidin' home," sitting in his rocking chair by the stove, his hat still on. John was gone to pick up a chunk of illegal moose from Ollie Crocker. So Jim and York had sat silent awhile, listening to the surf. Till Jim got up to poke at the wood stove. "I'sll jes ginger up t'kettle a mite la. Yeeess, an we'sll 'ave a cup o'tea." Jim seemed to drink tea anytime of the day or night. And padded around the kitchen, rinsing a pair of cups: special big cups with the King and Queen on them, King George V and Queen Mary. And fetched out the Gunpowder tea Ma Snook kept for special. And the sugar bowl with real cubes in it. Brushing the table clean with his huge hand and finding a few broken cookies in the pantry.

York watched him gather the monuments, watched him nurse the kettle and brew the Gunpowder in the newest of the old teapots. York had a package of cigarillos with him—his little cheapo cigarillos—to match the dignity of the occasion.

"Would you be mindin' a cigarillo, Jim?"

"Don't know as I could. Ain't niver smoked but cig'rettes, la." Jim pushing his cap back on his head. York got up and carried the cigarillos to Jim. Only a few feet away, but he wanted to carry them over and offer one. Jim looked at the package as he might at a strange bird. But took one and smelled it, then tucked it carefully behind his ear. Silence.

And when and York finally rose to leave, Jim said, "Yeeess, an' I guess ye'll be comin' back on bach'lir night next week?" York said yes, he'd like to.

And the second time he went, Jim just smiled and set up the

Gunpowder special again. Then went to his cubbyhole bedroom and came out holding the cigarillo from the week before. He held it for about half the tea. Then unwrapped its cellophane and slowly smoked it. And started talking about the early days in the Cove, before the road came in; only the boats.

After that York went every week on bachelor night. John would go off with Ma Snook, visiting, and York would bide with old Jim.

Then Jim would take his weekly cigarillo from storage behind his ear, feeling it over, warming it with scraggy fingers. And York stood up to light it for him, feeling so proud that Jim was going to smoke it at all. And for nearly an hour he nursed that little cigarillo, and they talked of "Hospree Cuv." How wandering fiddlers and pipers had been the only entertainment in the early days, coming in by boat once or twice a year. And the whole village became a "carneeval." And the "jannies"—mummers who went around during the twelve nights after Christmas. Villagers dressed up like transvestite ghosts. Mirth and the macabre. And Jim said, "Yeeess, ye niver knows when one on 'em hain't from t'far side of yonder, la." York could have listened all night.

And Jim looked content. "You and John loikes Hospree Cuv some good!"

"Like . . . ? We *love* the Cove, Jim!"

And that's when Jim had smiled his yearly smile. "Well, you an' yer John is livyeers now, I kin tell ye that fer sartin."

"An what's a livyeer, Jim?"

"Well, an' ye lives 'ere now."

Then silent as he finished his cigarillo. York knew it was time to go. And ran back to find John, to tell him, "We is livyeers now!" Because he and John had been worried. Had felt the villagers sizing them up over the past months, all thousand souls. Would they, or wouldn't they, be welcome to remain in the Cove? The villagers always friendly, of course. But if they didn't like you—you left! They'd seen it happen with one or two other visitors. The slow, silent pressure driving them away. . . . But now they were livyeers. And it was only a few weeks later that they'd gotten the Valentine cards.

York looked again at the photo. And laughed—old Jim tried to look so fierce. But always a covey of grandchildren scurrying around his rocking chair. They'd pretend to be afraid, and he'd growl, "I'se goin' t'wallop yer bottoms fer the lot o' yez!" And the kids would screech in delighted fear and press closer to his chair. His big gnarled hands would creep up and catch a child or three, and hold them tenderly.

York picked up the photo—heard Jim's voice, soft. "Ye'll be comin' back to the Cuv?" The very last day, when York was leaving Osprey Cove, he had gone to say good-bye to old Jim. And Jim made some tea, which was strange, because Ma Snook always did that when she was home. But Jim was doing the honors that day. While Sammy Snook tried to dump York out of his chair, saying, "Well, an' yer goin' t'play the swell in Londontown. . . . Hospree Cuv ain't grand enough fer ya!" Sammy laughing, poking his bluff affection at York. And little Jacob Snook was presenting John with a white kitten that John didn't want, " 'Cause we already got a cat, Jake, an' we calls him after yer family."

Jim had carried a big cup of Gunpowder tea over to York, "fer spicial." And York in gratitude took a big swig, which dumped him out of his chair spluttering! The tea hoarse in his throat, and all the Snooks stomping their feet in applause. Jim must have slipped half a cup of Screech into it. And when York recovered enough to glance over, old Jim was quietly rocking, pretending to pat Farley. But as soon as York looked over, he chuckled. "Jes t'tide yez over till the next time, Yark."

And suddenly the whole Snook clan was whirling all over York, and he got no further chance to speak with old Jim. Ma Snook chortling. "Give me greetin's t'the Queen an Prince Philip, la!" But York was upset; hadn't really said good-bye to Jim. And suddenly a hush, the other Snooks making way. There he was, Jim standing right beside the truck window, chewing hard on the remains of his cigarillo. York rolled the window down as fast as he could. Jim clamped his big gnarled hand on the window ledge as if to stop the truck. And practically shouted at York, "Ye'll be comin' back, then . . . back t'the Cuv!"

"Yes, I'sll be comin' back, Jim."

"Yeeess, an mind ye duz! 'Cause yez is a livyeer now, you an' yer John!" And with that Jim released the ledge and waved his boys back, because they were standing blocking the truck. And Ma was chasing grandchildren off the back, all wanting to come to the airport. John revved up with a final toot of the horn. And as the truck wheeled to leave, York saw old Jim. He was walking alone, down toward the surf, blowing hard on his nose with that big red polka-dot hankie.

"Yes an I'sll be back, Jim. . . . back to the Cove." But York wasn't in Osprey Cove, he was in bed, in Marrakech, amid the photos. The babble of pictures a babble of friends, relatives, family left behind in the Cove, like Christmas at the Snookery. A sudden knock at the door. Khalid? Claude? York slipped over to open. It was Bertrand, appraising York's underwear with a flickering glance as he entered. And then York abed as Bertrand stood in silhouette—classic Greek today, a blouse, simple leather belt, and baggy pants.

"I've just been . . . r-reading," York said, stammering, caught between Bertrand and Osprey Cove.

"I hear you have good news!" Bertrand swaying slightly, one arm hidden. "That's why I came."

"Oh, great news. My letter finally arrived."

Bertrand moved closer to the bed, tongue flicking his lower lip. "You've been waiting so hard for that letter."

"Yes, I suppose 'hard.' It was very important."

"I understand. Some letters *are* a matter of life or death." Bertrand smiled, bracelet jingling on his arm. "May I sit?"

York nodded as Bertrand composed himself across the end of the bed. "I hope it raised your morale, and maybe more." York still nodding to himself. "Yes . . . sure death, anyway, if it hadn't come." Bertrand's eyes flicked like his tongue. "I brought my flute." Producing it from behind his back. "Just for you." And putting flute to lips, he lolled back, spilling a sudden serenade around the room. Caught in the sunlight, eyes fluttering, lips in love with his flute.

"I wanted to celebrate the news." Flute at his side now, eyes on York. Lips parted, leg moving closer. Gold skulls dangling like little berries; Bertrand's eyes on York. Suddenly York saw his own skull hanging there. And flinched.

Bertrand pulled back.

"Those photos—he sent them to you?"

"What? Oh, he gave them to me before I left." York's eyes diving back to the pictures. "Osprey Cove, where I live."

"You live *there?*" Bertrand eyeing the display of Snooks, old Jim, the Citadel. "Bizarre-looking people, aren't they?"

"I love them."

Silence. Bertrand recoiling off the end of the bed. "I just wanted to share my music." And departed.

He dived into the photos again, the first one touched a lifesaver. Who? The lieutenant, in full Salvation Army uniform, parading down the main line of Osprey Cove. And Sammy Snook right behind, carrying the army flag—Blood and Fire. Mariam waddling behind Sammy with the big Bible. And *boom-ka-boom*, Sadie on the bass drum. And a scurry of kids with tambourines . . . Molly and Gracie, and Jed's two. All so proud parading for Christ.

The very day John and York moved into the cottage next to Mariam's. In Skinner's Lane, one of the Snook lanes. "Snookville" it was called, some thirty various Snooks living there. The pink-and-yellow Snookery of Jim and Ma the headquarters. And *boom-ka-boom!* the sudden roll of a big bass drum in Skinner's Lane. A wild bugle note right off their front yard, John and York rushing to the window to see. It was the Sally Ann, in full brigade. The Lieutenant at the head, with portable loudspeakers. "Callin' all hands fer Christ!" And John and York rushed outside a-goggle, Farley following in a fit of barking. The three of them joining the parade, marching down Skinner's Lane, and on to the main road alongside Osprey Creek.

A bright and breezeless day it was, as their little band grew—more children, with several of the fishermen's wives bundling out to join up. As the Lieutenant bellowed out, "Callin' all soljers fer Christ!" And marching right on down to the docks, because it was the hour the fishermen came home. Loudspeaker booming at the fishermen. "Are ye comin' home to Christ . . . or is the Divil king in yer home?" But the fishermen weren't saying too much after a hard day out on the waves. Old Ned Crocker hiding a bottle of Screech under the seat of his dory. But most of them liked the young Lieutenant, because he was young and hardworking. Besides, some of their wives were standing right there, hollering along with the Lieutenant. "Are *you* comin' home to Christ?"

Ollie Snook getting cuffed by Barney Crocker for cussin' right in front of the Salvashun Harmee like that, the first of the fishermen clambered clear of his dory and came over to stand meekly beside his wife in the brigade. And the Lieutenant announced over the speaker, "I feel a new touch o' power comin' down, Lard!" And *booom-ka-boom,* Sadie on the big drum, the kids going wild on their tambourines. And Molly Snook rushed up and thrust a tambourine into York's hands. John leaping around and around the group with his camera, clicking with glee. And the Lieutenant roaring, "We wants pictures of Hospree Cuv fer Christ!" While several local trucks rattled up, Covers clambered up on their backs to sing, "Glory, glory, halleloo-yaah!" Till a good portion of Osprey Cove was standing right at the docks, the ocean rolling at their feet. "Gloree, gloree . . . hallelooo-yaaa!"

The gathered band marched jauntily back up the main lane. "Onward Christian so-o-o-ol-jers!" Back toward the Citadel perched on a knoll; sheep grazing, and Mariam's big ram.

"Gloree, gloree hallelooo-yah!" York floating amid song and drum, abed in the Hôtel des Amis. And seeing the kids he taught in Sunday School at the Citadel: little Jacob Snook, and Walt Crocker, Susie and others. "What *happens* in t'fiery furnace, Mister Yark?" And Susie didn't know why Shadrach, Meshak and Abednego didn't get all burned up quick.

The words booming up. "You've given the Lard yer song, yer dancin' . . . will ye give Him yer life?" The Lieutenant's words. Just before York left for London. And John had come, though he didn't tell York why at first. They got to the Citadel a bit late, as everyone was singing, "I've got gloree in my soul . . . gloree, gloree hallelooo-yyah!" Citadel shaking like the big bass drum, hands clapping, and all their folk and family singing to make old-time Methodists seem weak of lung. Mariam and Ma Snook right up there on the platform near the Lieutenant. And old Jim, who rarely turned up. And Aunt Glad in full regalia, Sally Ann bonnet with bulging bow and red-tabbed uniform, looking as if she were leading the Charge of the Light Brigade. "Gloree-gloree in my soul!" And Molly and Gracie Snook leading the jangle of tambourines right below. Aunt Glad's podium, right below the sign.

J E S U S
A
V
E
S

York watching the Covers celebrating God. And he and John joined in, rattling and banging their tambourines like lost Gypsies.

And by the time he'd gathered his wits it was Testimony Time. The Lieutenant stepping briskly forward. "Who has a testimony t'give t'Christ?" And there was a buzz of silence, because Testimony Time was *very* serious. Even kids held silent, even Hilary Snook and a little fuss passing through the Citadel, because Mariam Barnes was standing up. Mariam rarely gave testimony, because she said, "It scares t'pimples right onto me, iveryone lookin' at I like that." But there she was, standing foursquare, hands fidgeting. And starting in a small voice. "I ain't never seen our Lard. . . ." The Lieutenant nodded, and Mariam spoke up stronger—"No, I hain't niver seen Christ. But I's watchin' fer Him, 'cause He'sll come back one time, I knows it!" And Aunt Glad murmured, "Haa-lay-looya!" And Mariam saying, "An He'sll be takin' all on us to His home—yis, an' He will!" And for a moment Mariam just stood there, eyes closed, the Lieutenant saying, "Yes, an' Christ'll take us to His home." While Mae Hann burst into voice, "An' that's enough to make us sing. . . ." The entire Citadel jumping in to join her.

Several more gave testimony. Old Art Crocker, save his soul, announcing he was "givin' up wit' t'liquor like, 'cause Our Lard don't drink that I knows of." Mae Hann on her feet, in full song. "My sins are all forgiven, and I'm on my way to heaven!" The Citadel shaking with the voices. And Mate Barnes standing so he could play the accordion stronger, while the Lieutenant clapped hands in time.

And all of a sudden Aunt Glad just grabbed old Willie Hart and began stomping the platform. Skipping and hopping like a ballerina in a bonnet, face crinkled in joy. And Sadie coming in on the big army drum so hard, the plastic flowers near the Mercy

Seat were bouncing in their vases. And Mollie Harris, Ma Snook's mother, was on her feet clapping her hands, all ninety-three years of her. Till John was up and over, catching Ma and pulling her out on the platform by the Lieutenant, dancing the Glory Dance. While York sat shaking with happiness.

The dance done, Ma Snook puffed back to her seat, and John beside York again. "You've given the Lard yer song an' yer dancin'. . . . Will ye give Him yer life?" The Covers huddled quiet under the Lieutenant's raised arms. "Will ye give Him yer life?"

York huddled in his pew, knowing what had to be done. He put his tambourine to one side, surreptitiously checked that his fly was closed. On his feet, making his way forward. Almost calm once started. And under all those sharp eyes that'd spot a partridge in the gorse at a hundred feet. Those rabbit-sharp, moose-smart, osprey-honed eyes of the Cove. Especially the kids; they could spot a fake a mile away. As York proceeded forward, kneeling just to the right of the Mercy Seat. On the plain board floor, in front of the platform.

Serene in his terror. And just above his head on the podium, the three blank crosses, lace crosses stitched by Mariam, saying all there was to say. The whisked arrival of one, two other bodies beside him. He couldn't see who. And the Lieutenant's voice high overhead, on the platform. "Our brother Yark has come farward t'give himself. An now is the time fer all of us t'give 'im our prayers. He's goin' on a long trip across t'ocean. Pray he comes back t'Hospree Cuv." York hearing the words, stunned. And a voice behind him singing out, "Christ'll watch over Yark, he'sll watch over all on us, Christ will." Mae Hann and Sarah Ward burst into duet. "He touched me, Christ touched me, an' made me whole." Mae's high rolling song, and Sarah joining in. And York afraid, eyes clenched in tears suppressed for generations. He reached forward to clutch the ledge of the Mercy Seat.

And glancing up saw the toes, feet, with large square-head iron clouts beaten through, and blood barely congealed. Right above his head. Weight of that man hanging above him, nailed. The man's words roaring, as down a funnel of fresh wind of two thousand years, saying,

You are beautiful, my daughter, my son, my brother. . . .

Voice pounding as unhurried waves into York's ears.

All beautiful in the eyes of Heaven, if you dare know. . . .

York trembling in the *presence.* Man walking so gentle between iron-studded soldiers. Walking of his own accord.

York's knees numb on the floor, ears listening to the man's voice over and over again, while the soldiers laugh and nail him. York certain that nothing remained for him but this man and what he was saying.

After the service was done, John and York walked back to their trailer. York pleased John had been with him for that farewell service. Perhaps he would start coming to the Citadel again. But John just said the Lieutenant had told him beforehand that special prayers would be offered for York's trip. "When we sees you, we sees Yark, an' when we sees Yark, we sees you . . . an' we wants ye t'know we likes the two of ye together!" So John had come but didn't seem very happy afterward. Brooding in the trailer, suddenly saying, "You just want to get Christed, Yo-yo; that's the truth."

For a while he lay quiet. John jealous of the Sally Ann that final time—so silly, when all their friends in the Cove were Sally Ann. . . .

The next photo was Mariam: Mariam with a large basket, and Ma Snook's daughter, Marie, and some of the little Snookery—all standing outside their trailer. York wondering why, till he spotted the pots and pans in the hands of the little Snooks. The day of the berry-picking party, that's what! A few days before York left for London, he and John were in the trailer, making plans for the winter. They'd follow the birds south to Mexico, where it was warm and cheap. Follow the yellow fellows for York's next book—*their* next book, because John would do the photography. Then migrate north with the birds in the spring, return to the Cove to build their home. They decided to meet in Toronto after York's holiday, then drive to Mexico.

An awesome war whoop outside their window, from behind the bushes. Farley scattered under the bed, and their cat, Littlesnook, into the closet. Tambourines, drumming, singing. Another Sally Ann parade? John flung the trailer door open to look. There they were—Mariam and Ma Snook banging on large pots, and Marie and Gracie and Molly with tambourines, and young Gary Snook blowing on a whistle. Mariam shouting, "Out wit' yez, ya pair o' friggin' jeezlies!" The whole shebang of them marching around and around the trailer. And when the din-and-dance had lowered to shouting level, Ma Snook clambered in the door of the trailer, hands on hips; glaring at York. "C'mon, now, Mr. Yark, ya cain't be warkin' an friggin' *all* o' the time. An' it's a marvel of a day, no breeze like." And John standing behind Ma, flipped his best wink at York. "C'mon, ya gotta come berryin' wit us. Parfict day fer berryin'." So that's what all the pots and pans were for.

The door had swung open—no knock, though perhaps it had been lost in the din of Osprey Cove. York looked up—Khalid's face peering around the door. Could he pick up the lunch tray? Yes. Khalid entering, and right behind him Claude. And behind Claude, Richard. "We couldn't resist, dear friend. It's been several hours." Claude swooping past Khalid to the end of the bed. Richard scuttling for his chair. All three of them established in the room, expectant. Silence. "But you haven't touched your lunch," Claude expostulated. "That's a *good* sign," Richard piped up. "Love feeds on air!" York staring from one to the next. And Claude surveying the photos spread across the bed. "Do you, perchance, have one of John?" No, no picture of John. Just Ma Snook and . . . "Ha! This is very Brueghel, no?" Claude reaching for the photo of Mariam and sniffing. While York tried to cover up the rest. And when Claude reached for another, he was suddenly out of bed, grabbing Mariam back and shoving Claude away. Claude protesting, "But Bertrand saw them. We only wanted to share!" And York spluttering, "Please, I need some time with my friends, my family." Propelling Claude Inc. toward the door. Khalid took his cue and scurried off, forgetting the tray. But Richard paused at the door. "Bravissimo! I can see the cure is taking."

York slammed the door and clambered back into bed. Back in that parfict day fer berryin'. "Okay, okay Ma Snook, we'sll go berryin' wit' ye. Or ye'll never stop bellyin' at us." Ma and Mariam had been at John and York for days to drive them up into the mountains, "T'fetch a slather o' them berries, very best kind!" Their truck could go way up the old lumber trails. And they could transport half the clan in the back. So, yes, they'd promised. And here was half of Snookdom, ready to be off. Mariam clanging on her pot. "Ye dasn't need t'warry fer food, 'cause I made a picnic fer us—rabbit pie t'way ye likes it."

And in minutes they were all swarming all over the truck. York just had time to grab his pipe, notebook and current reading. John already in the driver's seat, with Mariam and Ma Snook and a squad of grandchildren. The back of the truck crammed with the rest, all clattering on pots and tambourines. And just as John put the truck into gear, he stopped the truck, raced back to the trailer—coming out with camera, binoculars, and one of the collapsible rocking chairs. And proceeded to set it upright in the back of the truck. "C'mon, Yo-yo; you can't take a scenic drive without a rocking chair!" And York found himself ensconced in the rocker, holding his binoculars and smoking his pipe, just as he had been when the first war whoop had broken out. John gave him a wink and they started off, the little Snooks chanting, "John-an'-Yark . . . Yark-an'-John."

And John, always alert to the occasion, drove the long way, slowly, so they passed smack through the length of the village. The little Snooks banging on their pots, and John honking at assorted sheep and ponies careening to escape the green monster caravan. Ma Snook leaned out the window, shouting at Una, the postmistress, "Yis, we's goin' roight up into them mountains fer the best o' the berries." Knowing that once Una knew, so would all of Hospree Cuv.

York sat content, rocking and waving at the startled villagers, while they rode pageant through Greater Osprey Cove, as John called it. And turned up the steep road, on past the bush, and out into the Gulch. That lunar rock wasteland which, Ma Snook liked to say, "sep'rates t'rest o' the world from the Cuv!"

By the time they'd passed through the Gulch, miles of sparse spruce jabbing the eye, they had fallen silent. And the fisherfolk in the next village eyed them with stern doubt—a group like that could only mean trouble. But soon they were into full spruce bush. Ma Snook pointing urgently at a steep trail on their right. "That's t'one. Lots o' berries hidin' up thar, my son!" John dubiously nosed the truck up the trail in first gear, snout bulldozing through overgrown bush. And the little Snooks cowering in the back as the branches whipped past, and a lone grouse whirred irate. But the trail began to widen, and soon they were climbing steadily into the spruce forest. Gracie Snook standing up, leaning against the cab to see better, suddenly waving her hands wildly, pointing dead ahead. York peered to see about thirty yards up the trail—moose! Loping with enormous elegance up the trail. John slowed the truck, and Ma Snook leaned out, hollering, "Git along wit'ye, Mister Moose. Yer blockin' me berry crew!" Mr. Moose stopped short, turning to gaze disdainfully at the racket behind. Forcing the truck to a halt. But Ma took a pan and leaned out, banging with might and main. And Hilary Snook on a tambourine. And Mr. Moose gave a protesting snort and soared into the bush.

They lurched up the trail a few miles farther, till the woods opened out, road dissolving into a high meadow of daisies and rocks. The Lomond River plunging off on their right—sudden vista down to Bonne Bay and the ocean. Ma Snook banging on her pot again. "Stop! Stop right 'ere!" She hurtled out of the truck and announced to all who would hear, "We's to the top berryin' spot o' the world, 'cause no one kin git 'ere save Mr. Moose!" York couldn't see any berries. But Ma banging on her pot, summoning, "All hands t'berries! Mariam, ye wanta take the patch up past t'head of the track. An' Gracie, ye best strike straight on yonder. . . . Molly, you an' Hilary get t'where that big pine tree is, see't?" Ma parceling out berry territories like a field marshal. Till she glanced up, saw York sitting in his rocking chair, laughing at the trip, the dismissal of Mr. Moose, and the antics of their one and only Ma Snook. Ma wasn't having any of that. "Ay, an' thar's the Lard Yark hisself, la. An I'sll wager ye doesn't pick nary a berry t'whole day through!"

"But, Ma, somebody's got to guard the truck."

"Guard yer truck? Aginst what, my son? Thet moose? Ay, you an' John'll be at yer friggin' soon's we gets our backs turned. That's truth!" Ma blasting up a full gale. But John jumped out of the truck, tootling on his clarinet and shouting, "Ye better be good to us, Ma, or we'sll jes drive off an' leave yez all here fer the night wit Mr. Moose!"

But Ma went on. "Ye better pluck a pot an' join all hands a-berryin', if y'wants t'earn yer supper!" And John said a sudden okay; he'd go with Gracie. Ma told her brigade, "We'sll gather back at t'truck when the sun gits past that big pine, la." She pointed to the single pine standing high above the bush. "Now everyone on t'the berryin'!" And various Snooks scuttled off in the indicated directions, John with Gracie, who was smiling to bursting. And Ma herself sped into the bush with a chortle of conquest. Leaving York sitting in his rocker on the truck, Farley sniffing the little clearing around them.

He managed to relight his pipe, gazing down to the ocean. Long, rolling view. But now he felt a nagging loneliness. He'd gladly have gone berrying too. But John hadn't said a word, not even a wink. So York had stayed. Well, maybe he could relax, read awhile. But didn't feel a bit like reading. He clambered down from the truck, strolled to the edge of the vista that tumbled to the sea. Pure heaven: if only John were there! He'd just presumed John would stay, and they'd chat and John play his flute, or for a time they'd both read. As they often did. Or share the dance of love. There he went, jealous again, jealous of John's freedom. What Ma Snook said: "Ye dasna own yer John, that's truth. He belongs t'all on we!" York winced. Ma had a deadly eye for certain things. "Ya kin let us have a piece o' yer John now an' then, my son!" Ma really loved John. But all the Covers did, John so outgoing and frisky. The first to help in their work: a fishing shed to be moved and he'd be down with the truck and pulley, hauling it to a new site. Lumber to be carted, he'd be there in early morning, offering truck and a smile. Or a new dress for Ma Snook—that had been John's idea too. While York stuck at home, slogging away at the book.

He picked up a stick, began doodling with it. But no matter! If he wasn't going to be with John, he'd rather be back at the trailer. He glanced up. Farley was nosing through the rocks, taking a leak. A pair of birds flitting a nearby tree. Farley finished her business, turned toward the truck . . . and froze. Only did that when an interloper came near the trailer—someone she couldn't see or smell, the breeze going the wrong way. York looked around. Nothing. But Farley moving warily toward the truck, hackles up. Another moose? Tricky animals, dangerous. A rock crashed behind York. He spun around—no one. But Farley barking, running at the truck. When York looked again, there it was: the red head rising above the back of the truck. The wide smile—John, John of Osprey Cove! Standing on the far side of the truck, laughing. Had fooled even Farley.

"Didn't really think I'd go and leave you, did you?"

"Oh, that's all right." York feeling foolish. "You just gave me a scare."

"C'mon, Yo-yo!" John ambling forward, all shamble and glee. "Well, I still love you, you idiot." For a moment they stood quiet in the vista. Till John went to fetch York's rocker from the truck, set it on a flat, moss-covered rock. "Now you can watch the world in peace." And with that spread a blanket nearby, and sat down cross-legged. Nodding in his smile.

The daisies wide-eyeing the pair of them in this improbable oasis. The burble of river to one side, the sound lucid and rising. "Look, York—purple fellows!" John pointing at Ma Snook's big pine tree. York clapped the binoculars up. "Finches . . . *and* crossbills!" The splash of raspberry plumage. Crossbills working amid the pinecones. He passed the binoculars to John, who focused and chortled. "Hey! So that's crossbills! Bigger than purple fellows." John stomping his feet gleefully. "They're serenading us, Yo-yo!" It was the song of the finches that had burbled high beside the river, giving color to the stream. And Farley, catching their joy, frantic to join their excitement. Till John found a stick and threw it for her.

They sat listening to birds, seen and unseen. "You know what it is, Yo-yo? It's a welkin." And John winked. "East o' the sun and west o' the moon!" Always said that when he was happy. And suddenly up and running for his camera. Telling York not to move. John bouncing up and down as he focused on York and Farley. "I want a picture of my big black bear." And Farley barking because John was so excited, *snap-snap!* And John wanting another. "With your pipe this time, Yo-yo." And York obliging as John bobbed side to side, peering through the camera. "Now try smiling, luv," John shouted. "You can do it!"

And photos done, including some of John, they settled once again in their welkin. York gazing at John, who was browsing in a book now. Big Red! And John glancing up to pat Farley, his eyes that sultry phosphorescent blue. York had never seen eyes like John's. Velvet—or most dangerous, smoky. He always knew John's state through his changing eyes. And now they were hot velvet.

"Hey, Yo-yo, this book of yours; it's a first-class sex manual!" John flourishing the little paperback—the *Spiritual Canticle*. And reading a line aloud: love as fire, love burning and warming and consuming. John's own eyes burning as he looked up. And York chuckling—John could find sex in anything.

At that moment a portion of sky flustered down onto the picnic baskets. Gray, black—tails bobbing. "Giant chickadees," John whispered. Birds strutting, around the baskets, pecking closer to the food. And smack! Farley plunging into the birds, which hopped monkeylike up the closest tree. The birds drifted away in a splash of beauty over some tall blue spikenards. And John ran to the truck, burbling to himself. Returning to settle on the blanket with his clarinet. As York realized, those birds must have been Canada jays; never saw them up close before.

And beside him, John improvising now. Like the roll of the river, the song of the finches: John imitating the song of the purple fellows. His cheeks blown round, head nodding, eyes glowing up to York. As one of the jays returned and sat nearby, head cocked, curious. And York rocked in time with the music, scarcely daring to look lest it all dissolve.

Abruptly John stopped. "York, do you really believe a spiritual life can include sex?" His eyes hot velvet. "Like us, Yo-yo. Can we really be . . . contemplative, and hot rods, too, like you said that time?" John looking so serious, then winking.

"Of course I do, John-o." York startled. Focused full on John now. And John pivoting as he sat. They would have erupted into sex on the spot but for the realization that the Snook clan was spread all around them. So they just sat longing.

Then John was pointing at the sun. "Look, Luv, it's getting close to the pine tree." He winked, beckoning York over to the truck. But not till he had packed rocker, blanket, and Farley into the back, leaving only the picnic baskets behind, did York realize what he was up to. They drove the truck about a quarter of a mile down the trail, well below the dip of the mountainside, off behind some trees. Then leaving Farley locked in the cab, they crept back to the edge of their clearing, hid under some deep bushes. And just as the sun angled past the big pine tree, they heard the clanging of a pot, and the first Snooklets appeared. Their hands and faces smeared with blue, purple, like woad. For a moment they stood bewildered. "This kin't be t'spot, ain't no truck 'ere. . . . " "Well yis, an' 'tis,'cause Mariam's picnic's right 'ere!" And now Gracie and Marie cast up with a pile of berries and raised a hubbub, all of them staring at the picnic baskets and the spot where the truck had been. As John and York wormed deeper under the bushes, out of sight.

"An' by the Lard Jeezus, them two 'as gone on us!" Mariam trundling up with a giant pot of berries, standing quietly a moment. They all began poking through the brush, as if the truck might be hiding there. Another Snooklet, and now Ma Snook puffing up with her two pails brimming. Mariam fumed, thrashing at a bush. Ma watching. "What's her to? 'As she gone plum crazy?" Mariam wheeled in plump rage. "Well, an'ye kin use yer eyes, kin't ya?"

"An' there ain't nuttin' wrong wit' me eyes, Mariam Barnes! Jes look at them berries I plucked, two pails on 'em. More 'n you got, 'cause when I warks, I warks!"

"T'Lard be wit' ya, Kat'rine Snook. But if thir ain't nuttin' blind wit' yer eyes, p'raps ya kin tell us where t'truck be to!"

Ma set her berries down and stood looking. "Well, an' yez is right, Mariam Barnes. There ain't no truck that I kin see, la."

"Allay-looo-yaa! An what duz ya pr'pose we do—walk plum back t'Hospree Cuv?" Mariam quaking with indignation, as Ma set to howling with laughter.

"Ya might be tellin' us where t'humor be, Kat'rine Snook!"

"Well, an' Mariam couldn't walk nor a hundred yards an' she couldn't, 'cause her's like a whale, she's that big around, la." Ma Snook laughing so hard she knocked over one of her pails. Mariam turned to Gracie. "John an' Yark is jes down t'trail a mite, sure on 't. Ya best trot down tell 'em we's back, la." Gracie jogging off with Molly, while Mariam waddled back while plumped herself, on a large rock. In moments Gracie and Molly were back—no John; no Yark; no truck.

"By t'Lard, if them rangy varmins 'as gone off an' left we all 'ere fer t'night wit' Mr. Moose. . . ."

At which John blasted a colossal farting sound from between his cupped hands, the sound a moose makes in the bush. And Ma Snook spun around to see where it came from. Twenty Snook eyes scouring the underbrush. Till John and York erupted from their hiding place, yodelin' and dancin' around the lot of them. As Ma stood hands on hips, chewin' on her teeth. "An' I s'pose the two on yez 'as been doin' it, right there in t'bush. Friggin' some wonderful! While we wuz gone warkin'. Well, ye ain't gettin' none o' the berry pie. . . . Pair o' hard tickets ye is!" Ma

Snook beltin' it at them. They only got clear by going for the truck, driving it back with the horn honking full toot to drown out the mighty Ma Snook. As Mariam spread the picnic, spewing out fresh sandwiches and tarts like first aid. And John taking pictures of the whole blessed lot at their mountaintop feast.

John said, "Heaven's right here on earth, Yo-yo. Not just in your books of religion." As he slowly undressed in front of York that night, right at the supper table, and drew York off to early and energetic bed.

Well, he was in bed right now—but wrong bed! Though at least he had Osprey Cove back. The bedlam bands of Covers spouting wondrous din . . . like the Djema-el-Fna. He imagined John in Marrakech, in this crazy little hotel. John would love all the song and prance of Morocco, Marrakech, les amis. Yes, Osprey Cove in Marrakech! He saw John parading through the market, the old covered soukh. John in a blue burnoose, strolling the lanes, dropping into the antique shops. He'd dazzle all Marrakech, drive les amis voluble with lust.

And for a moment York lay in carnival. Ma Snook taking tea with Rebecca, pluckin' them berries right off Rebecca's hat. Herbert sharing Screech with old Jim. And John would delight them all, turn the gossip of les amis into full theater. John and Bertrand on flute duet, the pipes of Pan rollicking Khalid's garden. While Claude danced, endless houri. And Richard sat wise, his entire soul clapping time. York laughed; how John would have joshed the Colonel! And titillated James! And joined in their jaunt for the sheer lark of it, dancing highest above the flames. Singing out, "C'mon, you old Yo-yo, it's all for fun and games!" Yes, John *was* the magic carpet. Why not bring him here? Show him the Koutoubia. "As big as mine," he'd say, "and nearly as red!" Take him to Dmitri's for lunch, try to keep Dmitri's hands off him. Write the Colonel to come back, bring James. Invite Keb. . . .

Another photo, this one of Mariam standing by her sky-high mauve-and-red hollyhocks, just outside her cottage-shack. The yellow cottage bright as a giant goldfinch, nestled amid fierce flowers. There she was, shunting out the door, hurling a bowl of scraps into her yard. A scurry of hens from nowhere to feed. Sighting York. "An' 'tis yerself, Mr. Yark. Well an' I dunno as I should be seein' ya, after ye nearly left us up in them mountains yest'rday!" Mariam pulling York into her parlor. "C'mon wit' yez. I'sll bile up some tea t'last ye till London, la."

And in her parlor York went to *his* chair, the apple-green rocker with the cherub wings and hearts carved into the back. Mariam poking up the stove embers. "Ye likes honey wit' yer tea, dasn't ye? Jes got some frish from t'meadow. An' ye won't be mindin' if we fix wit t'ram now? I'sll jes rinse some cups, la. . . ." Mariam waddling back and forth. Bringing out her for-special teapot, old floral English pot with daffodils and robins on it. Pear-shaped like Mariam herself. As York sat blessing Maid Mariam, feeling immemorially at home. And just as he was rocking back relaxed, saw the long white face passing the front window, stuttering across the pickets of Mariam's fence, pausing beside the defiant rise of hollyhocks. Muzzle flickering, Mariam's ram, finest in Skinner's Lane. Just standing there by fence and flowers, then tearing off a float of hollyhocks. York was half out of his chair, go chase it away; Mariam's pride and joy, those flowers. And just as he was out the door, 'Arvey, Mariam's husband, grabbed the ram by the horns, leading it into the backyard to a ramshackle shed set amid a final blurt of flowers. Ram standing in front of the shed, chewing on the stolen hollyhocks, so nonchalant, lord of the lane. And 'Arvey's ax jumping from behind, high overhead, slamming down, unseen by ram. A muffled crack that spewed the hollyhocks out of its mouth. The animal slumped to its knees with a wheeze, eyes bulging. And York stumbling back into Mariam's parlor, feeling a friend had just died.

"Yer tea's jes ready, la." Mariam wading over with the pot, pouring a full cup with dainty flourish of wrist. "An' 'ere's some honey." As York wheezed into the rocking chair, his own head split by that sudden ax.

" 'Arvey always uses t'ax like that. 'E's some quick wit 'n; always fells 'n t'first time. Did ya see?"

York nodded. Yes, he'd seen. Saw again the ram kneeling in abrupt sleep. How often he'd seen it, king of the field, behind Mariam's.

"Yer gonna be wantin' more tea, isn't ye?" Mariam going over to her shelf, taking another pinch of her prize tea from the caddy with the coronation picture on it. And York feeling glad the ram had been chewing a final flourish of hollyhock. Words tumbling around inside him.

"Yez is into thet thinkin' o' yers again, my son. I kin see it." Mariam stopping mid-kitchen, surveying him. "Ye be wonderin' about yer trip t'London."

"No, I was . . . thinking that"—York hesitated—"unless it be holy, unless it be hallowed first, then it's we who are slaughtered." Words popping out, York feeling absurd, and quickly adding, "That's why I was glad it had the hollyhock, like an offering. . . ." As if that might explain. He glanced up, but Mariam just gazing at York, her arms folded, saying, "Now thet's jes like ya. Yer always thinkin' somethin', my son. Like what ya jes said, la."

"I guess I is . . . an' I guess that's some bad." York sat with lips tight, wishing he'd said nothing.

"Yer not drinkin' yer tea. Ya mustn't let yer tea fall cold on ya." Mariam shuffled over to the stove, to warm up the pot. While York sat gazing around the kitchen parlor, as if for the first time. The sunflowers on the floor, linoleum pattern of giant sunflowers. The print of clipper ship riding crest over the stove. And above the table the large framed verse with roses painted around it.

ONLY ONE LIFE,
IT WILL SOON BE PAST.
ONLY WHAT'S DONE FOR CHRIST
WILL LAST!

Yes, all of a piece. All the bright china birds, here and at Ma Snook's. And the lace doilies in the parlor but imitation ones for the kitchen. And the curtains with "All Hands" stitched across. As if a single Sally Ann vicarage spread through all of Snookdom. And this home ancestral to York now. As if his father's father's home, ancestral roof, centuries back in Devon, in the West Countrie. West Countrie croft it was, transported through the heart to bide in Newfoundland. York reaching for his pipe, starting to rock again. And Mariam back with a "cup o' the frish" for him, and one for herself as she clucked into the other rocking chair. Peering over at York.

"My son, an' I'se gonna tell ya somethin'—didya know that Kat'rine lost a son, la? 'Twas a wonderful lot o' years an' years ago, an' she lost a fine bye.'E was jes siventeen an all that flamin' red hair, like yer John." Mariam fidgeted with her cup, glancing at York. "Ya see, that son o' Kat'rine's were t'same kind as you an' yer John, duz ya understand me, la?" York understood. "An Kat'rine jes took after this son o' hers, name O' Boyd. She jes took right after 'n, a-bullyin' at 'im wit' her tongue. Ol' Jim paid no heed, an Kat'rine kept on drivin' at t'bye. An one day 'e was out huntin' partridge birds, up in t'Gulch. An 'e didna come back fer supper. . . ." Mariam got up, closed the door, plumped herself back in the rocker, the chair disappearing beneath her. "Sammy Snook found 'n. 'E had no head left. Head blowed plum off 'n. An t'Mounties said an 'twere an accidint. But Kat'rine wuddn' talk t'nobody till one day her sez t'me—'Tweren't no acceedint that. An' ya knows it. I druv me own Boyd to death. Boyd bein' a good hunter an all. I druv me own bye like that. Didna want that kind an' 'e was. An I'd niver do it agin, cause me Boyd was a wonderful bye, a right good 'n. . . ."

Mariam rubbing her knee, finally saying, "An' then all them years later, you an' John came long t'the Cuv. An' Kat'rine sez to I, 'Mariam, that John 'e's jes like me Boyd were. Looks a ringer for me Boyd, an is jes t'same kind, la.' She luvs yer John. Lard, an' she luvs 'im some strong." York sat bone-still.

Mariam nodded. "Y'see, us thought ye was hidin' from T'Mounties. Somethin' was a-chasin' ya both t'hide in our Cuv. Like ye was crooks. Lets o' times crooks comes 'ere t'hide." Mariam chased a fly from her cup. "But ya wasn't no crooks. Ya was jes John-an'-Yark, like us knows ya is. Yez 'as always got a 'ome in t'Cuv, my son. You an' yer John! So ya mustna mind what them grum fellers like Nat Hart sez, nor Hegdar Kelt . . . 'cause they be real hard tickets an' a bust o' wind. An' if they causes yez a mite o' trouble, why Kat'rine an' me we'sll jes call out t'Snook byes, an we'sll make gooseberry pie out on t'lot of 'em." Mariam had taken up her knitting, was knitting hard, not looking at York.

"An when yer over t'Londontown, remember we luvs ya. An' John luvs ya somethin' fierce. Yes, an' I knows thet. 'Cause I saw him ivery day after t'two on ye quarreled, la. An ya ran away t'Sain' John's, Yo-yo. Ya said 'twere fer yer wark, but ya was a-runnin' off an' leavin' yer John. An' John went 'alf loony. I know, 'cause 'e wouldna eat any o' me pie."

"Mariam, why did you tell me this?" York hesitated. "About Boyd, and . . ."

Mariam plopped her knitting onto her lap and gazed out the window. " 'Cause yer goin' away . . . an' I dasn't think ye'll be back t'the Cuv, not ever. No, I dasn't."

"Mariam, I'm coming back. This is my home. You're my people, my family . . . I *love* you!"

Mariam shook her head, began knitting fiercely. "Na . . . ya isn't comin' back, Yark, I knows that. 'Cause ya is doin' somethin', yis an' you is! And you is burnin', Yark, though no one in t'whole Cuv knows why. Not even Kat'rine, an' she's wonderful smart. But I'sll tell ya this, Yark . . ." She clashed her knitting needles and glared at York. "If ya iver leaves yer John, ye'll be dead. . . . One or t'other on ya, ye'll sure be dead. An' I knows that, right in me bones, la. An' that's why I had t'tell ya, afore ye flies off t'yer Londontown."

Mariam, who rarely said much, saying it all. And now with that winsome smile on her face. "An ye'll 'ave some tea now, 'cause ya hasn't touched nor a drop." And up again, trundling around the stove, poking and clucking. York had never really seen the little kitchen parlor. Nor seen Mariam, really *seen* her. Nor Kat'rine either. Nor old Jim, with his great hook of a nose; wry, serene smile. Never as they really were, nor as deep as they saw him. He glanced up. Mariam serving yet more tea with a little flourish of the wrist. Like a lady, if you please. But Mariam *was* a lady; that was the truth.

York settled back and drank in silent toast—to Lady Mariam. Calm inside himself, just because of Mariam's doomsday truth. When the bloody body came shunting through the door, chest split wide, head gone. Red-and-white carcass carried by two teenage Snooks and 'Arvey. Whoomph, the dripping flesh slapped onto the center of the big kitchen table. Mariam handing a huge curved knife to 'Arvey. And 'Arvey wielding it with the dexterity of a giant razor. Flesh fleeing the bones at each slice. Steam pouring from the carcass as 'Arvey thrust into the barrel chest of ram, emerging with the heart, passing it wordlessly to Mariam, who stood ready with a series of plastic bags. 'Arvey sliced deeper—liver, kidneys after heart. The two boys watching in silent trance, and a cat licking blood from the floor. As Mariam bundled each new item into a plastic bag.

The ram clean done, only a scatter of bones left. 'Arvey whispered to Mariam, who smiled, picked up two of the bloody, bulging bags, and trundled across to York with a sort of curtsy. " 'Arvey an' me wants fer ye t'have the 'eart an' the liver on 't. Fer John 'n' you." Mariam passing him the bundles like wedding cake. And everyone smiling as York sat holding the warm gut of ram. The musky, sweet odor of blood and intestines all through the parlor. While he sat, unable to get the pipe out of his mouth because his hands were full.

And right after the final remnants of ram had been scraped from the kitchen table, and the scraps of gristle thrown to that enormous cat, there was the face in the side window. Red beard popping at the window, peering . . . York wanting to shout, but John putting his fingers to his lips. And creeping in the door on all fours, unnoticed in the trance of children, cats, blood, packaged ram. John creeping in under the table as Mariam cleaned up. And giving her ankle a fine bite. "By the flamin' Divil, an' what's it be?" Mariam jumping back, staring under the table. "An' it's Red Beard hisself . . . an I'sll fix wit ya!" Mariam grabbing a length of gristle and walloping at John under the table till John crawled out. "But, Mariam, I can't resist; ya's got the prettiest ankle in all the Cove!"

And after they all had final tea, John produced a big envelope. "Came special fer you, Maid Mariam!" But she said, " 'Tis a mistake, I never gets no mail, la." And John winked at York. "This ain't mail, and you'd best open it fer all to see." Mariam prying the envelope open; it was a picture John had taken weeks before, of Mariam with all her family, sitting here in the parlor. Mariam in the center, in the rocker, with her knitting. And her best white blouse on. And 'Arvey beside, looking startled. And Coo Snook, who lived with 'Arvey and Mariam, because he said, "Gettin' married is jes too darned ixpensive!" And all the kids with their knit tuques on in the high summer.

It was the finest of a series John had taken, and he'd just had it enlarged. She sat gazing, silent. "A present fer ya, Maid Mariam, fer you an' Harvey."

Mariam nodded. "That's what it be . . . a portrait of me whole fam'ly. An I ain't niver 'ad anything like thet b'fore." As John and York got up to leave, Mariam came out with another bundle of ram's meat. "Would ye like some ribs fer extra?" But York shook his head. "Mariam, you always give so much."

The fuss from the garden, Bertrand shouting, "Where's that old busybody gone?" And Claude replying, "She's gone to the Medina, to find a hoopoo skin. I told her hoopoo feathers were protection against . . ." But York just lying there, seeing the long pebble beach in front of Snookville, glowing as if by moonlight. And old Jim walking down to his lobster pots, waving his red hankie like a flag. And Ma Snook standing guard in her imperial garden, beside Snow White and Lord Churchill. And Sammy Snook painting his dory in spanking gold. " 'Cause I plans a big ketch o' them lobstirs this year, la." Their daily ways of Hosprec Cuv. Singing and laughing. "I feel a new touch o' power comin' down, Lard." And around each of them a wild bright light, around Old Jim and his Kat'rine, and Gracie and Molly. Alleluia around each and all of them. York seeing them the way he'd always felt them, as he would see them in his heart forever. . . .

When he came to, the sun had long since passed his veranda. He got up gingerly, gathering pictures, pages of letter, that leaping sunflower of John's final page. Put them on the table beside the bed. "If you're lonely, if you ever want me, there's the special ones, just for you, Yo-yo." And half asleep, remembered the smaller envelope, sealed. He shuffled over to his valise. There it was. And back abed, feeling silly; he'd already spent most of the day in Osprey Cove. Of course, there's been no photos of John till now; John had taken them all. John the seeing eye but always absent from his pictures.

But now John was right in his hand. He felt almost smug as he lay holding the special photos. Which would they be? Which John? John of the freckled smile, all gangly? Or John Barbarossa, Viking John in his big bush boots? Or John of the pipes, clarinet serenading the world? York tried to guess, savoring the moment. And just as he was about to reach into the envelope, it struck him—it was John who'd found the Cove in the first place. When they'd been fleeing the Canadian mainland, John's mother threatening police yet again. She'd sent the Morality Squad, the regular police, the RCMP, even Interpol, and finally the Federales, toughest of the lot. Every time her own marriage became particularly barren, she'd send a new batch. "Mother's about due for a quarrel with Dad," John would say. "We'd better move on." And mostly he was right, could predict the next batch of police practically to the day. The last time they'd fled to Newfoundland; a short visit, they'd thought. York would do some research in St. John's. And they'd vacation for a week or so.

After the ferry ride they'd driven up the west coast of Newfoundland, parking truck and trailer at random every night. Small bays, forests, riverbeds. And one day after they'd parked the trailer, John went off for a drive in the truck. Came back smiling and wouldn't tell. But bundled York into the truck. "Something to show you, Yo-yo." Drove him along the coast, past scattered fishing homes. And up an inland road through a lunar gulch of stones, shattered spruce. Worse than nowhere. Till the road rose steep, and they nosed into improbably green pastures, ponies cantering wild. John nodding, driving them over a final hummock of green. And there, several hundred feet below, was the ocean—scimitar curve of a bay, with a giant arm of land flung into the sea on either side. And directly beneath them, a village.

John drove down to the village, along the beach to a cluster of homes by a waterfall. Homes painted blue, pink, yellow. . . . And the one house, pink, with moose horns atop the door, moose horns painted bright red. And plastic statuettes on the fence: Winston Churchill, Snow White.

They stopped right there, silent. And as they got out, a shadow loomed overhead: a large bird gliding over houses. And a voice nearby saying, "An' that's the heagle, 'e comes over ivery day, same time, a-fishin'." A man standing in front of the loony pink house. And John asking, "Where are we?" The voice replying, "Yez is t'the Cuv, Hospree Cuv."

"Osprey Cove? That must've been an osprey just flew over!"

"An thet's a sea heagle, us calls 'n."

"But he's an osprey, of Osprey Cove!" John jumping in glee. And the old fisherman smiling, inviting them in "fer a spot o' tea." It was old Jim Snook. And the pink house with red moose horns was the Snookery.

That was a year ago; they had never left the Cove since.

York smiled—yes, it was John who'd found the Cove. And in a special way it *was* John's Cove. Because if York was accepted by the Covers, John was loved by them. He owed the Cove to John. Must tell him that when he got back.

And suddenly his hand into the envelope for a photo. Took a quick glimpse—a china moose, statue of a moose; and a pump organ with red velvet frontal. The inner parlor of their house in Skinner's Lane. The lace doilies, and the wax-and-hair flowers done by Mariam's grandmother: "Remember me." And the picture of the Queen and Prince Philip, young. York grinned—typical Newfie room for best. With its ornate framed pictures of ideal farm, little boys and girls surrounded by plump geese, chickens. Frames all gussied up with silver paint.

The plush Victorian sofa in the center, its blue silk cushion. And John's silky red hair glistering under the flashbulb. Hair arterial-red in the light, mane of it right around to the lumberjack beard. And eyes green jade, watching expectantly. York following the line of John's head. One of the pictures from John's twenty-first birthday. John elongated on the green sofa, right arm propping him up on the cushions, as if his red-mane head too big for him. And his skin a flickering ivory against the velvet green. Right leg extended, left leg cocked up akimbo. Body stark to the camera.

And bull's-eye center, John's cock, distending cock dangling over his thigh. What the Covers called a man's cock, a "bird." "How's yer bird t'day?" they'd ask in Snookville, laughing. John's rising bird a face, and his naked body frame for it. And his other face, lips parted, swelling in the mane of beard.

"If you ever get lonely, Yo-yo, if you want me, here I am." And John's wild wink as he thrust the envelope into York's valise at the last moment. Little had York guessed. One of a series on John's twenty-first birthday. " 'Cause we're legal now, Yo-yo!" John bouncing into the parlor where York had been reading, yanking down the blinds, pinning blankets up over them as he always did when ready to make love.

He pushed the photo aside . . . difficult taking his eyes off John, even in a photo, much less a picture of John flashing naked, waiting for York to walk across the parlor, claim the big red bird.

York's own bird purring now, churning his startled balls. Always like that—to see John was to churn, burn. "C'mon, love, I'll show you the wonder of the Cove!" John had finished pinning the blanket up, slowly undressing and stretching out on the sofa. And gazing at York, his cock swelling.

York lay, trying to think but seeing only John's eyes, drawing him across an ocean now. Grappling him. Some days they were clear, as in this picture—waiting to be filled. Some days dancing, as with clarinet—like the berry-picking day. And some days smoky. Strange, hazy smoke, like the day when—

A sunny day. One of those few high summer days when all the elements stood still in Osprey Cove. The land a pool of flowers and meadows, and the gnarled gray carcasses of dead conifers standing eternal. And the inland lake—the pond, as the Covers called it. "Paradise regained," John said as they awoke in their trailer and gazed out on the morning.

York hoped they'd go for a swim. But John had promised to help Sammy Snook with his dory. "I'll be back for lunch, Yo-yo. We can swim then, go for a walk." John flashing his finest wink and driving off jauntily to help Sammy. York consoled himself and settled in to read. . . . Then had an idea. He'd seen Abraham Snook the night before. "I'se got a fine ketch o'trout, Yark, if ya wants some." Suddenly York was up and out the door of the trailer, cantering off to Abe's shack. Abe was home, had caught more trout that very morning. " 'Ere, an' ye best take eight of 'em, cause John's a big 'n." Abe plopping the lake-fresh trout into a bag. And in short order York en route back to the trailer. Stopping at Sarah's to pick up some partridge-berry pie. Sarah's pies were the best in the Cove; she mixed in other berries as well, but never told the secret. Then, as he walked along the river, he plucked some field flowers, chuckling as the goldfinches skittered by.

And as he trundled back to the trailer, was thinking of their book on the yellow fellows. Follow their migration, stopping where they stop, seeing as they see. In pictures and words. He got back to the trailer, put the flowers in the vase. Stuffing fresh tomatoes with bread crumbs and garlic; John loved them. No more truculent tomes about culture, but a book of celebration—seeing the land, nature the way warblers do. Then remembered the bottle of rosé they'd hidden for a special occasion, like a windless warm day in Osprey Cove. Yes, York would do the text for John's pictures. Where was that damned wine?—under the bed. He put it on ice. It'd cap the day. And they'd follow the warblers back to the Cove in spring. He had everything ready; was turning on their little tape recorder to the flute music John loved, when he heard the snort of a truck. And glancing out saw it lumbering across the open field, Farley's head barking out the front window. Enough of yellow warblers—here was the real bird!

He popped everything onto the stove and tried to look nonchalant, just another lunchtime. And now John clambering through the door, saying nothing. Maybe he smelled the garlic. York trying to block the view to the stove, hide the surprise a moment longer. But John's eyes darting past without even seeing York, spotting the frying pan, the fish set out to cook. And the wineglasses out. He broke into a big grin. York could never hide anything from him, not even an unexpected summer lunch. John grinning at the surprise, big flashing smile. But just as quickly the smile ceased, immobile. John suddenly remembering something. As he disappeared back outside the trailer York looked out, saw him taking off his work boots, socks. And hurried to cook the fish, get them onto the table, open the wine—just as John reentered, his smile gone, and in its place a pinched grin, eyes partly closed as if slitted. York served the trout, poured the wine with a flourish.

John sat with a grump of fatigue, looking at the trout as at something strange, not what he'd expected. Only gradually poking at them, prodding with his fork. That taut little grin, eyes hooded. At last he ate a single mouthful.

York couldn't detect anything precisely wrong in what John was doing. Yet felt the back of his neck going tight as he started eating his own fish. John still silent. A kind of steely politeness when York glanced over, as if John were meditating on something for a moment, please. Remained silent too. But the back of his neck kinking in an odd way, as if pressure on it. While John doodled another of his fish, shoving it around the plate. And just as York was about to make a whimsical toast to Greater Osprey Cove, John pushed his wineglass aside, abolishing it somehow, and York's toast with it.

York looked over, saw John's eyes shimmering—smoky, they were. Like smoke off dry ice. Wanted to ask, Was something wrong? But John's face was set in a half smile that denied comment.

York sat stiff, eating bits of dead fish, sipping flat wine. Tasting neither. He still couldn't put his finger on anything really awry. Perhaps it was just that lunch was flowing, as it sometimes did, in a thoughtful silence. John clearly had something on his mind, that was all. Except that York felt his eyes hurting, and an ache starting in the back of his head. The flowers he'd picked, and the summer day over the pond, all monochromatic now.

This is all in my head, York thought. And when he was done eating, asked, "Would you just like a cup of tea, John-o?" But John quietly shook his head. "I really wasn't hungry at all, you know." Got up brusquely, putting on his running shoes. Then went to the cupboard, poked out a few oatmeal cookies, shoving them into his pocket. For an instant he paused in the open door: Big Red, silhouetted in the sun. Then stepped casually out of the trailer, whistling for Farley to follow. And outside, stopped, glancing back at York as an afterthought. "I thought I might stroll down to the beach, if you're interested in coming." York couldn't get a word out, sitting over the remains of his lunch. Shook his head. John banged the door shut, set off toward the beach, Farley trailing behind.

York sat numb. Nothing he'd wanted more than to wander along the pond with John. What in hell had happened? He couldn't think. His head felt severed from his body now, as by guillotine, and his body burning. As he watched John stroll off toward the beach. Strolling so casually, yet looking wooden somehow . . . his back ramrod straight, that was it. And perhaps he felt York watching, knew he would be. Because he turned at the last moment, raising his arm at York, waving . . . doing a funny little dance, almost a jig. That's what it looked like in the shimmering sun. Then his hand slashed the air in final wave: Good-bye, Yo-yo. As he jaunted so concertedly to the beach.

York sat burning, John's wave like a fist in his face. Entire lunch a fist in his heart. In a single leap he was out the trailer door, tears of frustration choking him as he churned barefoot over roots and rocks . . . roaring like a mad thing toward John. And John turning calmly, nodding in a quick little smile, watching the mad locomotive churn across the tundra. Then with an almost gleeful yodel, he started running toward the rocky beach. Running past startled children at the edge of the lake, York raging after him, catching up at the edge of the lake. . . . John skirting the high antlers of a driftwood log as York hurtled through the branches. *Cra-aash* . . . dropping John like a shot beast onto a scatter of fist-sized rocks. And the last thing York saw was the look in those eyes, smoky eyes wide with amazement at York's total physical abandon.

When York came to, he was lying flat on his back on the beach, weeds straggling around his face. John standing high over him, nose and mouth flowing bright with blood, staring down. Smoky look completely gone, and in its place a look of wild satisfaction. Eyes blaring. "Yes, that's what I want from my Yo-yo!" But as he saw York coming to, he reached down all gentle, helped Yo-yo up. Saying, "Look here, you silly Yo-yo, you've gotta learn to handle your own hate, you know." Saying it so kindly as he helped York up and plugged his own nosebleed with a handkerchief. Crazy words, yet John grinning in satisfaction as he said them. "What in the world possessed you, love? I mean, you should've just come on the walk in the first place." John knelt down, carefully pulling a large slice of driftwood out of York's shin, blood spouting. John half whispered, "Besides, you've made a fool of yourself in front of all the kids." Yes, a group of children had run up, gathering around them, wide-eyed at the spectacle.

"An' what was ye doin', John 'n' Yark?"

"Oh, an' we was just runnin' on a dare, Hilary." John replying all jaunty.

"Well, an' t'aint wise what ye done there, 'cause o' them stones."

"No an' it weren't wise, Hilary!" John winked at the kids and started helping York toward the trailer. York feeling stunned and foolish, and John saying, "You should really take some diary notes, Yo-yo. You must be pretty psychically disturbed . . . acting like that." And York, all spent in that single demented crash, could only think, Yes . . . I must be insane. "Oh, don't worry, Yo-yo. We all lose control now and then. Besides, you've been under a strain, getting the book finished. You need to get away on your vacation!"

And when they got back to the trailer, there were the remains of their festival: uneaten trout, open wine bottle, and the vase of flowers smashed to the floor as York leapt out the door. John smiling sweetly. "I'll clean up this mess." But in the middle of the night York half awoke, bed shaking. It was John, his ass lurched full toward York—John masturbating and moaning, "Fist me . . . fist me!"

11
THE GOLDEN FLEECE

York slumped gratefully into the seat. If the market had been hot this past hour, the bus was hotter. A trio of young Moroccans had thrust their way onto the crowded bus and begun to chant, banging on a kind of tambourine and an instrument resembling an agitated armadillo. Bouncing vehement with energy and song. How could they, in such heat?

Was he insane, heading back to the mountains once more? Had leapt at the chance only moments ago. But now, with the music blasting sudden lust and his cock acting up, he wasn't sure. And worse, there was no Kebir beside him this time.

A final spasm from the trio at the back of the bus. And one of them working his way up the crowded aisle, collecting small money. York was glad to pay for silence; passed pennies to the boy, who smiled, bottom lip still quivering from his song. A head crawling up the steps of the bus. York, seated smack at the front, couldn't avoid it. A head? A man crawling up the steps on his elbows, stumps of his legs in the air behind him, lopped off at the knees. Head and arms clambering onto the gearbox beside the driver's seat. Aging head, face an open wound, pain twisted into it. Elbows rough from years of elbow walking. Chanting a high querulous wail above the bedlam of the bus itself—"Allah akbaah . . . All-laaah"—as chickens, goats and people continued loading at both ends.

Why was he heading back into the mountains? Suddenly the whole bus tilted sharply to the right. A massively fat man entering, official cap, sunglasses like pince-nez on his rotund face. He swept the wailing beggar off the box and plopped himself into the driver's seat, pressing four buttons and knobs at once. Bus grumbled, engine clanking like an aged trawler. The beggar tumbled down the steps and out the door. And a conductor blocked further entrances, human or animal. A final screeching, a blast of horn. The bus lunging forward. York certain live bodies under those wheels now, till they lumbered on through the marketplace. Past that café, scene of the brawl. Bus barging a path, swaying and grunting. The monumental driver paunched over the wheel, slamming the horn at an obdurate donkey, though not the brakes. Like being inside a giant rhino, charging straight for the Koutoubia, which stood imperturbable as they swung right, belching down the boulevard and through the ancient walls into the new town. That weird transition from the medieval Djema-el-Fna to the Art Nouveau of the French quarter. And the curving hulk of the post office.

York checked—yes, he'd brought the letter with him. Beautiful letter, it had blasted energy into him; blasted him right through to this trip into the mountains again. Had brought John's photo too. Energy for this final exploration of Morocco. He noticed his favourite café whirling past, the Hôtel des Amis nearby. He could still hear Claude pleading, "No more magic-carpeting, my dear. You need rest."

Yes, les amis had dropped by again this morning for fuller details of York's "good news." To fend them off, he'd shown them the pictures of Osprey Cove. But by some mischance the picture of John was still among them; Claude suddenly whirling around the room, flourishing the photo. "Ah, my dears, what *equipment!*" Richard and Bertrand battling to see too. But Claude wouldn't share. Till York bartered a look at his letter for return of the photo. And after Claude had pronounced the letter much like York himself—"all birds and big words"—York had grabbed it all and fled the hotel for peace. Fled down to the market in quest of Kebir. And right onto this thundering bus . . . or all but.

The bus swung right again, blasting its way out of Marrakech into the abrupt countryside. York felt like waving good-bye, relieved to be rid of Marrakech, certainly of le tout Hôtel. As the palm trees floated by and beneath the palms, rich orchards. And beneath these, flurries of corn. Three-tiered world of green, with stabs of intermittent junipers, bloody splash of red-flowering bushes. Bus careening through a steady stream of carts, bicycles, and motorbikes loaded with baskets, bundles, sacks bursting with vegetables. York looked out again, saw splotches of tortured flesh, flayed skin dangling like a Grünewald Calvary—plane trees, flanking the highway like a crucifixion. Boujma sitting beside York as if he owned the bus, the mammoth driver his personal chauffeur. And scarcely deigning to notice the landscape, much less the inmates of their bus. York knew nothing of Boujma, beyond the fact that they'd met in the market an hour ago. And suddenly on the bus together, headed in odd complicity into the Atlas Mountains.

Keb had come by the night before but York apparently was sleeping the sleep of the dead. Keb had left a message that he might be in the market this morning, at his regular café.

No Keb, just some of his friends, including big Jareeda. Keb had come and gone; his job had been extended for another two days. Shortly a new lad arrived: dressed rather in clean Western clothes—blue blazer, red flannels, polished boots. He was tall, a great mane of black hair making him even taller. And spoke Claude's kind of French, almost haughty. York was intrigued by a certain lordliness in him, but the others knew him and treated him with respect. "That's Boujma, a nephew of the Caid up near Demnat." Yes, spoken with reverence almost. Which intrigued York even more.

And evidently York intrigued the nephew of the Caid, who thought he was an American. York carefully explained that he wasn't, and glad of it. And by the time that was clarified, Boujma was talking of his family up in Demnat. He was en route that very morning to spend time in the old château. And York suddenly longing to go, immerse himself in Boujma's world. It would be safe, his uncle a sheikh. And when Boujma explained he was studying English at the university, York leapt. "I'll help you with English for a day or two!" Boujma eyeing him with apparent disdain, and just as suddenly smiling. "Yes, you will accompany me. We will talk English. And I will show you a world you've never seen." Kebir's friends remaining silent; they clearly didn't really like Boujma's lordly ways. But York was overjoyed—he'd tell the mighty Ma Snook he'd stayed in a sheikh's castle.

And moments later, armed with pipe, notebook and John's letter, York had set out for the bus, following Boujma across the Djema-el-Fna. Boujma proceeding through the crowd as if expecting paths to clear for him. York trundled in his wake, rejoicing in his good fortune. And when a young lad spurted toward him to sell hashish, or maybe himself, Boujma stopped, turned slightly, looked at the boy. And the boy fled.

The bus was already full when they arrived. Boujma summoned a man in a conductor's hat, spoke a few words. The next York knew, the man was hurling three people out of the front seat of the bus. Then bowing slightly as Boujma proceeded to this prime window location. York settling beside him, dazed.

Out the window, through a shimmering haze of heat, York could not see the distant mountains. Sullen, rising purple. The romantic seduction of a trip to a sheikh's château was dissolving. Something about Boujma was unnerving; he hadn't even said a word to York since they boarded. Then the bedlam of the bus itself, with chickens and a baby goat trussed in the aisle or on the racks. But worst of all, the mountains looming straight into York's gut. Their ominous reality, as if he'd never really confronted their meanings, the consequences of his trip with Tony and James. Indeed he hadn't, kept putting it all off.

And when he next looked out, there it was.

OUARZAZATE

The very sign for the turnoff confirming fears that had risen with the mountains. Their car crashing to a sudden halt. James shouting—"She's comin' straight at us!" And the young woman dancing, the morning sun, tambourine shaking madwoman, consuming their car in her dance of fire. They were taking the same route. Why hadn't he realized?

But the bus didn't branch off to Ouarzazate; it continued straight on. York began to perk up again. After all, he wasn't with a pair of kamikaze tourists this time but with the nephew of an evidently powerful sheikh, if Boujma's actions were any indication. And a different odyssey, no crazy sex safari this time. To see the inside of a world he'd only glimpsed the first time. To penetrate those kasbahs, enter the secret life he'd only sniffed.

He glanced out the window, startled . . . everything monumental in the sun, sculpted, shimmering. The palm trees long since gone. A circle of sheep grazing a bone-dry riverbed. A single heron bright as Pharaoh. Yes, he was seeing the landscape this time—before he had only witnessed its awesome grandeur. And the idiotic antics of James, racing into the mountains as if on a final fling—sure death, anyway. Well, James was back in London by now. Claude had said so. But York suddenly seeing flames, James hurling himself into flames, face ecstatic. . . .

He turned to Boujma, eager to talk. But Boujma seemed to be talking with everyone else. Many of the passengers coming up to greet him, all speaking in muted tones. York's gaze floated back out the window. *That's* what the Moroccan landscape felt like, a fire-breathing dragon! Sure as hell what the Sahara had been like, M'Hamid. Something about Morocco had frightened him deeply. Cane fields passing now, twice the height of a man. And testes atop the cacti. And fences of dead thorns, an endless crown of thorns. Matching those Grünewald trees, crucified land, whether you liked it or not—Calvary, cocks, and six-legged dragons.

He returned to the bus. The smells within were scarcely reassuring—rancid sweat, goat shit, and now a sweet-sickly fog of hashish. It was Boujma, smoking a small hash pipe, passing it around. And orating while several of the Moroccans peered at York over their trussed chickens, kid goats, sacks of oranges. York realized they were talking about him. Boujma nodding his head toward York while talking with the man in army uniform behind the driver. "What is it they want to know?" York asked. But Boujma kept right on, the fore portion of the bus nodding as a single head at his words. Boujma finally answering him, using English for the first time. "I tell them you are from North America. A friend of our ambassador. They are always interested in aromi." Aromi? "Foreigners. That comes from the early word for Romans. It went into Arabic, and Chleuh." Oh. "You are making a special visit to our château, for reasons of the family." For what? "Yes, the officer over there asked about your visa; he is the inspector for the region."

"But I haven't got a visa, not here."

"No visa?" Boujma switching to French again and scowling. And the officer scowling. Till Boujma laughed, waving his hash pipe. "*I* am your visa!" At which the officer quickly nodded, smiling graciously at York. But York felt less like a visiting pasha than a hostage on exhibit. His eyes fled back out the window, bus churning through the haze of sun. And the mountains ahead looking gangrenous, like the Grünewald trees, and the sallow red-and-yellow earth, and the intermittent crown of thorns. Safer to see it as biblical. Boujma continued his peroration to the captive crowd.

York felt totally disoriented now. Whatever slight perspective he'd achieved on Morocco in his time at the Hôtel des Amis, whatever wisdom, whatever wild desire he had had . . . all in tatters! He was in a situation far beyond his imagination. He shut his eyes; only made the pungent smells of the bus worse. Why do Moroccans keep all windows closed? Huddled in burnooses, djellabahs, turbans, towels, capes, they never feel it's hot, goddamn *hot!* York slumped in his seat, wishing he were anywhere else.

"Yes, and I'll be back to the Cove, Jim—I promise!" And suddenly seeing John recumbent on the big green sofa, his eyes beckoning to York.

He gazed out, low mountains floating on the left now. And vineyards . . . vines floating up to high, trellised platforms, like giant beds of seaweed. And on the right, larger mountains rumbling closer.

The bus yanked right, shuddered, came to a lopsided halt. People hurling themselves off in a seethe of sweat and flatulence. And when York could breathe again he realized they were on the outskirts of a small town: a few houses, a market, and dragon gas station. "Tamelelt . . . we rest here"—Boujma presenting the town, the sudden stop, as he, too, departed the bus. York sat a moment, disabled. Then, realizing there was fresh air and hopefully a place to pee, he forced himself out. A cactus field just beyond, and getting there he found a dozen passengers with robes up or down, variously squatting or standing, peeing contentedly amid the donkeys and turds.

When he returned to the market he looked for Boujma. There he was, at the center of a circle of admirers, include the officer, the bus driver and two conductors. All the officials of the trip. Boujma standing pageant, or so it seemed. Chatting with the officer as a near equal, the bus driver as a momentary equal, and the conductors as lesser aides-de-camp. The officer asking to be presented to York, with or without visa. The bus driver bowing from neck to nipples. And a conductor asking if he wished a Coca-Cola. York didn't. Nor did he want a whiff of Boujma's hash pipe, though the bus driver accepted it with pride.

By the time York had his own pipe lit, they had proceeded in cortege to a dismal café and were eating burning shish kebabs, courtesy of the house. York talking to a young lad Boujma had introduced. Lad in a short burnoose, Western pants. He, too, was en route to Demnat, in fact lived there. His name was Ranee, and he was impressing upon him the beauty of Demnat: its famous gorge, equally famous birds, and some high rock cliff. Had York heard of it? People leapt from it every year, disappointed lovers. No, York hadn't heard. York felt eager to depart the café, tour the market a moment. Soon he was strolling this local soukh, ducking the calls of vendors as he moved through the stalls. Any pretext for a quiet moment, unmolested by bus, protocol, impending cliffs. And was quickly lost at the end of the meat market, standing just past a freshly flayed carcass, staring. Staring up at a pair of storks. And glowering beyond, the Atlas Mountains. . . . For perhaps a minute he stood, transfixed by birds and mountains. Expecting James to appear, and *snap-snap*, those birds! Or John . . . John burgeoning out of the mountains, Mexico now. "What took you so long, Yo-yo—were you swimming?" But York wouldn't tell. . . .

"Here you are!" It was Ranee, grabbing York's arm. "They're waiting at the bus." Ranee weaving them back through the market, back to the bus. All passengers aboard now except York. And Boujma standing in front, preventing its departure till York found.

And with a final blast of the horn, the bus trundled onto the highway. The town receding into fields of sun-blitzed corn and cattle. And Boujma moving down the bus, orating to other passengers. Leaving Ranee beside York. Ranee so much gentler than Boujma, who seemed to exist in permanent processional—at once pasha and executioner. He stared out as the mountains surged past, a frieze of undulant pyramids on both sides now. York asking, "Do you know Boujma's uncle?"

Ranee hesitated, whispering, "I know of him. Everyone does."

York glanced over. Ranee was looking straight ahead. "Tell me about him."

Pause. "You know Boujma well?"

"We met by accident, in the Marrakech market. I'm going to spend the night."

They were both watching the fields now, soar of sunflowers. Ranee silent, suddenly glancing back to see where Boujma was.

"What are you doing in Morocco?"

"Visiting. In Marrakech, at the Hôtel des Amis."

"The home of Monsieur Claude."

"You know him?"

"Everyone knows Claude!" Ranee murmured, glancing at York. Outside, a man using a basket as sunshade. And a silver orchard. "Olive trees," Ranee said.

"Tell me about Boujma's uncle."

Ranee glanced over his shoulder; yes, Boujma was out of earshot. "A relative of the Glaoui. You know of the Glaoui?"

York nodded.

"Boujma's father owned the kasbah you are going to. The best land—" Ranee stopped, as if saying too much.

The mountains lurched up, tier on tier, a field of goats startled in the sun. "Where's Boujma's father?"

"Dead. They say he—" Ranee halting mid-sentence, his intimacy replaced by a flash of deference, fear. York looked up: Boujma standing beside them, so military in blazer, scarlet, the mane of hair. Boujma smiling quizzically at Ranee. "I trust you are delighting our guest with the splendors of Demnat?" Ranee nodded, shrinking back in his seat. And as suddenly, Boujma parading back down the bus again, talking as he went. And York remembered following him through the Djema-el-Fna, feeling something akin to the awe he saw on Ranee's face.

They had turned off the main highway now and were roaring directly toward the lowering mountains. York abruptly aware that his excursion was scarcely a picnic; even the landscape flashed fear. And the furor in the bus, people crouching, clutching turbans to their faces . . . a rooster, escaped rooster cackling the aisle, shitting on someone's head opposite, flopping out the one open window to freedom. Then relative calm, till the bus toppled off the road again, everyone out—clots of people flowing off the bus. And Boujma standing regnant out there, Lord of the Atlas.

York remained on the bus, Ranee beside him talking quickly.

Keeping an eye on Boujma. "If you want to see me in Demnat, it's the house with the double door in blue."

"I'll drop by for tea."

"Double door in blue, with a large star over it. Behind the meat market." York glanced up. Boujma was looking at them.

York tried to sort it out. Do I turn around, take the next bus back? What *am* I doing here? *Craaash*—on the roof, bundles heaved up, a goat. And after a final blast of horn the bus burst onto the gravel road, propelled by that behemoth driver.

As the road got worse, the driver went faster. Road climbing now, the sallow green-and-red soil clotted in dry crusts. And when the bus stopped again they were high into the foothills. Clutches of mud homes, goats, the first fir trees, and a donkey dong.

When they lurched on, the mountains began to blot out the sky. The road winding up through a steep valley—wild, primeval trees. "Arganiers," Ranee said, a kind of nut tree. The land fertile alongside a surging river. But wasteland beyond, cacti, rocks.

DEMNAT

York barely noticing the sign as they clanked through a large triple-arch gateway. And elements of flamingo-colored wall, fortress. Then little white homes and stores. The bus sagged to a halt.

The bus driver squeezed out the front door, leaving an immense gap in the front of the bus. For an instant York could see the long undulant valley of foothills. Then the rest of the bus seethed out, and he, too, was borne through the door to stand grateful in shade and fresh air. Ranee beside him a moment, murmuring, "Blue door with a star," and disappearing just as Boujma appeared. Boujma now standing on the step, as if expecting a salute . . . his eyes seeking York. And nodding for York to join him, proceeded up the single central road. Saying, "We have one stop first."

Boujma's strides seemed longer now, perhaps because he was

on home ground. As York struggled to keep up. The whole town seemed bicycles, not a car in sight. Cafés. And brilliant white. The town perched eerily on this high slope, as if about to tumble into the valley below.

Boujma swung left into an enclosed courtyard, as violent with colors as the town with white. Roses, giant sunflowers and trumpets . . . huge lilies, blasts of geraniums. And spouting up the center, a splashing fountain. Boujma crossed through the garden, York trotting behind. And as Boujma moved to one side York saw them—flayed skins, bulging heads hanging with bloody fleece, carcasses swinging. All through a vista of lilies, sunflowers, roses—heads, livers and testicles dangling as if food for the flowers themselves. And Boujma now standing at a meat counter. A courtyard of butcher stalls surrounding this garden; Boujma chatting with a butcher, testing a slab of meat. As a little boy popped out from under the counter with a pot of mint tea, tray of glasses. Boujma, butcher and finally York settling down between stall and garden to sip the fragrant tea. York's eye splaying through flying sunflowers, floating penises, and testicles staring at him like bloodshot eyes. All red and flayed and beckoning. Boujma prodding York to drink his tea. Boujma astride his stool like a scarlet hangman. The butcher raucous with deferential laughter as York split his tea. And presiding above, on the side of the stall, a picture of a man in white robe, on a white horse, under a gold canopy—the King. The boy offered York more tea, and a rose.

Boujma presided over the courtyard as he had over the bus. Others gathering around to hear his words, applaud his gestures in this court of flowers and blood. Till the butcher jumped up, brandishing a long knife, and slashed a quiver of flesh from a carcass, rolling it in paper, presenting it with a slight bow to Boujma. And a boy appeared, leading a mule with finely tooled saddle into the garden. Boujma loading it with his little bag, York's notebook and the gala of meat. And leaping onto the mule, beckoned York to hop up behind. York tried, failed, finally hoisted up by the laughing butcher—and out through the garden they clattered. On around behind the butcher-garden, Boujma nodding to various villagers as they went.

They were soon past the town, trotting toward a wall of trees. Till through the screen of trees the land fell sheer, a drop of over a hundred feet to a river broiling its way below. York almost falling into the gorge as the mule veered sharply, following a goat trail along the side of the cliff and then down. He clutched Boujma's waist, grateful that the animal had slowed to a wary step-by-stumble along the snaking path, down to the river's edge. Boujma leaping off, carrying York with him. York amazed at this torrent of water in a land that seemed to have none. Ice cold, thunderous . . . from the mountains. He glanced up—the town had disappeared behind the cliff. To the right the rising gorge, lush, sheer, impassable. And across the river, the rolling foothills, climbing to a slow purple. How in God's name could they cross here?

Boujma smiled and, yanking the mule, led them downstream a ways, to a tumble of boulders spanning the river like a giant's causeway. Boujma crossed first, hauling the wary mule from boulder to boulder, mule hopping like a giant rabbit. York clambering after as dubious as the mule, cursing his clumsy city shoes. But soon they were well beyond the river's turbulence, trotting along on the mule again.

The land alongside the river had been fertile, every inch of it under cultivation. But now they were moving on red-and-sallow soil, scattered with small boulders, cacti and scrub trees. Climbing a knoll, and from the top could see the body of valley seething down. To the right, pyramids of foothills, ringed at their base with tilled green lands.

Then they were descending again, past a clutch of mud homes, yelping dogs. But Boujma just cantered straight through the dogs, kicking one on the head as he passed. And once clear of dogs and huts, York prodded Boujma for a pee stop, his bladder battered and bursting. Walking off a few paces, behind a big cactus. The land desolate, with stabs of beauty.

They trotted on, climbing steadily again, mountains hoving closer like black-ribbed pachyderms. York arranging himself on the mule so that with one arm on Boujma's shoulder, one hand on the mule's thumping rump, he could nearly balance. Cursing himself for not bringing a hat, or Claude's sunglasses. Riding a mule with Boujma-pasha was certainly a far cry from touring in a stately Jaguar, far cry from tourist Morocco and picture postcards. Something whipping York's face, neck. Entering a copse of low stunted trees, hadn't even seen them coming. Boujma ducking and the branches slapping York. And as they surfaced beyond the trees, Boujma yanked to a halt, pointing to a lush belt of green spotted with mud homes. York nodding. But Boujma gesticulating higher—a cliff beyond the houses, cliff rising sharply above. And atop the cliff, like a predator lying watch, a four-towered chateau, a fortified kasbah.

Boujma kicked the mule forward. York sure he was riding into some Foreign Legion epic now. Only it wasn't romantic at all: sudden images of dungeons, burning oil, incarcerations. What Dmitri had said, in the crazy restaurant in Ouarza-what's-it. Skeletons—and James had shouted in glee, and made his speech about the Glaoui. Images from that trip and this fusing in York's addled mind: this disastrous landscape: the butcher-garden of blood, John. . . . Yes, that's where he was now—about to encounter a cousin of the Glaoui! But when he gazed up, the kasbah had vanished.

They were entering another copse of trees. Orchard amid the lava rocks. He ducked the clutching branches this time. As they followed a narrow path, a sudden rivulet. Lush green spurting alongside. Crazy, this landscape: you never saw what you saw, and when you did, it was already gone. Boujma belting the mule into a syncopated trot that banged York's balls at every step. At least it was cooler in this shaded lane, which seemed to divide every time York looked. Ending in a farmhouse and stable, surrounded by a cactus fence. The rivulet feeding a pond in front of it. A man appearing, scowling, then seeing Boujma and bowing. Boujma paraded on. York wide-eyed at this sudden farm. Only minutes ago, death valley, and now this idyllic cottage setting. Huts nestled like great hens under the trees. Farmyard animals ambling like friends. And an old woman in red shawl by the rivulet. They were already past, climbing steadily, canopied by trees. Hairy bulbous fruit dangling. And carefully tilled land beneath . . . corn, vines.

And rising before them, the stark red-brown of the cliff. And somewhere atop it, Boujma's castle. Boujma laughing now, scarcely slapping York on the thigh. He knew Boujma. And the boy on the bus had been so fearful York wished he were back in the Cove, out berrying with Mariam and John and Ma Snook. "Best berryin' spot in t'world." Not here. But Boujma was off the mule, clambering up the steep path to a final rise of the cliff.

And above it a giant stone wall running some hundred feet, a tower at the far end—the sheikh's kasbah! York wanted to bolt. How far had they come? Impossible to tell; over an hour on a cantering mule. He'd never find this way back.

He was at Boujma's mercy, if that's what Boujma wanted. What *did* Boujma want? To show York a world he'd never seen—that's what he'd said. And that's what York had wanted. To be right inside a kasbah, like the ones he'd spotted with Tony, James.

This one hunched over them as they climbed. They breached a canopy of trees, valley surging on their right, fortress like thunder on their left. A second tower, and the land leveling off beside into a belt of orchard and corn. Cries of chickens, goats. Five, six goats browsing high in one of the big trees. Primeval spread of tree and feasting goats. And beside the tree a swirl of blue burnoose, a young herder standing guard. Calling off a rush of snarling dogs, nodding to Boujma. The pair of them chatting, a reference to York because now the lad turned, smiled, his face dappled under the leaves, eyes of innocent amber. The boy standing like a breeze, baby goats at his feet. . . .

They trundled on past more chickens, scattered mud homes, into a courtyard ringed with lordly pines, elements of a formal garden. And before them the face of the château. A central monocular eye glaring—doors twice the height of a man, sheathed in metal with giant studs. A bundle of laundry jumping up as Boujma approached—a man grasping a rifle as iron and ancient as the doors. Man salaamed to Boujma, taking the halter as he descended. Tripped in haste to tether the mule, get back and unbolt the doors.

An archway led into an entry hall, arcaded walk branching off on each side. York suddenly out of the sun. Only slowly seeing the rising colors of a tile floor. And directly in front of him, a massive coffer, colors strident against the whitewashed walls. An enclosed courtyard just beyond, shouting with lilies, roses, sunflowers. A rampage of garden, shaded by a rambling tree. Boujma drew York toward a circular stairwell at one end of the hall. Stairwell winding up inside a corner tower. And through one of the slit windows, a vista of the burning valley.

Up into another hallway, another giant coffer, shout of color atop a red-tiled floor. Red and gold tiles running halfway up the walls. And in front of them a pair of paneled doors; light flared through the multicolored glass. Boujma strode to the doors, flung them open. York wanting to flee, till he saw Boujma had entered an inner room riotous with color. He crept forward, peering in. A large salon: ceiling twice the height of the hallway, peacock tail glittering at its center—a carved and painted mandala. York's eyes flickered with the flames on the walls: more gold-red tiles. And higher, light of iron grillwork over four windows open to the air. He yanked his eyes away, steadied himself—but saw instead a vast rug, echoing the walls and ceiling, the rumble of the valley itself. He turned to ask Boujma—

No Boujma! Ridiculous, he'd just seen him enter. Only one doorway. He forced his eyes around the salon: divans banking three walls, red cushions, circular brass tables, low. . . . But no Boujma. He slumped onto a divan. Some seventy miles and a mule away from Marrakech. His eyes fell into the coils of rug . . . turquoise, yellow, points of red—like a wild garden. And the black ankle rising at the far side. "No more magic carpeting"—Claude's voice in his ear. He looked up, expecting the dragon. But no . . . a blue flame swaying toward him. Boujma! Boujma clad now in blue burnoose with white lacings, and large yellow slippers. Crossing the carpet and handing a similar burnoose and slippers to York. "You'll be cooler in these!" Then elongating himself on the divan opposite, pulling out his small clay pipe, lighting it. More hashish. Offering a puff to York, who declined, lighting his briar.

Suddenly he started forward—gunshots! No, hands clapping sharp, voices giving orders from the courtyard below. Why was he so fearful? He decided to change into the burnoose. Quietly stripping to his underwear, pulling the costume over his head. Soft ripple on the skin, cooler. Proud of himself in Moroccan garb. . . . He glanced over: Boujma languorous on the divan, still sucking hash pipe, his left hand lost under the flow of burnoose, caressing, stroking. . . . York looked around the salon, the fiery walls, flare of rug. And back at Boujma so contentedly fondling his zeb. Well, that's what the room said to do. He'd better situate the room now, before any further magic started. Detach himself from the body of it spinning around him, caressing him through the burnoose. Sweet rape. He wouldn't change his shoes, that's what. Wouldn't put the yellow slippers on. Certainly wouldn't run his bare feet through the rug. . . .

He froze. Surging up from the core of the rug, a mountain of flowers, instant garden. Garden expanding, swaying . . . and topped by an enormous smile. A mountain of a woman, swathed in endless gaudy—blue, gold, billows of pantaloons, chemises, belts, jewelry and ornate slippers. If Kebir's mother was a monument, this woman was the Pyramid of Cheops itself. She was sitting on a large cushion on the rug. Silence palpable around her. York glanced to see if Boujma was still stroking himself. No, he was propped up on an elbow, beatitude rippling his face. An orb of light descended in front of the woman. A tray of tea, cakes. A girl in white burnoose wavering near la dame du château.

The servant child was suddenly gone, and Boujma was sitting up, orating once again. The woman nodding her eyes toward York. Boujma switching to French. "My friend is the friend of my friends. He comes from America; he is a writer who is known. . . ." Boujma making a formal presentation of York to the chatelaine.

The chatelaine whirled the first four layers of her robes, began pouring tea. And York suddenly removed his shoes and went over to sit on the rug before her. She handed him one of the enameled tea glasses and a warm smile. "We welcome you to our paltry home. You have come far to be with us."

"Oh . . . only the last part was hard. On the mule."

She adjusted a necklace. "Our Boujma never walks. Always rides. You will help him to speak English."

York nodded. And now she was chanting something, her voice unfolding like an orchid. "That is from the Koran. A guest is the flower of Allah." Ah. And now Boujma had joined them, sitting cross-legged on the rug beside York. The chatelaine arching her eyes in silent mirth. And the girl fluttering in with more cakes and burning incense. Then two, three small girls in white with silver belts, who came and dissolved in a silent tinkle.

"My daughters. They miss Boujma, now that he is studying in Rabat."

"So Boujma has many cousins."

"Many sisters."

A gong from below. The mountainous lady floated to her feet, poised between her flowering pantaloons and enormous smile. "The Caid is in the mountains today. Someone fell from a cliff." She laughed. "He returns tomorrow, n'shalla. Then we shall celebrate."

And before York could say a word, she was gone, and Boujma with her. Definitely gone. He peered around warily. But he couldn't seem to focus, everything shifting in the light. He retreated to the divan, ears perking. Yes, bright tinkling sound, yet earthy. Sound of the chatelaine and her daughters. His hackles twitched—damned salon felt alive, like moving flesh. He glanced at the center of the rug, blue form hovering there, eyes gazing down on him. Boujma. Boujma silently back, drifting over to sit beside York. "In our culture a man does not sit on the floor with a woman. Especially if the woman is raised on a cushion. I only sat beside you to cover the fault. Of course, my mother—"

"Your mother?"

"That was she."

"She's . . ." York managed not to say "a spectacle." "She's *magnificent.*"

Boujma frowned. "She's married to my uncle." Oh. "She talks too much. In our culture women must be silent. Except among themselves. But she's a Tazi; they talk a lot." Smoke of Boujma's hashish coiling around York with his words. "This ksar belonged to my father. But he died." Boujma passed the pipe to York, who puffed in commiseration. "My uncle will be suspicious of you. You are a friend of Boujma."

Oh. York passed the pipe back.

"It is said my father was stung by a viper."

"Here?" York shifted uneasily on the divan. "What do they look like, please?"

"Rabbits."

"I beg your pardon?"

"Coiled up in the sun: the silhouette, big head. Like the body of a rabbit, thick. And quick."

York shifted again, blowing hashish smoke away.

"I found the body of my father." Boujma nodded proudly. "Pushed under some rocks, a few miles from here. His throat"—Boujma puffing faster—"was cut. It was one of my uncle's knives. I found it."

York staring goggle-eyed.

"My uncle told me the same day he will share the land with me, when I'm older. He pays me to go away and study." Boujma passed the pipe back to York, who drew on it in slow consternation.

Silence. He glanced up at Boujma. But Boujma didn't look sad at all; in fact, quite pleased. Maybe he was just making up a story—shock the foreigner. But why? York peered around the room nervously. It seemed aflame again, creeping flames. Finally, "Are you sure it was your uncle who . . . ?"

Boujma rubbed his thigh. "Someone may have used my uncle's knife. But it is my uncle who has the land, and this château. And he took my mother to make sure."

"Took your—"

"Married her; one of his wives."

York thrust the pipe back to Boujma.

"My uncle became Caid. One of the few Glaoua who retained the favor of His Majesty. Hassan II, the king. . . . One of his wives is an Alaoua."

"The king's?"

"No, my uncle's. An Alaoua, from Rissani. The royal dynasty." Boujma nodded, as if confirming his own words. Then smiled winningly. "I'll tell him you are a lawyer."

"Tell who?"

"My uncle. He treats lawyers with care." Boujma placed his hand on York's knee. "You can help me."

York nodded uncertainly as Boujma's fingers caressed his knee. Such long, strong fingers. What did Boujma have in mind?

"You are a lawyer, a friend of ambassadors and Abdelhaq Tazi."

"I'm a what? I've never even heard of—"

"You are here to do my bidding," Boujma laughed charmingly, fingers rotating York's kneecap like a mushroom. "And when it's done, I'll give you a small house just past the château. And some goats. And as many boys as you want."

Is that what he said? It tumbled out so fast at the end. Boujma rising, pausing an instant, enormous hard-on projecting in profile through burnoose. As he made his way to the divan opposite.

York sat dizzy. Spun in the abrupt tangle of words, hashish, salon, sex, Boujma wanted something from him. But what? He glanced nervously at the rug. Expecting a rabbit—a viper? Perhaps it was all fantasy, Boujma's fantasy. And then he remembered the look on the boy's face, in the bus and at Dammit. What was his name? 'House with the double blue door."

He felt something touch his shoulder. Sunlight angling in from the ceiling. There at the center, a small dome with colored windows spinning fire down onto the rug, onto York. So that gazing up he fell into a vortex of light and gold and red, rug to ceiling—a flame in enveloping fire.

He yanked his eyes away to find something to cling to, but everything in the room part of the vortex . . . everything coiling, winding, roiling. His eyes found the doors at the end of the room. Doors were stable, yes. But not these . . . their silhouette ogival, shimmering—precise form of an erect phallus. Salon careening around him. Mind careening. Smoke of hashish floundering the room; York splaying at the edges, dissolving. Ready to acquiesce in the bidding of this salon, or Boujma, or even the absentee Caid.

He slammed his eyes shut. As deliberately as he could, he picked up his pipe and tobacco, stuffed them into his burnoose. Bent to put on his shoes. He glanced over—the body elongated on the divan there, head lolling, sucking on hash pipe, one leg cocked up. A sultry odalisque, one hand under his burnoose endlessly fondling, semi-erection nuzzling through the robe. York staring as Boujma turned his head, eyes wide, beckoning, entire body a summons. For an instant York tottered.

"Please," York mumbled, "I think I'll go outside, a walk, some fresh air."

"As you wish. My uncle returns tomorrow afternoon." Boujma grinning slackly. "Tonight . . . we do as we please." Yes, his eyes fragmented as he lolled there caressing his half-brandished cock. York wavered toward the door. He half fell through the phallic doorway, fumbling down the narrow stairwell, out the open portal into sun-blaze. And on into first shade, a group of trees. Cooler now, sun searing bright, but worst heat gone. York huddled under the trees, trying to gather his wits. Something about Boujma—at once purr and saber-toothed.

He turned. The rivulet gurgling behind him. And the hulk of the château pushing him farther into the trees. Following toward the primeval trees, lifting his burnoose to pee, relieve himself of that damned salon, of Boujma. And just as he flowed, saw the lips, slow sensual lips and tousled head, chocolate-gold face behind the next tree. About twenty feet away. The goatherd he'd met with Boujma, riding up on their mule. Yes, the same innocent smile as before. And as York peed, he felt the current between that smile and his exposed cock.

Then he was done, and they were ambling ahead under those archaic trees. Goats jumping from tree to rock to tree. The boy beckoning. For a few moments they strolled along, half following, half leading the goats. Maybe thirty goats ricocheting around them, udders flapping, farting. Boy pointing to another farm hut, several hundred yards up the rocky hillside. The orchard straggling up partway, then sparse brush. And when they'd climbed for a while York felt a weight gone from him, looked back. . . . The kasbah smaller now, crouching on its cliff promontory. And the boy beckoning him on, up to that first hillside hut and beyond. A fresh cluster of trees higher up, another feast for the goats. Wending up the mountainside, pausing, gazing down the valley. Tier on tier of rumbling foothills. The vultures overhead, questing the new dead. And, presiding over all, the Caid's castle, sentinel to the entire valley. . . . York glanced at his watch; plenty of time before sundown—why not go on?

They reached the farther copse of trees. And as they pushed through the copse, an unsuspected solitary hut. Barely sticks and straw, a few tattered chickens—and a fury of dogs. And after they'd been stoned to growling distance, York saw a figure in the hut. Woman in a frayed shawl, remnants of a dress.

She pivoted toward them: eyes hissing, teeth bared. Her face a shocking beauty, madonnalike—yet feral, like a cornered wildcat. And clutching a baby inside her shawl. She snarled, her eyes a broiling cauldron reflecting the valley,the tumult of rocks.

But Goat Boy merely saluted, smiled, threw stones at his goats to urge them forward. York stumbling after, anxious to get beyond those eyes. A hundred yards farther up, the rocks detonated into a screaming song: part yodel, part wail, like a bereaved animal. York shuddered, then saw the boy's head thrown back; it was he who was yodeling. And on they clambered, the château like a dissolving man-o'-war below them, redder in the declining sun.

Another hundred yards above them, a splash of green, more

trees. A cluster of farmhouses. Soon they were passing through a protective palisade of cacti, children popping over walls like dandelions to see. The boy herded the goats and York through a murky stable, on into a courtyard splattered with chickens, geese, children. Hard to know where the stable ended and the home began.

An older man appeared, bare feet and burnoose. He and Goat Boy chattering. Boujma's name mentioned. The man bowing, saying in wobbly French, "Be most welcomed to supper." And only then did York realize he and Goat Boy hadn't exchanged a word during the entire climb. And now the man escorting him with grave politesse up a rickety ladder, into a whitewashed room above the milling goat yard. He found himself sitting on a straw mattress in the shade, with a vista through the door onto the courtyard below. The old man squatting cross-legged beside him, little boys clucking around. A relay of girls passing tea, flat bread and honey up to the room. While the older man scooped oil out of a large clay jar, mixing it with the honey and a thick paste.

"Juba was rounding up the goats for the night. If you wish, he will escort you back to the kasbah in the morning." The man speaking a mixture of folk and military French. No, York wouldn't be spending the night. But he was glad to be eating the rich honey paste and oil; what was it?

"Umloo."

"Um—"

"Yes," the man said. "The oil comes from the goat trees." And smacked his lips in approval, pouring tea for York. The smile looming in the doorway: Juba, his goats bedded for the night, coming with a younger brother to sit by York. More tea and honey being relayed up the ladder. A pair of sheep pelts to spread over the mattress. And a small portable radio, carried preciously. The father tuning it to music that swirled gently around them.

"I regret . . . I must now visit my brother. Juba will care for you." The man bowed, leaving York with a diminished covey of children, teenage boys and the silences of Juba. The radio still weaving music through the room like incense on a coiling breeze. And borne by the music, York strolled out onto the flat open roof in front of the room. Watching the goats mill below, and sheep in a smaller courtyard beside. Children gathered on the flat neighboring rooftops to peer at the strange visitor. And as the sun settled lower, the valley changed to oxblood—from the tiptop of the world, view onto a lost universe below. York crouched to marvel, catching the white sparkle on distant horizon, ivory walls, towers: Demnat. Below him in the courtyard, the goats in their almond-eyed trance.

The air was cool now. Women weaving to and fro with large earthen jars, fetching water from a communal well just up the mountainside. Singing as they went. And Juba back down in the sheep yard, carrying grain. Prodding and patting the sheep, picking up a young one that was being trampled, putting it on a nearby teat.

York gazed down the valley again, vast bloodletting of the valley in the declining sun. The kasbah a black tusk, towers looming fierce in early sunset. He damned well was *not* going back there tonight. No, he was going to stay right here with the sound of the bees in that honey, the chomp of affectionate sheep, goats, scuttle of eager children. And Juba's poignant smile.

York went back into the room and in the gathering dusk found two of the boys on the mattress, hands buried under each other's burnooses. And only half glancing at York, who acted as if all was natural. No area of their shared body out of bounds. Till Juba entered and the boys drew back. And York refreshed, sweet hum behind his ears, as they all lolled in the embrace of the music.

The father returned, accompanied by his brother, who sat gazing at York as if he'd fallen out of the sky. Father saying how pleased he was York was staying; he'd known he would. And when York asked how, father laughed and said, "I saw you looking down the valley, back at the caidat. You can sleep right here in this room." And candles were lit, with more tea, followed by a platter of steaming vegetables and sauce. Lastly, a can on a plate. The children eyed it as something special—an unopened can of chicken. Till York saw it was meant for him, no! He contentedly munched the vegetables and meat sauce, the can remaining untouched.

Now the younger children had gone; only Juba and a teenage brother remained with the grown-ups, the father presiding cross-legged in djellabah and skullcap. Father announcing with pride that he had been with the French Army in the days of the Glaoui. Had fought at Monte Cassino. "There were more guns there than in all Morocco, ever! And more noise!" He was certain of that, covering his ears as if still hearing it. And saying, "But now I can't own a gun." Apparently the King forbade anyone who had fought with the French or the Glaoui to keep a gun. So he couldn't defend his home. The conversation veered, and no one except the father spoke any French. Room rippling with touch and fierce intimacy. And the meal done, York lit his pipe and passed it to the father, who smoked proudly, passing it on to his brother. Juba's smile growing. The two men departed with salaams, bearing the virgin can of chicken. Leaving York with Juba, and a variable number of younger boys floating in and out. Then they, too, dissolved into the night, only Juba remaining, swaying with the music and glancing at York. For a moment York hoped Juba would come over to the bed. But he finally rose silently, taking up the radio, passing back the pipe, and withdrew.

For some seconds York sat alone in the resonance of the room. Something about Juba was haunting . . . like an ancient message. He went back outside to sit on the roof, gazing into the night. A scuffle in the courtyard—goats in quick joust. Their heads in wild silhouette by moonlight, horns locked, eyes bulging, goat-beards flailing. York shivered, retreated into his room, carefully closing the door behind him. Wriggling under the sheepskin for warmth.

In the deep of the night he woke. Night birds quavering, an owl close by, a guttural wail. He got up, went out into the moonlight. Making his way to an outer corner of the roof. So that kneeling he could pee noiselessly onto the dense cacti below. Felt his cock perk, then his eyes probe, till he was scanning the dormant valley. Valley now a sallow ivory, patches of dried blood. The entire valley a single rumpling body, changeable—arterial by day, veinous and bone at night. He had felt that walking in it, riding in it. He stared over the roof, down past the lynx-woman's hut, down to that somber beast watching by moonlight—the fortress, sheikh's kasbah, staring right through him. He shuddered, tucking wary cock under burnoose, and retreated to the room. Bolting the door and pushing a large jar of grain against it just to be sure.

For a while he lay sleepless, his cock telling him something. Suddenly, he was lying with John, the body of this valley in all its mutations. John-freckled-body this lunar Moroccan landscape, day or night. . . . And not just up here in Juba-land, but out in the mountains with Tony, James—he'd felt it there too. John's eyes lurching out of that lava-scape at him. Big Red always there. Watching.

He awoke to a thrashing of bodies, blare of rooster . . . *arrk-arrrrkkk-arrr!* It was cold up here in the mountains beyond the kasbah. He'd come to escape Boujma and that raging salon. And ended here with the goats and Juba.

He sat up. Thunder from the thrashing bodies below, the goats, their shotgun farts, belches, blasting lips . . . goaterdämmerung! It was dark still, but he couldn't sleep. And, wrapping a sheepskin around himself, went to the door, tripping over the jar of grain—yes, the rooster was right, the first crack of bright slicing the mountains. He climbed steep wooden steps, up onto the roof of his room. Installing himself at its center, cross-legged, facing the slit of bright over the slowly rising mountains. As the slit brightened over the teeth of mountains, red to orange to first gold. The valley shifting from ivory to black russet. Slowly emerging into its cascade of rubble, jabs of green and sultry red. A skullcap: Juba's father stumbling into the courtyard, peeing serene among the goats, unaware of York's overhead vigil. Scuffles from the adjoining mud homes. Sky a golden rim with fleece of clouds. Yet black overhead: York's hackles telling him it was still night, his eyes that it was day. Now other shadowy figures moved in the courtyard. A woman in shabby shawl bearing an iron pot. And Juba hunching forth, slapping the butt of a goat in greeting.

York clambered down, finding father, Juba and teenage brother squatting in the room under his own. Coffee passed, and bread with a bowl of oil. As they huddled in this low mud room, a wide straw bed at one end, raised off the floor several feet: communal bed for four, five. The mother and several daughters skittered outside, scarcely daring to glimpse York. A goat butting half into the room, eyes slitted. And Juba rose, went whistling into the courtyard.

"Juba is taking the goats to pasture. He will be back before the sun is high; then we will escort you to the ksar." York on his feet, racing out through the stable, catching up with Juba thirty yards up the slope. The children shouting as he ran. Juba turned to see . . . and whooped as York arrived, dancing along among his goats, tossing more bread to the dogs to draw them on. And together they climbed into the fresh shards of sunlight.

But York was soon stumbling, whereas Juba seemed to skate over them, large rubber sandals made from old tires strapped to his feet. They reached a huddle of trees, the goats stopping to plunder new leaves. While Juba picked up a tardy kid, carrying it along. The mother blurted after him, anxious. The valley burst open in a scream, surging in an abrupt wail that rose and ranted oxblood and rubble, piercing York as if stabbed. Juba nodded at York, his eyes saying, "I told you!" York remembered his yodeling wail of yesterday. And looking down the valley, way back down, could see the figure, torn figure of that woman, near a clump of trees where her hut must be. Standing on a huge rock, wailing her soul over the valley in first morning sun.

As they climbed on, her fierce song drilled York's backbone. York scrambling in Juba's wake, steeper up the mountainside, not daring to look back. And for the next half hour all he could do was follow those agile sandals, the bleat of goats. The rocks dissolved in a splurge of green: wild grasses, oleanders, prickly oak. The goats pounced the final distance, butting into this oasis like children on a spree.

York stood in wonderment. The oasis . . . perhaps sixty yards around, garden floating a mile up the mountainside. Juba beckoning, pushing through an inner fence of stone and thorn. The sky scudding at their feet. A pool, deep spring, birthplace of the rivulet that surfaced at the sheikh's château and flowed on down the valley. And a spicy fragrance as Juba knelt, plucking a bouquet of green, holding it to York's nose . . . mint, a floral mint, pungent. The kasbah couldn't harm them here. While the goats rummaged and rutted in the verdure, though not permitted to enter the final close around the spring.

Juba sat on a half-petrified log and produced a small wooden flute, serenading the oasis. High birdlike chorale. The goats looking up as he started, then back to their browsing, such enchantment a part of their day. York watching as Juba played: a little hand-carved flute scattering gold to the passing clouds. He laughed and joined Juba on the big log. And arm in arm they sat, silent a moment. Juba ran over to shove a big billygoat back from the entry. Billy pretending to butt Juba, then turning and clearing a bush in one resounding leap. And Juba back beside him on the log.

But the dogs suddenly snarling, jumping at the sky. Juba and York lurched to their feet—a huge shadow wheeling over their oasis, bird swooping, then sheering away. Soaring on down the valley, gathering trees, rocks, huts and the château itself in its flight, as if the valley pendant from its wings. Juba's burnoose rising; his other, his hidden face prodding toward the sun, the departing eagle. . . . As the pair of them watched the rumpled fleece of clouds, still gold in the early sun. Silently touching. Juba's robe pulled up, strident against the leaves as they caressed each other's rods, gazing at the weave of sky and valley, small clouds scurrying like lambs. . . . Juba's face an ecstatic trance, hearing the ancient music. Till Juba was yodeling, warbling a vehemence of inner song, cock rampant in the sun, spraying flowers, shining white flowers across York's arm and hand.

For perhaps an hour they sat in beatitude, guarding the spring and its pelt of mint. Laughing at the ribald antics of the goats. And gazing down the long mountainside. Valley ecstatic with sun. And Juba played his pipe again, notes tumbling the air, the valley all one in his song. And the words floating up in York like the spring—"The Golden Fleece . . . the Golden Fleece!" He knew the ancient quest was true; he'd lived it in the morning trek with Juba, up to this oasis amid the clouds and flowers. As he sat gazing from the very top of the world, he remembering the singing he'd heard with Tony and James, up at the Lookout. York had so much wanted to go there, climb over to that floating oasis of green. And now he *was* there . . . with Juba.

Just before high heat began, Juba gathered a batch of mint, and slowly they wound their way down through the rubble of the stone furnace. And within an hour were approaching the cluster of farmhouses. Children cavorting around them, chanting, "Allah, Allaaah ak-baa" as they entered the mud sanctuary of Juba's home. Inside, York could see nothing, his skin and eyes seared by sun. He fumbled up the ramshackle ladder to the loft. And as his eyes cleared, he went out to peer down into the courtyard. *Crack-crack* . . . Juba's father crouched in the shade there, cracking nuts between two rocks. Father poised above the nuts, hands raised and *crack-crack*. And one of the littlest daughters fluttering over, scooping up the nuts in her shawl and carrying them to an older sister who was turning a round stone atop a larger flat one. And the crushed nuts flowing as powder into a basket below.

For a moment he watched. Father rhythmically swaying over the nuts, and *crack-crack*, one tap, at most two. And the little girl bringing more nuts. And mother chasing a chicken away from the basket of powder. They'd seen York now. And he was longing to talk with them, the daughters and the mother. But all they could do was smile and tease him with glints of mirth. He climbed down beside the father, who liked parading his French like an old sword. And the daughters, wife disappearing as York appeared.

Father glanced up. "You went up to the spring."

"Yes, it reminded me of a place I went with a friend. I killed another mountaintop oasis, full of berries."

"This morning, out past the trees"—*crack-crack*—"a big viper."

"What did it look like?"

"I buried it under the rocks." He flipped a nut to York. "You have to keep a sharp eye in the underbrush."

"They kill?"

"About an hour." Father shifting lower on his haunches.

"The land up by the spring belongs to the Caid." Father nodding and flipping a nut into his mouth. *Crack-crack*. "It used to belong to Boujma's father."

Father swaying over an extra large nut, hand poised. "They found him there."

"Who did?"

Crack-crack. "I did. I went to tell Boujma." Flipping the large nut to York. "His father was a true pasha. He died too soon." Father circling his hand high. And a daughter scooting over with a bundle of nuts.

"The Valley of the Eye, too many deaths."

York nodded, his eye caught by mother now, mother flashing across the end of the courtyard, transformed. Suddenly a gaudy mauve shawl, bright headband.

"The Evil Eye is death." Father's hand poised again. "He who has the Eye must kill." *Crack*.

"How can you tell the Eye if you see it?"

"Like the skin of a viper." Father picked up a stone, tossed it into a pail of water nearby. Water spraying onto the dusty mud. "Like that!"

"Like . . . ?" Yes, the whole courtyard swaying.

"That pattern in the mud." Father holding up his right hand to fend it off. "When you see eyes like that, hold your hand up *fast!*"

And York seeing Keb, his hand up against the madman down in Agdz, man who had hexed their car. . . .

Crack-aak. And the wife back at the end of the court again, gussied up full festival. A rainbow. *Raiment,* that's what. She was bent over, washing a few tin plates, crockery. Father humming to himself as she stooped, buttocks thrust up and back, high. Legs locked straight, yes, and torso hanging forward, head almost to the ground. *Crack,* and another nut in his lap. As he munched, nodding at Father but watching Mother. Something about her movements as she crouched now, deep crouch from the navel.

Craaack-crack. "You heard the woman. She always screams at sunrise." Father throwing his head back, rolling wild eyes. York remembered those rabid lynx-eyes coming up the mountain. "Her husband was struck by the Eye. And it started again."

York patted the chicken, back for another nut.

"The stories, about the Caid." *Crackety-crack.* "We found the body."

"The body of—" York swaying again.

"Her husband, the woman who wails." Father smiling. "Half his body, shish-kebabbed. We never found the other half."

Silence as York sat swaying, knowing what had really happened to James. Death of the soul. And York had done nothing to help.

Father stood up and clapped his hands. And gestured for York to enter a room right behind them. The shadiest room, with a real mattress and thick rugs. Picture of the King and Mecca and the Hand of Fatima. Father unwrapped a small object with care—the radio; switched it on, music swirling out. A daughter appeared with a pewter teapot, glasses. Father squatting on his haunches and filling the teapot with fresh mint Juba had picked.

Over in one corner York saw a small pile of canned food, including the can of chicken.

He fell back on a cushion, suddenly asking, "Can you tell me about the Glaoui?"

Father nodded, sniffed the tea. "Boujma's uncle is like the Glaoui." And then would say no more. Finally rose and drew out a knife. Fine silver knife in a scabbard. "I always use this. For the rites." Father smiled. "A gift to my father from Abd el Malek the Handsome." He drew it out proudly, returned and sat down. "My father saved Abd el Malek's life. He was Caid here, and my father was one of his guards." He carefully sharpened the knife against a whetstone. Testing the blade against his own throat. One of the little boys ran in nodding. Father rose. "It is time."

York followed the father through the courtyard into the manger yard. They were all there, assembled. Mother in her raiment, and the brothers, and the little girls hiding behind Mother. Father nodded, and Juba herded the sheep out . . . only a ram remained. Fine ram with full horns, one broken off at the tip. Mother stepped forward. She was holding a sprig of flowering herbs which she gave to the ram, extending them like a special treat. Juba returned, taking the ram firmly by the shoulders—half grip, half caress. "Allah karim," the father said. "Allah karim," the others echoed. And Father bent forward, raised the ram's head as it chewed serenely on the herbs and whisked the knife across its throat. The ram chewing another instant, as if nothing. Blood spurting as the ram sank slowly, gently from Juba's arms, eyes blinking onto the mud. Everyone silent as the blood coiled, sudden sweet smell of blood. A wheezing bleat from the slit throat.

York wanted to leave, couldn't move—it had happened so fast. The ram lying in the bloody mud. And Mother standing silent in her finery, twitching that final sprig of herbs. The one just younger than Juba standing with his lips swollen now, eyes fixed on the ram. His eyes in a wide slit, a trance, as he swayed over the slaughtered ram. And the silence, everyone silent. Only the buzz of flies and the pounding of the sky. And the final shudder of the ram.

Juba took another knife, making an incision in the back leg at the hoof. And bent down, starting to blow at the point of incision. The skin bubbled up along the leg, forcing the skin off the flesh. Father taking over from Juba and blowing up through the leg hole. Till the entire pelt of the animal rose like a giant balloon, clear up to the neck. And was slit and peeled off like a piece of clothing. Bloodied fleece lying to one side, the flayed body naked. Father slit the stomach, drawing out all innards in a single pull. And Juba's arms red with the fresh-cut heart.

York stumbled out of the courtyard, up to his room on the roof. Lying down, trying not to vomit. As if his own skin flayed. "Would ye like the 'eart on 't? 'Arvey an' me would like fer yez to 'ave the 'eart." Mariam holding up the plastic bag. And how in God's own name would he ever get from here, this wild magnificent mountainside, back to Marrakech, or even Demnat? Let alone back to Toronto, or to his beloved Osprey Cove? Would he ever leave? Or would he give up . . . follow Juba and goats and the thunder of sunrise up the mountain forever? Yes, everything in this valley, the presence of man since the first caves . . . welkin of the world alive. As down past Ouarzazate, on toward Zagora. Your body is my body, Juba, is that ram's body. Ram falling into Juba's final caress, holy dying; slaughter and love. Allah karim!

He sat up. The flesh still quivering and spitting on the skewer. Father holding out the fire-roasted meat to him: the ram, flesh of the ram already chunked and spitted. And Juba behind with mint tea and honey. The senior males of the family all in the room now, squatting. York reached for the meat, yelped, the sizzling piece landing on the floor. And was given another. As they sat silently devouring the fatty flesh, an innard, the soft rich meat of the heart. The still shuddering heart-flesh of the young ram. And eating it was to touch Juba, his quivering man. Smell the mint in that high oasis. Or see the valley soar in the eagle's wings.

"Juba will go with you shortly, take the mint and some meat to the Caid."

The words hitting York as a verdict. Knew he couldn't stay. And the meat partaken, his own flesh quaking with knowledge he'd have pledged his soul to evade—sure death, anyway. Juba gently rousing him, as the shadows began in the room. A covey of children gathered for his departure. Mother still in her raiment, a living rainbow. Father nodding and passing a jar to

York. "Best umloo in the valley." And he with no gift to give. Juba put the jar in his sack. And now they were going out through the stable, escorted by Father, children bouncing happily behind. Juba hoisted the sack over his shoulder, a bunch of newly picked mint in his hand. Soon they were stumbling down the tumbling hillside. York trying to fathom the father's final whisper. "Juba can help in the valley. He *knows* the kasbah."

12
THE EYE OF THE BEAST

They picked their way down the flank of the mountain. Only seemed able to see a few yards ahead at a time. Till they entered a grove of trees . . . that solitary hut, the wailing woman crouched under the thatch. York expected her wild cry again, but she was mild-eyed this time, clinging to her child as to a talisman. York wanting to run over, but he fled past, keeping Juba between them. And his eyes to the ground.

Down that avalanche of stone rubble, down. There was no way to evade it. Avoided as much as he could while at Juba's. What he'd fled in the first place—the Caid's castle. But it had kept watch on him. Kasbah crouched out on the promontory, waiting, its monocular portal black in the declining sun. And York urgent to continue on, ask Juba to take him straight on.

But they'd already reached the stand of firs, sentries before the keep. A donkey rubbing its flank against a tree. Wary as they strolled through the juniper garden, the red flowers, and implacable before them the hulking black doors . . . watching. The château itself looming over all. And the guard swinging the door open as they stepped among the white walls, sudden cool of cloisters. Flames quivering the edge of York's eyes from the floor, walls, and around that massive coffer. Flickering flames of tiles, and the brass studs of the coffer caught by the sun. A gong resounding. Juba still beside him, but so different now, tatterdemalion amid the splendor. The nervous look in his eyes as he whispered, "Boujma . . . *hatar!*" As a young man appeared in the final resonance of gong, beckoning to Juba, who followed. Leaving York alone in the entry hall.

"The stray sheep has returned!"—voice dropping on York from

the beams overhead. He glanced up. Over at the coffer, an unblinking eye painted on the front. Watching.

"*Salam alaikum* . . . we like to keep an eye on you."

York turned, caught the figure partway up the stairs—Boujma, in sandals, cape.

"I went for a walk."

Boujma gave a slight bow. "Indeed. A walk up the mountains with our beloved Juba. Then supper en famille, with the father and brothers in proper attendance, no? The father is a little strange. But very loyal." He paused, the sun flickering his face in violent silhouette. "Then a rooftop vigil over our valley, so romantic." Yes, his face like one of those rutting goats, eyes bulging wide. "And this morning up to the high spring, with Juba. Our spring; abode of the God of Skins." He smiled, descended a step, flicking his cape aside. "We are glad you enjoyed your time with our goat boy."

York felt naked. "I'm sorry it took so long. I didn't expect—"

Boujma down a step farther. "Ah, but you are my guest and in our care. We wish for you whatever you wish for yourself." He clapped his hands, descended into the hallway and stood expectant.

A shuffle: Juba emerged, clutching his empty shoulder bag and the jar of umloo. York had forgotten about it—Father's gift. Boujma nodded, and Juba passed the umloo to York. And Boujma a small coin to Juba. Boujma clapped hands twice. A metallic clanking: the portal cranked open, and Juba dissolved into the sunlight like an escaping sparrow.

"I thanked him for tending you so well." And with that Boujma strode back up the coiling stairwell. York following with a final glance back—the great entry door already swinging shut. And up the steep stair, across the hall, toward the gleaming phallus-doors. Boujma disappearing into the salon. York hesitated.

He entered slowly. But the salon felt smaller, shrunken somehow. York beginning to discern its outlines through the shadows, wondering what had upset him so much before. And trying to locate Boujma. Couldn't seem to keep track of him. Then the roar as the salon surged forward: rug leaping, walls flaming, ceiling exploding up. Boujma flaring huge beside an iron grille, a window, standing in flames beside a shutter he'd just swung open to a rage of sun. York stared—yes, the room asleep in shadows till he'd opened that shutter. But now it was all back: the shout of colors, the blast of rug. And Boujma himself, his flowing cape, mane of black hair and glaring eyes. He smiled, gestured at York's shoes. York stooped to remove them, resisting abrupt impulse to kiss the fringe of carpet. Boujma laughed, motioned him to sit.

York dropped into his original place opposite the windows, clutching his jar of umloo. Dizzy from the peaks of Juba-land, the dying ram, arrival here—and now Boujma. He shuffled his feet on the rug. "How did you know where—"

Boujma bowed slightly. "Everything you do here is known. Télégraphe arabe. You declined to eat their one can of chicken; very kind of you." He was nudging the shutter to and fro, shunting the sun back and forth across the rug. "They are poor; they live on nuts and argane oil." Boujma savoring the words—and suddenly pointing at the bottle of umloo. And York involuntarily sheltering it, as if it held his entire voyage up the mountain. While Boujma stood silent, lips pursed in hidden smile. And York's eye splattered by a spasm of seething sun—eruption of red, blue. He fell back staring. Then gazed up at Boujma, who was almost imperceptibly swinging the shutter back and forth again, flashing the rug with sun. "Don't worry, honored guest; I do not covet your precious umloo."

Boujma smiled, waving something. "You left your notebook." York flinched, had completely forgotten about it. "Since my English requires your gracious help, I studied it with care." Boujma waving diary and shutter . . . sun stabbing York's eyes. Along with the realization they hadn't spoken a word of English since arriving. "The notebook is most curious, no?" York shifting back on the divan, molested somehow. "And who, may I inquire, is John?"

Silence. Boujma dallying shutter, sun and diary.

"He's my . . . friend. In Canada, not here." York protecting him from salon, château.

"You write many notes about this John." Boujma opening the diary, nodding over a passage. "You say, 'John is protean, changes form, color, and intent.' What does that mean?" Boujma stumbling over the names. "But John's letter is also most curious."

The rug surging, snapping in front of York.

"He draws most unusual pictures on the letter—like zebs!" Boujma laughing. "Does his zeb fly?"

Another slash of bright across York's legs.

"You must explain this John to me."

York felt his skin slit and flay. Sat start upright. Gaped at Boujma, who was lounging on a divan now, slowly waving notebook and letter. York endeavoring to light his pipe, focus somehow. Get that letter back from Boujma . . . But another flash of rug, sun crashing the rug. And York's mind sliding, splaying—*crack-craack*. Father cracking those nuts and saying, "It's a difficult valley—too many deaths!"

Boujma glanced across, waiting.

"Valley of the eagles." York managing to get his pipe lit. "You don't need a diary with eagles."

"What did you say?" Boujma raising himself to look.

"An eagle's diary is the sky!" York swaying, puffing on his pipe.

"That doesn't sound like the letter. Or like your notes."

York blew a smoke ring. "*My notes all lie!* I have to watch the sky and the play of the goats."

Boujma set the letter down, watching York warily.

"That's why the ram had to die." Another smoke ring, larger. "Our body and blood!" York blew a small ring through the large one. Boujma's eyes following words and rings of smoke. And York laughed, sending rings through more smoke rings.

"I need that." Boujma gesturing.

"Need what?"

"Your pipe!"

York nodded, swaying around the pipe. Boujma stopped dallying shutter and notebook. "The Evil Eye is like the Faa." York sat back, savoring his pipe. "The pattern of the Faa is the splashing water. And both are the Eye." He jabbed his pipe forward through a ring of smoke.

Boujma sat straight up. "I *must* have that pipe!"

York paused, then nodded. "The pipe for my notebook and letter. And your unfailing hospitality."

Boujma wove forward, passing the hostages to York in exchange for the pipe. York taking them with a small bow. And surreptitiously leafing through the pages of the letter: yes, all there.

Meanwhile Boujma dandled his prize, reaching into his burnoose to pull out a small bundle of hashish, filling the pipe. And fondling his crotch as he fondled the pipe. "Do you want your picture too?"

York shrank back, Boujma waving the photo of John. He'd forgotten it completely.

"It's most unusual." Boujma smiling contentedly. "Very sexy."

York felt flayed again. He glanced around, as if the room were an accomplice to Boujma. Sun plucking at the carved woodwork like sharks' teeth. Rug shunting forward.

"I'd like to keep him." Boujma grinned.

York stared. No time to think. The whole body of the salon raging at him. As the room invaded the last remnants of York's toppled mind, he slumped down on the divan, hands over his ears. Caught in a terror he could neither name nor understand.

When he finally opened his eyes, the flames pouring in from the door, spreading across the lower walls. And voices. He jerked himself up, eyeing two robed figures rising from the carpet, rising amid the flames. And the sun itself hurtling into the room—no, one of the figures flashing a large brass platter. The other a mountain of pink, yellow . . . giant daffodil.

"You slept long, honored friend." The spreading daffodil speaking. "You were talking to your dream, we heard." Boujma's mother speaking.

York gazed around, sheepish. "I thought the room was on fire."

She laughed, so pleased. "It is always flames when the sun sets. We shall soon be dining. Here is fresh tea to waken you."

Dining? York glanced at his watch—it was after seven. Had slept several hours. He looked up at the chatelaine; she was seated as before, by the window. On a cushion. Sunset flooding in behind her. And the brass platter with bright glasses, a large pot. All rising out of the flames of sunset. And Boujma off to the left, sitting up now, eyes dilated, York's pipe in his hand. At least his burnoose quiescent. For a short while they sat in the holocaust of the declining sun. Boujma's eyes embracing the room, carnal gaze devouring all.

"You went for a little visit up the mountain." She held out a glass of tea. And York went over to take it, sitting as before, cross-legged on the floor beside her. Till he realized he shouldn't be. The hell with Boujma. "Yes, a little visit."

"It is very beautiful up at the spring. I once wanted to build a house there." She nodded. A floral oasis herself.

But Boujma was orating again. "That spring is under a curse; the gods no longer visit it." His face swelling as he spoke. York staring—another of Boujma's transformations. But suddenly Boujma's face sagged, blood abruptly drained from it. Eyes suddenly fugitive. And the chatelaine herself falling back, gazing toward the door. The room caught in a vibrant hush.

Resounding hush already in possession of the salon—in a single swoop, white tusk of presence occupying the very space Boujma's eyes had fled. York sat immobilized, unable to look, simply aware of this great white tooth. The chatelaine dissolving as if her space preempted. And Boujma sitting amid the shreds of his own receding flesh, head floating as if severed from his body.

York wanted to slap himself out of the trance. That animal had taken possession of the hush within him. And sat, arraigned beyond fear, body glowing with the flames of the room.

"The sun is dying. We shall dine." Voice stabbing the room even as it caressed.

"Yes, the sun is falling. . . . Yes, we shall dine." Answers burbling from Boujma, and a voice by the door, the chatelaine. And the Caid turning to her, conversing without relinquishing the core of the room. York stared ahead blankly . . . never seen anyone enter, possess a room this way.

York sitting there, cross-legged on the rug, head bowed and eyes lowered as Boujma's had been. Hadn't really seen the uncle at all. Just that white tusk of presence impaling the inner eye, dismantling the outer. . . . He peered up. A pair of white slippers, long pointed slipper-shoes riding the rug. Flowing white burnoose. And at the waist a large curving knife, silver with massive ivory handle—tied into its sheath with a red cord. York's eyes drawn cautiously up. . . . Tall man, slender, a silver chain around his neck. Iron-gray beard trimmed sharp. Nose curved like knife. Lean face declaring the skull, but eyes opulent . . . *eyes right on me!*

York stood up shaking, bowed his head. And when he glanced up again, the Sheikh was flowing slowly toward him, though no discernible movement of his limbs. Eyes calmly absorbing York, who felt his body expand as the Sheikh rippled closer. Sheikh looming twice life size now. York saw arms, his own, floating slowly forward, palms open. And a pressure on his hands as if they had received touch. The Sheikh arriving in front of York, with his own arms open. As if they were embraced, though they remained fully four feet apart. And before he could respond . . . the Sheikh had dissolved.

A pistol shot of hands. And a soar of gold. Young servant bearing the brass table across the rug, setting it up past York. Giant teapot and glasses descending onto the tray. And glancing over, York saw the hand. Hand floating above the tray, gesturing him to be seated. The Sheikh . . . enthroned in the corner beyond the tray. Face a peaceful smile, small white skullcap on his head.

York settled on the divan, half facing the Sheikh. Tray to his left on a low table: domes, pinnacles, spires—colored glass, silver hammer, embering brazier nearby. And arching over all, teapot inlaid with enamel. The Sheikh's head glowing above, master of the keep as he broke chunks of sugar with the small hammer, dropping them into the teapot. And maneuvered glasses to center tray, sniffed a bundle of mint, adding more sprigs to the pot. Then sat back, content. Boujma sifted over beside York. The rug embracing them amid the flames of sunset.

Till the teapot soared two, three feet—an iridescent scimitar of tea spouting forth, steaming, arched frothing into the glasses. York stared. Would a figure rise naked from the carpet, dragon above the flames of rug? No, just the Sheikh lowering the teapot onto its brazier. Serenely indicating York's glass while raising his own, sniffing the mist of mint, tasting in a slurp of incisive elegance. Nodding to York. York followed, slurping loud, but no elegance—damned tea scalded his tongue. Barely managed to hold on to the burning glass, get it back to the tray.

A young man lighting candles inside high suspended lanterns. The myriad light of candles flowing through colored glass to mesh and match the last of the sun.

The Sheikh took one of the silver containers, lifting the dome, exposing a cluster of small white petals. Sprinkling a few in his glass, his hand floating across, strewing some in York's glass, in Boujma's. The burning tea biting fragrance from the petals, the

Sheikh imbibing it, half closing his eyes and swaying on the divan. York swayed too. The Sheikh nodding, content at the way his guest moved.

Again the Sheikh leaned forward. Hand fluttering to the silver hammer, opening another container, prodding uncut chunk of sugar, hitting it, and shooting it directly into his glass . . . trajectory of two feet. Doing the same for York, Boujma. Tea now in its third phase, and York swept on in its wake.

"It is like a bird. Each flight differs. Each movement of plumage creates a new bird. So, too, our tea. . . ." The Sheikh intoning in precise, if halting, French.

"Yes, like a bird." He heard his own reply, knew the Sheikh was right. The entire ceremony fluttering and flying. The tea itself alive, bird or butterfly.

"Our mountain tea is a rejoicing. The mint comes from a spring that was my father's. It greets only the morning sun; it drinks the first dew." The Sheikh purring. York saw the embroidery lining his robe, as elegant as the tea. "You sat there, honored guest"—the Sheikh nodding "with my herder, the handsome Juba. Up at the spring, I preserve that pasture for the mint alone. I permit nothing else to grow there. Did you observe?" Sheikh crooning around his glass, as York sat stripped, sensing the Sheikh *knew*.

"Our valley is particular; our mountains have their own flowers and scents. Their own mysteries." The Sheikh's voice a garland of flowers around a curved blade.

"Your oasis, sir, has a mystical quality."

The Sheikh smiled. "You see, in early times the rites were performed there to the God of the Skins . . . the Goat God!" And as the Sheikh fondled his glass, York saw Juba standing beside him by that spring. The Sheikh's eyebrows flickering at York as they talked through their tea. "You see, honored guest, the tea and the dance and the valley are one. And when they are not . . . it is death." His very voice issuing from within his glass. And a glint of mirth. Boujma sat silenced . . . his every movement miming those of the Sheikh. Whether or not the Sheikh had murdered his father; whether his aunt was also his mother, preempted by her mate's killer; whether this château itself was barbaric plunder—Boujma now merely a bowed head, a mimic sway, a slurping glass. During the tea the Sheikh had not glanced at him once; and York had not dared.

Another gunshot crack—teapot, sugar bowl, flower bowl, glasses, hammer and tongs . . . minareted tea tray floating up, up over their heads and off to one side. A servant lowering it to the left of the Sheikh. And placing a large lantern by the table now . . . lantern catching the colors of walls, rug, spewing them over the glistening tabletop. A second servant arriving, bearing another massive tray high over their heads. For just an instant the youth stood before them, waiting. The Sheikh nodded imperceptibly; the tray descended directly in front of them. Tray a full three feet across, topped by a high silver dome. Again the Sheikh nodded; the dome soared up in a volcano of steam and fragrance, combining herbs, flowers and carrion. Rotting flesh and petals, garlic of rosewater and death. York trying to place it, that musky smell . . . from where? And through the rising vapor discerned the Sheikh, eyes closed in beatitude, lips pursed, nose climbing in the wake of that first eruption. And the mist slowly dispersing to York's staring blank-eyed at him from a mound of vegetables and flesh, there in the center of the platter—*a head*. A pair of horns, one broken off at the tip . . . the head of Juba's ram! Tongue lolling forward, and caught in its teeth the remains of green sprig Juba's mother had placed so gently just before the knife. Before the final spew of blood, ram coughing softly to its knees in Juba's embrace. All roiling York's own flesh as he inhaled the rancid, rabid fragrance, the platter before him.

He wobbled on the edge of the divan, pretending avid pursuit of such divine aroma. Sheikh nodding appreciation. But York's body beyond control, last bleat of the ram in his ears, sprig of green in his eyes. The smell of sacrifice bellowing, "Timbuktu—52 jours." For an instant he thought he must faint, his body possessed by recognitions he dared not accept but could not avoid. Here the blood and snort of beloved beast resounded the dinner plate. And food itself proclaimed a sacrifice saved only by prayer, and the last mercy of flowers.

With a shudder, his mind collapsed in the rampage of his body, floating in the flames of lanterns, rug, the salon itself. As if the room had dissolved, roasted with this ram, and passed into York through the steam from the platter. As if every action of York's since arrival was served back to him now as blatant fragrance and food. And as he floated, saw the servant retreating, the chatelaine seated beyond on her ample cushion—and past her, a man standing guard . . . with a gun?

York heard the cough, the Sheikh summoning him back to their banquet. York floating back from his own auto-da-fé, back to the edge of that sacrificial platter. Catching a glimpse of Boujma extinct: regal zombie. And the Sheikh's eyes awaiting the return of York's. Sheikh smiling a glinting pardon as York returned to platter and presiding ram's head. And intoning "Bus-millah," the Sheikh reached forward with right hand, pausing above the reeking platter, fingers hovering like eyes over the cowering chunks of meat. Then, swooping down on a piece of flesh jutting beside the severed head, bore it sizzling to his lips. Closed his eyes and savored the chosen meat, chewing with elegant, sucking care. And morsel swallowed, he nodded, and Boujma nodded, and York nodded.

Till the Sheikh reached again over the platter, appraising further prey. Finally diving onto a piece rich in fat, plucking it to the edge of the platter. And placing it between thumb and forefinger, shot it clear over horns of the ram . . . *splat*, to land at platter's edge in front of his guest. York gaped as the meat hurtled toward him. He let the meat cool a moment, then weaned it from the burning rice and sauce, got it to his mouth. And without thinking, closed his eyes, smacked his lips, tilted his head back—chewing with concerted gusto and swallowing. He opened his eyes. The Sheikh gleaming delight at his achievement and setting out to find a choice piece for himself. Boujma followed suit. Giving York time to savor the meat. He'd tasted nothing during the actual eating of it. But the flavor lingered . . . like suckling kid, not ram at all. Meat melting like marrow. Steeped in that buttery sauce, but with a pungence that was palpable seeping through his palate, echoing from his gullet. As if butter gone rotten, aged in dead flesh. "No, not armpits—smen!" Words leaping in York. "*Smen!*" Tony bellowing as the vapor rose from the platter. Camel couscous en route to the desert, that sauce! And the blood on James's floor, after, when the Commandant came. "Give a girl a chance, wot?" York teetered, steam rising from the immense platter, bouquet of live innards steaming as if they were coming out of the ram at slaughter—innards of James, Tony . . . or himself?

The teapot surged up. York grabbed for a glass in self-defense. Sheikh shooting tea clear across the ram platter. Then circular, heavy dark bread passed. And another bullet of meat soaring over John the Baptist head, *plop*, into the butter sauce in front of York. While the Sheikh broke his bread, deftly nuzzling sauce and meat with it . . . raising it all to his mouth in a joust with gravity. And licked his fingers, glancing at York as if to say, "That's how." York broke off a piece of bread, maneuvering the second offering of meat with rice and sauce, getting it all to the edge of the platter, raising it . . . and *splat*, the meat plummeted to the floor. York wanting to dive after the truant morsel, ask pardon on hands and knees. Certain the Sheikh had seen his dereliction. He peered up. Sheikh smiling at the ceiling, benign. But his right hand circling over the platter again, diving for an even larger piece of meat and propelling it with deft finger flick across the table to his guest. This time shortening the trajectory, the meat falling farther from hazardous edge of platter. Grateful, York leaned over, took the meat in his fingers, determined to manage. Got it halfway to his mouth—but too unwieldy for a single mouthful. He sat paralyzed. A cluck-cluck from far side of platter. The Sheikh drawing his long silver knife, offering to cut the meat. Thank God! York started to pass the meat over the ram's head. But the Sheikh flicked his left hand high in the air, splashing fingers wide, drawing York's startled eye. York felt a slight pull in the hand holding the meat. He looked down—the meat had fallen onto the platter in two pieces. And the Sheikh wiping the blade between folds of bread, laying it down beside him.

York gaped. Had the Sheikh really—yes; there the meat lay, cut in two, ready to eat.

He sat numb, wanting to bleat, run. Glanced up. The Sheikh fondling the silver collar at his throat, silver glint in his eyes as he foraged for more meat. And Boujma probing the sauce, foraging with bread. So calm they seemed. Perhaps York was just overwrought. He picked up one of the sliced portions of meat, hand trembling as he got it to his mouth. Sheikh nodding at this success. And yes, it was delicious. But as he ate, the room took over again—shunted yellow of the tiles like the bittersweet of sauce, red the biting pungence, mauve the underriding touch of garlic. The very body of the meat and rites of the meal become his form of knowledge here . . . the way he saw, was seen. Any failure on his part, any failure to flow, was insult to life. The benefit great if in living faith he ate this flesh, but likewise the danger great if received unworthily.

He leaned forward, shaking, hand following rhythms of the Sheikh's hand. The adept dipping of bread into sauce, balancing of meat on bread swung in high arc to mouth. Laws of gravity suspended. As shreds of tripe, splatters of kidney and groin flew into his mouth. Whether by luck or abandon, he didn't miss again. Though his face, beard, hands amok with sauce, flying vegetables and meat.

The Sheikh then plucked up a large bone, placing one end in his mouth. Sucking on it, cheeks puckering as he sucked till the bone showed hollow . . . and the marrow rolled around his darting tongue, his eyes rolling with it. And again he nodded benignly at York, who found a smaller bone, sucked on it with no success, no marrow. But the Sheikh's hand floated up, hovering over a bigger bone, rounder one. And York soon drawing on the bone, sucking out its innermost flesh of marrow. Sheikh swaying content on divan, sucking his own lips in pleasure for his apprentice guest. And bones no sooner finished than gun-clap of hands, and the remains removed. And when York glanced down, a cornucopia of fruit on the table: dates, figs, pomegranates. Coffee and almond nuts. York nodding as if all were normal, furtively wiping his smen-soaked hands on the bottom of burnoose. . . .

Another clap of hands. A youth bearing a silver object, like a giant salt shaker, and a towel. Sheikh holding forth his hands as the servant sprinkled water across them . . . fragrance of spiced water. York creeping his own hands back up from his soiled burnoose. And the Sheikh clucked, brandishing the tall shaker and leaning over to York. Boujma poking him again, "Hold out your hands!" And the Sheikh elegantly sprinkling water over them. The servant following with towel so he could wipe hands, face. Then Boujma—the spiced water shooting out, and suddenly squirting all over his face. The Sheikh apologized lightly as he subsided back on the divan in a satisfied belch. Boujma mopped his eyes. While York stared at the silver shaker: tall and slender, with small water holes at the top. Boujma scowled, miming a smile. The Sheikh simply smiled and, taking the shaker, held it out to York, who didn't know whether to duck or extend his hands again. Boujma silent this time. But the Sheikh proffering the shaker, passing it to York. Who took it uncertainly, testing some of the water: yes, sharply perfumed. And the Sheikh waving his hand. "Allah karim! A gift to mark your visit."

"A gift?" York stared at the shaker—a kind of water ewer, really. Finely chased and embossed. Then back at the beaming Sheikh.

"We wish you to have it. It is the first time you have seen one, no? Please accept our gift." The Sheikh firm.

York nodded. Finally stood and bowed, still holding the ewer, which dribbled down his burnoose. And suddenly ducking past Boujma, returned with his bottle of umloo. Bowing again and passing it to the Sheikh.

"Ahhh, donnant donnant," the Sheikh murmured, appraising the bottle. "You will permit me to open it."

York sat down as the Sheikh lifted the top, sniffing in anticipation, then delight. "Umloo, one of the precious secrets. Most foreigners—you will excuse the word—do not know of umloo."

York nodded. The Sheikh nodded. Boujma half nodded.

"But allow me to guess which region, which plateau, which valley this umloo comes from. You see, honored guest, each district produces its own umloo. Each is different. In the Marrakech plains it is very sweet. Up by Telouet, sharper yet deeper, darker." The Sheikh crooning to himself as he swayed over the open bottle.

"Like different wines," York ventured.

"We do not drink wine." Suddenly the Sheikh shot a finger into the bottle and back up to his mouth. "Ahh . . ." The Sheikh closed his eyes in delectation. "The sharpness of the rocks, the lush of waterfall, the high flavor of mountain and mint. As fine as our own valley, no?" His eyes rolling open. "As sweet as our Juba's smile."

York stared.

"You met him, did you not? His father makes the finest umloo in the valley. We allow him the use of our spring."

York squirmed.

"We thank you, dear guest, for bringing our valley home to

us. You have brought the finest gift, hamdoulla." The Sheikh whirled his knife. "Will you have a fig?" York nodded as the Sheikh passed a fig skewered on the tip of his knife. "And some coffee?" He reached for the pot, poured. Then again for his knife, slicing a pomegranate, as York made a furtive sign of the cross.

"You are a Nazarene?"

A what?

"A Christian," Boujma whispered.

"Yes, a Christian." The word skittering the salon, echoing off the walls, to drop into the flames of the carpet.

The Sheikh smiled, knife dallying his pomegranate. "You believe a man nailed to a tree can live, can fly to heaven?"

York nodded—at the Sheikh, or at the question?

The Sheikh slurping his coffee. Finally saying, "Are you waiting for anything to befall us except victory or martyrdom?"

"I beg your pardon?"

"Hell lies in ambush. . . ." The Sheikh passing York part of the pomegranate, skewered again.

York tried an appreciative smile. The Sheikh reciprocated as Boujma whispered, "The Koran, lines from the Koran!"

"Ah, the Koran reads you, honored guest." The Sheikh belched contentedly, producing a silver pick with which he cleaned his teeth. "Please feel welcome in our unworthy home! Allah has purchased of the faithful their lives and worldly goods. . . ." Boujma nodded and belched.

"Our Boujma tells us you are a lawyer, and a friend of ambassadors."

York stared at the Sheikh.

"We are honored to receive a guest of such importance." The Sheikh had finished with his teeth, was doing an ear. The silver pick had an ear scoop at one end.

"But lawyers do not usually enjoy this region. They have been known to disappear."

York stiffened, eyeing the Sheikh's knife. Was that guard still at the door?

"The last one fell down a well. Thirty meters down. Eavesdroppers are pursued by fiery comets." The Sheikh now reaming his right ear with the silver scoop amid grunts of delight. "We have very deep wells." The Sheikh smiled, offered York another fig.

"My knowledge of law is quite slight, really."

"We know that. Indeed, we rejoice that you are not a lawyer at all. Nor a friend of ambassadors." The Sheikh's eye pierced York, who turned away. "So you are under my protection, a cherished guest."

York's eyes on the rug, the red rising there like blood.

"Which is why I wish you to have our water ewer. Emblem of our indissoluble friendship, n'shalla." The Sheikh popped a date into his mouth, closed his eyes, chewing. Then shot the date pip out of his mouth, ricocheting it off his hand onto a plate. And, with a smile, reached for his knife.

York froze.

But the Sheikh simply whirled the knife above his head and down into his sheath. And slowly stood up. "I must go to prayer . . . to the one God, yours and mine." Sheikh towering over the table, head showered in red, gold, blue . . . lantern swaying beyond. Towering there, as if already in prayer, the room before him void. Then gone. Doors closed. And the rug soaring where the Sheikh had stood.

For some moments York sat enmeshed in that departure. And when he looked up, saw the flames of rug and salon, all whirling in a cone above the table. A whirlpool of colors there. The ewer—the Sheikh's ewer gathering the colors of the room into its single glistening body. Silver catching the light, the flicker of candles, the storm of rug. Flashing the salon into York's eyes as single flame. Ewer expanding as if the Sheikh himself, towering there. A man whose slightest gesture held keys of life and death. A man who held such power simply by holding it over himself. Not as construct of mind or will, not as ideology . . . but some marriage of body and being.

He glanced up—the salon as permanent aureole of the Sheikh himself. York's eyes drawn to where the Sheikh had first stood. The Sheikh's very being fusing this world and a world beyond. In a way that unmasked the secular as a cowardice more devious than other-worldliness. And sainthood, even sainthoood, a refuge for fools.

York suddenly on his knees. "I've met a man whose sense of justice, kind or killing, is linked to majesty. A man for whom death might rightly be less important that the arc of fresh-roasted ram, shot over a host's platter to his unknown guest. A man who might well commit murder, and even the son of the victim would join his dinner, grateful for access to a reality larger than the murder itself."

York crouched in terror on the rug. Aware that he was not the source of the words, but saying only what the entire valley had been saying since his arrival. Magnificat. And if insane, then insane in some right way. And if the Sheikh himself a tenant of hell . . . at least within the eye of the transcendent gods.

He flopped back on the divan, glanced around the salon. How long had he been there? Dinner tray gone, coffee and fruit gone. Everyone gone. He probed the flickering light, unable to distinguish lanterns from wall, floor . . . all moving, breathing. Room of the dragon, it had never left. Shadows from candles rumbling the salon in carnal arabesques; glint of eye from lanterns; tusk from walls.

He fell back. A shadow on the far wall: shadow rising, elongating, head swaying. *A cobra!* Caught in the lantern light, no mistaking that contour. York's eyes splaying left, right—nothing, no one. Yet the swaying shadow of snake still there, rising beyond the second lantern. A cobra—as finale, farewell from the Sheikh!

He yanked his feet up on the divan. Began piling large cushions. He glanced at the doors—shut, bolted. Trapped. He crawled atop the cushions. Then moved only his eyes to locate the cobra. Eyes traversing the rug, to lamp on the far table by a divan. Serpent-shadow rising on the wall beyond that lamp. He forced his eyes down, down, to the space between shadow and lamp. There! Cobra stark, swaying. He tried to see more clearly over the lamp. Caught the swollen head above the swaying body . . . and a hand! York craned to see.

And saw a hard-on: massive cock, erect beyond the lantern. Hand serenely stroking cock in the shuddering light. Heard a sigh. And shifting further, York saw the body lying along the divan, hidden below lantern and table. Lost in the folds of a burnoose, adrift in the colors of the salon. Boujma lying there, gazing beatifically at his own hard-on.

A spasm of relief shook York. He wasn't locked in with a cobra, but with a young Moroccan, calmly masturbating after a copious meal. And smoking York's pipe, he could see that now too. Smoke mingling with candle flames, and the floating smell of hashish. York staring as Boujma varied his stroke: one hand, then the other. Up at the tip . . . and down, rolling his balls. Completely unconcerned whether York was there or not. Cock-cobra still swaying the wall, and York wondering what to do. A discreet cough? Irrelevant. Part of the decor so to speak. Flames of the room into flare of Boujma's magnificent cock. York nodded—if the decor convoked a man like the Sheikh, it also convoked a man like the Sheikh, it also convoked an acolyte of the God of Skins. Convoked a Boujma, lying serenely with giant erection.

York shifted position slightly; Boujma glanced up. Eyeing York on his cobra-proof cushions. York tried to grin—about to climb down. But Boujma thrust a hand up and slowly rose from the divan. Towering above the lantern, moving forward, cock first.

Boujma smiled. "C'mon, *Yankee!*" And with that he turned, and holding his burnoose up with one hand, hard-on displayed with the other, began parading around the room. Past several lanterns . . . pausing in each angle of light. Burnoose pulled higher and higher—silhouette of cobra flashing. Smile spreading his face as he pivoted in the light, displaying cock, legs, arse—Boujma rampant. Then turned again . . . strode over, taking York's arm. Leading him over to the divan where he had been lying before.

Boujma lying back, hard cock still on display. And York sitting beside, eyes fixed on helmet head glistering by candlelight. Tusk of flesh shimmering with the reflected colors. And the hooded shadow dancing a yard high, the swaying shadow on the flaming walls. Cobra once again. And Boujma, following York's gaze, thrust his cock farther into the light. The shadow larger now . . . poised beast readied to spring. Like the final head of the Sheikh, more real than any flesh. Of course, this cobra-cock, beast of prayer, it's what this salon is. Helmet of all flesh, dragon, hidden god this salon celebrates. Man. What the Sheikh fulfilled . . . Sheikh's every movement enacting the verity, conjugating this salon as eros absolute.

York's blood throbbing, his own cock rising hard. As Boujma reached over, grabbed York's hand, placing it on his immense dark cock. York stared, motionless. Both of them staring at Boujma's cock. Boujma wanted sex, but this salon, this valley, so much more than sex. Sex ending where this salon began. Salon and valley demanding life, sensate celebration. But Boujma was just cock.

Volubility of room and York rising with his own hard-on. As Boujma thrust donkey dong harsher into York's hand. York looked down, Boujma's cock bursting for attention, jutting a full hand above York's clasping hand. A spasm of lust shaking York. As Boujma whirled onto his belly, ripping burnoose up to his chest, buttocks moaning the air, pleading, please, *please*. Boujma at one moment all pasha, at another a flaunt of cock, now anal dervish writhing in his necessity. Necessity York there to fulfill, hostage from the start.

Boujma slapping his own butts. York's head whirling amok. He looked up . . . shadow writhing on the wall. Flailing shadow amid the rising flames. Big Red moaning "Please, Yo-yo, fuck me, fuck me hard!" John rotating his buttocks in the air, stroking red-cock. York lurched to his feet, caught by the throb of his own hard-on. "Please, please, do it *now!*" York pulling his burnoose up, hand on cock to plunge, impale that shouting flesh. But glancing down, saw Boujma's ass rioting there. For a second he stood, tempted. Then started to laugh . . . laughter booming the room, walls . . . crazed cackle of laugh. As he gave Boujma's ass a sharp slap and stumbled back to his own divan.

Moments later the moaning ebbed and died. And trickling in the air, the saline-sweet smell of a man who has just come. And knowing the mighty Boujma wouldn't trouble him again tonight, York crumpled into tormented sleep.

He awoke to rooster call and the first slant of sun. Twinges of gold, red, floating beams—the salon rising in the morning light. *Arrrk-arrghk*, right outside the windows, must be in the front court. And the sun flickering along the line of beams from the high cupola. Never seen such a room. Never lived such an evening as last night. He glanced across: there was Boujma, asleep, burnoose still half up, huge knob of cock distending with the dawn. *Aaark-aaarrk*. Salon rising, light catching the upper walls, the carved cornices. Beautiful, like this whole wild valley. Like the oasis, with Juba. What he'd spent a lifetime to find.

Boujma shifted on the divan, half turning. Not awake yet, but already fondling his massive cock. And the sun creeping down the walls. *Aaark-aaarghk*. York propped himself up. And suddenly it all spewed up in him. The talk of murder, what Juba's father had said. The boy on the bus. And Boujma. The sun was striking the first of the red tiles. In half an hour Boujma would be active, trying to rape York, or inveigling York to rape him. Boujma was hardly interested in the finer points of English. Sun slicing the room. Another day like yesterday and he'd be locked in this salon forever. Locked psychically, if not physically. Hostage to the gold and shimmer and captured sear of sun. God, locked into the very balls of God!

He staggered to his feet, still in the burnoose, looking for his own clothes. Where? Under Boujma's head. He looked again—his clothes and notebook all in a tumble at Boujma's head. No way to get them now. Found his shoes; bent to put them on. Then crept toward the door, unbolting it . . . only locked from the inside. And just as he was about to quit the salon, turned. Imbibing the majesty of the Sheikh last night. On the brass table: the ewer. The Sheikh's gift. No need, it was all burned inside him. He *was* a ewer; get out!

He bowed, moved silently through the upper hallway to the stairwell. Sneaking down, pausing at sudden vista out the slit window. The valley, cascade of rock and rumble. And far beyond, to the right, a glint in the angling sun: white walls, mosque tower . . . Demnat! The tip of the town rising above the winding run of green—the river, must be. York half ran, half fell down the rest of the snaking stairwell to the hall below. No one; only the sun.

He shot out the portal door—then stopped, as if merely sniffing the air. The guard rigid at first, but smiling as York nodded, sauntered on. Through the row of junipers first, toward the tinkle of the rivulet. He'd follow it as far as he could, toward the river. . . . He found the little stream and stumbled along the embankment, eyeing floating turtles, orchard of figs overhead and those gnarled trees the goats had climbed, where he'd first seen Juba. No sign of Juba. He thrust ahead to a cluster of mud farm huts, yards enclosed in thorns. A young woman approaching, wide eyes and smile, carrying mint, a bundle of mint. And for a wild moment wanted to accompany her to her hut, sit for morning tea. Just stay in this enchanted valley—why go anywhere now? But pounding behind him, the black eye of the iron portal, the guard staring.

The sun was already hot though day just risen. "Damnet? Damnit?" York gestured in what he presumed was the direction of the town. The startled woman nodded, pointing along the rivulet as it fell below the kasbah. York pushed into the swaying network of trees and vines, till he came to the path winding down the cliff. Rivulet tumbling beside. And after falling twice, was down into the maze of gardens lurking like a nest under protective branches. Visual lagoon of cucumbers, corn, trumpeting flowers. Till he realized he was lingering, wanting to sit down. . . . "Get a move on, Yo-yo, this ain't Osprey Cove!" And spurted past the huts where he'd seen the old woman in red shawl—weeks ago, it seemed. Following the rivulet down the slope till it divided under an orchard. He swerved onto the right-hand path. Another five minutes . . . rivulet dividing again, part of a complex irrigation system. Again he bore right as he followed a narrowing donkey trail. Another five minutes, till his face smacked sharply by sun. The glade had ended, the rivulet dissolving into mud. Beyond that, a tilted ocean of rock, foothills, interspersed with stunted trees. And in the distance, the low mountains, gaunt-ribbed mountains encircling the valley. But no town—only the valley blaring into him.

Where was Dammit? He bore right again, lurching out onto the crackling rock, following a winding trail. Toward a hump of land—might see the big river from there. His eyes clinging to a few scrub trees as he went. My God, everything upside down here. All penetrating him. . . . Get the hell to Damnation, York! The trail snaking forward in the tilt and furor of the land. Ten minutes and he'd crossed this first lava blast, grateful amid the writhing shade of an arganier orchard. His head tinkling: a portion of the rivulet surfacing amid the trees. He squatted, splashed his face. Laughing—the way the Sheikh had squirted water in Boujma's face. Wily old bastard! "I must go to prayer . . . to the one God, yours and mine." He glanced at his watch: only eight-twenty. Suddenly racing toward that high knoll again. Trees and stones chattering, land eliding with his body. The rivulet had dissolved into the rocks once more. And the land now dropping, not rising as he thought. And once clear of the orchard—the rapacity of sun, the air fatally still.

He glanced back. Château looming against the sky like giant antlers, over a mile behind him. Arrived at the trees, puffing.

His eyes splaying across the land for clues, data. The sun implacable. He'd have to turn back. Rooster shout ahead. Maybe a farm.

He shuffled into a run—hitching up his torn burnoose, following rooster cry like a road sign. It crowed again.And one scraped knee later he was panting amid a sprout of green. A donkey ambling by, an old man peering from a hut. "Denmit!" York bleated. "Damnet?" Old man jerked his head in the direction of the knoll, and a higher rise of land beyond it now, pine trees just visible. Close, closer now. But his stupid shoes took half an hour to get there. Land rising and falling, then higher. He crouched over his fear, shitting. Yes, burnoose good to shit in, doesn't get in the way.

He scrambled to the next height of land, desperate to see a glint of Damnation, or even that swollen river. Nothing, except the blast of rocks, the demented forms of cacti. He cowered under a pine tree. Another hour and the sun'll be full strength. His eyes stuttering with the staccato of rocks. I've come too far, should never have left Marrakech. Never left Osprey Cove. I came too far, John! John's letter, photo, still with Boujma, final hostage. Yes, when Boujma took my pipe, it was my cock he was after. He glanced up, a shadow floating overhead. A vulture coasting, rising the next hump of land several hundred feet ahead. His eye followed, followed the trajectory of vulture toward the higher knoll. If he could just get there, maybe he'd see the town.

He forced himself on down the slope, up, running so as not to fall. No path; rivulet long gone. Hot blast of noisy silence. But scrub bushes suddenly taller. Land leveling off. And a hand—hand raised at him, *stop*! No, just an oak leaf silhouetted by sun. Scrub trees, some kind of oak. And beyond the oak, pines looming. Improbable surge of green oasis tapping underground moisture. He pushed forward into pine grove, vines. And softness of his shoes now, dead leaves, pine needles underfoot.

And as the mottled shade swarmed around him, saw a path. Mirage? No, a path there, path trampled through leaves and loam. He leapt to it, running, stopping at abrupt sound. Heard the voices, raced toward them. And stood gaping at a circle of yellow flowers hiding under the trees. He knelt beside, caressing them. Carillon of flowers as he knelt in their song. And ducked and peering up, saw white-and-black mask, falcon alighting in nearby pine tree. Falcon preening, scouting the underbrush, marauding on. York touched the flowers again, thanked them and ran, tossing himself along the path. The trees closing in, shade deepening. Insane land: one minute fiery furnace, next a primeval orchard, then greenwood and chorale of flowers.

My God, the path gone. No, just trees shunting closer, shrinking his passage. Path passing beneath lowering branches, like a long tunnel. He bent on all fours, snouting through the underbrush. Path still there, leaves and needles well trodden, wide enough for a small donkey to pass. Natural beds of earth, deep leaves on each side, but one of the beds to the left hurtling up. Had he fallen? No, the earth detonating, glaring at him. He toppled to a halt, staring along the thundering tunnel of green. Staring . . . into an eye. *Eye*—maybe ten feet away! Don't breathe, Yo-yo. . . . The eye moving now. Amber-red eye, size of a prune, boring into him. Coming toward him? No, angling to the right.

York frozen on his knees, flesh fused to the slowly moving eye. Unblinking single eye stabbing like fang. And beyond the eye, sharp rising ear, bristle of shoulders. Beast in profile, part hidden by branches—great hump of head, neck . . . barrel chest. The rest hidden by green. As the eye turned toward York. Chest hidden, but haunches so elegant, antelope. Walking on tips of its feet, hooves. And barrel body pivoting around that eye pointed . . . directly at York.

Slowly the animal turned its head straight toward York, like unsheathing a knife. My God, *is* a knife: great sabering tooth . . . ivory tusk. York impaled to the ground. And even as he lay, slashing the air in single fling of that massive head. And loped off elegantly, silently into the underbrush.

York dared look up. It must have been lying in that hollow of earth, mattress of leaves its berth, cool. Surprised from sleep. No sound of beast. And York up on his knees, humming to himself, hands held out, palms open to where the beast had been. Crooning to himself.

He crawled over to the hollow of earth. Bent his head down, sniffing, catching a subtle musk. And sniffing again, breathing musk in deeply . . . energy spiraling up his spine, through his arms, fingers. Right hand floating forward, right forefinger. Finger thrusting into the warm earth—and tracing an eye, jab of ear, hump of back to long, tapering haunches. And pausing, finger jumping up, poised high, then down in the sudden stab of curved ivory tusk. Beast traced in the soft earth. Motion of beast just seen, caught at fingertip. York throbbing as he knelt, gazing at this animal outlined there. And bent down, kissing the body in the earth, wed in their joined eye.

And even as he kissed, heard the rumble, seething up within the soil. Clear and deep as from a giant underground cauldron. And felt it through the palms of his hands on the earth. He put his ear to the ground; yes, thunder of some huge hidden cauldron, underground geyser. And scrambled up on all fours, muttering, "Follow it, follow the eye of the beast!" Lunging after the fresh imprints. Scrambling for his life . . . fifty, a hundred yards. Bursting into a clearing. Only the sudden sun, more scrub oaks, larger. And grass, thick grass and sparkle of flowers.

York still crouching as the land flared over him. He stood up, trembling. Came too far, John . . . was on my way back. As he slapped himself on the face, hard. He churned forward, chasing the roar of earth and ear. Grass spurting higher, strange fleshy plants. And *crash*—smashed sideways onto the ground, grabbing at a tree trunk. His face buried in vines, feet plowing the ground as brakes. The earth shuddering as he lay clinging to the tree. And only slowly raised his head.

He was at the edge of a gorge. Thundering gorge directly below him: a hundred feet, more. And at the bottom, river pounding through a cauldron of giant boulders. York gaping into a watery inferno as violent as sun above it. Yes, the river he'd crossed with Boujma and mule. He stared . . . sudden lush of gorge, trees, grass, vines. And the rage below, drawing his eyes down and down. Entire body sucked forward by river race. And the bleeding, weirdly beautiful red rubble of rocks. Longing to dive, float out over the fragrant floral edge of chasm, swim in sun and air. . . . River funneling him in like an airborne tributary.

Kee-rist! Pull back, York. He shoved with both hands, back from cliff edge. Slowly stood up, clinging to a scrub oak as anchor. And saw above the far cliffside a tower, two, and encircling walls. . . . Damnation! About a mile to the right, perched on the endless cliff.

He crept forward to the edge again. Eyes tumbling to rocks below, the mist rising vehement from waterfall, iridescence of sun. And that silver python river. His body quaking as he peered dizzily over the edge. And perched about halfway down the rubble face: a patch of green, suspended oasis of grassland—and animals. Goats grazing. How did they get there? Path down the cliff? If he could find it, follow . . . then down to that jumble of boulders at the throat of the river. Yes, a straggle of boulders spanning the river there. And across . . . the cliff on the far side not nearly as steep.

He glanced down again. Cliff wall almost vertical—might as well try to fly. He looked along the torrent of river. Surely there was a path to where he'd crossed with Boujma. But the gorge wound out of sight. Maybe that crossing lay beyond the town; two, three miles away. Couldn't be sure of getting there. He looked back, the large knoll he'd just come from, tunnel of trees, the beast. . . . No, must cross here. Become a goat!

He crouched down, edging his face over the cliff, sighting a few small bushes, hand holds, a winding path of ledges . . . A sudden, wild, raucous screaming. Massive black body hurtling at him, a hundred feet of gorge spinning in the air, wheeling from black to bronze and diving. "Get back—*back!*" He jockeyed backward, ears and eyes torn by the eruption. Thousands of blackbirds swooping, shimmering . . . and gone, vanished back up the throat of the gorge. Their metallic cry careening off rocks and hanging vines.

York clung to the oak tree. When he looked again, the town was still there. He had no choice. Crawled over to the cliff, positioning himself directly above the goat hummock some sixty feet below. Trying to spot, place, the bushes: possible hand grips down to that hummock. Suddenly seeing Juba scrambling with his goats, using every shrub, root, as purchase up the mountainside. . . . And with that inched himself backward over the cliff, grappling to a scrub pine, lowering himself slowly, sliding, half catching a root . . . dropping to a halt on a narrow ledge. And below that, a large rock jutting out. . . . He pressed his belly flat against cliff wall, sliding again, burnoose ripping up, skin ripping . . . *plop*, onto the rock. Now could see a slight path worn into the rubble. Goat trail! . . . He leaned forward, roots projecting below the rock, large vine. And clinging to the largest root, lowered himself, trying not to see the gorge. Down another ten feet. Straddling a wobbly shrub. And the thunder in his ears, dizzy. Unable to see the path at all now, only another ledge some fifteen feet down. And a clutch of vines. He aimed himself at the ledge, sliding, falling, clutching at roots, shrubs, body splayed wide like pinwheel, feet, fingers, chin as brakes—missed the ledge, missed, grabbing for vine, roots, a cactus . . . rocks rumbling after his one-man landslide.

He opened his eyes to green, lush green. And a face against his own—face licking, nuzzling. A baby goat. Other goats prancing around. And hoisting himself up saw the spring rising, water bubbling. The cliff rising straight above. And the roar of the river below. His shoulders throbbing, he pulled a shard of root from his palm, watching the blood. More goats returning to the hummock. They must have scattered as he crashed onto their oasis.

He crawled to the edge of green . . . forty feet to go. And that broken causeway of boulders across the neck of the river, just below the waterfall. He glanced upriver: rock walls narrowing into a high chasm, huge vines dangling fifty feet and more into the red-black gorge. Like a giant bird's nest . . . where that phalanx of birds came from. He looked down again—a plummeting rubble wall. . . . He flopped back amid the nuzzle of goats, hands over his ears. How could he get to the goddamn river? Another crash landing? He lay trying to think, his hand, body burning with bruises, abrasion. A goat licking his leg.

Suddenly he was up—growling, shouting, snatching up rocks that had fallen with him. Pitching them at goats; shouting and chasing them. Goats spewing off the hummock. Most of them scattering up the face of cliff. But three young ones, and a nanny, making their way down toward the river, slowly picking their way. The young ones following with care. He watched; whenever they stopped, he threw another stone till they moved farther down. Yes, on a path he could just discern, shrubs and boulders marking the turns. And now York began to follow, clutching at the scrub, a few vines, sliding, catching a large clump, clinging an instant, slithering down the massed vines, falling, hitting a gnarled tree, falling again, rolling . . . *craash*, into a pile of wet rubble. Roar of the cauldron in his ears and the tossed spray.

He was down, river about twenty feet away. Goats scattering

along the river. He wanted to weep, run after mother goat, thank her. His body rubbery, numb now.

He counted the boulders . . . nine of them spanning the river, water rampant between them. The first few close together. The middle ones farther apart. But the last two . . . four feet to the first and a large leap to the second. Then a short jump to the far bank. Could he? One slip and he'd be swept into the torrent. He looked at the final big rock. It was flat—a mound of moss in the center, large as a double bed. Thick moss? Had to get to that.

He pulled back. Right to the bottom of the cliff, some thirty feet from first boulder. Took off his shoes. Then sprang forward, sprinting toward the brink: first rock, hop-skip, leaning his weight forward dangerously, hop-jump . . . second, third rocks . . . skip-jump, across the middle rocks and leaping to the second last, rock just large enough to gain footing, take one firm stride at speed and, thrusting his head forward, yanked his body into a dive, diving as high and as far as could, hovering over that final spewing stretch of white water, heading wide-eyed for the final rock, that stretched bed of moss. And as soon as he saw the clutch of green hurtle up at him, balled his body somersault-round, hitting the ground with his shoulders, head under, protected by hands.

When he looked up he was lying on green . . . not moss but a cushion of succulents and dead vegetation. Miniature island with a layer of green earth breaking his fall instead of his neck. For a moment he lay, peering out of one eye. Only a few feet to the far shore. Then saw covered with blood his arms, legs and ripped burnoose. He probed . . . no breaks. And coughed, more blood spewing out . . . cracked his nose on landing. And suddenly lunged for shore, half missing, falling up to his waist in the torrent, but shoulders, arms flung onto land, one hand catching a root, the other around a knob of rock. Current churning his legs as he hauled himself out and stumbled, spouting blood, up the shore. Tripping over tree roots, vines, and falling flat on his back.

When he came to, John standing there, shaking his head. "Whatever possessed you, love?" John looking so satisfied as he reached down to help York up. York reached out, sat up. . . . No John. Turning, the birds, hundreds of them, surging from the dark neck of the gorge, wheeling into sunlight.

He yanked himself to his feet. And clawed his way up the near cliffside, up to a small path . . . till he reached a rocky road at the top. And a donkey approaching, boy on a donkey. "Damnit . . . how far to Damnation?" Boy halting, contemplating York. Finally jumping off and prodding him toward the donkey. Propping him on its back, the three of them trundling along the edge of the gorge toward Demnat. Boy shouting above the roar of water . . . something about a bridge. But his French bad, and York too deaf to hear. The gorge trotted by.

13
KEBIR

It's high morning hot, but not half as hot as that damned gorge. What day? Who gives a fuck what day? Today's the day I see this butterfly. Fluttering back at red flower, flip-flop of flutter sound. What are you searching for, butterfly?

Gone again & garden shrinks as if sun behind a cloud.

Lucky to find this garden nook, shade in a nest & I the bird peering, all unseen. Flip-flop, my butterfly says to see is to touch.

Khalid passed a while ago with Rebecca talking flowers. And she said, "Why don't you come to our gala dinner?" But Khalid replied, "I haven't gone out for dinner since the old King died!" I was so proud I nearly cried.

Claude said sunstroke again & why hadn't I taken sunglasses or even a hat? I said because I had no intention of going into those damned mountains again.

York sat back musing. His second day back now; the first had been mostly blank. All he remembered was returning in a collapsed taxi. Arriving at the gate of the hotel with no money, no clothes, no shoes. . . . Had staggered through the gate in his torn burnoose. To find les amis gathered at one of their lunches. They hadn't seen him at first. Till Rebecca glanced up as York stood silently there. "What's happened to you?" And they all looked up at York as at a ghost. York saying, "I need to pay the taxi." From where? "Dammit . . . Damnation!" But Richard saying, "Demnat?" York nodding. While les amis collected money for the taxi. Khalid tried to bargain the driver down, but the driver honking, honking and honking till paid in full. And les amis gathering around York at the lunch table, offering wine, shrimps and advice—but endlessly eager to know, "What in God's name did you do *this time?*" And York sitting numb, saying over and over, "The silver knife, he was like his knife." Till Claude took him up to his room and put him to bed.

And this morning they'd all duly appeared with questions and commiserations. Richard presenting him with a new tropical shirt. Rebecca contributed a gold cravat. And Herbert in league with Claude and Bertrand to offer a new pair of shoes. In return York promised to tell all—tomorrow. Reveal all about his trip at their farewell dinner. Yes, tomorrow his last full day in Morocco. And Herbert and Rebecca had kept their promise, inviting le tout hôtel to feast at one of Marrakech's most glamorous restaurants. A former palace, now a gourmet dining spot. And the following day, York's departure. Claude had already booked his plane ticket, saying "We've got to send you home in one piece, before you reduce the whole of Morocco to a pâté!"

York sitting in the garden of the Hôtel des Amis, watching his butterfly, knowing he now saw butterfly the way he'd seen that beast, beast of the tusk and burning eye, up in Dammit.

The next evening they were gathered in front of the hotel, ready to leave for the gala dinner. Richard debonair in a fading white suit and his sempaternal Order-of-What's-It. Claude in black with a red rose: black shirt, hat, cape, boots. Richard declaring he looked "very Comte de Montesquieu." Rebecca: "Do you mean *Proust's* Comte de . . . ?" He did. And Rebecca herself in a triumphant ensemble of flannel, coral beads, Moroccan gauze and a parasol. Claude asking why the parasol, and she why his cape. And they all laughed. Even Herbert, handsome in a pale blue tropical suit, cane and Panama.

"But where's our divinity?" Claude stamped his foot.

Khalid was dispatched to find him. While York stood eyeing this elegant assembly and his own new clothes—floral shirt, gold cravat, shoes. Yes, le tout hôtel had certainly rallied around after his return. He was proudest, however, of the silver hand hanging once again from his neck; the Hand of Fatima, courtesy of Kebir.

Khalid reappeared, announcing Bertrand en route. Yes, the divinity glowing down the walk in cossack attire, blue and white with gold belt. And Brigitte on his shoulder, attached to a leg ring and leash like a pet monkey.

"You're not taking that bird to our dinner," Claude snapped.

"Why not? She rarely gets out for dinner."

"It's a gorgeous idea," Rebecca said. "I've never dined with a macaw."

Settled, provided Bertrand kept her on the leash. Khalid hailed a pair of calèches. They would ride to dinner "in state." Rebecca's idea again.

Claude performed as master of ceremonies. "Rebecca, Herbert and Richard will proceed in the first calèche. Richard knows the way. Besides, he's Rebecca's favorite." Khalid aided the ample lady into the calèche, which acknowledged her advent by tilting wildly. Richard soon grinning beside her as aide-de-camp. Herbert facing them, hat askew, vaguely suspicious.

The others followed as soon as the macaw could be persuaded. York perched beside Claude in the backseat. Khalid and Bertrand opposite, Bertrand rattling his bracelet in anticipation. In minutes they were trundling down the bright night mall. The orange trees and palms parading past; Rebecca bobbing her parasol at the night strollers. Claude waving at a boy. "That one's a fallen angel, but the fall was worth it." York just beginning to relax in the splendor of it all, when Bertrand winked. "It's better than your ride from Demnat, remember? Your little visit to Demnat!" At which York sat up, staring over the side of the calèche as if the Sheikh himself might suddenly appear. And Claude upset, telling Bertrand to behave himself, at least till dinner. But it was too late. He'd gotten from the gorge to Demnat by donkey. And by sheer luck found the house with the blue door and Ranee, who gave him food and shelter for the night. And next day had tried to catch a bus to Marrakech. No bus. It was a holiday. But York terrified that the Sheikh was lying in ambush somewhere. And Ranee went off to find a car, someone to act as taxi. And left York sitting in a café opposite the butcher garden. Just as York had given up hope, a tawny vintage sedan clattered up, sagged to a halt. Driver's door falling open and a pear-shaped man plopped out, tying his door shut with a strap. That would never make it to Marrakech! But the driver bundled over, stationing himself beside York as if listening. "Marrakech!" York bleated.

Driver shook his jowls. "Sixty dirhams to the main highway."

Main highway? Only halfway. "A hundred to Marrakech!'

Driver sucking his lips sadly. "My car is tired. It's a holiday. One hundred and ten to Tamelelt."

And the bargaining finally done, York climbed into the sagging car. The pear-shaped man wheezed orders. Someone cranked the front of the car, which stuttered to life. The driver sank into his seat. Car surging forward as Ranee whispered through the window at York, "I saw Boujma earlier, told him you'd gone sight-seeing, up to the natural bridge." He winked. And two hours later, the sun at its zenith and the engine boiling, they saw the Koutoubia tower rising majestically through the front window. And soon entered the main boulevard, York desperately trying to remember the location of his hotel. Telling the driver to stop, he'd ask. But driver didn't want to stop, car mightn't start again. York shouting out the window, "Hôtel des Amis . . . Hôtel des—" till finally a policeman stopped them, decided it was easier to direct York to his hotel than to arraign him.

Gorge, Demnat and mountains far behind now. They were in a calèche, en route to a festive final dinner. And Kebir was going to join them at the restaurant, n'shalla! Their calèche had pulled abreast of Rebecca's now. That worthy lady leaning out to announce "I feel like a Roman charioteer." Claude shouting back "Marrakech by night, the Paris of all Africa." And Bertrand preening for passersby, kids ogling his macaw. York agreed; it really was Paris by night—an exotic, medieval Paris. Battlements and scars of ancient wars, cannons and huzzahs and heads impaled on spikes, wasn't that what James had said? Yes they were leaving the old French quarter and entering ancient Marrakech. Rebecca waving her parasol frantically at the Koutoubia, illuminated by night . . . illuminating the night, its high arcades booming, sentinel to an entire city. York surged to his feet and saluted. Bertrand asked what he was doing. York nodded at the Koutoubia. Bertrand laughing as the calèche lurched and York fell into Claude's lap. Claude saying "At last," and Bertrand announcing, "York's gone crazy again." But as York crawled into his own seat, Claude was saluting, and Khalid. All of them saluting the tower. Claude declaring, "We should always come by calèche." As the tower wheeled by and they turned into the Djema-el-Fna, Rebecca insisted they go through the market, because Herbert wouldn't venture there after dark. And Claude waving his cape as if conjuring up the sights and sounds of the place. York peered ahead at the small restaurant where he'd first eaten with Kebir. Would Kebir be there tonight?

Next thing York knew, they'd stopped, Khalid leaping out to help Rebecca onto the cobblestones. And Herbert protesting, "This can't be the spot . . . such unruly smells!" But Khalid led them down past shuffling beggars and through a gloomy portal . . . into a glittering foyer, large torchères and a servant in green pantaloons. A bell rung—a man appearing in red waistcoat, gold bow tie. Reservations? "Yes, the party of monsieur Claude Montamagny de la Vallette!" And the maître d' became all smiles and bows till the macaw let out a squawk. The maître d' froze. No—the restaurant didn't accept birds! Bertrand would have to check it along with the capes, canes, parasols. Bertrand refused. And Khalid stepped forward, smiling and waving his eyes. The maître d' grinned sudden recognition of him. And when Claude produced twenty dirhams the matter was settled by recourse to principle—parrots in general were not allowed in the restaurant, but this parrot was.

They followed the maître d' through a long hallway, old spears and rifles glinting the walls. Rebecca saying, "How thrilling." Claude and Richard gurgling at the prospect of a free feast. They were entering a room, fully three stories high, balcony and colored dome over head. Room of divans, pillars, arcades . . . and hidden pleasure nooks, all giving onto a central dance floor. Claude whispered something to the maître d' and slipped him more dirhams. And the maître d' lead them to a corner at the far end. "We'll have privacy here," Claude said.

They spread themselves around the corner on divans and poufs, peering at the room. Richard declaring it had been one of the Glaoui's palaces, which explained its grandeur. Herbert averred he'd never seen anything quite like it: "A cross between a Roman bath and an opera house." The maître d' reappeared with a waiter offering hors d'oeuvres and a wine list. Herbert insisted that Claude "choose the very finest of Moroccan wines." And Claude set to. "A blanc de blancs to begin with, and a gris de Boulaouane as follow-up, then . . ." The waiter bowed to another waiter. A chain of command, or at least of waiters, which rapidly produced several open bottles and wineglasses.

York gazed around the room. So this was a former Glaoui palace. The enormous carved entry doors, painted and rising to the balconies above. The lanterns swaying, spraying polychrome amid the pillars. A trio playing in the far corner. Flute, muted drum and a violin, the musicians all wearing the red fez, tassels revolving as they played. They seemed almost dwarfed by the room. Only a few guests as yet. About a dozen, sprinkled between pillars and arcades, mostly in suits, dresses and cameras. One group in djellabahs and yellow slippers, older Moroccans. The room gazing down on all of them, as if to say . . .

"To the Hôtel des Amis!" Herbert raised his glass.

"Le tout Hôtel des Amis," Claude corrected, "including our most generous English hosts."

Glasses clinked, the macaw snapped, and Khalid's eyes rolled in delight as he sipped wine for this special occasion. Rebecca's idea that Khalid be included. "He's privy to all the gossip . . . he *must* come!" And there he was, all grin and pride, like a dusky Frenchman of the 1930s in his old blazer and tie.

"And to our intrepid Canadian, on his last night," Rebecca added, smiling at York. Richard mustered a "Hear, hear!" for the toast. And Claude was on his feet to announce he'd never "met a tourist quite like our dear York." Hear, hear. "Never knows what he's doing, never knows where he's going. And returns each time with a satisfied and undiscussable smile!" Rebecca thought this magnificent. But York protested. "I'm no bloody tourist!"

"Then what are you, dear?" Rebecca asked.

"An escapee. . . ." York moaned.

"From what?"

"*To* what, is more important!"

Rebecca was thrilled. And Claude still up speechifying, about fallen angels and risen demons till he reached into his cape with a flourish and produced a postcard. "It arrived this very day." All except York nodded as if aware. "So I kept it as a treat to start our soiree." He passed it with a bow to York. A picture of Tangiers by night. Tangiers? York knew no one in Tangiers. "Read it! Read it!"

> Dear Archbishop of York,
> Spent a splendidly seditious evening here in memory of all turrets, towers, kasbahs and marabouts of old Morocco. Phone me as soon as you reach London. Hunt's awaaaay!
>
> Colonel Tony

York stared as if the Colonel had suddenly dropped out of the ceiling. He glanced up. They were all watching him as if they knew. As if the card might bite, or start to sing. Or the Colonel himself take his place beside them now. Suddenly he started to laugh, laughing at the preposterousness of it all. And they were onto his mountain adventures, Rebecca leading the way. "You simply must tell us of your most recent escapade, haven't told us a word!"

"We know you were in Demnat," Claude said. "We paid the taxi!"

York nodded and ducked behind his wineglass.

"But what were you doing in that hellhole?" Bertrand sniffed.

"I don't really know."

"But you were up to something special," Claude insisted.

"I fell down that goddamned gorge!"

"Gorge?" said Rebecca. "What was in the gorge?"

York paused. "An army of blackbirds."

"But that still doesn't explain . . ." Rebecca wasn't letting up.

"If you must know, I was fleeing the Sheikh's fortress." York gulped more wine. "A castle on a cliff past Dammit."

"Who with?" Bertrand asked.

"He had a magnificent silver knife, I told you—a salon that . . ." York peered around the restaurant nervously.

"But what happened?" Claude leaning forward. "My dear York, you arrived back virtually naked, no money, no memory. We were perturbed. We have a right to know." Les amis nodding, and Claude adding, "*Tony* will want to know!"

"Boujma was sleeping on my clothes!"

"On what?" Bertrand asked.

"After the cobra on the wall. I was wearing that burnoose he loaned me."

"Snakes and poets," Herbert declared inscrutably, swigging Bertrand's wine.

"My wallet was with my clothes. He bartered for my pipe. Like in the market . . . bartering souls."

"And you lost your diary, as well," Richard murmured.

It was clear to everyone that he'd lost everything—including, Bertrand snapped, "that photo you promised to show me!" Not to mention his watch, which had disappeared while he was staying at Ranee's in Demnat.

Bertrand's tongue flickered. "At least he didn't lose his virginity."

"Perhaps more important"—Richard leaned forward—"he didn't lose his life!"

Silence, as the music of the restaurant swirled on. Rebecca gazed at York, trying to decide whether he was a lunatic or a poet. And Herbert vouchsafed that he was "no clearer about York's trip than before!" But attention happily passed to the next table. The maître d' escorting a group of four to their seats. The restaurant had been slowly filling. Various small groups, and now the foursome right next to them. "Boches!" Bertrand whispered after cocking an ear to listen. Les amis finally appraised the newcomers. Deciding they were harmless—a husband and wife, teenage daughter and son. "Quite respectable!" Rebecca stated.

And conversation shifted on. To khalifas and caids, which was what York must have meant when he said *sheikh*. York nodded, sipped his wine. He'd found Ranee, who hadn't seemed at all surprised to see him, even in his battered condition. But some of the things Ranee said! "Yes, I've met Claude!" How? "The way all of us meet him. Outside our school." What? "Claude parks his car near the school at the end of the day. And picks one of us." Oh . . . and Boujma? "A friend of a Saudi prince who comes every year to Marrakech." I see. "He likes, you *know*," Ranee tapping his butts and laughing. Yes, York knew. "And that's why the Caid doesn't harm Boujma. He knows the prince is a friend of our King." Ranee saying it so casually. "But how is it you know so little about us, about Moroccans?" York replied that it was his first visit. And Ranee suddenly bitter: "You buy us like a glass of wine, then dump us." York had been shocked. Ranee continuing, "Forgive me, friend. I knew you didn't know. But I had to say it, say it to one of you . . . Europeans, Americans." And after that, so kind. Finding a car the next morning. Persuading the driver to take York all the way to Marrakech—assuring him he would be paid when they reached York's hotel.

Claude had procured more wine. And a waiter was weaving around them; passing a lightly spiced pâté that Rebecca thought tasted like head cheese. But Claude quickly diverted attention to the wine. And Rebecca suddenly asked York if he'd seen any religious rites. Rites? "During your stay at the Sheikh's." And York pondering. "The God of the Skins." Which silenced Rebecca. Richard was holding forth on the Aissaoua, and an even stranger group that used snakes. Though Herbert hated snakes. "Snakes and socialists!" he said, emptying his glass. "Socialists and snakes!"

But chitchat broke up as more tourists arrived, shepherded to the far side by the maître d'hôtel. "More damned Boches!" Bertrand muttered, clutching the macaw protectively. Herbert noting that it seemed a completely tourist restaurant. Richard replied, "Most Moroccans can't afford to come here." Claude adding, "That's why we brought you, show you a piece of old Morocco." York suddenly blurted, "It's the Sheikh's salon." A great mistake, because Rebecca pounced. "You still haven't told us what your Sheikh was like!" York replying, "Kept changing shape and color. . . ." What did, the salon or the Sheikh? "Both!" Rebecca looked uncertain. "And what did he say?" York laughed. "Eavesdroppers are pursued by fiery comets."

The conversation looped on in music and wine. But York silent now . . . watching the restaurant. He shifted nervously. Something about their soiree; all their chitchat felt like sacrilege. Couldn't put his finger on it. But every time he looked up at the ceiling, lanterns and balcony, the Sheikh seemed to be gazing down. And suddenly York wondered where Kebir was. He looked around anxiously . . . no sign of Keb. Just more tourists. And he sat solacing himself with remembrance of their lunch the day before. At a small restaurant in the Medina, a rabbit tagine. And York content, basking in the presence of Keb. Finally York telling Keb he was leaving. Keb sitting fingering the necklace, the two-headed falcon—John's falcon. Yes, in a couple of days York would be en route to John. He'd fled John to see him more clearly. And now there was Kebir, the whole of Morocco in his face. And after, Keb had taken York back to the hotel. Sitting in Khalid's garden, Keb taking off the falcon necklace. Offering it back to York.

"Please, keep it for now, Keb . . . till our dinner tomorrow."

And suddenly Keb was standing, both of them standing, embracing. Keb rising hard against York's groin. And saying, "Do not leave, ami . . . I'm your Marrakshi." Silence. "Then take me with you . . . *anywhere.*" And before York could reply, gone. York standing like a breach of promise, knowing he *must* leave Marrakech.

He had hauled himself up to his room, closed the door, and lain a moment on the bed. Then hurled himself to the floor, smashing his head again and again against the floor, bellowing. And when he looked up, there was Claude. Claude gaping. "Dear friend, what's wrong?" And York had rubbed his bruised head, sitting up slowly. "It's all right, I feel better now."

These past few days, the battle inside him—John against Kebir. And Kebir winning, because of something sinister in John that erupted in violence or pain. As if John liked that. His smile of satisfaction after causing pain.

But he wasn't with either Kebir or John right now. He was with le tout Hôtel des Amis in an old Glaoui palace. And maybe Keb wasn't going to turn up at all. "You seem to be in a trance," Rebecca whispered. York glanced up, saying it was the music that did it to him. "Like prayer." Prayer? "Yes, don't you see? Sights are sounds, sounds are sights, and both are prayer. . . ."

"Did you hear that, Herbert?"

"Fortunately not." Herbert laughed.

Claude adding, "York is dangerous now. Ever since he returned from Demnat, he's been saying the most bizarre things."

"Bizarre?" York spluttered. "I'm talking sense for the first time in my life."

"Well, my dear, last night you orated at me. Remember? Said 'butterfiles are the eyes of angels'?"

"But he's right," Rebecca said.

"And quoting the Koran left and right, as if you wrote it."

"I just started reading it yesterday!"

"Precisely," Claude said. "But this afternoon, you may recall, you asked me if I expected anything except victory or martyrdom. And when I expressed a certain surprise, you said, 'The Koran, lines from the Koran!' "

York paused. "You've lived in Morocco four years now. Have you ever read the Koran?" No. "Then you're still a tourist here!" York laughed, almost adding, "Parked outside the school!"

But their exchange was interrupted by the maître d' soaring over and giving a vast menu to Claude. And as Khalid knew not only the maître d' but at least two of the waiters, their corner seemed immune from touristic invasion. Claude's finger swooped around the menu, diving to an item halfway down.

"Oui, m'sieur, we have the *bstilla . . . bstilla à la Glaoui.*"

Claude rapped the table. "Tonight, madame, messieurs, we dine on bstilla! I forbid you to choose anything else." Richard gurgled joy. But Rebecca asked, "And what is a pustilla?" as if she might have been consulted.

"I advised Claude to choose the most Moroccan dishes," Herbert said.

"Oh, of course," she replied. "How clever of you."

But the maître d' was retreating to deal with a crash from a table of Americans. One of the men had tripped, half fallen across the tabletop, and his friends were applauding him. The German family at the next table watching with surprise. The wife sitting erect in disapproval, the daughter following suit, the father pretending not to notice. "Snakes and Americans," Herbert intoned as the clatter increased. "Americans and snakes!" But the musicians stepped forward now, tassels on their caps whirling with their eyes. The man with the large banjo breaking into impromptu dance, while the one with the violin made it jump and cavort. Sudden mirth of music flashing the room, igniting hidden corners and crenellations. And even the waiters caught in the romp of rhythm, balancing leaded trays as if a trapeze act. The room rising in triumph over tourists again.

But les amis were no sooner devotedly tasting another wine and pâtè when a further commotion broke out—a skirmish at the entrance.

"Just what we need, a flamin' fight," Herbert muttered.

"Don't worry, they have a bouncer." Claude grinned. "Demolishes drunks, strays and undesirables."

York glanced up, then hurtled out of his seat, past the Americans, the musicians, toward a pair of embattled waiters. One of them finally demanding, "Are *you* m'sieur York of Ospree?"

York drew himself erect. "I am, and this is my friend!" Kebir standing there, clearly upset and prepared for further battle. One of the waiters stared from York to Kebir. Keb scarcely looked like a client of this majestic restaurant—Keb in a scruffy shirt with tar on it, worn army jacket, picking up an equally scruffy bundle from the floor.

But now the maître d' bustled up, to quell this new commotion. "What's wrong?"

York bowed and said, "Your waiters are what's wrong!" Smiling at Kebir. "This is our guest of honor. He is under my protection."

The maître d' desperately trying to overlook Kebir, but unable to overlook York, acquiesced. Though the expression on his face as he escorted them to their table said, "Well, they have a macaw, why not a vagrant?" But Kebir paid no heed as he floated past, his head high, his body moving with both room and music.

"And *who* is this?" Herbert inquired as the maître d' found a place for Kebir. "Who is this . . . gentleman?"

"Oh," Rebecca said, quickly appraising York's smile, "remember, dear? York asked to bring a friend."

Herbert clearly had not expected a Moroccan. Much less a— He inspected Kebir's garments with unhappy eye. But Claude rose with a bow. "Kebir, of Marrakech and Ouar-za-zate, and York's guide on his historic voyage into the Sahara." Herbert slightly reassured.

And Rebecca cooing. "Now we'll get all the details. . . ."

But Kebir no sooner ensconced than he requested the washroom. And disappeared. "A dramatic entrance and quick exit!" Bertrand sniffed. "He does look like a tramp in this setting," Bertrand continued. Which Rebecca thought unkind, but Herbert thought true.

"Kebir has special qualities," Claude said, catching the glint in York's eyes.

"Qualities no one here knows anything about," York stated.

"Nonsense!" Bertrand snorted.

York glared, clenching his wineglass. Herbert, whose wineglass had been knocked over, asked what the fuss was about.

"Wait and see," Richard intervened.

"Won't see any of it here." Bertrand laughed.

"See what?" Rebecca asked.

"What York came to Morocco for!"

"We need more wine," Herbert intoned.

"We need peace and quiet!" Claude added.

Khalid summoned a waiter. As York spluttered, "I came to Morocco for—"

Before he could finish, Kebir was back. No longer in work clothes, but a dark blue burnoose, leather belt and tooled pouch at his waist. And yellow slippers. Kebir in full Moroccan garb. John's two-headed falcon glittering his chest.

"My!" said Rebecca as Keb took his seat beside York. "So . . . *aristocratic.*" Yes, the transformation complete. Keb all washed, garbed and quietly smiling. Explaining he had come directly from work, not wanting to miss the evening. Keb put his foot on York's under the table. And York swelling with pride. As Rebecca declared, "He looks like one of those Blue Men. All he needs is a rifle."

A group of girl dancers joined the musicians out on the floor. "Chleuh," Claude said. "An ancient Moroccan dance." The girls in long robes and massive jewelry, twirling and yodeling. The musicians stamping their feet to keep time. The German behind Richard, eagerly focusing his movie camera, his wife surging erect again. Kebir's eyes flowing on up the walls to the balcony above, the glitter of paneling. York's gaze followed—yes, the room expanding again, expanding in dance and chant, the walls shimmering, lanterns swaying . . . the tourists dwindling beneath. And for a moment he just watched, watched as the restaurant became grand salon, became palace, became . . .

"You have chosen?" The maître d' with his back to any rumpus, as if to buffer their table.

"But yes"—Claude waved a hand—"bstilla for all."

The maître d' bowed and summoned a waiter bearing yet another bottle of wine and a hot pâté en croûte.

"You must try this Ksar rosé," Claude bowed to Herbert. "It's prephylloxera."

"Aha." Herbert hastened to his glass. As all tasted, declaring the rosé admirable. And the pâté, which Rebecca thought must be game. Though Bertrand thought just goats. "They graze in the wild." Adding with a glance at York, "Basic Moroccan morality. You can fuck goats, but you mustn't steal them." His words fortunately lost in the rising music. A final spasm of the dancing girls, gauze whirling, jewelry clattering. As they went spinning off the floor in a cascade of tourist applause. The German with camera looking mournful as they went. His wife looked relieved.

In the calm that followed, Claude announced he'd done a portrait of Kebir. "How splendid," Rebecca exclaimed. Well, not a full portrait . . . a sketch. Done while dear York was "terrorizing Demnat." Kebir said that wasn't possible—he hadn't spent time with Claude. But Claude explained it was done from a photograph left by Colonel Tony. He was going to give it to York as a keepsake.

"York's guide has such wonderful eyes," Rebecca announced.

"I hadn't noticed." Herbert leaned forward to locate Kebir's eyes. Kebir sat silent, serene smile flickering his face.

"Kebir has eyes that . . ." She hesitated as Kebir's eyes floated over her and on into the salon. And everyone staring at Kebir now, trying to find the word.

"That behold," Richard finally murmured.

"But Richard has eyes that eat you." Bertrand laughed. "Gobble what they see."

"Don't you think we should compare the Ksar rosé against a vintage Cabernet?" Claude interrupted. "If we're to give our English friends a true taste of Morocco." Herbert was delighted.

But Rebecca was hot after eyes. "York's eyes"—appraising York till he squirmed—"are afraid of what they behold."

Bertrand smirked, but Richard murmured protest.

"Speak up, dear." Rebecca tapped Richard's arm.

"York is only afraid"—Richard chuckled—"because his eyes are larger than his heart. . . ."

"Now that's worth the entire dinner, isn't it, Herbert?"

But Herbert was testing the newly arrived Cabernet. "This wine holds up jolly well against the pâtè." Richard winked at York. And Kebir swayed invisibly to the music while Rebecca toured the table after eyes. "Claude's are malicious . . . Richard's are Socratic . . . Herbert's eyes . . ."

"Are in his wineglass," Bertrand whispered.

Till she reached Khalid and faltered, saying something about Khalid's eyes "seeing twice as much."

"And your own eyes, dear madame?" Claude inquired.

"See more than they ought but not as much as they'd like." She laughed delectably and switched nonstop to a question about the greatest eyes they'd ever known.

But all conversation was again broken by a blast from the American table. One of the young women on her feet, dancing disastrously out of time with the music. Two men joined her, all stomping, waving their arms. It hurt York's eyes to watch. . . . The rest of that group clapping and stamping. York glanced at Keb, wondering what he thought. Kebir sitting alert now, seeing the Americans yet avoiding them; his gaze flowing along the walls and up, up to the giant lanterns, painted balconies, the entire salon. And the salon gazing back imperturbably, as if viewing yet not deigning to see. York squirmed, uncomfortable, remembering what he'd felt earlier—their chitchat as a kind of sacrilege here. And now one of the American girls tripping into the lap of the blond tour leader and rewarded with applause and a big kiss. Kebir blinking. And Herbert bleating, "I don't mind them invading Europe, but couldn't they leave Africa alone?"

But the musicians were making way for a man sweeping forward in a long burnoose, wild frizzy hair, playing a deep woody flute. Behind him a boy carrying a large box. Conjurers. The box was opened and a black head whipped up, two, three. The flautist whisking one from the box, and another. An American girl screeching as the cobra glided toward her table. And York dismayed as several more snakes swished out of the box. One with diamond markings and a hammerlike head. Fatter than the lithe cobras. Keb leaning over and whispering, "*El Faa.*" Boujma had said they're fat, like rabbits coiled in the sun. And the boy picking up *el Faa* and dancing with it. Then the blond leader was on his feet and draping one of the cobras around his neck. His girls ogling as he did so, dancing with the wriggling cobra. Claude held up an empty wineglass and gazed at snakes through the glitter of glass, murmuring, "How voluptuous!" And Rebecca demanded to see, too, see through Claude's glass that way. Peering through. "Oh, Herbie, you *must* look!" But Herbert categorically refused to contemplate "any more damned snakes," retreating to more wine.

The maître d' appeared, and behind him a waiter bearing a large platter with high domed top. Another shudder through

York. But when the top was raised, no ram's head appeared, thank God . . . merely a voluminous pie. Richard twittering as the maître d' took a small silver trowel and sliced into it. Geyser of steam pouring forth. Claude cramming his face into the vapor. Fragrance combining sweetness, musk and lurking memories inside of him. The maître d' leaning to whisper in Claude's ear. Claude nodding, "Ah, ecstasy!"

"But just a touch," the maître d' noted, disappearing. As Claude, possessed of the trowel, proceeded to cut into the pie. Rebecca trumpeting, "You haven't told us what it is."

"But he has," Herbert reprimanded. "It's the pastella."

"The bstilla," Claude corrected, "though tourists corrupt the word to pastella." Khalid grinning. The true bstilla à la Marrakech." And Keb squeezing York's hand under the table. This was what they'd eaten at Kebir's home . . . a pie, a special meat pie. And Herbert thrusting Rebecca back from the pie and shouting as he slashed out with his cane. York certain the man insane or drunk. Till he saw the face at the edge of their table, black face coiling up over tabletop, tongue flicking . . . unexpected image of Amelia. And Herbert half falling across the *bstilla*, smiting at the snake there, smiting and bellowing, "Goddamned cobra, tryin' to eat our pie!" The German suddenly up with his movie camera. And an American with flash camera rushing up, *snap-snap*. And the maître d' following. "It's just for show, m'sieur, for the pleasure of the eye."

"Sodding serpents and fat-assed Americans!" Herbert ejaculated, whirling his cane like a propeller and swiping at the agitated snake. Claude trying to rescue flying wine bottles. And Herbert getting the snake in the air on the tip of his cane. "Hold it there a second," the American shouted. *Snap-snap*. The cobra flailed off the end of the cane, onto the German's table. And into the wife's lap. Wife screeching, daughter fleeing and the table collapsing. Till the snake charmer ran up and rescued the battered cobra from amid crockery and broken glass.

"Darling, it's just a cobra." Rebecca whimpered, wiping wine and bstilla off her bosom.

But Herbert with his cane at the ready. "I saw that damned cobra *in the loo*!" Bertrand sat delighted, jingling his skull bracelet to calm the macaw. And the music played louder to cover the debacle. A battery of waiters trying to right the Germans' table, calm the wife and inveigle the daughter back. Richard overacting as ambassador, explaining that "we have an Englishman in our midst with a *phobia* about snakes."

It was Kebir who retrieved the bstilla. A rather mangled bstilla, wobbling hazardously at the edge of their own table amid fallen glasses and bottles. And the stupefied maître d' marshaling fresh wine, glasses and commiseration. While Khalid assured Herbert that such snakes were quite harmless, "just a part of the show. . . ."

"Of course," Claude said. "They've been defanged!"

For a moment they sat quiescent, Herbert muttering that a macaw at table was quite enough, "without flaming *serpents*!" The German lady staring as if she'd just been violated. And York staring at the ceiling, wondering if he'd gone mad, or was it their entire table? Only Kebir seemed serene, as if everything was as should be. Two more groups arriving. A large one, cameras at the ready. And the maître d' propelling them over to one side. And a threesome, Claude grimaced, but waved at them. York turned to see . . . that little doctor and his two pals. Kee-rist, that little doctor bouncing up with a little cry of "*Toro . . . toro*!" Claude rose for introductions. And Herbert struggled to stand. The little doctor laughed. "Do remain seated, I can see it's an . . . epic evening." And Herbert fell back muttering, "Indeed!" The doctor saying, "You're engaged with the bstilla, I see—best in all Marrakech." And congratulating Bertrand on his macaw.

"He insisted on bringing her," Claude said.

"Why not?" said the doctor. "Brighten the old place right up." But the little doctor turned to York. "At last we catch up with you and . . . your friend. We keep seeing the pair of you in the distance."

York mumbled.

"And you still haven't given us the details of your jaunt to Zagora and the deeper Sahara."

But Claude whisked his cape. "Our Canadian friend is still sorting it out."

"How wise." The doctor smiled at York. "But do join us for a brandy later, share stories."

York nodded, anything to get rid of the man. And with a flash the doctor turned and left, followed by his two cronies.

"Who was *that*?" Rebecca asked.

"The most dangerous tongue in all Marrakech," Claude said, regaining his seat.

"Well, that's precisely who I want to talk to,"Rebecca said.

York sat stupified. Why hadn't he gone somewhere else, anywhere else, for this final evening with Kebir? Gone with Keb alone. Should never have come to this lunatic dinner with les amis. But his eyes cleared as he felt Keb's hand again, glanced up. Yes, Keb resplendent in burnoose and smile. As if all hell could pour down and Keb would still smile, and have the sense to rescue a tottering bstilla.

Claude was cutting into the bstilla again. Richard murmuring something about soprano and basso, which seemed arcane till they tasted the pie: an elegant arabesque, high-pitched sugary crust and deep inner earthiness. "If carrion were . . . sugarplum foie gras," Herbert opined. Which Rebecca thought the brightest comment thus far.

The maître d' appeared with an extra bowl of sauce—some of the sauce of the bstilla had been spilled over the cobra. Claude was savoring it and announcing another ecstasy. Herbert inquiring about its "unusual odor," but Claude's answer lost in a fresh barrage of music. A trio of dancing boys whirling onto the floor, *ka-boom*. Their legs spinning with the drums, their heads flung back. Herbert glancing up and quickly away. But Richard stopped even the bstilla to watch. And York stared for a moment as the boys leapt over each other like gazelles, higher and higher. Keb engaged with the bstilla and extra sauce. Dipping his bread into the sauce and sniffing its musky sweet aroma. "A pigeon pie," Claude said, "with many spices." And, as York delved into pie and sauce, he saw them—Tony and James—delving into camel couscous . . . Tony fondling the waiter boy and bellowing, "Smen!" Voices and faces rising in the very fragrance of the bstilla now. That omnipresent sign for Timbuktu. The Colonel bellowing at James, "Stop fuckin' that chair of yours!"

York fell back, blinking, head spinning with drums, dance and voices. The same sinuous pandemonium of dancers here as in Zagora, M'hamid . . . same madness of music. The salon surging forward, flaring colors of walls, lanterns, as virulent as the sauce and pie. *Ka-boom*. Everything in Morocco a single ongoing experience—sure death, anyway.

"It's the touch of *smen* does it," Claude noted. "Delivers the coup de grace."

"Touch of what?" Rebecca shouted above the drums.

By the time the matter was resolved and Rebecca satisfied, a black teenage acrobat had replaced the whirling dancers. The boy executing back flips across the floor like a flying panther. Then walking on his hands up onto the American table, up atop a wine bottle now, balancing on one hand. The camera buff shouting, "Hold it!" *Snap-snap*. And the ladies desperate not to ogle the boy's flipping zeb through the loincloth too overtly. And Bertrand bouncing with pleasure as the boy floated off the bottle onto the floor in a spin of cartwheels, legs flashing. Bertrand grabbing Rebecca's arm and pointing at the boy. "That's Morocco's heaviest industry."

"Heavy what?" Rebecca snapped.

And for no apparent reason Bertrand suddenly talking about Amelia, saying, "I always like them black."

"Black what?" Herbert inquired.

"Snakes!" And in moments the secret was out. Bertrand kept a cobra by the name of Amelia at the Hôtel des Amis. Rebecca sitting up in momentary shock. And Herbert bellowing, "I knew it, *knew* there was a cobra." Bertrand and the macaw ducking as he reached for his cane. Claude explaining, "She's perfectly harmless. . . ."

And Bertrand laughing. "Yes, she's a virgin! I've never had her defanged!"

"That's not true," Claude snapped. "And you know it."

But Herbert sat moaning. And Rebecca sitting erect, glaring. "How *dare* you have a cobra in *my* hotel." As she leaned across the table and slapped Bertrand sharp across the face. Bertrand's eyes popped. Suddenly a scream rose reverberating the pillars, dome. The macaw, screaming bloody murder! The best efforts of the musicians couldn't contain the fact. Music and murder rampaging the restaurant, Bertrand trying to prevent the macaw from assaulting Rebecca now. And the maître d' over to quell the uproar. Claude slipped him a wad of dirhams, which momentarily quelled the maître d' but not the screaming parrot. The German at the next table too startled to take a photo of it. But Bertrand began feeding bstilla to the parrot, which finally shut it up. York wondered if the maître d' was going to expel them from the restaurant, but he finally waved an arm, all his arms. And a waiter appeared dispensing free bottles of wine. To their table and the molested Germans—the Americans as well. Everyone seemed reassured, including the macaw with its bstilla. And Bertrand suddenly leaned over and gave Rebecca a kiss, saying, "You're worse than my mother." Which appeased her too. Kebir was rocking in his seat with laughter. Herbert, both hands to his brow, protested, "This city cracks a fellow's head."

Richard intervened gently. "Marrakech was always called the city of blood, from the earliest times! So many murders, feuds, wars . . . always exciting."

At which Herbert swigged his entire glass of wine, looked around the table. Looked at them all as if at some dire revelation. "Kebir is right," and started laughing and laughing till the tears came. And all of them laughing nervously with him.

They were barely done with the battered bstilla when a flaming sword headed for their table. And when smoke and flames had cleared, it was a large skewer of meat flambé, several skewers, held by a waiter. Herbert muttered, "City of blood *and* fire!' And the maître d' appeared with a special wine. Claude nodded approval, then pointed to the kebab. "See if you can guess." Offering the first chunks to Rebecca and Herbert.

"Venison, rather like venison," Herbert declared.

Claude shook his head.

"Camel," Rebecca said doughtily, about to spit it out.

"Sanglier!" Claude announced. "Wild boar from the mountains." At which Richard dived for the meat. And Keb grinned, saying his father used to hunt with the French—wild boar tusks as long as his hand. "As beautiful as a gazelle, as strong as a lion." Keb speaking in French. "But very dangerous, the tusks, people killed every season."

York seeing that eye down a long tunnel of green. Red eye, size of a prune, red eye buzzing, shifting toward him. And bristles of ruff, great hump of neck, barrel chest. Yet haunches of antelope.

"That's it!" York almost shouting. "Up by the gorge, by Dammit. A tooth . . . walking on the tips of his feet. I was crawling on hands and knees, fleeing the Sheikh's."

Claude stared; they were all staring.

"I was in a tunnel, low branches. . . . The earth exploded!"

Herbert was gazing at York as if he were a cobra. But Richard crooning to himself now.

"A wild boar!"

Herbert trying to remove York's wineglass.

York insistent. "It showed me the river, the gorge. That's how I got back!"

"Showed you *what?*" Rebecca asked.

"I drew a picture of the boar and kissed it . . . and I heard the river!"

Yes, all staring at him, except Kebir, who had placed a hand on York's knee. And York shouting with joy. "A wild boar! I saw it the way it sees!"

But the floor had exploded again, musicians in a new fervor of drums and woodwinds. A woman in a spangle of jewels, gauze, a tiara, shimmering the center floor just past the Americans. Colored lights thrown onto her swiveling hips. Midriff bare . . . getting barer. As she swayed around and around in drums and spotlights. Tossing a veil aside, another . . . shawls and robes tossed onto the floor while she circled, whirled. As if her thighs must fly open in embrace of the entire salon. Bertrand flopped back in disgust. But Herbert was in euphoria, suddenly talking to the German, who was jamming film into his camera at the next table.

"Herbert, would you pass the wine, dear?" Rebecca's voice cutting across the scene. And Herbert, flustered, finding wine and pouring it into the first empty glass at hand. But no, Keb never touched wine. York caught in the whirl of the room. Floor tilting, tables floating, tourists swirling by. *Ka-booom*.

"Morocco is unlike any country I've ever heard of." It was Rebecca, as the music ebbed.

"It's the light, dear." Herbert nodded to his glass. "It's fanatical."

And Richard piped up. "Moroccan sun stabs objects."

"You do make Morocco sound like murder," Rebecca murmured.

"But that's why we like Morocco." Bertrand gleamed. "It *is* murder!"

And York, half listening, half watching the flesh of the floor, suddenly turned on Claude. "What happened, what *really* happened . . . to James?"

Claude's eyes flapped. "I told you, dear friend. . . . He's en route to London. You received the postcard, after all."

"James didn't sign that card!"

"He may have taken a plane from Casablanca." Claude smiled. "He said he might, after driving there with Tony."

York sat dazed . . . thud of drums from the floor pummeling his spine. He turned to Kebir. "So nothing happened in M'hamid . . . under the knife?"

Keb silent.

"Did that knife finish James?"

Keb suddenly turned, gazing at him. "Ami . . . James was not worthy of such a knife!"

Had York heard right amid the whirl of dance and drums? But knew he had, and felt foolish. As if he still understood nothing about Morocco. Keb's Morocco—he could only understand it through Keb himself. Till Richard suddenly tapped his arm. "You've had a privileged experience, my dear."

"Of what?"

"Of Morocco. You've seen what few visitors ever see."

York nodded, knew that much. "You helped me to see. I'll always remember that, Richard."

The old man chuckled and whispered. "You see, I passed a flame to you." Richard squeezed York's arm. "All I knew. . . ."

York nodded.

"I realized moments ago, I won't be here when you come back."

York stared, Richard's face aghast with his own words. But talk impossible. In the wake of the belly dancer the Americans had surged out onto the floor, the entire group of them. Led by their handsome leader, who was now sporting a long Moroccan cape and dagger. One of the girls donning a handkerchief as a veil. And another wearing large chunks of Moroccan jewelry. All whooping and laughing in imitation of the Moroccan dances that had gone before. Claude gazing disdain. But Herbert watching, finally saying, "I've already made a fool of myself tonight, why not again?" And he staggered to his feet. "Come, darling, it's time we danced!" And he drew her along with him out to the dance floor. Les amis staring in disbelief. As Herbert and Rebecca joined the Americans, bouncing and bobbing. Rebecca trying a pirouette but skidding on the polished floor. And

Herbert waving, laughing. Claude announcing, "It's a disgrace, but at least it's an international disgrace!" The blond leader whirled with his cape, cape flying out, slapping across Rebecca, who fell back. The tour leader swaggering to the applause of his girls. And whirling again, cape catching Herbert, tripping him to the floor. The Americans too caught up in the antics of their yodeling leader to notice. And Kebir suddenly on his feet, going out to help Herbert up. And leading the pair of them back. Rebecca thoroughly upset. But the Americans laughing and clapping in their wild dance. York staring as if hit in the face when Rebecca jostled, Herbert knocked down. And now all of them watching that jamboree. Seething mass of bodies preempting the salon with their war whoops. Blond tour leader parading his new cape in a series of wild turns, semi-pirouettes. Girls heaving bosoms and butts . . . thrusting their bellies forward in mime of Moroccan belly dances. And one of the men busy with camera to catch it all.

York glanced at Herbert, so deflated now. Rebecca too. No one wanted to talk about what had just happened. But Kebir sitting taut, his eyes smoldering. Blond leader performing another flamboyant pirouette, flailing his dagger. The girls loud in applause. And blond leader suddenly raising both hands over his head, and down. Allah, Allaaah . . . as he mimed the Muslim way of prayer. York flinched, the salon itself mocked. Allaah . . . Allaaah—blond guy raising his arms and bowing down, and up grinning, flicking his ass. And York angry, the majesty, the magnificence of the place, carved painted walls, lanterns, dome . . . all sullied, betrayed somehow. Blond leader going up to the musicians, borrowing a small drum with tails hanging from it and barging back to the floor, battering on the drum, shaking the furry tails in the faces of his fans as he danced the Sheikh of Araby.

York cursed. Blasphemy, that's how it felt. But Keb rising from the divan now. Was he leaving? York trying to catch his arm, stop him. But Keb gone with that smolder in his eyes onto the dance floor, taking his place to one side of the Americans, the circus of bosoms and frantic butts.

"What's he doing?" Rebecca found her tongue.

For a moment Kebir stood quiet, scarcely seeing the Americans at all. Just gazing at the soaring walls, balconies, head tilted to one side. So slender beside the squad of Americans.

"Why don't we leave . . . have a brandy somewhere else?" York blurted to Claude, "I'll get Kebir."

But slowly, like a sapling in a breeze, Keb had begun to sway. Swaying from his very center, as though the music were his own core. This the music he'd been reaching for as he stood, head cocked, eyes soaring the room an instant before. York stared. Yes, the motion growing from Keb's loins. Thighs moving as if possessed of a long furry tail. Keb's flow defining an invisible tail swishing, flicking to its tip. His torso rising from this sway of legs, thighs, waist. York's eyes tracing the coil and recoil somewhere in Keb's backbone, lower spine—fulcrum of unfolding dance. And York feeling the tremor of his own body as Kebir slowly unfurled in the beat of drums.

"They'll knock him down too," Rebecca bleated.

York had almost ceased to see the Americans. But with Rebecca's words his eyes reinvaded by the flaunt of Americans in dance. And seeing both Keb and the Americans now jarred his head. One ear catching the music of Keb's dance, the other catching the American din.

But now Kebir unfurled further within his dance, a wider motion of body. Keb a blue flame in his burnoose, that leather belt and pouch at his waist . . . yes, like the men of the south, men of the caravans. And the angry star gleaming his chest, two-headed falcon. As he raised one foot, stamping the floor—abrupt, muffled thump. The American girl next to him turning in surprise, Kebir suddenly visible to her. She watched his rhythm, fumbled to imitate. And abandoned her attempt in a pout. While Keb danced as if the girl were not there, though barely a yard away. And *thump*, stamped his foot harder, the girl retreating to her table. His dance now occupying his own space and hers.

Keb's sway amplifying now. *Thump-thummp* . . . both feet hitting the floor in muffled thud. The sound reverberating deeper than the music. For the first time York saw that Keb was dancing in bare feet. All the Americans watching him. Opening a space to include him in their frolic. But Keb oblivious, his head tilted slightly back, eyes high on the flickering walls. As if contemplating something there.

"In a trance," Rebecca murmured.

The Americans staring at this bizarre presence in their midst. One of them mimicking Keb and tripping. Others trying to catch the hidden flow. The girls trying first, rocking their bellies and buttocks.

The girls squealing appreciation of their own efforts. Ogling Kebir and grabbing at their guys to follow their new dance. Several of the younger men trying, but the girls laughing as they did. Till they circled in a ring, around Kebir, staring at his ease of motion and clapping at odds with the music. Kebir paying no attention—his eyes high, as if it were the salon he was dancing with, the swaying lanterns. The Americans moving closer to watch. And *thump-a-thummmp*, Keb stamping urgent foot again, dispersing more of them to their table.

But the younger girls were determined. And thrust toward Kebir—one-two, one-two . . . three-four—their feet clacking, faces in drunken concentration. And still Keb didn't notice, as he whirled once, and again. Till one of them barged right up and grabbed Keb's arm. *Thump-thump-a-thummmp*. Keb's foot stamping hard. The girl caromed away, back to her table.

"Such an effective method," Herbert murmured.

But York didn't hear, his eye catching the glint of Keb's eyes. As the remaining Americans, about eight of them, shunted and rolled around their own bodies. And the German camera rolling at the neighboring table.

Keb stamped again. *Ka-booom*, the drums picked it up. The restaurant shaking. Two more men crept away, back to their table. And seeing their men desert, the girls flocked back to the table too. Entire table staring at this strange Moroccan, as at a wizard, medicine man in disguise.

Only Kebir and the blond tour leader on the floor now. The musicians shunting forward and increasing tempo with a flick of their heads. Blond leader took his cape off, whirling it at Kebir. And for the first time York saw Keb checking . . . yes, the floor clear of all Americans but this tour leader.

"Herbert, this isn't fair."

Kebir whirled full circle, pirouette seeming to acknowledge the presence of the leader. Yes, nodding ever so slightly at him now. And the American circling, flaunting his cape in front of

Kebir, then stepping back, waving to his fans back at their table. His compatriots shouting, "Go, boy . . . *go!*"

For an instant York lost sight of Keb. The blond leader strutting around him, swishing and swooping his cape like a matador on parade. Keb so slender, invisible behind this display. Then reappearing slightly off to one side, lost in his own dance.

"*Mano a mano,*" Claude purred.

Blond leader stepped forward, flicking his cape at Kebir. Keb falling back, imperceptibly drawing the American into a series of moves, half turns. Blond guy following with a flail of cape and winking across to his harem when done. And again Kebir drew him into a simple pirouette. The blond following, flaunting the cape, suddenly swishing it under Keb's feet—

"Herbie, you've got to stop them."

"I doubt there'll be time." Richard chortled.

As Keb spun clear of the cape, blond leader stamping his foot, *ka-thump*, and following Kebir. Keb in another pirouette, the cape snaking under his feet again. Keb half tripping, then spinning clear. And blond leader strutting for his girls.

The tempo rose, musicians following the pace of cape and pirouette. Keb's arms swimming out from his torso now, head swaying, eyes rolling from side to side. His lithe figure expanding with the tempo. And the American bearing down, cape whirling, flicking it under Keb's feet from the side. Keb jumping, spinning. *Boom-ka-booom*. York's hackles perking, something in Keb's eyes, the rhythm of drums, as Keb whirled faster. American puffing to keep up, spinning with his cape, spinning in poor imitation of Kebir. But Keb whirled again, shooting both arms straight out, jumping, landing with a double stamp of feet right at the American's toes. Blond leader hesitated, swayed and collapsed in a swathe of cape and carnage onto the floor. Keb swayed an instant over the fallen body, then bent down and quickly stripped the man of cape and burnoose . . . tossing them to the grinning musicians. Leaving the leader in his blue jeans and fat shirt wriggling on the floor.

"Splendid, absolutely splendid!" Herbert intoned as the American gathered his shorn body up from the floor and slumped back to his buddies, who clapped him on the back, one of them again.

Les amis sat triumphant. The German photographing them

now and the wife granting their table a benevolent smile. "A brandy," Claude said, "to celebrate." Herbert and Richard quickly agreed. The maître d' appeared shortly, waving a brandy list. "What do you recommend, my dear Claude?" Herbert asked. "They have Cognac, Calvados, Poire Williams, Armagnac . . ." Claude suggested they start with the Poire Williams, then a Cognac—then see. "Splendid."

Kebir was still held in the rhythm of his dance. And several other couples now venturing out to dance as well; some tourists, and a cluster of Moroccans. Kebir's face serene, as if there'd never been any adversary . . . only the majesty of the occasion. Just music now, the salon surging up in the music, as if all this had been dismantled while the Americans danced. Surging back now, the Glaoui's palace once again. And Kebir dancing as if he would never stop. His body coiling, recoiling, winding in hidden helix. Starting at his ankles, flaring up, expanding, till at his groin the circle large, strong. Kebir at once master and seducer. Lord of the Two Ways. York's eyes drawn to this flow of Kebir. Keb dancing proud, arms forward as in gift, his swaying body its own generosity.

And *thump-thump*, stamped his feet lightly, head flicking imperceptibly toward York. The rhythm of his dance spurting to mirth. The musicians speeding tempo as Kebir laughed, clapping his hands. His arms spinning, body spinning, as if juggling. Yes, hands juggling the air in a whoop of joy . . . as he tossed invisible batons to York, and his eyes with. Eyes a sultry pool now, and York falling again—

"Brandy, York?" Herbert, or was it Claude, passing a glass. But York already had his—Kebir out there, miming that day in the Djema-el-Fna, in the circle around the juggler. Keb suddenly marching, scrunched over himself as if thickset, with stocky legs, as if on mission, scowling. The musicians catching the change, beating a determined march on the drums. Keb stopped, whirled around and presto . . . all tall, lithe in a new pair of pants.

"Cigar, York?" York nodded as a small cigar floated into his hand. And someone offering to light it. But York's eyes on Keb. As he remembered the morning he'd marched out of the Milkbar, through the market to buy the new red pants. Keb so proud afterward. But Keb dancing something else now: tall, erect, shoulders back and chest out as if rows of medals, swagger stick.

Yes, Colonel Tony, pausing, hands cupped to his face. "Hunt's *awaaay*!" York laughed, then stopped. Keb dancing with head tilted wild, feet nimble. A lilting song of body, as if playing tambourine—My God, that young woman, mad woman nearly crashing their car en route into the mountains. Yes, Keb holding right hand up now, fend off such mad dance. York closed his eyes. And when they reopened, Kebir standing as if in full oration, hand raised, face flushed, addressing the world. Yet silly somehow, sad. . . .

"Haven't touched your brandy, York." Face peering at him, Claude's face. Oh. . . . He slurped a quick brandy. And gazed back . . . yes, Kebir as James. James making that speech in the restaurant. Words silent from Keb's mouth, yet ringing York's ears: "I give you El Hadj T'hami el Glaoui—" And *Craaash!* Glass smashing to the floor. But now Kebir dancing in solitary sway, as if standing so casual beside something—plucking fluff off his shirt, adjusting his belt, like a cat preening. Kebir as . . .

"What's he doing out there?" Rebecca asked.

York shook his head, couldn't explain. But now Kebir mimed "Hunt's *awaaay*" again, spun around and started lurching as if drunk. Jumping into the air, dancing an incantation. And leaping as with a knife. Yes, that shaman leaping at their car, leaping at York. He winced, but Keb again holding up his protective hand.

"Very odd," Herbert said.

But York kept his eyes fixed to Keb's dance. Kebir parading toward the musicians, patting one of the boys, prettiest of the boys, and the boy laughing. And Keb in a Pooh Bear dance—Colonel Tony caressing all boys beautiful. As Keb stroked the air, long strokes of hands, eyes rolling. The valley itself in Alleluia as Tony's boy came. . . .

Keb fleshing events so fast within his dance, York barely had time to respond. And doing it all with a flick of hand, roll of eye, gesture. Doing that Commandant in Zagora, Commandant surveying James's room in debacle, and James himself. And Tony, "Hunt's awa-*aaay*," Tony's "view halloo" marking every stop and start. As they soared the sun and the Sahara. Keb's dance recreating it all as song now. Their song. York-and-Kebir. And doing it as sleight of dance, invisible to anyone who didn't know. Just Keb doing some odd Moroccan dance out there on the floor, one of perhaps a dozen dancing now. Keb sometimes serious, sometimes playful, that was all. Now someone with a long cigarette holder. Prancing and pirouetting as on display, chin bobbing out like a pointer . . . Claude, of course, m'sieur Claude. And someone else, another face as if talking to Claude, chitchat of faces, endless chitterchatter. Several faces, bodies in the melee of Kebir's mime. . . .

And Rebecca laughing. "Les amis, he's imitating le tout Hôtel." Yes, Keb presenting the gossip sessions of Claude, Bertrand, Richard—complicit faces, pursed lips, high prurience. . . .

And someone asking, "What do you think?" York couldn't think. "Which painting should Herbert buy?" It was Claude, Claude and Herbert discussing the acquisition of one of Claude's paintings. But York sat silent, all his attention still out on the dance floor.

Thump-a-thump . . . Keb spurted into savage life, stamping, whirling. "What's he doing now?" Rebecca asked. Keb's arms, body whirling in a frenzy. Then still, one hand drawing something from his belt, holding it high overhead. Then down, slicing a line across his forehead as if with a knife. And *boom-ka-boom*, dancing mad dervish again, musicians keeping up. And York expecting blood to sprout . . . from Blond Boy of M'hamid or Keb or himself. But already Keb changed again. Standing august, like White Robe in M'hamid, like the Sheikh himself. And suddenly leaping . . . leaping as onto a horse, up into high saddle. Yes, thighs wide astride a war-horse, galloping. And musicians thudding in his gallop . . . *boom-ta-ta-boom*. And Keb leaning forward, arm as though wielding a javelin, hurling. *Boom-ta-ta-boom*. Music and gallop churning York, churning inside him, walls of restaurant rising as flames. And Kebir riding stallion across some endless plain. Javelin poised. As he galloped, face a holy joy, *boom-ta-ta-boom*. . . . And York agasp, fingertips aflame, body roaring. . . . Kebir towering inside the music like war chant convoking the entire salon. . . . Keb as sheikh, God's own sheikh. . . . Till quivering, his feet slowed. And *thump-a-thump*, he whirled full circle, stopping abruptly . . . *eyes right on me!* Keb immobile, arms held forward, eyes burning wide. Walking slowly toward York.

And when York could see again, Keb almost to the table. All distance, space abolished in his dance. Keb's movements as smile, pride of his eyes . . . gentle warrior. And only after he sat down, placing his bare foot atop York's foot, only then did York realize from the slow seep in his own pants that he had come.

The restaurant so tranquil now. And the immense dining salon soaring around them. Salon as aureole, and quiet flames. World of the Glaoui. . . . Are you waiting for anything except victory or martyrdom? York glanced up—Keb nodding. Salon nodding. It was victory.

The maître d' broke the silence, appearing with a special bottle of cognac and a plate of honey cakes. Apparently a sumptuous millefiori had come and gone. The cognac was a prewar Hennessy, "réserve du patron." Herbert was in glory. Bertrand feeding cake to his macaw. Richard crooning to himself. But York wasn't paying attention—muttered something about nature's call and made his way toward the wash room at the far end of the restaurant. Wobbling through tables, divans, tourists. And as he passed an alcove someone waved. "Toro, toro!" The little doctor. But York fled on. And in the bathroom swabbed himself as best he could. Stuffing his handkerchief inside the front of his underwear. Perhaps it wouldn't show. But on his way back the doctor darted from the alcove, pulling York into the alcove and offering him a brandy. "You did promise to have a drink with us." And presenting his two friends again; York didn't catch the names. "We know you've had a stunning visit."

York gulped brandy, ready to flee.

"What was it?"

Was what?

"That dance! Something very special, we could tell." Little doctor flashing his hand, grinning. "Come now, it was virtually sexual semaphore."

York shook his head.

"Darling"—the doctor flashing something in his hand—"he had an enormous thing, we saw!"

What was the doctor flashing there?

"You've hooked him, you know, bonded . . . man to man, à la marocaine." Doctor gleaming approval. "*Sexworthy*, that's what he is."

"But it's not like that, it's spiritual."

"*Spiritual?* He's hot for you, it's coming out his eyes!"

Coming what?

"His pants! We thought he was going to cream his drawers right there out on the dance floor." Doctor grinning at his chums, adding, "We ran into him in the Djema-el-Fna a few mornings ago. He was desperate to find you, dear."

And York suddenly listening.

The doctor nodded. "You'd gone off with that other boy, the one in a blazer, so regal. On the bus. . . . We *had* to tell your friend."

York stared.

"We were at the Café du Glacier, saw you depart. Your boyfriend was heartbroken!"

York stunned—Keb looking for him the very morning he'd left for Dammit. Could've . . .

"We did try to console him. But he refused even to sit with us. As much a snob as you." Doctor waving that silver thing—what was it? "Do have some of my snuff, best London club." Doctor dropping a whiff on York's hand from the silver snuff box. And sniffing some himself. York followed suit . . . sneezed violently, eyes streaming.

"Splendid," the doctor cried. "That boy loves your *appearance*. . . . Ferocious, that beard of Jove, your piercing black eyes. Don't you understand . . . you're a perfect little butch. All stocky and chesty and scowling." The doctor paused, York wordless. "You see, you *never* smile, just that fierce old scowl. You always look as if you're about to detonate."

What in hell was the man saying?

"You look the part to perfection. That's why your boy—"

"Leave Keb out of this!" York grabbing the doctor's shoulder.

The doctor pulled back, delighted. "There, I told you, a perfect S and M master. Pique him and he attacks!"

York spluttered incomprehension.

"High sadomasochismus, and he doesn't even know it. The most delectable kind. It exacerbates them to a frenzy." The doctor so pleased. "And your boy's so tall, such a lot for you to work on. . . ."

York sat numb.

Little doctor nodding—"But if you refuse to tell us about yourself, at least tell us about your boy . . . or boys!"

"I didn't come to Morocco for *boys!*"

"But that's what we all come to Morocco for, isn't it? Even you!"

York downed his brandy. "I came to Morocco to think, dammit. And I hate people who come for . . . *boyos*." York struggling to his feet.

"I see," the doctor purred. "And I suppose your friend went to Timbuktu to think, the same as you."

York stared. "What friend?"

"Why, James, of course."

"James?" York peering down at the doctor. "James is in London."

"I see. They've been protecting you. Your colleagues at that ridiculous hotel. . . . They didn't tell you the truth." The doctor beaming.

Silence.

"Tony did try to get James out of M'hamid. But he refused to budge." The doctor paused. "Do sit down, dear, and I'll give you the *straight* goods, as you Americans like to say."

York slumped down.

"How kind of you. You deserve the truth." Doctor flaunting his snuff box triumphantly. "By the way, what was that scream we heard a while ago?"

"Scream . . . oh, that was the macaw—Bertrand's parrot."

"A pity. We thought it was you!" Doctor winking at his two chums.

"What happened to James?"

"Of course. . . . We have the latest information for you; a friend of ours returned from Ouarzazate yesterday." The doctor pursed his lips. "Had lunch at Dmitri's there. And Dmitri told him in private—"

"What happened to James?"

"Exactly. You see, he had a fix about the Blue Men." The doctor cocking his head, watching York. "Had it for years, you know. You see, you also stopped at Dmitri's on your way back from M'hamid. Not that you noticed. And the Colonel took Dmitri into his confidence."

"Doctor, where *is* James?"

"Dmitri reports that Tony had his hands full trying to get *you* out of M'hamid in one piece. You were raving about someone called John, or 'Big Red.' " The doctor smiled inquisitively. "At least that's what Dmitri said."

"Please, for God's sake . . . *James!*"

"And while the Colonel, as they absurdly call him, was busy with your little hallucinations"—the doctor grinned—"James made off with an entire caravan. Or perhaps the caravan made off with him. In either case it was bound for Timbuktu."

"Oh, *Jesus!* When's he coming back?"

"Darling"—the doctor fluttered his eyes—"you're so innocent, it's a miracle! James chose a one-way ticket!"

York wrenched himself up, staggered toward his table. And for a moment he sat paralyzed. At least Keb was still there, serene. And Claude chattering with Herbert. Yes, Herbert wanted to acquire one of Claude's paintings. Rebecca saying, "We must have one of the hotel garden." But Herbert wanted "something a little more exotic. . . ."

York heard nothing. Just sat gazing at his hands. Blood all over his hands. Blood—was it pouring from his head? Had he held the knife over James in M'hamid? James's face leering right against his own, shouting, "You're cruel, York . . . *cruel!*" And *slaaap*.

Herbert liked Claude's suggestion. "Yes, we'll buy two paintings, why not?"

"Another cognac to celebrate," Claude said.

And the maître d', cognac amply poured, was summoning a waiter. Waiter bringing a tray with tall silver ewer on it. And floral water to cleanse the last of honey cakes and crumbs. Fragrance of petals—and flames up the walls, flames of rug and lantern. York rubbing his hands to get rid of the blood. It was all blood, his entire stay. He'd sensed it . . . death as lurking guest, everywhere. Keb's foot was back on his again. Healing touch of Kebir.

And Claude warily eyeing York. As Herbie offered cigars all around again. From Sumatra. What was? As Claude finally said, "So you talked with him. . . ."

York nodded.

"He's all malice. Don't believe the half of what he tells you!"

But York did. Knew the doctor had told the truth, if only to hear York scream. He put his nose into the cognac, to steady himself. Yes, Claude had been protecting him. So had Richard, all of them. And what could he do? Go find James? Search the whole damned Sahara . . . to find what? His own skeleton as well as that of James? He glanced up, Richard's eyes on him, eyes murmuring, "Better just one, than all of you."

"We're coming back next year, aren't we, Herbie?"

"Whatever you say, dear."

And Kebir, he'd known too. What was it he'd said—that he'd known there was trouble by Ouarzazate. He glanced up. Keb gazing straight ahead, unblinking. But his foot pressing down hard on York's.

One of the Americans was over with a camera. "Hi, you all. Would you mind if I get a shot of your table?" Herbert muttered. But the American saying, "We just voted you the most colorful group here tonight." And one of the girls coming up, adding, "We wondered if you were theater people, or opera?" Which Rebecca thought exciting. And soon they were posed around the table, smiling into posterity.

And then it was finished. The maître d' produced the bill. And Herbert gaped. "It was all the brandies and wines, m'sieur. You were drinking doubles, triples. . . . But I didn't charge for Khalid. He is my guest tonight, m'sieur." The maître d' so pleased. "We grew up in the same village, near Ouarzazate!" Khalid gleamed with pride, giving a little bow.

Keb nodded and stood up. Taking off York's necklace, the two-headed falcon that had marked their days together . . . Lord of the Two Ways. He put it around York's neck firmly, gently. York taken by surprise and standing up beside Kebir. Gazing into each other's eyes. Keb stepped forward, embracing York, kissing him on each cheek. Then turned, striding without a word across the floor. The room swirling around him. Kebir-Sheikh . . . gone. Out the door.

York fell back on the divan. Rebecca eyed him, finally taking his arm. "Thank you for sharing him with us, his dance. You'll be back," she said, "and he'll be waiting." And York hurtling up from the divan, pounding toward the door past startled waiters, maître d', doorman. Out into the alley. "Keb . . . *Keb!*" His cry as he churned down the winding alley. Too late. But as he turned the corner at the end, saw the loping figure. "Keb!" And reaching him, stood stock-still. Their eyes meshed again. York hearing inner drums. . . . Then slowly he took off the falcon necklace, holding it out. Keb bending a little as York placed it around his neck again. And when it was done, Keb murmured, "*Ami . . . York d'Ospree, ami!*" And straightened up in that silent salute that was his very being, eyes like swords. And turned and strode into the black night.

York groped his way back into the restaurant, back to the divan where les amis were finishing final brandy and cigars. He sat in a stupor. That final sight of Kebir . . . and abrupt premonition of what was coming. Crossing a bridge of a thousand years, ten thousand. Crossing back from the Valley of the Eagles, and Keb's dance—back to John and Toronto and the launching of *Identikit Canada*. "Hey, York—you gotta tell us about Morocco sometime. Get any photos? A fun place, eh?" He could hear it all now. And suddenly he leaned forward, weeping. Herbert stared in amazement. But Rebecca's voice was quick and stern. "Herbert, if you say one word, I'll slit your throat."

The next morning they were all waiting when he came down. Khalid and Bertrand, Rebecca and Herbie, Claude and Richard. Standing in the garden of the hotel. To say good-bye. Richard with his cockatoo grin and a quick whisper. "The gateway's here! Come back, and go farther . . . for me." Bertrand jingling his bracelet. "I'm glad you're not a skull yet!" Kissing York, licking his cheek as he did so. And Herbert presenting him with their London address. "We'll lunch at the Garrick, frighten a few artists, maybe an archbishop or two." And Khalid kissed him twice, saying his room up by the palm tree would be waiting. York stood stammering. Finally Claude ushered him to his waiting car. Just as York was about to enter the car, he straightened up and turned. Waving, shouting, "I love you, all of you." Rebecca shouting back, "Remember, dear, we're convening here next year, le tout Hôtel des Amis!"

Soon they were rolling down the main boulevard and around the spraying traffic circle. A final salute from the Koutoubia, and on through the flesh-colored walls. Skirting a donkey, a camel, sheep. . . . York trying once again to hold his door closed with the rope. But this time Claude noticed, slowing down without being asked. He looked so pleased. "I'm going to buy a new car. With the money from those paintings!" York nodded, silent. Palm trees swaying alongside of them, flames in the sun.

"She's right, you know." Claude grinned.

Silence.

"He'll be waiting!"

They were entering the terminal, the glass doors swallowing York into another world. World of posters advertising Morocco. Claude cleared his ticket for him.

Then York crossing the gray tarmac toward the plane that would carry him back to London, then Canada . . . and John. And only as he got closer, seeing those dark shadows, soldiers, Sten guns. He'd forgotten about them. Didn't care this time. He turned to glance back at the air terminal, wave to Claude.

It wasn't Claude who caught his eye. On top of the airport, up on the visitors' gallery—that tall slender figure, red pants flaring in the sun, arm raised in last salute . . . York gulping. For a moment York hesitated.

A soldier stepped forward, motioning him onto the plane.

As he waved, shouting, "Keb, Kebir . . . Marrakshi!"

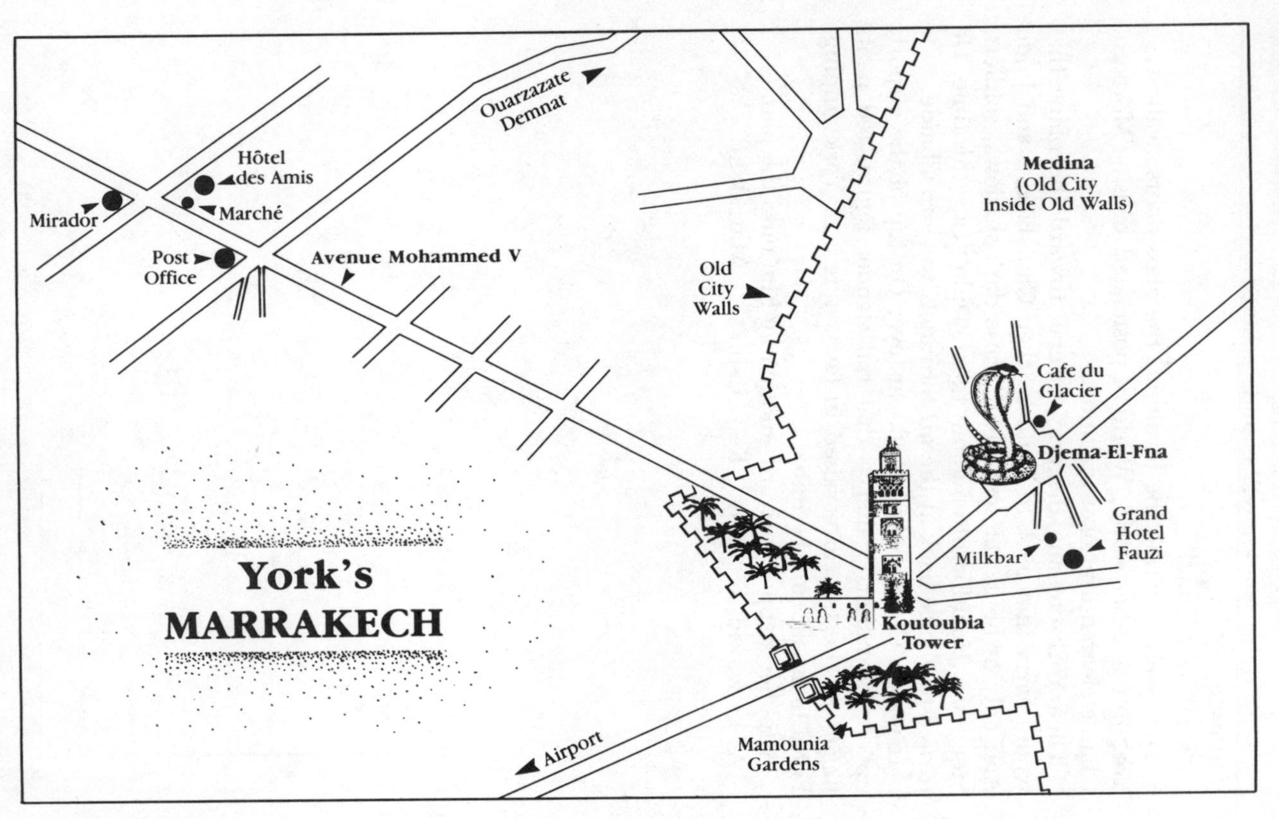

York's
MARRAKECH
Hôtel
des Amis
Mirador
Marché
Post
Office
Avenue Mohammed V
Ouarzazate
Demnat
Old
City
Walls
Medina
(Old City
Inside Old Walls)
Cafe du
Glacier
Djema-El-Fna
Grand
Hotel
Fauzi
Milkbar
Koutoubia
Tower
Mamounia
Gardens
Airport

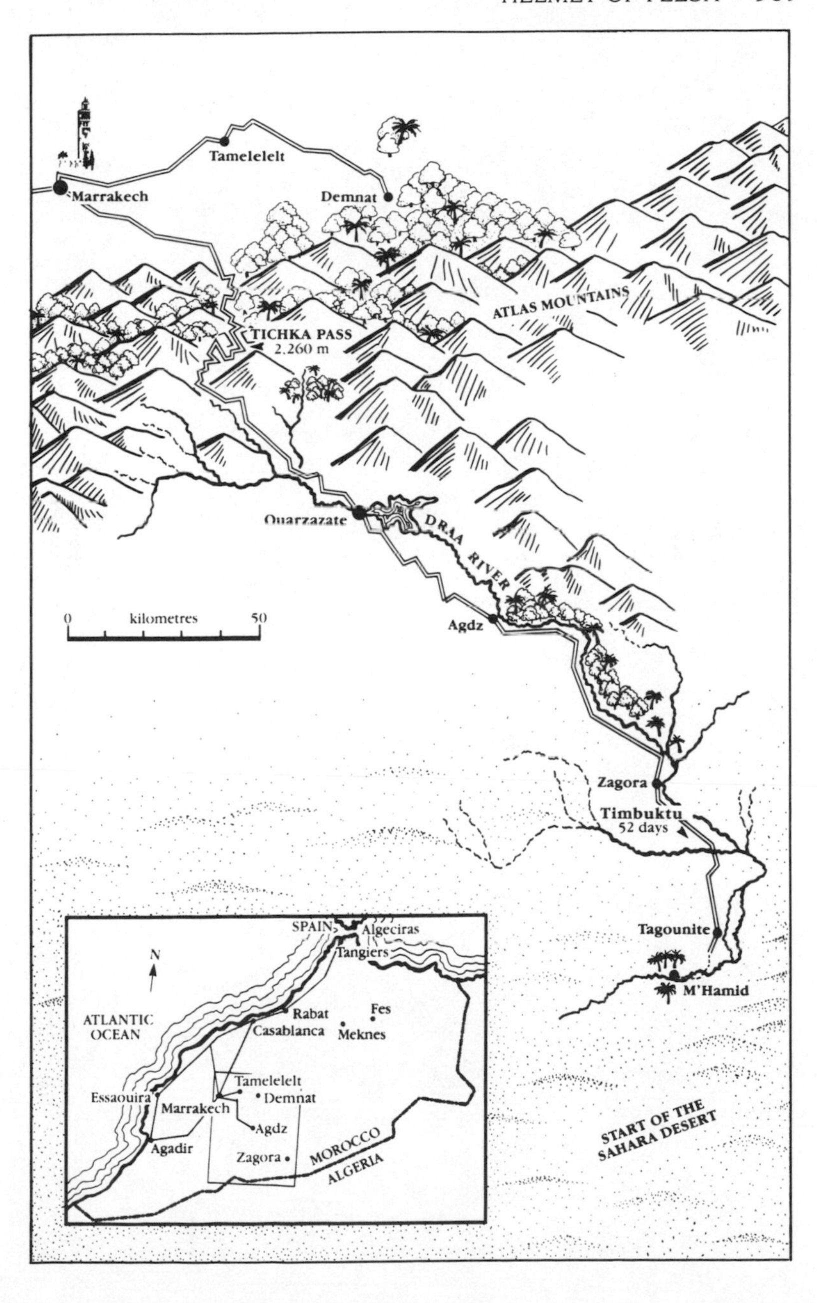
Tamelelelt
Marrakech
Demnat
ATLAS MOUNTAINS
TICHKA PASS
2,260 m
Ouarzazate
DRAA RIVER
Agdz
0 kilometres 50
Zagora
Timbuktu
52 days
Tagounite
M'Hamid
START OF THE
SAHARA DESERT
SPAIN
Algeciras
Tangiers
N
Rabat
Fes
ATLANTIC
OCEAN
Casablanca
Meknes
Tamelelelt
Essaouira
Demnat
Marrakech
Agdz
Agadir
Zagora
MOROCCO
ALGERIA